Katie peeked through her eyelashes at Branch, then her eyes flew open wide. "He's got a knife!" she cried aloud.

"And he's going to use it," Branch replied. "You know I won't hurt you, Sprite. What's the matter?"

Katie's gaze was glued to the wicked curve near the point of the forged steel blade. She swallowed hard. "What . . . what are you going to do?" she asked.

Branch gave an exasperated grunt. "What do you think I'm gonna do? I'm gonna cut you out of the blasted cane."

"I knew that," Katie said. "But listen, couldn't you just pluck away the thorns and lift me out? I think it would be better . . ." While she argued, he slipped the cold steel blade inside her bodice and split the yellow dress from neck to hem.

Before she could let loose with the words he felt certain she wished to hurl at him, Branch yanked her up and out of the vine.

She clutched his shoulders to keep from falling. "Mr. Kincaid, you have to be the most conceited, offensive, predatory animal to walk the face of this . . . Oh . . ."

He could no more have stopped than man could fly. With a groan, he pulled her to him and lowered his mouth to hers. . . .

THE TEXAN'S BRIDE

Geralyn Dawson

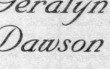

BANTAM BOOKS

NEW YORK · TORONTO · LONDON
SYDNEY · AUCKLAND

THE TEXAN'S BRIDE

A Bantam Fanfare Book / May 1993

ISBN 0-553-56175-8

Published simultaneously in the United States and Canada

FOR STEVE.

*Thanks for the time, the understanding,
and the support. You've shown me
what a true Texan hero is all about.*

THE
TEXAN'S
BRIDE

⚒ PROLOGUE ⚒

*R*OB GARRETT LAY DYING. He knew it. He wanted it. But Dear Lord, why was it taking so long?

Unbearable pain radiated from his spine, eating through every inch of his body, searing his soul. Still, he remained conscious. Penance, perhaps.

He cradled the child to his chest. She was cold now, cold and still. Eternal sleep. I'm sorry, Pumpkin. I tried. But the smoke. At least you were spared this.

Fire. What irony. And Britt, nowhere near this time. He'd never know the score was settled.

Another wave of pain. He clenched his jaw against it. Please, Lord, let me die. Tears escaped his eyelids. Left a trail of salty pain down his cheeks. He smelled charred flesh.

What was that sound? His tortured eyes opened. Tried to focus. Recognized the face. White as the child in his arms. Then the gun. Praise God. A gun.

"Shoot me," he begged, barely moving his lips. "Shoot . . ."

The baby was lifted from his arms. He watched the gun. "I tried to save her. She didn't burn. I tried."

Wide, blank eyes stared at him.

A voice spoke from somewhere beyond the face. A boy's voice. Young. Scared. "He's burnt bad," he said. "All across his back and legs. I think we should do it, Katie."

"Who did this?"

Oh, Lord, the pain! His, hers. Words a mountain to climb. "No name. Pitchfork. Flames."

1

The boy again. "He's hurtin' somethin' awful."

"Please!" Rob begged. "I went after her. You owe me."

He saw the barrel of the gun rise. Point straight at him. He smiled. Good-bye, Eleanor. Heard the click as the hammer cocked. Pa, the fire was my fault—not his. Closed his eyes. Sorry, Britt.

Crack.

✍ CHAPTER 1 ✍

REPUBLIC OF TEXAS, 1845

*R*IDING THROUGH THE VAST expanse of pine forest, Branch Kincaid failed to notice the black cloud rising above the horizon. Land fraud, murder, dusty dreams, and promises swirled in his thoughts. He broke from the trees at the crest of a hill just as the storm darkened the afternoon sun.

"Aw, hell," he muttered, looking north. A smoky blue mist billowed across the land in front of the tempest. It tumbled forward like an ocean wave breaking on the shore and approached with ominous speed. He should have known it was coming.

For the past couple of days, the early January weather had been passing close to hot. When a cool breeze had awakened him this morning, he'd been so busy enjoying the change, he never considered the obvious—a blue norther headed his way.

He leaned into the horse and Striker lengthened his stride. "You'd think I was a greenhorn, the way I dawdled this morning," Branch grumbled. Two days of oppressive, warm air, a few hours of chill—why any Texian who'd spent a single winter here knew what was bound to happen next. Damnation. What had he been thinking of?

Rob, of course. His older brother. His murdered brother. For almost as long as Branch could remember, Rob had been the fair-haired son of the Garrett clan. He had been the man who rode beside Sam Houston when Texas won her independence from Mexico. He had served the Republic as commissioner of the General Land Office, a position of power that reflected favorably upon the family.

While Branch struggled to survive, Rob married the woman Branch wanted and accepted the designation as sole heir to Riverrun, the family sugarcane plantation on which Branch was forbidden to step.

Now Hoss Garrett, grieving over the loss of a much-loved son, found himself willing to do anything to punish his son's killer, even offer reconciliation to the second son. All Branch had to do was find and dispense with a murderer, and he could go home to Riverrun.

Shrugging as a chill whipped over him, he grumbled, "So here I am, smack-dab in the middle of East Texas, a good three miles from the inn where my investigation begins, and the weather is fixin' to get colder than a witch's kiss. Kincaid, you're one damn fool Texian."

The wind picked up, whistling through the trees. He urged Striker even faster. Reaching behind his back, he fumbled with the strap on his saddle pack. Once he opened the leather bag, he felt inside for the coarse texture of his blanket coat. He yanked the coat out, knocking a tin of tobacco to the ground.

Branch cursed but kept on riding. Shelter seemed more important than a smoke right now. The mist bounded toward him, and he slipped the brightly colored poncho over his head. The wool had absorbed the tobacco's woodsy scent, and the aroma teased him before being swept away by the numbing blast of cold air that suddenly enveloped him.

Within moments, he was chilled to the bone.

The wind shrieked against man and horse; they fought for every step. Branch yelled an exceptionally vile curse as the gale whipped his favorite wide-brimmed felt hat from his head and carried it south.

He looked above and saw that the edges of the tumultuous storm were tinged in green. Well, that's a little better, he thought. By the looks of it, this promised to be a typical blue norther. Although they appeared pretty nasty coming at you, clouds like this rarely held any moisture. "Maybe this is the worst of it, old boy," he told the horse through dry, chapped lips. "At least we won't get wet."

The howling wind captured his brittle laugh when he

felt the first bite of sleet on his face. His ears ached and tears blew in wrinkles across his temples. *I reckon this is a fittin' way to arrive at Gallagher's,* he thought. He'd been ice inside anyway since his father's messenger had found him at the South Texas ranch where he'd been working.

Finally he caught the scent of burning cedar and saw a glow of light filter through the trees signaling road's end. With renewed strength, he and Striker pushed for Gallagher's Tavern and Travelers Inn.

The barn door groaned against the wind as Branch pulled it open. Light spilled into the structure through the open doorway. He counted nine horses tied wherever room allowed, with probably the ugliest mare he'd seen in his life occupying the single enclosed stall. "Waste of good space," he said, shaking his head.

The animals stirred when he led Striker into the barn. "Barely enough room to turn around in here," Branch grumbled. Without hesitation he moved the mare, tying her to a support post. Striker deserved the best accommodations available.

The big dun was Branch's truest friend. Striker had helped him out of more tight places than there were Indians in the Llano Estacado. He owed the horse his life, and he never forgot it.

Quickly he uncinched the girth and pulled the saddle from Striker's back. He used a blanket lying in one corner of the enclosure to rub down the horse. After adding more oats to the bucket hanging in the stall, Branch left the barn to seek his own comfort.

Hunching his shoulders against the elements, he trudged the short distance to the inn. When he pulled the door open, a gust of wind yanked it from his numbed fingers. The door banged against the log wall, and a good measure of the storm blew past him into the room.

A voice rang out above the clatter of tankards and whiskey-pitched conversations. "Shut the door, mister. We'd just as soon keep the weather on the outside if you don't mind."

Branch was tired and hungry. One thing he didn't want

right now was to listen to some smart-mouthed fool. He shut the door and turned with a caustic remark on the tip of his tongue.

He swallowed his words, choking.

The source of the carping voice carried two dead squirrels by the tail, stood all of five foot tall, and wore a high-necked, long-sleeved calico dress that stretched tight across a positively bodacious bosom.

Branch stood there, staring at the barmaid. "Well, well, well," he drawled, "but couldn't you turn a blue norther red hot, little honey." He wouldn't mind a bit scorching some sheets with her a little later.

She glared at him through narrowed, bluebonnet-colored eyes. A flush crept over highly placed cheekbones, painting her fair skin an appealing pink beneath the light dusting of freckles. A long auburn braid fell over a shoulder. She tightened her full lower lip into an angry frown.

I wonder what's rattled her slats, Branch thought as his gaze swept her body before lifting to fasten on her chest. A blaze of lust melted the norther's chill from his bones. Plenty of curves for such a tiny package.

He was somewhat surprised at his reaction to this little bundle of femininity. He'd not dallied with a tavern chippy in years. Although never a man to shut his eyes when offered a spectacular view, he'd always looked for more in a woman than mere physical appeal. In this case, however, he desired to search no farther than the obvious set of features that even now approached.

A slow grin spread across his face as she walked toward him. He never lifted his stare above her neck. I do believe I'd rather watch her walk than eat fried chicken, he decided.

She stopped less than an arm's length away. He vaguely noticed the tapping sound her foot made against the puncheon floor; he was fascinated by the effect such a movement created.

She caught him completely by surprise and square in the face when she slapped him with the two dead squirrels.

"Thunder in the valley, woman!" Branch raged. He

backed up a step and wiped his face with a corner of his coat. The blasted squirrels left something wet behind.

She dropped the animals and, with hands on hips, moved forward. He felt the wall against his back. Why, she wasn't the least bit cowed by his bellow, he realized. Male pride reasserting itself, he put *his* hands on *his* hips and leaned forward. Glaring down at her upturned face, he growled through clenched teeth. "What in Sam Houston's name do you think you're doin'?"

She punctuated her words with a surprisingly powerful jab to his chest with her index finger. "I think, mister, that you had best keep your eyes to yourself, or you'll be back out in the sleet looking about as healthy as these squirrels."

Branch shook his head in amazement. Nobody, especially not a hundred-pound little-bit, had dared to pull a stunt like this on him since his voice stopped cracking.

The only sound he heard was the slurping of ale as the occupants of the room watched the confrontation with rapt attention. He wondered what would happen if he gave the tiny termagant what she so obviously needed. He decided to settle for less, for now. What he had in mind required more privacy than the tavern presently offered.

He brought his right hand to his chest, rubbing the spot she had stabbed. His left hand snaked out to grab her wrist. Angry blue eyes widened at his action, and trepidation glimmered across her face. So she does have some sense after all, he thought, and grinned.

He looked deep into her eyes. Loosening his grip, he slid his hand over hers in a gentle caress until he held only her fingertips. He bowed low and pressed a honeyed kiss to the back of her hand. "I humbly beg your pardon, ma'am," he said in a loud voice. "I fear the bitter cold must have affected my sense. I acted the rogue and I apologize."

She tugged on her hand but he held it tight. In a lowered voice only she could hear, he continued, "One thing though, Sprite. From here on out, *I* do all the pokin'."

With a gasp, she yanked her hand away as though burned. She whirled and darted toward the exit. Branch laughed aloud when she stopped short at the doorway, turned, and marched back to retrieve her squirrels. With her perky nose high in the air, she flounced outside, not even bothering to don a cloak. The door slammed behind her.

"That was a right gentlemanly apology, boyo." The voice, a curious blend of Irish brogue and Southern drawl, boomed over the noise that again filled the tavern. A grizzled man stood behind an oak bar that ran half the length of the room. He gestured for Branch to approach, then placed a shot of whiskey before him. "Welcome to Gallagher's," he said. "The first one's on the house, on account of your reception."

Branch laughed. "I've been greeted at the door with dinner before," he said, "but never quite like that." He drained the whiskey in one gulp and signaled for another. For a travelers' inn in Texas, the liquor wasn't half-bad.

He grinned and shook his head. "I didn't mean to insult your help," he told the barkeep, "it's just that seein' something like that when you come in out of the cold, well, it warms a man up right quick."

He raised his glass to his lips for a sip as the older man tossed back a drink of his own and lamented, "I know just what you mean. Me daughter looks just like her mother did at that age."

The whiskey spewed from Branch's mouth. Chuckling, the bartender reached across the bar and pounded the visitor's back. "I'm John Gallagher," he said. "Me Katie's the one with the squirrels. She's not exactly the help—'general' comes closer to describin' her position around here."

"I'm Branch Kincaid," he groaned, figuring he was destined to sleep with Mother Nature tonight after all.

"Pleasure to meet you, Mr. Kincaid," Gallagher continued. "Don't let the girl be botherin' you. She was cross before you arrived, and I'm afraid her storms tend to blow as fierce as the one goin' on outside."

Branch nodded, uncertain how he should respond. He hadn't exactly planned to make this sort of first impression around here. Ogling the owner's daughter wasn't usually the way to secure a job. Still, Gallagher didn't seem to mind too much. Probably with a gal like that around the place, it happened all the time.

A disgruntled voice demanded another drink, and the tavern keeper moved to refill the cups of a group of card players at a table in front of the fireplace. Branch shifted his position and took a lazy look around the room. The limestone hearth filled most of the wall farthest from the door, and a dozen or more rough-hewn chairs sat scattered through the room. Shutters hung on rawhide hinges allowed a good bit of frigid air into the room through the single window on the south wall.

By the look of the place, Gallagher's had begun as a typical dog-run style cabin. The narrow steps built in one corner probably led to one large sleeping room upstairs. He hoped he'd not be asked to share a mattress with a stranger tonight, as often happens in a Texas inn. He'd be damned before he'd bed down with a man, and that attic floor would sure be cold tonight with only a blanket between him and the pine.

Branch's gaze fixed on a sampler hanging on the wall. Tiny stitches embroidered the quotation: "There is nothing which has yet been contrived by man by which so much happiness is produced as by a good tavern or inn—Samuel Johnson." Couldn't be her handiwork, he thought. Somehow he just couldn't picture the spitfire sitting passively before a hearth with needlework in her lap. A shotgun, maybe.

Gallagher returned to his place behind the scuffed and dented bar, interrupting Branch's train of thought. The Irishman studied Branch. "You look familiar, young fella. You been here before?"

Branch frowned. "Nope. First time through East Texas. Pretty country up this way, though."

"Aye, 'tis the evergreens a keepin' the land from lookin' so barren." Gallagher poured another drink. "So where do you hail from?"

"Virginia originally. My Pa brought me and my brother to Texas back in '18. For the last few years I've been makin' my livin' down south, ropin' mustangs."

"Really now. I've heard that's a good bit of work to get into."

"Used to be," Branch said. He took a sip of whiskey. "Too many people now, drivin' the herds too far west. I'm not anxious to lose my scalp to a Comanche."

Gallagher shrugged. "Where you headed?"

This is it, Branch thought. Make it good. "Well, I don't rightly know. I'm lookin' to file my headright and claim the land the Republic of Texas is willin' to give me."

"Is that so? What class of headright do you have?"

"I came to Texas before Independence Day in '36, so mine is first class. I'm a veteran of the Siege of Bexar, so I've also got a donation grant comin'. That qualifies me for a good amount of land, but I'm wantin' to ranch. The more sections I can claim, the better."

Pausing, he swirled the whiskey in his cup, carefully considering his next words. His brother had been killed while tracing a trail of counterfeit land scrip in East Texas, and Branch intended to find that path himself. He said, "I've got a bit of coin saved, and I'm willin' to put it into scrip for additional acres if I can find the right piece of land. What do you know about the availability of good ground around here?"

"I'll tell you the truth of it," Gallagher said, scowling. "If there are two words that mean the same thing in Texas these days, they are 'land' and 'fraud.' You be mighty careful, boyo, before you give your hard-earned money to an agent dealin' in land scrip. Check him out all the way back to his great-great-gram to make sure you're not gettin' took."

Branch held his excitement in check. "What do you mean?"

"When the government decided to authorize agents to sell certificates for land as a way to raise money, they made a big mistake. There's enough counterfeit scrip out there to paper the road from here to San Antonio de Bexar."

You're right about that, Irishman, Branch thought. Rob Garrett had discovered that some of it led to Gallagher's own door. Casually, he asked, "Well, who's makin' it? Can't the law do somethin' about it?"

Gallagher's eyes narrowed, and he gripped the spill cloth in his hand until his knuckles whitened. "The law is part of it," he stated flatly. He made an obvious effort to relax before he asked, "So, you got a family you'll be a'bringin' to this ranch?"

"Nope." Branch shook his head. "I'm a single man."

Pursing his lips, Gallagher nodded. "There's your problem. You get a league and a labor of land if you're a family man, rather than the third of a league single men receive. You'd be safer to get yourself a wife than to spend your money on risky scrip."

Branch laughed. "I think I'd rather take the risk of bein' stuck with counterfeit paper than a false woman. Good women are hard to find in Texas—they get snapped up before they're out of pigtails."

Gallagher fixed a considering gaze upon Branch. "You might just be surprised, boyo. Tell me, now, are you hoping to settle 'round here?"

"Yeah, I'm in no hurry, though, what with winter comin' on. I'm gonna look for work and take my time huntin' the best piece of land."

"Funny you should mention hunting." The tavern owner rubbed a hand across his whiskered jaw, his light blue eyes steady as he gave Branch a measured look. "That's one of the things that had me Mrs. Starr in a huff when you blew in."

Branch lifted an eyebrow. "Mrs. Starr?"

"Katie. It's a widow woman she is. Well over a year now."

The way the old man tilted his head and the satisfied gleam in his eyes caused Branch to shift uneasily. The fella shouldn't look so pleased, seeing how not ten minutes ago he'd eyed the man's daughter like she was hot peach cobbler.

Gallagher continued. "Those squirrels she belted you with were the last of our fresh meat. Our hunter quit a couple of weeks ago." A ghost of a smile hovered on his lips. "Seems he couldn't get along with the cook."

"The cook?"

"Katie. Anyway, me boy, Daniel, is not able to use a shotgun." John lifted his chin defensively. "His right hand is crippled."

"Sorry to hear that. Must be a hard prospect to live with," Branch replied.

Gallagher appeared pleased with Branch's answer. "An accident. Hard for a youngster to accept what happened. He wants so bad to pull his weight around here, but he just can't provide meat enough for the family and the guests. Think you could handle the job? It'd be a good way to get a look at the land around here."

"You offerin'?" Branch asked.

"If you think you can do it, the work is yours."

Branch grinned. He'd never hoped for something to suit this well. He offered his hand. "You've got yourself a new hunter, sir. I'm proud to take the job."

Each man smiled at the other while they shook hands on the deal. Branch knew his own motivations, but he could only wonder at John Gallagher's.

"If you want," John told him, "you can head out to the kitchen and tell Katie I said to fix our new man a meal. She ought to have those squirrels ready in a while. The kitchen's out back to the left. After you've eaten, Daniel will be showin' you where to put your gear."

As Branch rose and started for the door, Gallagher called out to him. "And never you mind what Katie says, you're hired. Don't let her scare you off about how she made the last hunter leave. What she's liable to tell you would be only a portion of the truth."

That made Branch pause. He lifted a hand to his face where every so often he'd pick up the scent of dead squirrel. He owed her. This just might be fun.

⚔ CHAPTER 2 ⚔

COCOONED IN THE WARMTH of her kitchen, Katie struggled to dismiss that overgrown oaf from her thoughts. But as she tested the cutting edge of a carving knife against her thumb, she pictured glowing, golden eyes, a cocky smile, and shoulders that filled the doorway. She stabbed the pumpkin before her with uncharacteristic viciousness.

"Were I not a good Catholic girl, I'd send him on his way," she grumbled. The sharp knife bit into the tabletop; two hunks of orange gourd rocked on either side. "Without a coat." She chopped each half into quarters. "Barefoot."

Certainly he deserved no better. Only his size and the voice that had rolled over her like warm molasses made him different from any other first-time patron of Gallagher's. Katie placed the pumpkin into a Dutch oven and set it onto the coals to bake. I should be used to it, she thought. After all, hadn't O'Dell Thompson pinched her behind right before the stranger came in? And hadn't the card player from Austin just asked her to show him to his mattress and stay awhile?

"Men!" she exclaimed. She ought to know by now that the majority of the men who walked through the front door followed the divining rod in their pants. They took one look at her and wanted to dig for water. And Da—half the time he'd pull a shotgun on them and the rest of the time he'd invite them to stay a couple of days extra—on the house! She'd realized right off that he was husband-hunting for her.

"And isn't *that* just what I need," she mumbled. She

13

peeked into the brick Dutch oven built alongside the fire-place. The aroma of baking cornbread escaped to mingle with the other tempting scents wafting through the room.

He'd smelled of tobacco.

She shook her head as though that would dislodge the memory, then turned her attention to the skinned and dressed squirrels, muttering, "Seven men, Daniel, and my-self to feed with two measly squirrels."

She sucked her lower lip, considering the best way to stretch the small amount of meat. "Brunswick stew is the best I can do," Katie decided. Picking up a large kettle from the hearth, she carried it back to the worktable. She dropped the squirrels into the pot, then gathered vegetables from shelves, bins, and baskets that sat around the room.

"Better add extra of everything," she fussed. "No doubt that scapegrace will eat for three." Da ought to charge a man that big more than the usual fee. Gallagher's surely would lose money boarding him.

Katie added lima beans and corn to the pot, and then picked up her knife to peel the last of the fall tomatoes. Actually, he wasn't that tall. Why, Steven had stood to six feet, and the stranger was only a bit taller than that. He just had a lot more meat on him than had her husband.

Dear Steven, how she missed him. A friend long be-fore he became her sweetheart, Steven had loved the per-son she was beneath these female characteristics men seemed to find so fascinating. While they *had* enjoyed the physical side of marriage—after all, they had wanted a family—the true strength of their love had been the friend-ship that had bound them together since childhood.

The kitchen door flew open and the bitter wind swirled into the room, displacing the warmth and cozy aromas with hollow chill. She looked up to see Daniel wrestling to pull the door tight against the gale. "Do you need a hand?" she asked, then immediately cringed at her thoughtless words.

Her brother secured the door, then turned a sullen face toward Katie. "Yeah, you got an extra one you can sew on for me?" he asked, holding out his right arm. From the cuff, the crushed, mangled hand drooped pathetically toward the floor.

"I'm sorry, Daniel. My mind's full of clover this afternoon. 'Fraid I had some trouble with one of the guests, and it left me a tad flustered."

The boy's expression lit. "So I heard," he said with a smile. "Squirrel slapping's something new for Gallagher's." He walked over to the table and grabbed a handful of shelled pecans. He pulled out a chair and sat down, plopping a nut into his mouth.

"Oh, posh. I don't need any sass from you, young man," Katie said.

"Sass?" he asked with innocence.

Katie rolled her eyes. That look reminded her of the stranger. Do they practice, or are men just born with it?

She reached beneath the table to grab a potato from the bin next to the dough box. "Have you finished with the beds?" she asked.

"Yeah, except we don't have enough blankets," Daniel answered. He looked at his sister expectantly, as though he knew what her words would be before she said them.

Katie frowned. "Well, any traveler this time of year ought to carry his own blanket, even if he does plan to sleep at inns. And they shouldn't be complaining, either. We're the only hotel in a hundred miles that offers each guest his own mattress. They're lucky to be staying at Gallagher's!" she finished in a huff.

Daniel peered into the kettle, now piled high with vegetables, and licked his lips. "They're extra lucky 'cause you're the cook," he declared.

Katie smiled. She was a good cook. She'd worked hard to learn. That first year after Mama died, she'd almost run off all the business with the meals she'd put on the table. Of course, even then, Gallagher's food wasn't much worse than what the average hotel in Texas offered.

She cut up one last potato and added it to the stew. From a basin she took fresh water and poured it over the mixture, before adding salt and pepper as the final ingredients. She looked at her brother. "Would you carry this over to the fireplace for me?" she asked.

"Sure," the boy said matter-of-factly, but he stood a little straighter as he grabbed the handle and toted the kettle across the room. He hung the pot on the iron crane that pivoted in and out of the fireplace so that Katie could tend her victuals away from the heat. He pushed the metal arm into the opening that was big enough to roast a small steer. "You need anything else, Katie? I thought I'd help Da for a while."

Katie shook her head, clicking her tongue. "Don't you help him like you did last week. You get into that corn liquor again, and he'll skin you alive."

Daniel shuddered, moving toward the door. "Not likely. I've never been that sick before in my life!"

Katie laughed, remembering the boy's green face. "There is one thing, Daniel," she said. "We've got all the horses inside the barn because of the storm. I'd hate for any to get loose. Would you check on them please?"

"Yes'm," Daniel answered. Passing the table, he grabbed another handful of pecans.

Katie slapped at his hands and laughed. "Get out of here, or I'll make you eat one of those doughballs I fixed for breakfast," she warned. She'd attempted a new recipe for the rolls, but it had failed miserably.

Daniel held his hand to his throat as though choking. "That'd make me sicker than the corn brew, for certain." Laughing, the boy scampered out into the cold, heading for the barn before his sister could scold him.

That boy, Katie thought with tenderness. It's so good to hear him laugh again. For more than a year following the fire, Daniel had wallowed in guilt; he'd survived and the others had not. The mischievous little boy transformed into a melancholy young man, and she'd begun to fear he'd never deal with his grief. But eventually time began its healing, and now, in these last few months, he appeared to be putting the horror behind him.

That's why she'd been happy to be the target of one of his pranks yesterday. Before the trouble, he'd pestered everyone in the county with his practical jokes. When he'd tripped her with that hidden rope, she'd wanted to shout for joy, but she'd boxed his ears instead. He needed to believe everything was back to normal.

Katie's heart lifted. Things would be just fine around Gallagher's Tavern and Travelers Inn. She walked to the fireplace, took a spoon from a hook hanging above the hearth, and stirred the stew. Well, they'd be fine once Da got the food problem solved.

During that first disastrous year as mistress of the inn, Katie learned how much a well-laid table meant for business. Stories of burnt meat, decaying vegetables, and predictable menus commonly offered at hotels across the Republic made an indelible impression on the young hostess. She realized that a reputation for fine food would stand Gallagher's in good stead.

So she bent herself to the task of learning new methods for preparing the staples—corn and pork—and oversaw the planting of a variety of vegetables in the garden. She learned the location of every fruit and nut tree in the area. At her insistence, a hunter had been hired to provide an assortment of game for the table.

Then, as a combination wedding gift and bribe not to move to the Starr family land, Da had built the new kitchen to her exact specifications. It came complete with a connecting bedroom for Katie and her new husband to share. She stayed and cooked, and now Gallagher's was well-known for the fine fare served to guests. Why, not a month ago, a visitor told Da that he made a detour on his journey in order to stay here and sample the delicious bear steak he'd heard so much about.

"Of course," Katie muttered, "a month ago we had a hunter."

She bent over to look into the oven at the cornbread. Frowning, she remembered their last hunter. He'd worked for the inn almost six months before he decided to try his trapping skills on the cook. She shuddered as she recalled his rancid breath against her lips and his groping hands. "I wonder if he can walk without wincing yet," she mused, deciding the bread was just about done.

A frigid draft encircled her exposed ankles and shimmied up her skirts. Without turning, she called, "Daniel,

either get in or stay out. You're almost as bad as that
yellow-haired wolf I tussled with earlier over the very
same thing."

She straightened and stepped back—into a wall of
muscle and two very large hands that grasped her firmly
around the waist.

"Grr . . . ," the blackstrap voice growled into her ear.
"What big muffins you have, my dear. Care if I take a
bite?"

Her outraged gasp preceded a screech that made the
lamp chimneys vibrate. "You! Take your hands off me this
instant, you—"

The overbuilt animal released her before she could finish her outburst. She twisted to face him.

He wasn't looking at her.

He gazed past her into the oven, and she almost could
see the halo above his head. "I sure do love the taste of
cornbread right out of the oven," he said.

He's perfected that look. I've got to keep him away
from Daniel, she told herself. She pushed past him and
marched to the worktable. Armed with a rolling pin, she
demanded, "What in heaven's name do you think you are
doing?"

He flashed a cocky grin over his shoulder. "I believe
I asked that same question a little earlier. Only I didn't
much like your answer." He moved to check the contents
of the kettle. Squatting down, he peered into the pot and
asked, "Is this where my squirrels ended up?"

Katie dragged her gaze from his behind. Really, those
buckskins stretched indecently tight. He'd caught her looking, and as he rose, his grin became a knowing smirk.

She felt her face flush. Oh, saints above. Get hold of
yourself, Katie, she silently fumed. She should be scared,
alone in the kitchen with this muscle-bound brute, the
wind howling so fiercely outside that no one would ever
hear her screams.

But she wasn't afraid, just very, very aware.

Embarrassed and ashamed, she declared, "Listen to
me, you uncouth man, I don't know why you came into
my kitchen, or what possessed you to paw me, but I tell

you this: You just lost yourself a place to stay tonight."
With each word her voice became more strident until she
ended with a shrill, "Get out of my kitchen and this hotel!
In fact, leave the blessed Republic this instant!"

He pivoted and walked toward her, his magnetic eyes
capturing her own. "Sprite, you use the words 'man, pos-
sess, and me' all in one sentence, and you're liable to cook
up more than squirrel stew."

With a yelp, Katie scurried to the far side of the table
and raised the rolling pin. He stopped with the table between them, grabbed a chair, and straddled it.

He folded his arms on the back of the chair and said,
"To answer your sweetly asked questions: Branch Kincaid,
dinner, you backed into me, and I'm not leavin' because
your father just hired me to be Gallagher's new hunter."

The rolling pin clattered against the wooden floor. "He
what?" Katie had to force the words.

Branch cocked his head to one side and answered, his
golden eyes twinkling. "Yeah, I'm now gainfully employed by the famous Gallagher's Tavern and Travelers
Inn in the capacity of game procurer. I assume that means
the four-legged kind. Although I have nothin' against the
two-legged variety. It's just that things tend to get a little
messy tryin' to stock the stable, so to speak."

Katie sank into her chair, then buried her head in her
hands. In a minute, she told herself, in a minute I'll pitch
a fit. I'll get this all straightened out. What was his name,
Limb or something?"

"Brunswick," she finally muttered through dry lips.

He arched a blond brow.

"The stew. Not just squirrel, Brunswick stew."

He nodded solemnly. "Heaven for the senses, I'm
sure." He launched into an explanation of the travails of
his journey and what had led him to Katie's kitchen. She
comprehended about one word out of every three. But
while her mind was a mass of confusion, the rest of her
was busy reacting to the hunk of masculinity across the
table.

His voice flowed across the table, touching her, bringing shivers to her skin. Tendrils of heat spiraled through-

out her body, and she tingled in places that had no business tingling. It was all she could do not to squirm in her seat.

Slowly Katie lifted her head and looked at him. He rested his chin atop his hands, and she heard words like "storm," "barn," and "card game." But his compelling eyes spoke a different language, and she understood every word.

He fell silent. His lips curved into a slow, secret smile.

"You had it wrong, you know," she eventually said.

Again, he quirked one eyebrow.

She watched his mouth. "You said it backward. The muffins. Red Riding Hood says what big teeth you have, not the wolf. He says . . ."

Kincaid interrupted. "The better to eat you with, my dear." With that, he picked up a doughball from a bowl on the table and took a large bite. He chewed once, and a peculiar look crossed his face. As he continued to chew, his brows met in a V, and he began to blink rapidly. With great effort, he swallowed.

For a moment, the only sound to be heard was the nervous tap of Katie's foot.

He hiccuped before he shuddered. "I swear, woman, that was worse than eatin' Mexican grapeshot."

That broke the spell. Nobody crawled in here and criticized her cooking—even if it *was* deserved. She jumped to her feet and grabbed the carving knife. "If you like that so much, it's a shame you won't be around to taste the roast wolf I'm serving up for supper."

He stood suddenly, sending his chair banging against the floor. "Sprite, if you can't take a little honest evaluation of your cookin' skills, maybe you're workin' in the wrong room of the inn."

Katie groaned and raised the knife. He retreated from her advancing figure toward the half-open door opposite the pie safe.

Backing into the room, he threw a glance over his shoulder. Katie saw her mistake in the delight reflected on his face. She'd chased him into her bedroom.

He lunged for her, and in a flurry of movement, he

knocked away the knife and pinned her beneath him on the bed. He smiled that wicked-wolf smile and said, "I'm glad to see you're taking my advice."

She spat in his face.

The teasing light in his eyes died. How could they be so hot and so cold at the same time, Katie wondered?

"Enough!" His voice grated like corn in a gristmill.

Katie bucked and wriggled, ignoring the tight, grim set of his jaw. He yanked her arms above her head, pinioning both wrists with one hand. His free hand traced the gentle curve of her cheek, and for the first time, she feared him.

"Go ahead," she forced the bravado into her voice. "I goaded you into it. No one will blame you. Why—" she gave a brittle laugh—"my father probably will say I asked for it." She blinked away the blur in her eyes. "For some reason, he's been trying to foist me off on a man, any man, for some time now."

The anger drained from his features. "Silly little girl. So brave and so foolish. Next time, though, try making your point without a knife."

He pressed a feathery kiss to her forehead, then rose, pulling Katie up to stand before him. "Now, listen well, Sprite. I've accepted this job and I'll be around for a while. You'd best get used to the idea."

He smiled at her again, and it touched her clear to her toes.

He said, "I won't disappoint you. Don't worry. I always get what I aim for." He stared into her soul. "You can count on me to put something in your belly."

CHAPTER 3

$\mathcal{B}$Y THE TIME the norther moved out, after three *long* days, Katie knew something must be done. The man made her life miserable.

In the space of seventy-two hours, Branch Kincaid had ingratiated himself with her father by accomplishing a multitude of chores and repairs around the inn. He had deluded poor Daniel into thinking he deserved hero status on a level equal to Jim Bowie. Really, he had a nerve, claiming to have been gifted with those fancy guns by Commodore Moore himself. Most likely he'd stolen the revolvers he called Texas Patersons.

"Well, at least that scoundrel's good for something," Katie told herself. Thoughts of him kept melancholy at bay. She sat back on her heels and surveyed the small grave she'd been tending. Fragrant pine nettles and waxy holly leaves with their lush red berries provided a splash of color to the image of decaying grass. Spring would bring a blanket of green to cover the father and child who slept side by side, but for now, the meticulously arranged twigs of evergreen softened the image of the winter grave.

Katie rose to her feet and dusted the dirt and clinging leaves from her skirt. She clutched a finely sewn baby quilt to her bosom as she fought back tears. "Someday I'll find him, I promise."

She'd never give up. If it took her entire lifetime, if it cost her life, she would find the devil responsible—him and his pitchfork and flames. Her words were satin steel as she swore. "When I do, he'll pay."

Mary Margaret would have been walking now, speaking a few words, saying "Mama." She'd be hugging and kissing, returning the affections Katie would have showered on the girl. A single tear spilled from the mourning mother's eye, one of millions she'd shed during the past eighteen months. Would she ever overcome the grief? Would she always have this great, yawning hole in her soul?

The baby had been two months old when she died. Katie pictured in her mind dark curls and china-blue eyes, a toothless grin newly mastered, a smile criminally cut short.

Katie buried her nose in the quilt, hoping desperately to catch a lingering whiff of that cherished, unique infant perfume. There, so faint, was a tangible assurance that for a little while, Mary Margaret Starr had lived.

Losing a husband was hard. Losing a child, too, well— Katie wondered if any experience life held could be more devastating. Especially when a mother was at fault. It was a mother's responsibility to protect God's gift from harm, and Katie had failed in her duty. Though her faith assured her she was forgiven, she'd yet to forgive herself. She doubted she ever would.

Staring down at the limestone marker her father had tearfully carved, Katie prayed she'd someday have the chance to atone for her sin. If sometime in the future, the Lord ever placed another child in her care, she would face hell itself before she'd allow any harm to befall him. Perhaps in some small way, it would redeem her.

Stooping to brush a rock from the top of Steven's grave, Katie said a silent good-bye to the loved ones buried on that picturesque bluff above the Angelina River: Mama, who'd died so long ago; Steven, her husband; Mary Margaret, her daughter; and Mr. Garrett, the visitor unlucky enough to be at her home the night of the fire.

Katie turned her back on the row of markers and started down the hill. "I'll think no more sad thoughts," she said, stroking the quilt. A gloomy day would better serve such bleak memories.

Today's azure sky triumphed over the dreary gray of the storm. Sunshine toasted her back and the air's fresh scent tickled her nose. She flung the covering across her shoulder. On this dazzling morn she'd devote herself to finding a solution to the problem that called himself Branch Kincaid.

"The audacity of the man, moving that hulk of a horse into Pretty Girl's stall," Katie fussed, bristling at the memory. Never had a person presumed so much. Even worse than that were the comments he'd made just this morning concerning Pretty Girl's looks.

"Just you wait, Mr. Know-Everything Kincaid. Before I manage to send you on your way, I'm going to let you in on a little secret. I do believe a horse race is in order. I think I'll show you just how my horse lives up to her name."

A worried frown replaced Katie's self-satisfied smile when a breeze whipped the quilt from her shoulder. She watched the multicolored coverlet fly over her head and snag on a high, leafless branch of a red oak.

"Oh, saints a mercy," she groaned, eyeing the treasured blanket flapping high above the ground. The quilt was one of the few things of Mary's that she had kept. She had to go after it.

She walked to the edge of the tree and kicked off her red russets. The ugly leather shoes would be more hindrance than help climbing the gnarled bark of the oak. Luckily the trunk veed about four feet from the ground, so she didn't have far to climb for a foothold.

Struggling up to the perch, Katie grimaced at the new stains and snags in her faded yellow homespun. At least she'd worn her oldest dress today, knowing she'd be working at the graves. She hadn't planned to be imitating squirrels, however.

Looking above toward the patchwork coverlet, she planned the best route up. A thick, sturdy limb stretched beneath the dangling blue-trimmed corner, and she figured she just might be able to grasp it if she stood on her tiptoes. She climbed to the branch and, straddling it, began to ease her way out.

Directly beneath the quilt, Katie stopped. This would be tricky. The only thing she had to hold for balance when she stood were thin twigs growing up from the limb that held her. She positioned one bare foot atop the branch, yanking her skirts out of the way. The breeze whistled in her ears as she placed her other foot upon the limb. Cautiously, she stood. Weaving back and forth, Katie fought to maintain her balance. She grasped a twig and finally steadied herself.

With care, Katie extended her arm above her head. She stretched. The quilt swayed just outside her reach. Taking a deep, steadying breath, she inched up on the tip of her toes. Her fingers brushed a soft cotton edge. Clenching her teeth she tried again. Up . . . up . . . "I got it!" she cried.

Then she tumbled from the tree.

Katie screamed as she fell backward into the jumbled clump of wild blackberry vines growing at the base of the red oak. Dust rose around her as dozens of spiny thorns pierced her skin. She sneezed and the thorns pushed deeper. She tried to rise, and a frustrated, pain-filled screech exploded from her lips as what felt like half her hair was plucked from her scalp.

"Kincaid," she cursed. "This is all your fault!"

Branch had four rabbits to his credit this morning, but that wasn't near enough to satisfy Colonel Kate back at the inn. Honestly, if William Travis had been blessed with Katie Starr at the Alamo, Santa Anna would never have breached the walls. A more organizing, demanding, persnickety woman he'd yet to meet. She had every male in the place dancing to her tune—and half of them didn't even realize it.

"Well, she's fixin' to learn a brand new jig," he declared. As much as he wanted this job, he'd about taken all he was going to from the tiny tyrant.

Never had he been so pleased to see dawn break clear as he had been this morning, although after three days of constant harassment, he'd probably have gone hunting in a blizzard. To top it all off, she'd met him in the barn with that . . . list. As if he'd actually hunt according to her whims. "She'll cook what I bring back, and if she doesn't like it, she can suck a green persimmon," he grumbled.

He tugged in his line and checked his bait. He couldn't remember the last time he'd had the chance to fish, and by damn, he wasn't going to ruin this pleasure thinking about Katie Starr. The worm-baited hook landed with a plop in the middle of the gently flowing Angelina River.

Of course, he thought, propping one boot against a bleached hunk of limestone, pleasure didn't necessarily preclude that saucy short-stuff. She'd felt mighty nice beneath him. Branch shook his head and pulled a straw from a dried-up clump of wildflowers. He placed one end between his teeth and snickered as he remember just how he'd fired her fury. He mused, "I guess I might've asked for a bit of the grief she'd been giving me, after all."

The late-morning peace was shattered when the biggest bass Branch had ever hooked exploded from the water.

At the same time, a female scream blew through the trees from somewhere behind him. His cane pole bent toward the river. The caterwaul sent shivers up his spine.

"Help!"

"Damn." He dropped the pole and grabbed his gun. "This had better be good," he muttered, racing through the woods toward the commotion. He stopped when he saw the baby quilt lying on the path. He couldn't see much of Katie, but there was no missing the clamor she made. He grinned. "I'm shocked, Mrs. Starr. I wouldn't have believed a lady like you would have knowledge of words like those."

She lay on her back in the middle of a large clump of thorny vine. Blackberry cane wrapped her from head to foot, completely entrapping her with its clinging briar.

At the sound of his voice, she froze.

"Mrs. Starr," Branch observed, unable to keep the humor from his voice, "you seem to be in a bit of a tangle."

She kept quiet for at least a full minute. A sigh preceded her words. "Mr. Kincaid, as much as it pains me, I must request your assistance."

"What are you saying, Sprite, the briar is thornier than

the Branch?" He burst into laughter. This was almost worth losing that black bass.

He could just see over the top of the bramble. It'd be a task to comb through them or even cut a path with his bowie knife. "How in the hell did you manage to wind up in the center of a blackberry patch? If I'm not mistaken, blackberry season's long gone."

Katie didn't answer.

What was it about this woman that gave him such pure pleasure to tease? Obviously, she'd fallen from the tree; a low-hanging limb stretched above her. He eyed the red oak. Probably be easier to lift her out of there than to cut her out, he thought. The tree looked sturdy enough. Of course, he did outweigh her by at least a hundred pounds.

"Mr. Kincaid, are you going to stand there all day, or are you going to help me?"

"Keep it up, lady, and I'll go back to my other fish."

Branch didn't like the idea of thrashing through the thorns to retrieve the prickly female, but he didn't relish climbing an oak either. After all, there was his questionable history with tree branches to consider. That's what had earned him his nickname to begin with.

"Aw, hell," he finally muttered. Shucking out of his jacket, he walked to the tree and, grasping a lower limb, began to haul himself up. While he worked his way to the branch above Katie, he wondered how she could have become so entangled just from falling. He inched his way out along the arm of the tree, gripping the coarse, corky bark with his hands and his thighs. "Since I'm up here risking life on limb, don't you think you should show a bit of gratitude? The least you could do is tell me how you managed to get up to your—"

"All right, all right," Katie interrupted. "My quilt got hung in the tree and I slipped. I'm afraid I lost my temper a bit when I tried to rise and couldn't."

"Pitched a bloomer-bustin' fit, huh?"

"Just get me out of here, please," Katie implored.

Branch grinned. That "please" must have cost her a full measure of pride. He lay balanced on the limb, his long, powerful legs wrapped around its width, and reached below to pluck the vines from the Irish-Texian bundle of trouble.

He started with her hair. As gently as possible, he un-wrapped the mahogany strands from the cane. She had beautiful hair—he hated to see any of it torn from her head. Fine and silken to his touch, its soft texture soothed the prick of the thorns his fingers encountered.

He talked as he worked. "I'll have you know, I was on the verge of landing a huge bass when I heard your scream. You ought to appreciate me more. I'll bet there's not a dozen men in Texas who'd have dropped a catch like that at a woman's holler." He looked down at her. Each breath she took lifted her breasts toward him. He almost fell out of the tree.

"Of course," he clicked his tongue, "my daddy always taught me the best fishin's found in a brush patch." He grinned at her. "You ever tried a worm, Katie Starr?"

She glared at him, then puckered her mouth into fish lips. "Your bait wouldn't land a minnow, Branch Kincaid," she retorted.

"Well, we'll just have to see about that now, won't we?" He'd loosened most of her hair, and he went to work on her clothing. This could take all day. He sat up to stretch his cramping muscles and came to a decision. He eased his way back to the trunk of the tree and hopped down.

"Mr. Kincaid. Hey, Mr. Kincaid, where are you going? Don't leave me here. Branch!"

"I'll be back in a few minutes," he called over his shoulder. Quickly, he made his way back to the river and his gear. "Shame about that fish," he said to himself as he pulled his bowie knife from the trunk of a cottonwood tree. Earlier he'd used the weapon to cut his fishing pole, and he'd grabbed only his Colt when he heard the scream. He headed back to Katie with a merry whistle on his lips.

She was reciting the Hail Mary when he returned. "I'm back," he called. She switched to the Lord's Prayer. If he didn't know better, he'd think she was scared.

Katie grimaced as she turned her head to watch him climb the tree. He winced at the thought of her pain. Even scratched and tattered, wrapped in thorns and remnants of spiderwebs, she attracted him like a drink of cold water on a hot afternoon. He stretched above her on the limb. Katie peeked through her eyelashes, then her eyes flew open wide. "He's got a knife," she cried aloud.

"And he's going to use it," Branch replied. "You know I won't hurt you, Sprite. What's the matter?"

Katie's gaze was glued to the wicked curve near the point of the forged steel blade. She swallowed hard. "What . . . what are you going to do?" she asked.

Branch gave an exasperated grunt. "What do you think I'm gonna to do? I'm gonna cut you out of the blasted cane."

"I knew that," Katie said. "But listen, couldn't you just pluck away the thorns and lift me out? I think that would be better." While she argued, he slipped the cold steel blade inside her bodice and split the yellow dress from neck to hem.

He peeled away the cloth, trying not to hurt her as he pulled the thorns from her flesh. Her drawers remained relatively free of spikes, so he left them intact. The chemise, however, went the way of the dress. Engrossed in his task, Branch ignored what he'd uncovered. At least, he did until he touched her.

Sliding his arm beneath her, he intended to pull straight up and free her in one quick motion. But the vision of those bare, bountiful breasts, rising up to meet him, was his undoing. His body's immediate reaction made his position on the limb downright painful. He jerked his arm away and sat up, disregarding Katie's grunt of pain as she sank heavily into the brambles. He stared stupefied at the woman displayed beneath him.

Her glorious breasts rested proudly upon her chest with dusky tips erect. Their fullness served to emphasize her incredibly narrow waist, and the thin cotton of her drawers did nothing to conceal her gently flaring hips and shapely legs. Fair, unblemished skin provided the perfect backdrop for her thick, auburn hair. Even the scratches looked good on her. Consumed with lust, he absently wondered how mingled pain and pleasure would feel from loving on a bed of thorns.

"Branch Kincaid, when I get out of here, I'm going to beat you like a tied-up goat." Katie's voice sizzled with angry embarrassment and broke through the haze of his desire.

"You're gonna do what?" Damn, but the woman had a mouth on her. He tossed the knife to the ground.

"Listen, lady. I'm gettin' cotton-pickin' tired of your complaints and your threats and your highfalutin ways." He glared down at her. "I'm of a mind right now to leave you where you are till the buzzards gather."

Her outraged gasp didn't faze him in the least. He continued, "Now, if you want my help, we've got to get a few things straight. First, you keep that tongue of yours off me unless I give you leave to do otherwise. Second, your father hired me to do a job. I'm gonna do it in my own way on my own time. I don't need any advice from you on how to hunt."

He looked into her irate blue eyes and slid his arm around her waist. "I admit maybe I came at you a bit strong, but seein' how you're a widow woman, I didn't figure you'd complain." Before she could let loose with the words he felt certain she wished to hurl, Branch yanked her up and out of the vine.

It was no mean feat to get them both settled on the limb without either landing in the briars. Branch managed to straddle the limb with his back supported by the upward-reaching trunk of the tree. Katie sat sideways, nestled between his thighs.

She clutched his shoulders to keep from falling. "Mr. Kincaid, you have to be the most conceited, offensive, predatory animal to walk the face of this—Oh!"

He could no more have stopped than man could fly. With a groan, he pulled her to him. Ever so slowly, he lowered his mouth to hers. Softly, gently, he wooed her lips, the tip of his tongue tracing a seductive path across the trembling surface of her mouth. "Ah, Kate, let me in, open to me," he whispered. And she did.

He plunged into the scintillating pleasure of her kiss.

She tasted sweet as the sugarcane grown at Riverrun and, despite her fall, smelled as fresh as the forest after spring-time rain. So tiny and soft, so fragile—he felt as though the slightest pressure from his hand would break a bone.

But Katie was anything but fragile. To his surprise, she met his invading tongue with a demanding passion that stole his senses and left him heavy with desire. She took control, teasing, exploring, plundering. Swept into the vortex of craving she created, Branch relaxed his arms and allowed her to move as she wished.

Impatient fingers worked the buttons of his chambray shirt, and she pushed it from his shoulders. One hand brushed a feathery caress across his back while the other gathered the shirt and flung it to the ground.

Katie broke the kiss and pulled back. Her eyes beckoned with sultry promise. Then she reached to grasp a limb above, and her breasts lifted in pagan offering. He leaned to accept just as she pulled herself up to stand upon the wood. The vision of the thinly veiled triangle right at eye level held him spellbound as she raised one leg and wrapped it over his shoulder.

"Oh Lord, Kate," he murmured. His chest heaved, and it took all his restraint to allow her to proceed at her own pace. Apparently the merry widow knew exactly what she wanted and far be it from him to deny her desires. A tree. A doggone tree. This one would certainly give a new dimension to his name, that's for sure.

Ever so slowly, he felt her weight shift as she brought her other leg up. She straddled his shoulders, holding herself away as she shifted her hands, getting a firmer grip upon the limb. He could stand it no more. He reached for her, his hands cupping the softness of her buttocks. Her throaty laugh filled his ears, and she flattened her feet against his back. Then just as he brought her to his mouth, she pulled up. She rose over his head, and before he knew what happened, Katie planted a mighty shove to his back, and pushed him from the tree.

He hit the blackberry vines face first. Cane snapped beneath his weight, and biting thorns jabbed deeply into his skin. Stunned silent, not from the fall but from disbelief, Branch listened as that conniving little witch descended from the tree. Her bubbling laughter poured salt on every damned scratch on his body.

Branch roared with the savagery of a rabid coyote. Thrashing to his feet, he spit dusty spiderwebs from his mouth as he pinned his gaze upon Katie. Laughing with delight, she was buttoning *his* shirt over those remarkable breasts and wearing a disgustingly smug expression.

"I swear, I'm gonna kill her!" he growled.

At that, she lifted her chin and looked at him, her brilliant blue eyes alight with mirth. Standing there amid the winter-stark forest, her mahogany-colored hair in tangled disarray, with his shirt all but swallowing her in its voluminous folds, Katie Starr smote him with her heart-stopping beauty.

"But first," Branch promised himself, "I'm gonna have her."

Yanking his way through the cane, he ignored the pricks of the thorns and marched toward her. Clenching his jaw, he fixed her with his most ferocious look.

Unbelievably, the audacious minx put her thumbs to her ears, wiggled her fingers, and stuck out her tongue. And he wanted her as he had never before wanted another woman.

Katie's laughter filled the forest like songs of returning birds in spring. She scooped up the baby quilt and darted off in the direction of the inn.

While watching her flee, a lazy grin crept across Branch's face. He fought on through the vine and finally broke free. He winced when he looked down at his bare chest and saw blood oozing from a myriad of cuts, not to mention the splinters that lay embedded in his skin in a dozen places. He lifted a knuckle and wiped at a warm trickle of wetness that ran down his cheek. The grin reappeared as he gathered his gun and knife and walked back to the spot by the river where he'd been fishing.

Branch knelt and washed in the cold, clean water of the Angelina, whistling a bawdy tune he'd first heard in a Mexican bordello. This situation would require careful consideration. The little general had declared war and could claim victory in the initial skirmish. "However"—he lifted his chin, clasped a fist to the breast in mock solemnity, and quoted John Paul Jones—"I have not yet begun to fight."

Rising, Branch gathered his belongings and picked up the rabbits and a stringer of fish he'd enjoyed catching before he was interrupted. That's it, he decided. He'd plan the next assault with the strategic finesse of Alexander the Great. He'd storm her defenses like Saxons at England's castle walls. He'd conquer Katie Starr as Napoleon had conquered Europe, and within a month, the spoils of war would be in his bed.

Confident of victory, Branch headed for Gallagher's and the field of dishonor. He broke into song, his baritone forming the ribald words that became his battle hymn.

He did his best to forget the niggling thought that even Napoleon had his Waterloo.

CHAPTER 4

OCCASIONAL BURSTS of laughter split the muted hum of after-dinner conversation in the main room of the tavern. Pine logs crackled and popped in the fireplace, working to displace the January chill seeping through cracks in the log walls' chinking. Overall, the atmosphere in Gallagher's was cozy and comfortable as the inn played host to eight guests.

The two ladies, sisters traveling with their husbands to visit family in Liberty, had already retired for the night, seeking their beds upstairs. Their mates had joined a dice game in progress and were now expansively detailing the beauty of the Sistine chapel to two buffalo hunters headed west and a patent-medicine salesman who eyed their pocket watches with interest. The aroma of roasted turkey mingled with the pungent scent of cigars and lingered with the soulful notes Daniel Gallagher pulled from his harmonica.

The inn's other guest sported an elegant frock coat of dark blue broadcloth over a red satin vest—quite a contrast to his poker opponent's buckskins and wicked smile. Katie worked behind the bar, polishing spotless glasses as her gaze returned time and again to the gentleman and Branch Kincaid, who apparently had taken this night off from the siege he'd declared on her virtue.

For the past three weeks, Gallagher's Tavern and Travelers Inn had served as the staging area for a war equal in intensity, if not in violence, to Texas's War for Independence. Not that the skirmishes between Branch and Katie lacked for havoc; they just weren't as mortal.

Although she was a skillful strategist and had evaded most of his maneuvers, Branch had managed to capture a few stolen kisses over the days. More and more she felt like the walls of the Alamo; another kiss, and Santa Anna Kincaid would breach her defenses.

She filled a cup with water and drank from it, glancing over its rim to the golden-haired warrior whose eyes set fire to her fortress. Honesty forced her to admit that sometimes, in the middle of the night, defeat sounded *so* good.

Branch lifted the tankard of ale to his lips and sipped. His opponent laid down his hand and said in a voice that carried, "Two pair, jacks high. My win, Kincaid."

Branch tipped back in his chair, grimacing. "That brew is green. Next time you buy me a drink, William Bell, make it whiskey. Gallagher's Irish is pretty darn good."

"I'm not here to discuss the relative merits of this establishment's beverages," the visitor said with a wry smile. He paid careful attention to gathering his small pot of winnings from the middle of the table. "Branch, cease with the evasions. I rode through a two-day snowstorm to reach this rustic little dwelling, and I believe I deserve some answers. Now, what have you learned since your arrival at Gallagher's?"

"Hah." Branch's scornful scoff caught Katie's attention. Her long, auburn braid swung across her shoulder as she gave him a curious look. He flashed her his rakish grin and winked. Loud enough for her to hear, he said, "I've learned that war can sometimes be a helluva lot of fun." Katie rolled her eyes and returned to her business of dusting the various bottles and glassware behind the bar.

"Branch?" William Bell inquired.

"What have I learned?" The front legs of his chair thumped to the floor. He fastened a frigid gaze on the impatient messenger and said in a low, deliberate voice, "I've learned that if Hoss Garrett wants me to do this job, he'd best stop sending you to check up on me."

Bell calmly swept an imaginary speck of dust from his well-tailored coat. "Your father wishes for a simple status report. That should not be too much to ask."

"Don't call him that! Around me he's Hoss Garrett!"

Branch swiped up the deck of cards and shuffled them, his movements abrupt and angry. His voice snapped as he added, "But I guess if Hoss wants a report, I'd best give you one. I like you too much, William, to send you back to Ol' Splitfoot empty-handed."

Bell thumped his tankard against the tabletop. "That is enough."

Ignoring Bell's outburst, Branch continued. "Here it is, short and sweet." He slapped the card deck onto the table. "That envelope you gave me when I signed Hoss's contract contained more than just the anonymous note sent to Riverrun informing the family of Rob's death. There was a packet of letters my brother had written to Eleanor and Hoss. In one of them he wrote that the principal players in the counterfeit scheme met regularly at a tavern outside of Nacogdoches run by an Irishman and his daughter. It was easy enough to determine that Gallagher's was the place. I've been spending all my time"—he stopped and looked again at Katie—"well, *almost* all of it, buying drinks and playing cards with every visitor to the tavern."

He paused and took a sip of his ale. "You know, if nothin' else, I've proved I can hold my liquor with the best of 'em."

Bell sighed impatiently. "But what have you learned?"

"Most of the men who come in here are members of an organization they call the Moderators. From what I can figure, it's a vigilante group formed to oppose another bunch of rabble-rousers who call themselves the Regulators. Actually, Will, it seems to stop something just short of an all-out war. Last August, Sam Houston sent in a militia and rounded up the leaders, forcing them to sign a treaty of peace. All that did was send the brawlin' underground. Now nobody really knows who's fightin' who."

He briefly considered the story he'd heard the previous evening about a Moderator who'd been bound to a log and whipped to death. "It's been a bloody little feud, this Regulator-Moderator thing. Neither side is all good or all bad; it's basically the old-time settlers against the newcomers. I'm fairly certain, though, that an inner circle of one of the two gangs is the source of the counterfeit land scrip. The problem is findin' out just which group."

He leaned back in his chair and folded his arms across his chest. His voice grated as he said, "So you can trot yourself back to Riverrun and tell the old bastard that I'm hard at work on the case. I'm sure he'll have his doubts, considerin' it's me he has doin' his huntin' for him. But at least he ought to have confidence that I can finish the job once I find Rob's murderer. After all, I *am* a killer."

William Bell's face flushed as red as his vest. He slammed his fist against the table. "Boy, I bounced you on my knee when you were young, and I have *always* defended you to your father. Don't spout such stupid things to me. Your fath—" He stopped as Branch shot him an icy look. "Hoss Garrett is offering you a chance, Branch, to grab what you've always wanted. I know how you feel about Riverrun. And Eleanor is a widow now; she's as beautiful as ever. Don't allow false pride to get in the way of your heart's desire."

"I've had little luck with my desires of late." Branch's gaze went unerringly to Katie. Eleanor Garrett wasn't the only beautiful widow in the Republic of Texas. "Buy me another drink, William, a real one this time."

He glanced toward Katie, who had dropped all pretense of ignoring the whispered conversation taking place at the table in front of the fire. "Sprite," he called, "as your father is fond of saying, I'm in need of a wee drop of the Irish."

Katie approached carrying two glasses and a bottle of John Gallagher's best. Undisguised curiosity put a glow to her face that made Branch want to laugh. It made him want to throw her over his shoulder and carry her up the stairs to his bed and answer all the questions that *really* mattered.

She poured each man a drink and waited expectantly. Branch looked up at her. "I guess you want an introduction."

She shrugged. "Well, this gentleman is the first of our guests to inquire after you by name. Obviously, you are acquaintances, and I'm always interested in learning more about our employees."

Branch shook his head at her demure look. Really, the woman should be on stage. "Mrs. Starr, may I present Mr. William Bell. William is a friend."

Bell had stood as Branch spoke, and both he and Katie waited a moment for Branch to expound on the relationship between them. When it became obvious that Branch had no intention of doing so, Bell bent over Katie's hand and gave it a courtly kiss. "I'm honored, madam. Please allow me to tell you how much I enjoyed the meal this evening. The turkey was roasted to perfection, and that cornbread dressing was the most delicious I've ever tasted. You must share your secret so that I may tell my wife."

Katie's smile beamed her pleasure. "Why, thank you, Mr. Bell. It's rewarding to know that my guests enjoy my cooking." No one but Branch knew she punctuated that statement with a kick to Branch's shin.

She's never goin' to let me forget those doughballs, he thought.

"I normally do not share my recipes, Mr. Bell, but since you are a friend of Mr. Kincaid's, I'll make an exception." A teasing twinkle in her eyes, she looked first over one shoulder, then the other, and whispered, "Two pours of Irish whiskey."

"Aha." Bell chuckled. "What an innovation!"

Katie nodded. "Actually, one might say it's my father's discovery. He's the one who tipped the bottle over in my kitchen one afternoon." She smiled warmly at William and added, "Welcome to Gallagher's, Mr. Bell. Make yourself at home. If I may be of any assistance, please let me know."

Watching her, Branch suddenly got a picture of Katie standing on the front veranda at Riverrun, welcoming guests in just the same manner. The thought cut like a knife.

"Sprite, I haven't checked on Striker yet this evening. Would you find Daniel for me and ask him to make sure he's settled for the night?"

Katie accepted the obvious request for privacy and left

the table, stopping to inquire as to the needs of the dice players before exiting the room.

"Mrs. Starr is a pleasant young woman," William commented.

"Don't believe it. She's as ornery as a mule colt, I'm here to tell you. And take a hint, never go near the woman when she's within squirrel-swingin' distance."

Branch sipped his whiskey and dealt another hand while thoughts of the Widow Starr mingled with memories of Riverrun. After a few moments of quiet he said, "Listen, William, I know you want to help me. I appreciate that, and I appreciate all the work you did searchin' to find me when Hoss ordered it." He sighed. "This is hard for me, William. I apologize for acting like a mule's hind end. It's just that, well, you were there that day, you know what it was like."

Bell studied his manicured fingernails. "It wasn't much of a party, was it?"

Branch's twisted grin agreed. Oh, the trappings had all been there. No matter how hard he tried, he could not forget the details of that night. It had been the end of his innocence—the payment for manhood. "Recollect the lanterns? Must have been four hundred of 'em hangin' from the live oaks that lined the drive up to the Big House."

Bell nodded.

"They cooked for weeks gettin' ready. The music, the dancing—I loved that song 'Possum up a Gum Stump.' The fiddler sure made the strings sizzle." He chuckled, remembering. "Rob danced with every pretty girl there and even some of the ugly ones. He told me that if he'd known turnin' seventeen could be so much fun, he'd have done it sooner."

Branch absently rearranged his cards, reflecting that his brother's dancing days were done. *I'll find the bastard who did this, Rob, I swear it.*

Bell sipped at his drink and commented, "You were thirteen."

"No, fourteen. My birthday was two days before Rob's. Not many people knew it."

Conversation ceased as the men stared at the cards in

their hands. Bell frowned and tossed a coin onto the table, but his next words proved the direction of his thoughts. "Hoss was wrong, Branch. Terribly wrong. I know that in his mind he recognizes it. I believe that he has been looking for a way to bring you home for years. The problem is that you two are so much alike. That damnable Garrett pride is keeping you apart. This is your chance, son, seize it. Be the better man. Forgive him."

Branch turned his head away and stared into the flames dancing in the hearth, the memory of a blaze in another time, another place, searing his heart. How different a life would he have lived if the fire in Virginia had never happened, if his mother and grandparents had not met their deaths when Eagle's Nest burned?

Certainly Branch would not now be a Texian. Hoss Garrett joined the many Southerners who painted *GTT*— Gone To Texas—on their front doors only because he fled painful remembrances. Hoss and his sons would not have established Riverrun. Branch wouldn't have been banished from his home. Rob wouldn't have died in East Texas.

Hell, why waste his time wondering about it? What's done is done. Nothing could bring Rob back to life.

But Branch *could* return to Riverrun.

When he spoke, his voice betrayed his emotion solely by the flatness of its tone. "Hoss's bellow rose above the music and laughter, everybody heard. Do you remember, William? I'd ridden his prized thoroughbred tryin' to impress Eleanor, and he cursed me for it, condemned me before all of South Texas. He declared his hatred of me and demanded that my friends and family hate me too."

"Branch, he may have said that, but no one—"

"William, we talked about this before when you ran me to ground at the Colby's ranch. I took only my nickname and my mother's maiden name when I left Riverrun that night. I've done fine with my life up till now. Why should I want to change? I've got a good thing going here at Gallagher's."

He looked toward the door through which Katie had exited moments earlier. "In fact, I'm presently embroiled in a skirmish that's makin' life more interestin' than it's been for quite some time. Maybe I'll forget what brought me here and simply enjoy myself instead."

"You won't."

"Why do you say that?"

"Because you loved your brother. Because even if you choose not to admit it to yourself, you love your father."

Branch's words blazed across the table. "Go to hell, William." His chair banged against the floor and he stomped outside into the bitter winter night.

Above the small clearing the thinnest of horned moons hung in the west, and stars died beneath the dawning light of day. Under the cold air a rounded roll of fog followed the twists and turns of the creek that meandered across the meadow, while at the forest's edge, indigo shadows hid from sight the tearing, splintering progress of a tree choosing the moment of dawn to crash to an ignoble end.

As daylight burst upon the land, thirteen-year-old Keeper McShane peered furtively at the motley collection of humanity gathered around Regulator leader, Colonel Watt Moorman. Goramighty, Keeper thought. It's a good thing it was dark when I got here, or I'd a been pure-dee scared of these creepy-crawly folks.

At least thirty men and horses now crowded into the small clearing. Grubby hands passed a bottle half-full of clear liquid from man to man, and Keeper grimaced while watching a chaw of tobacco balloon a fellow's cheek as he took a long, thirsty pull. "Goramighty," he murmured.

The cold stung his nostrils as he breathed air scented of sweat, saddle leather, and last night's whore. Watching the bottle with a wary eye, he wondered what he should do when it came around to him. He didn't want to look less than a man on this, his first ride with the Regulators, but someone had laughed that it was Willie Thompson's home recipe they were passing about. That rotgut had damn sure killed somebody just last week!

His hand trembled as he accepted the bottle from the man beside him. The neck was warm in his hands. Wondering if he could get away with skipping his turn, he sneaked a look at Sheriff Strickland. Amusement crinkled the corners of the lawman's eyes, and the dimple in his chin deepened as one corner of his mouth lifted in a crooked smile. When he raised his hand and ran a finger along his thin, straight nose, Keeper knew what he was supposed to do. It was the sheriff's way of telling a fella to get on with a thing.

Sheriff Strickland got more talking done with his eyes and his fingers than he ever did with his mouth.

Keeper brought the bottle to his lips. The liquor's kick about knocked him off his horse. The man next to him pounded his back as he choked and coughed, fire burning its way to his belly. "Good stuff, ain't it boy?" the man said. "Tastes like the backwoods of Kentucky, just like Ol' Willie said. Family recipe, you know."

Keeper ignored the man and turned watery eyes to Strickland. The sheriff smiled an encouragement. Despite the burn the liquor caused in his innards, the boy shivered and the tears in his eyes took a bit to dry. Shee-e-it, he thought, glancing around. An ocean of men surrounded him; he couldn't run away and puke even if he did get the nerve. When Watt Moorman started talking, he listened with half an ear.

"Glad to see so many of you turn out today," the colonel said, hooking his thumbs under his arms. "This council has much to consider on such a fine January morn."

Attempting to ignore the rumbles in his gut, Keeper watched the Regulator chief and tried to figure why he'd been chosen as leader rather than the sheriff. After all, since the group had organized in order to take the law into its own hands, it made sense to pick its only real lawman to be the headman.

Moorman was a strange character; he always dressed like he was late for the Battle of the Alamo. Today he had on a half-military coat and a black hat with a red feather in the band. He carried a brace of single-shot pistols and a bowie knife, and rode with a hunting horn hung on his saddle cantle. But in Keeper's eyes, Colonel Moorman couldn't hold a candle to the sheriff. Jack Strickland was tall with coal-black hair. He had a mouthful of straight white teeth that sent womenfolk to swoonin' when he smiled. Sheriff Strickland could draw a pistol slicker than snot and shoo the stinger off a mud dauber at fifty feet.

But most important of all, Strickland was the one that got him out of the whorehouse.

The boy snapped back to attention when the men around him all raised their right hands. He didn't have a clue what was being voted, but when Strickland's hand went up, his did too.

Moorman said, "It's unanimous. We continue our war on the lawless group Edward Merchant formed to oppose us—the Moderators."

The band of Regulators cheered. "We are the leaders of our communities," Moorman continued. "We own the towns and the courts. We will use the power of our positions to squash the rebels like pesky mosquitoes."

Some men fired pistols into the air. Keeper about fell off his horse.

Moorman smiled and held up a hand, signaling for quiet. He said, "It has come to my attention that many of the Moderators have made it their habit to do their drinking at Gallagher's Tavern outside of Nacogdoches. I propose we direct this evening's efforts against that establishment. Although I have a course of action in mind, I will consider any ideas you may have on this subject."

Hissing like a nest of copperheads, the Regulators whispered among themselves. As different kinds of punishment were proposed to their chief, the noise level rose. The snakes loved violence.

Listening to the talk, Keeper began to feel like one of the vipers had decided to crawl down his spine and settle in his belly. He knew the Gallaghers; they seemed to be fine folks. Being as how him and Daniel were of an age, he'd talked to the fella a couple of times in town. You had to respect a body that learned to shoot a slingshot so good using just one hand and his teeth. And the lady—she once bought him a peppermint down at the mercantile.

Overhearing what a couple of the more unsavory Regulators whispered about among themselves, Keeper considered retching. He'd seen that kind of stuff go on when he still lived with his mama at The Mansion of Joy. Miz Katie didn't deserve that.

He chewed the inside of his cheek as the vote was taken. Still, he knew he had to vote with Strickland. As Moorman directed a fifteen-man squad to don their hoods and head north, Keeper figured that things could've been worse. Burning and beating's better than killing. It was just too damn bad about Miz Katie.

The thudding rattle of hooves on the mud-packed road chased away the serenity of early morning in the forest. With ears pinned back, the mare listened to the words of encouragement crooned by the rider, stretching, seeking to hold her lead.

The dun pulled beside her, his nostrils flared and sides heaving with exertion. For the space of three ground-eating strides they ran even, the back-and-forth rhythm of the headlong gallop placing first one, and then the other, ahead at the nod.

Suddenly, as though he'd been toying with the mare all along, the dun charged ahead, a flash of black and gold, and his rider's victorious shout thundered into the pale Texas sky.

Katie Starr muttered an unladylike oath. "Branch Kincaid, I'll beat you yet."

Slowing Pretty Girl to a canter and then to a walk, Katie followed reluctantly as Branch turned off the road onto a path that led to a bluff overlooking the Angelina River. Branch swung from the saddle and stood beside Striker, rubbing the gelding's glistening neck.

He turned to her, eyes alight with victory—and something else. He gifted her with a courtly bow. "I believe the forfeit was a kiss, milady."

"You cheated," Katie declared as she slid from Pretty Girl's back.

A mock expression of pain sprawled across Branch's face. "You wound me, madam. 'Twas a contest fairly won. Fie on your attempt to cast aspersions upon my honesty."

"Oh, hobble your lip, Kincaid. I had you beat from the

start. That course you marked was a good bit longer than half a mile, and Striker caught Pretty Girl at the dogwood, well past the distance we should have run."

Katie hated losing, and his blatant delight only made things worse. She sulked, trying to figure how to avoid settling the bet, distracted all the while by the way his shirt clung to his sweaty back.

They walked briskly, giving their mounts a chance to cool. Below them, occasional ripples disturbed the rusty colored surface of the slow-flowing Angelina as bream surface-fed on midges. In the trees, titmice whistled *peter-peter-peter.*

A gentle peace stole over Katie. "I was foolish agreeing to your terms," she admitted. "You and Striker are well matched." He had fooled her by repeatedly refusing to accept her almost-daily challenge, and it wasn't until she upped the wager that he had agreed to race.

Now she owed him a kiss.

She gave him a sidelong glance. Toned and tapered, he worked on her senses like a spinster's dream. She wanted to touch him. She swallowed hard and chewed at her lower lip. When he chuckled, she felt it in her knees.

"What's the matter, Sprite? Not thinkin' of welchin' on the bet, now, are ya?"

"Of course not," she scoffed. Actually, she was beginning to wonder if she'd lost the race on purpose.

They walked silently for a time. He caught her hand in his and she didn't pull away. He began to whistle that same tune he'd been humming off and on since the day she left him in the brambles. "What's it called, the song, I mean?" Katie asked. "It must be a favorite of yours."

"Lay the young . . . oh, I don't remember the name. Just a catchy tune I can't seem to forget," he answered.

She looked at him suspiciously. He's up to something, she told herself. He's wearing that angel's face again. "I thought perhaps you wouldn't want to race today."

"Why did you think that?"

"Well, after the way you stomped out of the tavern last night, I wondered if you'd even be here this morning. Who was that man, Branch? You and Mr. Bell didn't exactly look like friends during all that whispering between you. What did he say to upset you so?"

Her eyes widened as, for just a moment, he became a cold, forbidding stranger. His golden eyes shuttered, and his body tightened into a long, angry line. Automatically, Katie took half a step back.

He visibly forced himself to relax his stance, although the tension in his eyes lingered. "He's a friend, I told you that," he said. "Anything more is not really your business."

Stung, she looked away. For all their bickering and bantering, nothing he had said had actually hurt her feelings before now. Suddenly she wanted to cry.

Their wanderings had led them to a spot not far from the graves of her family, and upon that realization, she murmured a distracted, "Excuse me," and left.

He didn't follow her at once. She had cleared the refuse of dead leaves and pine needles from both Mary Margaret's and Steven's graves and had begun to work on her mother's when Branch spoke from the edge of the graveyard. "How did your husband die, Kate?"

Kneeling beside Steven Starr's final resting place, Katie's back stiffened. "Murder. He was murdered. My daughter, too. She was just a baby, a beautiful, healthy little girl."

Branch's curse was short and explicit. "Texas is a damned hard land, isn't it?"

"No." Katie shook her head as she brushed brittle dogwood twigs from the base of the cross that marked Mr. Garrett's grave. "It's not the land that is hard, Branch. It's the people. But people have to be hard to survive in a place such as this. The problem is that mixed with the toughness is the evil. Texas has more than her share of evil people."

She saw the scuffed tips of his boots as he walked to her side and squatted down. He took her hand. "You want to tell me about it?"

She couldn't help herself. She said, "It's none of your business, Kincaid."

He grimaced. "I deserve that." Gently, he brushed an

errant curl from her forehead, an apology in his touch. "I've got some ghosts in my life, too, Sprite. Sometimes, like last night, they rise up to haunt me."

Dirt clung to the fingers she lifted to rub at the pressure building behind her eyes. He took the hand and pulled her to her feet. They walked to the riverbank, where he wrapped her in a comforting hug, and in silence, they watched the water drift slowly past.

Katie shivered as emotion swelled within her, and when the words stumbled out, she spoke as much to herself as to Branch. "I made a promise the night they died. I promised them I'd find the one responsible and make him pay. It's been so long now, and I haven't learned anything, I haven't done anything. I feel so . . . so . . ."

"Powerless," Branch concluded. "I know, Katie, I know."

"But you don't, Branch, you can't." The trembling began, and she clenched her teeth against it. The thing that lived in the darkness of her soul, the animal that had teeth sharpened by hatred, blood pumped by rage, and a roar given voice by anguish, strained against its bonds here beneath the warmth of the midmorning sun. "I want revenge."

Branch squeezed her tightly. "I do understand. More than you can guess, I understand. But don't get yourself all worked up over it, Sprite. What you are feelin' is warranted. You have a right to want justice."

"Not justice, Branch. *Vengeance.* I want to make the murderer suffer like he made Steven and Mary Margaret suffer." She pictured in her mind the events of the night that had ended lives and torn apart her own. "I want to make him hurt."

She heard the frown in Branch's voice as he slipped his hand along her braid. "Aw, now, Katie. You may think you want that, but I know you really don't. It's only natural to want to hurt someone when they hurt us. That's human nature. But it's not civilized, and though it doesn't seem that way at times, we are civilized here in Texas."

He pressed a quick, friendly kiss to her cheek. "Come on, let's start back. Graveyards are poor places to reason."

She chose to accompany him, though in her thoughts she protested his claim of empathy. He couldn't grasp how she felt. But then, there was no reason why he should. He'd never lost any family to a murderer's gun. He'd never felt the guilt.

Some fifteen minutes later, they walked their horses through a meadow not far from Gallagher's. The sun warmed the gentle breeze as Branch reached down and pulled a withered stalk of grass. He stuck it between his teeth, saying, "I bet this field comes alive in the spring."

Katie nodded, the topic of spring a welcome direction for her thoughts. "Oh, it does. The birds sing and wildflowers blanket the ground. They're mostly buttercups and black-eyed Susans, but every so often a few blues sneak in. I'm kind of partial to blue."

"Me too." He said it with a purr in his voice, and when she looked at him, she knew by his expression that he referred to the color of her eyes.

Nervously, she glanced away. She lifted her gaze to the sky, where high above, a bird soared with the current. "We're busiest in springtime," she said, anxious for a safe topic of conversation. "Every year we get more and more settlers through on their way south and west. I'm always worn out at the end of the day during spring and summer."

"I've often wondered why you have no slaves at Gallagher's," Branch said. "Running your place is too much work for three people."

Katie shrugged. "During the busy season Da tries to hire some help from town. He won't hold for owning slaves, though." Pretty Girl stopped to pull at a clump of grass, and Katie tugged on the reins. "Actually, he'll tell you all about it if you ask. My father ran from his indenture in Tennessee. That's what brought him to Texas to begin with."

They reached the edge of the meadow and took the forest path that led back to Gallagher's. Katie continued. "It's quite a romantic story, he and my mother fleeing in the night, hitching a ride on a flatboat down the Mississippi to New Orleans. They sailed on the *Good Intent* to Texas in '22."

"And you were born here?"

"Shortly thereafter."

"Sounds more harrowing than romantic to me," Branch drawled. "But since you brought the subject up, I seem to recall something about a wager."

"Now, that's harrowing." Katie stopped with a sigh and rolled her eyes. The wolf look was back on his face. She should have known he wouldn't forget. "All right, do it," she demanded.

He halted, arching his eyebrows in innocence. "Do what, Mrs. Starr?"

"Kiss me. Get it over with."

He threw back his head and laughed. She almost punched him in the stomach. "Ah, but, Kate, that wasn't the bet. You're to kiss me."

"Oh," she said. Pretty Girl snorted and tugged at the reins. Katie started walking, her thoughts in a whirl as she tried to figure an advantage to this development. So she was supposed to kiss him, was she? She'd best not allow it to happen.

She liked the idea entirely too much.

Then the answer came to her. "If I do the kissing, then I get to choose the time and place." She smiled smugly. "Fifty years from today sounds good to me."

Branch just looked at her and grinned. She felt his gaze on her backside as he followed her, whistling, until they reached the remains of the old stone fence that stood a short distance from the tavern. That's when he grabbed her.

"Now," he demanded, backing her against the wall. He rested an arm on either side of her and stared at her lips.

"Now what?" she asked, but she knew. "Y— you said I was to do it. I get to say when." Her tongue nervously circled her lips.

"Do it now." His whisper soaked through her skin. She felt him everywhere, but he never touched her.

"No. I don't want to. I don't have to. It's the rules. You said so yourself."

He shifted to the right, still not touching, and blew a

gentle stream of breath into her ear. "The lady doth protest too much, methinks," he said.

Heat seared her body, and Katie surrendered. After all, she'd been dreaming of this for six weeks. "Shakespeare from a Texian drifter?" she asked, trying to keep her voice steady.

"Taming of the Shrew." His gaze melted her mind.

She pressed herself against him, shaking her head. *"Hamlet."*

"Oh," he said, and his lips captured hers.

Liquid heat coursed through her veins. Her arms snaked around him, and the hard cords of his muscles flexed beneath her fingertips.

Then Branch pulled back. He turned his head and listened, a wild thing sensing danger. Katie gawked at him until the crackle and scent of burning pine broke horrifically through her senses.

Crack . . . crack. Gunshots drilled the air.

"Da! Daniel!" she cried, pushing at Branch's chest. He held her like an afterthought, his brow wrinkled, his eyes topaz hard, as the whoops of destructive, victorious men reached their ears. "Let me go," Katie cried.

"I'm goin'. You stay here." He grabbed her chin and glared into her eyes. "You move so much as a jackrabbit's whisker, and I'll tan your hide." He gave her a shake. "Do you hear me, Kate?"

She nodded.

The moment he let her loose, she darted off. Da always said she moved quick for a gal with such short legs, but Kincaid reached her in three strides.

She lost her wind when he tackled her. "Blast it, woman, I can throw you farther than I can trust you," Branch said. He pulled her to her feet as she struggled for breath and dragged her back to the horses. Katie twisted and kicked, fighting him desperately. "Let me go!" she screamed. "I have to help my family!" She viciously bit the hand that clenched her arm.

"Damn it, Kate. Settle down. This tantrum's wastin' time. I'm gonna take care of your people; you'd just be in the way." He lifted a rope from his saddle and proceeded to tie her to the nearest sturdy tree.

"Please, Branch," Katie begged. "Don't do this. They're in trouble and I've got to help." Tears of fright and frustration streaked her face.

Ignoring her pleas, he grabbed the weapons he always carried on Striker, making sure to snatch up extra ammunition and loading equipment. Branch never went anywhere without his bowie knife, Texas Patersons, and plains rifle.

When her little brother's agonized scream filled the air, Katie whimpered. Only the rope held her upright as she gazed helplessly at Branch. He looked cold as a January norther.

"I can't lose them, too," she whispered.

"You won't." Branch kissed her forehead and ran toward the shroud of smoke.

ᴈᴤ CHAPTER 5 ᴤᴈ

*T*ONGUES OF ORANGE flame licked the sky. The inn, the barn, the storage shed, even the vegetable garden—all were in the throes of destruction. Chaos reigned as hooded men atop prancing horses held torches aloft, shouting and whooping, with violence and ruin riding their blood like a fever. Men afoot cackled at the spectacle of squawking chickens, their feathers alight, darting about the barnyard in a frenzied dance of death.

Branch stood motionless just inside the tree line, and the apocalyptic sight before his eyes flashed him into the past. Instead of the inn's roof crashing to the ground, he saw the Virginia plantation's huge Doric columns tumble into flaming rosebushes. He heard pops and crackles and screams—oh, God, the screams! The clouds of gray smoke engulfing him stank not of pine but of burning flesh—animal flesh, human flesh. Fear clutched his belly, slithered around his feet, and he could not move.

Mommy, I'm scared. The man looked to his fist and saw a seven-year-old boy's hand holding a matchstick.

Then the groan, a long, agonized wail of pain, snapped him back to the present. The Gallaghers! John lay facedown beside the horse trough. Alive or dead, Branch couldn't tell. Daniel, strapped lengthwise on a tanning log, his shirt ribboned and bloodied, was sobbing. Damn the bastards, Branch thought. Flexing his fingers, he ached to pull his Colt and drop the bear of a man who wielded the whip.

Rage constricted his throat as he quickly searched his mind for a way to help the Gallaghers. Outgunned, any of *his* shots would likely be answered with bullets plugged into his friends. Think, man! Considering and discarding several options, he arrived at a plan. Risky, not much more than a gamble, but a plan nonetheless. He took one bold step from cover when the sound pierced his heart like a Comanche arrowhead.

Katie's shriek stopped every man in his tracks as she burst through the trees and launched herself at the man holding the whip. They tumbled to the ground. When sunlight caught the knife blade she raised above the man's chest, Branch reacted. "Holy hell," he exclaimed, and fired off two shots.

The first bit the dirt at her knees. The second sailed wide of her hand. Together they grabbed her attention, buying him time to reach her. Where in the hell did she get a knife, he wondered as he pointed his Colt square at her head. Deliberately, he said, "Drop the knife and get up, Mrs. Starr."

Katie stared at him, her eyes frozen blue ice. Her gaze never left him, even when she reeled from the force of the backhanded blow delivered by the man dressed entirely in black, the one who'd been shouting orders earlier.

Branch's thoughts turned savage. Fury pounded through his veins. He reached deep for control and swallowed the bitter taste in his mouth. Pasting a friendly smile on his face, he extended a hand to the tall man. "The name's Branch Kincaid, sir."

The Regulators closed in on Katie, yanking her to her feet. Branch inwardly recoiled at the hate she hurled his way, and when one yellow-toothed blackguard reached out and cupped her breast, he went rigid. His jaw muscle twitched as he inhaled a deep breath.

Turning his back to her at that moment was the hardest thing he'd ever done.

The leader's dark eyes gleamed through slits cut in the black cotton hood. He brushed dust from his coat and asked in a muffled voice, "Have we met before?"

Branch looked up a bit to meet his eyes.

The scoundrel may have been taller, but Branch outweighed him by a good twenty-five pounds. And someday he'll feel every one of them, he promised himself. "No, we've not met, but you men are pretty famous in these parts," he said aloud. "I've been looking forward to makin' your acquaintance."

At that, Katie found her tongue. "Damn your hide, Kincaid," she screamed. He looked casually over his shoulder. Spewing venomous curses, Katie bucked and squirmed. She tossed her head in violent frenzy and twisted to rake her nails down her captor's face. "Da! Daniel!" she shrieked, straining to free herself.

Then she stilled and centered all her energy behind her words. "The devil take you, Branch Kincaid, the devil take you all."

She laughed hysterically. With her hair in tangled disarray, eyes frantic and breasts thrust forward as she arched away from those who held her, Katie looked like Bedlam's daughter. And as such, she unknowingly helped his cause.

He whirled on her, eyes blazing. Nobody stopped him when he grabbed her by the shoulders and shook her hard. "Shut up. I've had all your mouth I'm willin' to take." He stared into her wild eyes, trying to reach her, reassure her, but she was beyond seeing. He grasped her upper arm and yanked her away from the Regulators. She stumbled as he dragged her toward the horse trough and threw her to her knees beside John.

"Tend to your old man, woman. Don't let me hear so much as a swallow out of you." He lowered his voice and pleaded, "Trust me, Sprite."

Wearing a disgusted sneer, he walked back to the dumbfounded group of Regulators. "She's a loon, you know," he told the man in black. "Her old man told me she's had these spells ever since her husband died." He shook his head. "Dangerous thing, too. Why, one mornin' I woke up and she had a hammer raised above my head. Ready to kill me in my sleep she was. And after a right pleasant night of pokin', too. I should've known her Pa wouldn't sell her so cheap without a reason." He shrugged and said, "But she's an Anglo woman, unattached and clean. They ain't too easy to find in Texas, you know."

"It seems as though lack of sense runs in the family,"

the Regulator replied. "All I intended was for us to burn the place. It wasn't until the boy started shooting and the old man swung his fists that things got personal."

Branch waved a hand in a dismissive gesture and said, "They are a strange bunch of pups around here, that's for certain. I've been wantin' to talk with you about joinin' up with the Regs. I've got a hankerin' to get involved in this little war y'all got goin'. How do I go about it?"

The Regulator threw back his head and laughed. At the sound, a chill brushed the back of Branch's neck. "Just what kind of fool are you, Kincaid?" the fellow asked. He turned to his men and said, "You men take care, the woman isn't the only crazy one here today."

He shifted his gaze back to Branch, shaking his head. "You show up out of nowhere, help me out of a little difficulty, take control of one of my prisoners, then calmly announce you want to join our organization." He chuckled, but amusement never touched the sinister gleam in his eyes. "For all I know, you could be a Moderator spy!"

Now the gamble, Branch thought. But the stakes were higher than he'd planned. *Dammit, Kate, why didn't you stay put?* "You're right." Branch nodded slowly. "That's what I am, or at least that's what I told the Moderator leader, Edward Merchant."

The Regulator held up a hand, halting his men, who were going for their guns. "What's your story?" he asked.

Branch looked around guardedly. "Well, I hate to go into any detail right about now, what with all the company." He flicked his thumb toward the Gallaghers. Katie had helped John to his feet, and together they had staggered over to Daniel. She worked feverishly at the knots that bound his hands. Tears flowed down John's dirty, wrinkled face as he comforted his son, whose soft moans drummed in Branch's ears.

"Do you think we might could find a more private place to speak?" Branch asked.

Cold eyes stared at him a full minute, then the man nodded once and pointed toward the kitchen, which had not been set afire. "In there, after you."

"Hey, boss, can we have the gal now?" one of the men called as they crossed the yard.

Branch shot the leader a hard look. "The woman is mine," he stated flatly. "I meant what I said about liking my women clean, and I aim to make sure she stays that way. I've got four thousand dollars in land certificates that come with this deal, but nobody touches the Gallagher woman but me."

"You know, I could have you all killed with a single word," the muffled voice shot back. He tilted his head and studied Branch. "Four thousand?"

Branch nodded.

The Regulator shrugged and called over his shoulder to his men, "Leave the woman be."

Only then did Branch relax the viselike grip on his gun. With total concentration focused on maintaining his restraint, Branch followed the scoundrel purposefully into the kitchen.

They sat at Katie's worktable, where a white linen towel covered a wooden bowl sitting to one side. Branch lifted a corner of the cloth, then helped himself to a wedge of cornbread left from breakfast. "Needs a pinch of sugar, but still pretty good," he said. "Want one?"

The black hood moved from side to side. "Anonymity protects us from individual reprisals by the Moderators. That's the mistake Gallagher made. It's become well-known that the inn was a meeting place for Edward Merchant's band." A gloved hand pulled at the collar of a black shirt. "Enough of this. Tell me about the four thousand."

Branch stretched out his long legs and crossed them at the ankles. Mentally modifying the story he'd intended to tell all along, he began, "I'm a chemist, a very good chemist. With the aid of my special mixture of acids, I can erase figures in ink from the face of notes without destroying or damaging the paper. Unfortunately, I have some very bad people after me. I need protection, and I'm willing to pay whatever it takes to get it."

"Chemist, huh?" The Regulator crossed his arms over his chest. "Who is after you, and what does any of it have

THE TEXAN'S BRIDE   57

to do with your telling Edward Merchant you'd spy for him?"

One corner of Branch's mouth lifted in a mocking smile. "Well, mister, like so many others, I came to Texas ten steps ahead of the law, in this case a pair of New York detectives. But I didn't realize I'd be jumpin' from one hot skillet into another. This clan war of yours is cookin' pretty hot, and I want out of the pan."

"No one forced you to get involved, Kincaid."

"You are right about that. It's the woman. Isn't it always a woman? I was just lookin' for some clean commerce, and I end up gettin' shot at." He shrugged. "Hell, I've got enough people gunnin' for me without gettin' caught in the local cross fire. I figure that if each side thinks I'm workin' for them, they'll leave me the hell alone."

"Kincaid, I'm sitting here trying to decide whether you're somewhat smart or real stupid. You're telling me you're playing both ends against the middle?"

"I'm telling you I'm trying to cover my ass."

Dark eyes narrowed with suspicion. "You're a nervy sonofabitch, aren't you? What's to keep me from shootin' you where you sit?"

"Money. Lots of it." Branch leaned back in his chair and folded his arms across his chest. "Listen, I knew within a week of coming here who was going to win this fight. The Moderators don't stand a chance against men like Watt Moorman. In another year the Regulators will own East Texas."

The lingering scent of burned pine blew into the room on a breeze, a grim reminder of the destruction that lay beyond the kitchen's walls. Branch's gut clenched, and it took a conscious effort to appear relaxed. "I'll feed Merchant whatever information you want him to have, and I'll pass along whatever I hear from him that you'd be interested in learnin', as long as it doesn't tip my hand." He sat up straight, folded his hands on the table, and leaned forward. Make this good, he told himself as he said, "But that's not what I'm dealin' today. Eventually, those detectives on my tail are goin' to find me. If you'll put your

Regulator guns against 'em when they do, I'll get you enough money to own *all* of Texas if you've got a hankerin' for it."

"How?"

"Why, make it, of course."

Trust me.

The words echoed through Katie's mind. But he betrayed me. Betrayed us. Or had he? I could have ended it right then. The Regulator would be dead. I would be dead. I thought Da and Daniel were dead. Sweet Mother Mary.

Trust me.

Katie hung her head in despair. Daniel needed some salve for his cuts. She'd washed his back, but he needed the salve. It would sooth the burn. Five lashes, as best she could tell. A boy, he's just a boy.

Another boy had brought well water when she asked. She knew him, she recognized his voice. Keeper McShane. Another boy, freckle-faced beneath that awful hood. She had bought him candy, and now he held a gun on her, on them. She remembered what Branch had said earlier about Texas being a hard land. Perhaps he was right. What kind of country was this where boys suffered from the cruelty of men, where boys acted with the cruelty of men?

"Mavourneen," John croaked, interrupting her thoughts. "Water. Please." Katie lifted the pail to her father's split and swollen lips. Tears burned her eyes. Da, poor Da. Bruises covered his body. When she could get into the kitchen, she'd get something to bind his ribs. If she ever did get in, that is.

They'd been in there for an eternity.

The Regulator leader had left the kitchen once, long enough to send a man after Striker and Branch's saddlebags and to order all but three of the Regulators back to Nacogdoches. Now, along with Keeper, two men guarded her and her family.

Keeper seemed nervous. Every few moments he'd shift his pistol from his right hand to his left and wipe his palm on his dirt-streaked trousers. Katie began to wonder who was guarding whom.

Sweat ran in rivulets down her back. Was it the heat from the fire? The coppery taste of fear wouldn't leave her mouth. *Damn you, Branch Kincaid, what are you doing in my kitchen?*

Trust me.

The door swung open. The Regulator and Branch stepped outside, both all smiles, the hooded man gripping a handful of what looked like bank notes. Katie watched them walk toward her and was struck by the similarities between the two men.

Each carried himself with arrogance. Broad of shoulder, a swagger to their steps, they both exuded strength and tenacity. They both could be cruel.

The Regulator hid behind a mask. Who was he? Where did he live? How did he make his living? Was he a neighbor, a customer, someone she called friend? The thought made her shudder.

And what of Branch Kincaid? He hid behind that innocent expression and wicked grin. Who was he and why was he at Gallagher's? He asked her to trust him; did she dare? And heaven help her, he gave her an entirely different kind of shivers.

The Regulator looked her over, eyes gleaming. "I don't know, Kincaid. Perhaps I made a mistake including her in the deal. I've seen the lady in town before. Calmed down and cleaned up, she's an attractive woman."

Branch shrugged and said nothing.

Katie couldn't stop the shudder when the hooded man sat on his haunches and reached for a strand of her hair. He let it slide between his fingers. "Beautiful," he said. "Silky, a bit of red. What color are the rest of your curls, honey?"

He grabbed a handful of auburn tresses and wrapped them around his wrist. Yanking her so hard that tears sprang to her eyes, he pulled her to within inches of his masked face. "Come at me again, bitch, and I'll carve you up so bad that even a blind man can't stand to look at you."

He threw her into the dirt and stood. Keeper retrieved his horse, and taking the reins, the Regulator leader swung into the saddle. The sorrel snorted as he called, "Come on, men. The boss will be waiting in Shelbyville for a report. Let's ride."

Glancing at Branch, he added, "Report to Sheriff Strickland in Nacogdoches in a week, Kincaid. He's been asking the town council for a deputy, and I'll see that you get the job. It'll give you quick access to Regulator guns should the need arise. One more thing—don't make me look back on this day with regret."

"I'll be there, and I'll have what we bargained for," Branch promised solemnly. "Trust me."

During the night it rained, a long, soaking downpour that extinguished any embers left burning and turned dry ash into acrid clumps of clinging mud. Everything was gone but for the limestone fireplace that rose from the rubble like a monument on a battlefield, which, in truth, it was.

The day had dawned gray and lifeless, a fitting accompaniment for Katie's state of mind. She stepped carefully amid the debris as she searched for salvageable objects. She worked alone. John Gallagher tended to Daniel, who lay on his stomach in Katie's bed, passed out from the liquor his father had coaxed down his throat to alleviate his pain.

Branch Kincaid had disappeared sometime during the night.

"Good riddance," she told herself. She was glad he was gone, pleased that he had slunk off into the darkness like the wolf that he was. "Trust me, hah," she scoffed. The fairy tale was over—Grandma had been eaten.

She bent to retrieve a shapeless bit of metal that once had been a tankard. Damn the man. Perhaps she should have listened when he attempted to explain, but she'd been so upset, so worried about Daniel and Da.

Poor Daniel's back was raw; cleansing and applying the salve had caused him so much pain. He didn't deserve this. First his hand, now his back—boys weren't meant to have this kind of pain. And Da, he'd seemed to age ten years overnight. For the first time ever, when she looked at him, she saw an old man.

Damn Branch Kincaid. He had planned it. He had been part of it, she was sure of it. Branch and his charming friend, Mr. William Bell, had whispered and plotted the destruction of the very inn under whose roof they had sat.

You don't really believe that, a voice inside her whispered. "I do." She brushed sodden ashes from a misshapen Britannia teapot, then set it gently into the deep pocket of her apron. The voice argued, *The Regulators would have hurt you if not for Branch Kincaid.* "I'd have killed them if not for him." *You'd be dead if not for him. He saved you and he saved your family. You should be grateful to him.* Katie kicked the ashes and said, "Then why did he run away the first chance he got without explaining himself?"

"You didn't give me the chance to explain, Sprite." Branch leaned casually against the fireplace, his expression anything but relaxed. "And I didn't run away, I went after a doctor for Daniel. Some of those cuts are pretty deep, and I'm afraid of infection. Doc Mayfair's in the kitchen now, workin' on your brother. You could've had a little faith in me."

After the first fierce rush of relief came a wave of anger so great that she sputtered from the force of it. "Faith in you! Why, you . . . you . . ."

"I'll bet you've got it all figured out, don't you? I could hear your brain clickin' away from over here." He straightened and took a predatory step toward her. "What am I, Katie Starr, a good boy turned bad or a bad boy turned good?"

She gulped for air and said the first thing that came into her mind. "You're no boy."

"You've got that much right." He moved closer, his eyes glinting like sharpened steel.

Katie stepped backward. Her ankle twisted as her shoe slid across the slick surface of a bottle lying on its side, and she stumbled, flinging her hands out as she fell.

She never hit the ground. Instead she found herself

yanked against a solid wall of muscle. "Dammit, Sprite, I told you to trust me."

His lips swooped down upon hers, hard and demanding. He delved into her mouth with his tongue, deeper and deeper, searching and hungry. Angry.

Katie pushed against his chest, her emotions at war. Fury. Jubilance.

She was scared.

She shivered as his lips trailed down her neck, his teeth nibbling at sensitive skin. She gasped for breath and cried, "You don't frighten me!"

Savagely, he shoved her away. "I swear, woman, you don't have the sense to spit downwind. You may have a helluva lot of things to be scared of, but I'm not one of 'em. Don't you recognize help when you see it?"

Katie steepled her fingers and pressed them against her mouth. She gazed at Branch, her thoughts a whirlwind.

Disgustedly, he swung his boot at a half-buried remnant of a window shutter. Weariness etched his face and his shoulders wore an unfamiliar slump. "Lord knows why I care. You've been nothin' but trouble. A distraction, that's all you're supposed to be. I've got business to see to; I don't need to hang around coddlin' an old man, a boy, and a woman who thinks I'm dancin' with the facts."

"What facts, Branch?" Katie flung up her hands. The questions that had been swirling inside her for hours, for days, for weeks, burst from her lips. "Just what do I know about you that should give me reason to trust you? Why are you here? You're more than just a drifter, I'm certain of that. And just who is William Bell?"

Her voice rose as she stepped toward him. "Are you a Moderator spy or a Regulator? Where did you get four thousand dollars' worth of land scrip? Are you responsible for what happened yesterday? Have you been lying to us? Were you lying to me when you spoke of justice?" She ended her tirade in a shrill, "Why are you here, Branch Kincaid? What do you want?"

He stared at her. She stood in ashes to her ankles, the pockets of her smudged and dirty apron bulging with the fragments of her livelihood. Soot clung to her hair, streaked her face, and soiled her navy homespun dress. She was an Irish virago raging at fate.

She'd never looked so beautiful.

Lust tied his tongue and he spoke only one word. "You."

"What?"

"You, Sprite. I want you." He tugged her back into his arms and lowered his mouth to hers, kissing her desperately, the memory of his fear for her at the forefront of his mind. He tightened his hold on her as he tasted that fear along with the sweetness of her lips. Tearing his mouth from hers, he whispered against her cheek, "You little fool, you could've been killed."

She kicked him hard on the shin.

"Ow!" he exclaimed, releasing her to rub his tender leg. Katie glared at him through narrowed eyes, and she flung her words like arrows from a bowstring. "How dare you! How dare you play that game now after all that has happened. Are the only feelings you have those between your legs?"

The barb struck. "Feelings?" he repeated incredulously. "You think I have no feelings? Dammit to hell, Sprite, do you actually think I'm playin' a game here? Do you imagine I was amused seein' a man beaten and a boy whipped half to death? Do you think I enjoyed watchin' the wanton destruction that took place here yesterday? Tell me true, Kate Starr, do you honestly believe that I liked seein' that goddamn bastard manhandle you?"

Katie put her fists against her temples and grimaced at the sky. "I don't know what to think or believe or imagine anymore. You've answered none of my questions, Kincaid. You ask for my trust without offering your own. Why?" She flung up her hands. "Is there a reason you won't talk to me, Branch?"

"Yes."

She waited. He said nothing more. Her voice trembled with her fury. "Yes. That's all, just yes?"

With his thumb he nudged his hat back farther on his head. "That's about the size of it."

She took a breath to speak but then stopped. She

frowned at him as a speculative look replaced the anger in her eyes. Folding her arms, she tilted her head and asked, "Are you a government agent, Branch? Did President Houston send you here to collect information about the Moderator-Regulator War? Is that why you're so close-mouthed?" Had she not watched him so closely, she'd not have noticed the flicker of surprise in his eyes.

"Aw, Kate," he drawled, smirking, "don't you know that next to horse rustlin', curiosity's the most dangerous crime? Besides, you oughta know from my kisses that I don't keep a closed mouth."

Katie looked down and with the toe of her shoe nudged a charred wooden frame that once had held a family tree done in embroidery. "You're not going to tell me, are you?"

"Nope. You just have to trust me, Sprite."

She shook her head and said, "I can't."

Six days had passed since the fire. Six days of cutting, hauling, and stacking logs. Six days of sore muscles and even sorer tempers.

"Absolutely not." Branch plunged a hand into the ooze and withdrew a fistful of Spanish moss mixed with dirt and water. "I'm leavin' tomorrow." He packed the mud between two logs on the north wall of the newly erected barn. "Not the day after, or next week, or next month, or next year. Get it through that thick skull of yours, Irish-man. In the morning, I'm gone!" Red globs plopped up onto his face as he slammed his fist into the bucket for more chinking.

Tomorrow couldn't come soon enough as far as Branch was concerned. Life around the old inn, or kitchen, to be precise, had become downright unpleasant. Katie wasn't speaking to him. In fact, she went to considerable trouble to avoid him altogether. When he walked into the kitchen, she walked outside. When he went out to work on the new barn, she stayed in to nurse Daniel and spin thread and do what other womanly chores she could think up.

She was madder than a red-eyed cow, and Branch had plumb had enough. Katie Starr could take her temper and stuff a mattress with it. He was going to town and getting on with the business of finding the man who killed his brother. That's what was important. Not his sparring with a squirrel-slinging termagant. He'd find Rob's murderer, and then he'd head back to Riverrun and woo the gentle, beautiful, even-tempered Eleanor Garrett.

To hell with the Gallaghers and their problems. They weren't his responsibility. Besides, he'd done all that could be asked of anyone when he arranged in town for carpenters to come and build them a spanking-new inn.

John Gallagher scowled and said, "Aach, very well. I double your pay."

"You double my pay! Well that's a good one," Branch said scornfully. "Considerin' that I've worked for you a month and the only thing I've gotten for it is a hand-me-down hat, I'd have to be dumb as a rubbin' post for that to change my mind. Your promises are as empty as your pockets." The woebegone expression John adopted didn't sway him either. Since he'd announced he was leaving, he'd seen it far too often to be bothered by it now.

The wily old Irishman wasn't prepared to give up, however. He folded his arms and waited as Branch completed the finishing touches on the new barn.

Actually, the term "barn" said too much for the structure. It'd been years since Branch had helped build the log cabin that had been the original building at Riverrun. By the looks of the crude shelter he stepped away from, he'd forgotten what little that experience taught him.

"Hell, it'll last till spring," he grumbled, making a mental reminder to have the carpenters do a bit of work on the structure. Anyway, it wasn't like the Gallaghers had a bunch of stock to protect from the weather.

"It's a fine barn, Branch Kincaid," John said, nodding solemnly. "I thank you. We'd never have managed without your help. If you're set on leaving, I guess I just have to make the best of it." He rubbed his bristled jaw with his palm. "I'm unable to imagine what we'll do once you've gone, though. Why, even though he's on the mend, Daniel still cannot do much more than fish. It's too old I am to be starting over, building a new place and everything."

"Uh, John," Branch began. This figured to be as good a time as any to tell him about the new inn, and if Branch had any luck at all, John wouldn't ask where he had gotten the money for it. That he'd come to East Texas richer than the dirt in an old cow pen would be difficult to explain.

Gallagher was too caught up in his performance to listen to Branch. He hooked his thumbs in the armholes of his leather vest, stared up at the puffy white clouds floating slowly across the pale blue sky, and sighed. "I'm a'thinkin' perhaps the thing to do is to move into Nacogdoches. I believe the Mexicans would hire me as their barkeep at the cantina. Katie could wait tables."

Rocking back on his heels, he added, "Of course, as her father, I'd hate to see her have to dress like one of those Jezebels. It'd be nice if Billy Preston would hire me to work in the Anglo tavern—his women wear more clothes. Seein' how he's a Regulator, though, he'd never hire me. Unless"—he lifted his brows innocently—"unless *you* could get me on, seein' how you're one of them."

Branch gawked in amazement. "You're remarkable. You'll try anything to get your way, won't you, old man? I tell you what, I'll stay an extra day if you let me be there when you tell Kate she's gonna have to whore in Nacogdoches." He hooted with laughter, knowing Gallagher would sell his soul before he sold his daughter.

Picking up the rag lying next to the bucket of red mud, Branch wiped his face and hands. His gaze strayed to Katie, who stirred a tub of laundry with a battling stick. She'd rolled the sleeves of her calico dress up past her elbows and had hiked her skirt beyond the reach of the flames dancing beneath the kettle. Trim ankles and a good bit of shapely leg were displayed in a most enticing manner.

Steam rose, bathing her face, and she lifted a weary hand to brush back twisting, wet curls from her forehead. "John, what has she said to you about that day? Has she asked about my deal with the Regulator?"

Gallagher's brow wrinkled with worry as he, too,

watched his daughter work. "The only thing she men-. tioned was something about fools and misplaced trust." He looked quizzically at Branch. "That mean anything to you?"

"Yep," Branch said, grimacing. He'd never answered Katie's rapid-fire questions. How could he possibly explain the story he'd given the Regulator boss? The Gallaghers were smack-dab in the middle of this clan war, and he just couldn't risk exposure of his true purposes.

It was a dangerous game he played, with the highest of stakes. Of course, he didn't believe that Katie's family had anything to do with Rob's murder, but they were involved enough for Watt Moorman to have named them as a Regulator target.

Branch had no choice but to play his cards close to his vest, even though the regard in Katie's eyes had melted away like ice on a July morning. Not that he cared. Why should it bother him that she just wouldn't trust him?

With an oath, Branch flung the rag to the ground. "John, you know I told the man I'd contact him four days from now. I'm sorry if I'm lettin' you down by leavin', but I've done my best to help y'all get settled after the trouble, and it's time for me to move on. The Gallaghers are not my responsibility!"

"If you don't have a nerve, boyo," John said, scowling.

"Yeah, well, I'm gonna go wash." Branch looked down at his hands. In the red mud he saw his brother's blood, the lashes crisscrossing Daniel Gallagher's back, and Katie's disillusioned heart. "I've gotta go wash."

The afternoon was a sun-kissed promise. Almost every winter, this part of Texas was blessed with a couple of weeks that prophesied the coming of spring. At the Angelina's edge, Branch pulled off his blue chambray shirt and allowed the sunshine's heat to soak into his bones.

Tired, Lord he was tired. A cardinal's *whoit, whoit, whoit,* broke the silence, and Branch absently studied the trees, attempting to spot the bright red bird. He splashed icy water on his hands and arms, pulled off his boots, and tossed them away from the bank. Dangling his feet in the frigid water, he lay back and balled up his shirt to pillow his head. He closed his eyes.

The thought whispered, unbidden on the breath of sleep. *Sprite, forgive me. You see, I'll be his son again.*

A whiff of lye soap together with a tug to his scalp pulled Branch from sleep's oblivion. He wrinkled his nose and opened his eyes to the sight of Katie's calico-clad breast dangling inches from his mouth.

She knelt across him. He didn't know what she was doing and honestly didn't care. The scooped neckline of the dress teased with a hint of cleavage, and the trailing edge of a yellow ribbon tied at its center brushed a soft caress against his temple.

She must have heard him choke because she dropped her gaze and froze at the sight of his wide eyes. "Your hair is twisted around a button," she stammered. "I tried to untangle it so that I could take your shirt." Her voice faded as her tongue flicked out and danced along the ridge of her full lower lip.

Branch swallowed hard. "You can take anything you want."

Katie sat back, her gaze fastened on his mouth. "I ought to have your pants, they're the only ones that didn't burn."

"You're wrong." He wouldn't be surprised to see smoke rising from them just then.

She mumbled her words. He picked up only "need," "ready," and "hot."

"Hot?" he croaked.

"Boiling." Katie nodded slowly, her voice husky and low. "Da told me you're leaving. You confuse me, Branch Kincaid. I have the feeling that there is much more to you than you've ever let on, and I've attempted to understand why you'd make a deal with the vermin who burned our home. Are you trying to protect us still, Branch? Is that why you're going to work for him?"

He didn't answer. He couldn't answer.

"I don't want to believe that you're one of the evil ones, Branch. But I don't understand you. I hope you find whatever it is you're looking for."

"Holy hell, Sprite."

"Since you're headed to town . . . well, you've done so much for us, it's the least I can do for you."

He groaned hoarsely. "Sprite, I never thought you'd offer," he said, crushing her to him. He took her lips in a long, lazy kiss, then pulled back in puzzlement when she struggled against him. "What are you doin?" he asked.

"Why . . . laundry!"

"Oh." Undaunted, he rolled her beneath his taut frame and bestowed a kiss that rivaled the temperature of the wash water. By the time it ended, his own battling stick was anxious to agitate.

Weeks of frustration overwhelmed any chivalrous intentions he might have been fostering. She'd fought with him, played with him, talked with him, teased with him. The time had come for her to love with him.

He'd have her this one time before he left.

She didn't fight. She was floating in a soap bubble besieged by a storm of sensation, aware that any moment now her filmy sphere of resistance would pop, leaving her victim to mutual desire. Sluggishly, she tried to rise above the tempest.

But the first, feather-light touch of his fingers as they slipped beneath the neckline of her dress burst the bubble. Although she didn't trust him, she wanted him. He trailed wet kisses down her neck, following the path of his hand. She wanted to be a woman with him. He nuzzled the hard tips of her breasts through the thin calico. It'd been so long and he was leaving tomorrow.

He was leaving tomorrow. The warning flashed through her mind, piercing her passion like lightning splits the sky. He'd take her, then leave her. He'd disappear just like everyone else.

Katie felt his arousal hard against her thigh. "No," she said, pushing against his chest. She wouldn't love him, she wouldn't. She just might not survive it.

He didn't stop; he wove magic that threatened her will as nothing before. Her thoughts became disjointed fragments. She drifted in a carnal haze.

Ironically, it was the very expertise of his seduction

that pulled her back to reality. Steven never did this to her senses. Steven. Her husband.

As Branch's overbold fingers swept beneath her skirt, the question flared in her mind. Did she really want the memory of a drifter she didn't trust a whit to supplant the whispers from the past? No. She called upon the past to thwart the present and said, "We've got to stop, *Steven*. Oh, *Steven*, not here, not now."

It took a moment, but Branch rolled off her, onto his back, and lay with his forearm flung over his eyes. The cords in his neck protruded, and Katie thought she heard his teeth grind. His chest rose and fell with deep, lung-expanding breaths. He looked dangerous.

Katie sat up and straightened her clothing. She twisted the ribbon around her index finger as she edged away and stood. He never said a word.

Cautiously, she bent to collect his shirt. He shifted his arm and opened one eye to stare at her. His piercing gaze spoke volumes.

She looked away, out over the water. "I'll . . . I'll take th— . . . th— . . . this back and wash it. There's a pair of man's breeches in my trunk if you'd like to borrow them and add your pants to the laundry."

A muscle in his cheek twitched. He ground out his words. "Wasn't your husband's britches I was thinkin' to wear. I'll do my own goddamned wash." He jerked to his feet, glaring, and dived into the winter-chilled waters of the river.

By the time his head broke the surface, Katie had fled. Damn good thing, too, he fumed. He couldn't remember the last time he'd felt this kind of impotent rage. No, not impotent. Definitely not impotent.

He swam with angry strokes until the near-freezing water accomplished what he'd intended. Never, in all the years since he'd set out to do justice to the designation "rakehell," had a woman, in the midst of amorous pursuits with him, with *him*, had the audacity to voice the name of another man right in the blessed middle of things. Sonofabitch!

Cold replaced the tension in his muscles created by the

pressures of the past weeks, and he hauled himself onto the riverbank. He peeled the wet denim from his body. Standing, shivering, he looked around for something he could use to dry himself.

Mrs. Starr had left his shirt. He picked it up and rubbed the absorbent cotton across his chest. He remembered how she looked wearing it the day he got friendly with the briars. Teasing witch. She'd wanted him then. Hell, she wanted him today. He knew it.

The idea slithered into his thoughts. He grinned. Grabbing his boots and soggy clothing, he walked back toward the cabin and the laundry kettle. Naked. Whistling his battle hymn.

A norther blew in overnight, and the morning dawned gray and lifeless. Katie remained closeted in her room, where she'd retreated after yesterday's final confrontation with Branch Kincaid. He'd been naked as a newborn when he dropped his clothes into her laundry kettle. After he'd kissed her thoroughly and said, "The name's Branch, don't be forgettin' it," the rope that had tied her tongue tasted suspiciously like regret.

Now she heard stirring in the outer room, and something stronger than regret, she couldn't put a name to it, filled her heart. He was leaving.

The rumble of muffled male voices reached her ears. She smelled the aroma of strong coffee. I should have cooked him breakfast, she thought. He liked her hoecakes. But he'd make Nacogdoches by noon, and last night's leftover biscuits would hold him till then.

Nothing would ever hold Branch Kincaid.

Wood creaked as the front door opened. Katie sat on the edge of her bed, her hands clasped in her lap. Minutes passed as she pictured him walking to the barn and saddling Striker.

A gust of wind buffeted the kitchen, and she rose and walked to the window, telling herself she merely checked the weather. Bitter winter air swept into the room as she cracked open her shutter.

He was in the yard, mounted on the dun, his brightly colored poncho the single vision of warmth in the world outside. He wore his hat pulled low on his head, and a kerchief wrapped his nose and mouth. She saw nothing cold in his eyes, however, as his gaze met hers.

He nodded once, and then, as he gigged Striker and rode away from the remnants of Gallagher's Tavern and Travelers Inn, sleet began to fall.

✎⁍ CHAPTER 6 ⁌✎

$\mathscr{T}$HE DAY FOLLOWING Branch's departure, they had come armed with axes and saws and hammers, what seemed like an army of men ready to attack the task they'd been hired to accomplish. With them they carried supplies to last the length of the job: food, canvas tents—one man even brought his wife. The wages were good, with bonuses promised for speed and quality work.

Behind them had rolled wagon after wagon loaded with expensive milled lumber. Now, after weeks of constant toil in weather that ranged from pleasant to bitter cold, Gallagher's Tavern and Travelers Inn existed once more.

Katie, Daniel, and John anticipated a month or more of hard work ahead readying the hotel for guests. The Gallaghers would make many of the needed supplies themselves—some of the furnishings, mattresses, and decorative touches like window curtains—but many of the necessities were on order out of Jefferson, where riverboat traffic gave access to imported goods. Some had arrived already, but most were due within the next month.

With a little luck and a lot of hard work, the Gallaghers hoped to reopen the inn by midspring, when East Texas saw the greatest number of travelers.

While the workmen readied for their departure, Katie wandered from the parlor to the dining room, picturing the rooms filled with furniture and guests. Never had she imagined such splendor for Gallagher's Inn; it was too extravagant, too costly.

It was financed by a stranger named Finian Trahern.

She crossed the wide hallway that ran through the center of the structure to the long room that would serve as the new tavern. Da stood behind a long, polished wooden bar, whistling as he lined up bottles of liquor delivered from Jefferson earlier that morning. He went about his work with a vigor that had been absent from his movements for weeks, and the sight dissuaded Katie from mentioning her doubts yet again. Instead, she asked, "Da, where's Daniel?"

"He's upstairs. Our order of linen arrived with the whiskey, and he's lookin' for a place to store it. Most likely he'll be a'needin' your help, Katie-love."

"I'll keep the sheets in that wardrobe Mrs. Craig sent us from Nacogdoches House. You know, Da, I don't believe her claim that she had too much furniture in her boardinghouse. It's charity."

"Now, Katie," Da said, frowning a rebuke. "I have the same sort of opinion as you about charity, but Martha Craig is simply being neighborly. Don't be a'readin' problems into kindnesses."

"Yes, Da." But as she made her way upstairs, she grumbled, "Just like I'm not to be a'questionin' the largess of Mr. Finian Trahern. I swear Da is wearing blinders."

She found Daniel playing marbles in room number eight, a stack of sheets beside him on the floor. "Hard at work, I see," she commented in a wry tone. His guilty grin made her smile, and her pleasure at watching him move without pain prompted her to ruffle his hair and challenge him to a game.

She was on her hands and knees with her head lowered near the ground lining up a shot when a voice behind her groaned, "Good Lord, woman. Offer a man a target like that, and he's liable to misfire his shooter."

Marbles scattered everywhere as Katie flopped over, protecting her backside by sitting on it. Daniel shouted gleefully, "Mr. Branch! You're here!"

"In the flesh," he replied, never taking his gaze off Katie.

Her pulse hummed like honeybees swarming a sunflower. The very last person she had expected to see today was Branch Kincaid.

He wore his blue chambray shirt beneath a fleece-lined vest. Her stare snagged on the tin star pinned to the leather, and her stomach sank as hopes she hadn't realized she harbored were dashed. He *had* gone to work for the sheriff. What was he doing here today? Why did he come back?

Katie forced herself to meet Branch's gaze. His topaz eyes gleamed as he drawled, "Howdy, Sprite. Daniel."

He shouldn't have come here. Not now. Not when she'd been working so hard to forget him. Slowly, she climbed to her feet, paying careful attention to the dust she brushed from her skirt. "What brings you to Gallagher's," she paused and emphasized snidely, *"Deputy?"*

He frowned down at the star on his vest, then back at Katie. He opened his mouth to reply when Daniel interrupted, "Wow, a turkey!"

She hadn't noticed the bird dangling at Branch's side. His hands were not what attracted her attention. "Yes, Daniel," she said cattily, "it is a turkey, and it looks as though he's brought dinner with him."

Branch retaliated with that slow, wicked grin. He laid his free hand against his chest, batted his eyelashes, and chirped, "Why, Miz Starr, you do say the sweetest things to a man."

Her throat was as dry as the West Texas wind. "Pluck it, Kincaid."

"Only if you have me for dinner," he shot back. He held the bird out. "Now, Kate, I've hauled my turkey a far piece to visit with y'all, and I'm lookin' for an invitation."

Sometimes silence was a speech. Eventually Branch's expectant expression faded. He shoved his burden into Daniel's hands and took a step toward Katie. "Come on, Kate. Let me stay."

"We don't serve Regulators here."

"I should hope not. They're a whole lot tougher than turkey."

"You're disgusting, Mr. Kincaid," she said, lifting her

chin and squaring her shoulders. "I thought we'd seen the last of you. What brings you back?"

He grimaced. "Careful, now, you'll hurt my feelings. I'm a tender sort of man, you know. Anyway, to answer your oh-so-sweet question, the talk in town is all about this place y'all are buildin' out here. I wanted to see it for myself. You see, I once worked for Finian Trahern. He's a right nice fella."

"You know Mr. Trahern?" Katie asked, her pique forgotten at his words.

"Yep, right well, if I say so myself. You gonna cook for me, Kate?"

She wanted to, she really did, and she hated herself for it. Nodding slowly, she said, "Yes, I'll roast your turkey for you. It'll be my pleasure. Excuse me now, I have work to do." She brushed past him out of the room, aware that he moved to lean against the doorway and watch her descend the stairs. She exaggerated the swing to her hips for good measure.

They sniped at each other all afternoon. After John gave Branch the grand tour of the new inn, the deputy appointed himself kitchen assistant and nearly drove Katie mad. He made an art of innuendo and a science of innocent touches. She considered shoving a drumstick down his throat and taking a carving knife to roaming hands.

He made her feel so alive.

By the time they sat down for dinner, Katie had mellowed just enough to call a truce. Her curiosity had yet to be satisfied. As she passed him the platter piled high with roasted turkey, she commented, "Earlier you mentioned Mr. Trahern. Tell us what you know of him, won't you?"

John Gallagher's brows lifted. "You know Trahern?"

Branch nodded and took a long draw on his tankard of ale. "Prince of a man. I worked for him awhile. He's got a huge place down near Refugio in South Texas. Cotton mostly, some sugarcane. Racehorses are his passion."

"He must be a saint," John replied, dabbing at the corner of his mouth with a white napkin. " 'Twas the damnedest thing I ever saw, the carpenters and such a'ridin' up like they did. Just set to buildin' with nary a word. Picked the spot and everything."

Branch licked his lips, then winked at Katie after swallowing a particularly succulent bite of meat. "In town they're saying Trahern's your new partner. How did you come to know the man?"

Daniel chimed in, "That's the damnedest thing about it."

"Daniel Benjamin Gallagher!" Katie warned.

He rolled his eyes. "That's the *darndest* thing about it. We can't remember. Supposedly, he stayed here a couple years back and he and Da shared a bit of the Irish."

"Just a wee bit, I'm sure," John added, frowning.

Even Katie smiled at that. Daniel continued his story. "Anyway, Mr. Trahern has enough money to choke a horse, and he was travelin' through Nacogdoches when he heard about the fire. He remembered Da's hospitality, so he hired the men and bought the materials and sent them our way, asking only that we pay him back out of the profits from the inn." Daniel turned to Katie. "Is there a saint named Finian?"

Katie very carefully sliced her turkey into tiny pieces. Absently, she nodded. "Fifth- or sixth-century Ireland. St. Patrick's successor."

"Maybe our Finian's not a saint; maybe he's a leprechaun. What do you think, Da?"

John made a show of pondering the question. "Well, son, you may be right. Mayhap I found a pot-o'-gold and never knew it. What be you a'thinkin', Katie-love?"

"I'm thinking I'd feel much better had we met the man. What sort of person makes this type of arrangement with strangers? It makes no sense. It worries me."

Branch asked casually, "Did you sign anything?"

"Yes," John answered. "He sent a contract through an attorney. A straightforward agreement it was. Katie, you read it, you needn't be so fretful. 'Twasn't charity—after all, I wouldn't be a'takin' charity. Trahern'll earn a good profit from this deal."

Katie shrugged as she passed the bowl of mashed potatoes to their dinner guest. "I just wish I could remember him. Tell me, Branch. Why would Finian Trahern help the Gallaghers?"

Branch took his third helping of potatoes and passed the bowl to Daniel. He stared solemnly at Katie and answered, "Maybe when he was here, you helped him in some way. Maybe his money is all he is able to offer in return."

"You think so?"

He nodded brusquely and returned his attention to his plate. The way he pushed the food around gave Katie cause to wonder if she'd missed something in the exchange. No, she told herself, he's just full, finally.

Frowning slightly, she said, "I've molasses cookies for dessert if anyone cares for some."

Three male faces beamed at her.

Crouching in the shadows of the forest as the last red tints of sundown flame edged the sky, a man continued his vigil on the Gallagher homestead. Since his arrival earlier that afternoon, he'd watched and speculated at the activity he beheld. Soon now he would ask his questions and hear the answers he'd traveled so far to find.

Illuminated by the frosted light of the rising moon, a bead of nervous sweat dripped down his temple and fell onto his bare shoulder. He'd shed his traveling costume soon after leaving the more populated lands around Nacogdoches. Now he wore the clothing of his youth. Dangerous, certainly, to dress as such in East Texas, but the declaration came from within. Even the weather conspired with his soul, a pleasing change from the bitter north.

During the long afternoon he'd witnessed the commotion as the laborers put finishing touches on the new structure and departed. He'd wondered as one stranger remained behind, his familiarity with Kathleen obvious and troubling.

Nighttime had arrived. Soon he'd have his answers.

But would he have the help he so desperately needed?

· · ·

The aroma of roasted turkey lingered in the air as Branch sat at the kitchen table and brooded, staring at Katie. Damn, she's beautiful tonight, he thought.

Weariness from the day's hard work had drained the color from her cheeks, and her mahogany hair fell across her shoulders like a warm tear. Sitting in the rocking chair carding cotton, she reminded him of a porcelain doll. All she needed was a ruffled silk dress and a parasol.

Or maybe a ruffled corset and silk stockings.

"Damn!" He rose from his seat and walked to the window. Outside, a full moon and countless stars bathed the yard in a silvery glow. He could almost see her out there with moonlight melting over her creamy skin, the plump white globes of her breasts, their tips erect and straining . . .

Branch thumped his forehead against the log wall. It was a good thing he was only staying overnight. This place and the people in it were making him as crazy as a loco'd calf.

His dinner rested in his gut like grapeshot. Uneased lust for Katie plus all that talk about the mythical Mr. Trahern plain didn't make for good digestion. When in the hell had it begun to bother him to lie?

He never should have come here today, but he'd let his curiosity get the better of him. He'd wanted to see the inn he'd bought for them; he'd wanted to see their reaction. One thing he knew without a doubt, the money had been well spent. "Finally somethin' good comes of Hoss Garrett's riches."

"What's that, son?" John asked from his seat before the hearth, occupied with his evening ritual of filling his pipe with the woodsy-scented tobacco he smoked every evening.

"Nothin', just thinkin' about town."

"Been meaning to ask, how's the new job suitin' you?"

Branch looked over his shoulder. "Fine. Nacogdoches is a friendly place, and I like Sheriff Strickland. He seems to be a good man, and he cares about the town."

Katie glanced up from her work, her eyes wide and innocent. "I guess hunting men is more exciting than tracking food for the table?"

Daniel answered, "Of course it is, Katie. The only thing that shot back at him when he was workin' for us was a skunk." At that Daniel and Katie shared a look that set his blood to boiling. Smart-aleck pair—someone should take a switch to their behinds.

A vision of his hand cupping Katie Starr's bare bottom beneath the moonlight burst upon his mind.

He turned away from the window and returned to his seat. He picked up the week-old newspaper from the table and pretended to read. He should have headed back to town straight after supper. Instead he'd let Daniel's beagle-pup eyes and John's hound-dog face persuade him to hang around long enough to help move a few things in the morning.

Stupid move, Kincaid. She'd goaded him into it, acting like she didn't care one way or the other. The ornery little witch, she'd chatted all the way through the dish washing, happy as a two-tailed puppy. She'd thanked him for bringing the meat for dinner, then yammered on and on about her plans for reopening the inn. Even now she was humming a happy little tune in rhythm with the brush of the cards.

She was puttin' on, he knew it. He bothered her every bit as much as she plagued him. He was tempted to hang around a little longer, just to put a hitch in her gitalong. But one day away from town was all he could afford right now.

In the past few weeks he'd managed to learn the names of a dozen Regulators; he was slowly working his way into their trust. Soon he hoped to learn the identity of the man with whom he'd bargained the night of the fire.

He had a hunch that man had information Branch could use. After all, a fellow willing to beat an old man, whip a young boy, and take phony money in exchange for gun hands wouldn't hesitate at murdering a government agent—or inform on the one who had.

That's what his presence in East Texas was all about. He was here to do a job—to find his brother's killer. The little interlude with Katie had been pleasurable, but it was over now. He had to put a stop to the meanderings of his mind. He had to quit thinking about her at inappropriate times, like when he rode a Regulator raid or ate breakfast at the boardinghouse where he roomed. He had to stop the dreams that haunted the dark of his nights when he'd wake up aching and hard with a blue-eyed wraith lying beside him.

He turned away from the window and ambled over to her worktable. He sat on it—something he knew she hated—and swung his legs back and forth while he watched her and thought, Course, I'll always wonder what it would have been like to scratch the itch that was Katie Starr. *Damn*, but I hate to leave a job undone. His gaze fastened on that fabulous bosom that had attracted his attention from the start. Maybe when this was all over, he could breeze back by Gallagher's on his way to Riverrun and provoke just one more battle in their little war.

Katie bent to take more cotton from the basket at her feet, and he caught a glimpse of her breasts.

Yes, the idea definitely had merit. He reached for a leftover cornbread muffin and, popping it into his mouth, chewed thoughtfully. He had to go. Wandering around like a pony with the bridle off didn't get a man to the end of the trail. But nothing said he couldn't follow the same path on his way home.

Feeling measurably better, he swallowed the bread, licked his lips, and grinned. Katie was watching him. She didn't look as happy as before. Branch nodded to her and said, "Nothin' like good home cookin' to comfort a man, Miz Kate." He bit into another muffin.

She carded cotton furiously. "Jeez, Katie," Daniel said, "at that rate you'll be through the entire harvest before Christmas."

Branch choked back a laugh and searched the room for a deck of playing cards. Whistling his hymn, he took a seat at the table and dealt a game of solitaire.

Just a temporary cease-fire, Sprite. The war would be won, the shrew tamed, and then the conquering hero would go home. It was a right fine plan. The room fell quiet except for Branch's low whistle, the squeak of Katie's rocker, and the rustle of paper as Daniel turned the pages of a battered schoolbook.

The mournful wail of a screech owl cut through the night, and all four of the occupants of Katie's kitchen jumped.

With widening eyes, Branch watched the Gallaghers react to the sound. John's head snapped around at the noise while Daniel scrambled to his feet and asked in a querulous voice, "Da?"

Katie sat stiff as a three-day corpse, her eyes fixed and glazed. Branch jerked to his feet, intent upon going to her, when the sound came again. "Ooo . . ." It sent shivers up his spine.

His chin dropped in amazement when John's face lit with a smile, and Katie threw the cotton cards to the floor and dashed outside.

"Da, it *is* him!" Daniel rose as though to follow his sister, but John held up his hand.

"No, son, let them have a moment to themselves," Gallagher instructed.

Well, hell. Branch didn't like the sound of that. He turned and looked through the open window just in time to see Katie fly into the embrace of a near-naked man.

The visitor lifted her at the waist, twirling her around, and she covered his face with kisses. When her joyous laughter danced across the night, the stars seemed to flare in response.

Branch worked to swallow the lump that blocked his throat. Cornbread must be caught, he absently thought. Through hooded eyes he watched the tall figure wrap Katie in his arms and merge the two outlines to one.

"Well, sonofabitch." Only his pride kept him from tearing through the window and forcing the lovers apart. With fists clenched, a muscle twitching above his jaw, he waited.

The silhouette separated. Katie pulled the man's arm, dragging him toward the kitchen. Then he said something and motioned sharply in Branch's direction.

Both Katie and the stranger halted, and she glanced anxiously at Branch. The night obscured the man's features as he looked Branch's way. Words tumbled from Katie's lips, and although he couldn't see it, Branch felt the intensity of the stranger's gaze. Branch answered the unspoken challenge with a hard stare of his own.

Finally Katie raised both her voice and her fist and delivered a loud, frustrated declaration punctuated by a futile punch to her companion's stomach. "Trust me, you stubborn Cherokee!"

Indian? He's an Indian? Well, that explained the breechclout. It also meant this freehanded fella wasn't her beloved Steven. *Wait just a minute!* If this wasn't her husband risen from the dead, then who the hell was he?

Branch didn't get much of a chance to ponder the question; the Indian's reaction to Katie's jab stole his attention. The devil laughed uproariously. He bent down, scooped her up, and threw her over his shoulder. With one quick slap to her bottom, he carried her boldly into the woods.

The ladder-back chair that stood between Branch and the door hit the floor with a bang. John reached the portal first and planted himself firmly in the middle, arms crossed, facing inside. "Whoa there, boy. Settle yourself down."

Branch exploded. "What the hell are you doing, Irishman? That Indian bastard is stealing your daughter!"

Gallagher's reply hit him like a Mexican cannonball. "Shaddoe isn't stealing Katie. He loves her." John shook his head. "And weren't we a'thinkin' he'd died in the Cherokee War? Sure that me girl nearly cried herself dry over it. A miracle, that's what it is, a holy miracle."

He motioned to Daniel. "Get the playing cards, son. Let's have a game of euchre, what do you say?" He all but dragged Branch back to the table, where Daniel sat separating cards lower than seven from the deck. He dealt the thirty-two cards into three hands, but Branch just left his on the table. He stared out the window into the empty yard. *And don't I just love a water-walking act?*

·   ·   ·

"Shaddoe, you put me down this instant!" Katie said, sputtering with laughter.

"I think not, woman with the feather fist." Shaddoe chuckled as he marched toward the river. He pulled off her shoes and proceeded to tickle her feet while continuing in a stern voice. "Once again you have dared to strike the fierce warrior, Dances In The Night, and you shall be dealt the traditional punishment."

Katie pummeled his back. "You'd better not throw me in the river this time, I'll take a chill." An uncharacteristic whine entered her voice. "Besides, I washed my hair before dinner, and it's just now dried. You know how long that takes."

"Still vain about your hair, I see," Shaddoe said, reaching behind his back to give those locks a tug.

"Ouch. You're just jealous that my braids have always been thicker than yours."

"Bratling." He swatted her rump again and continued toward the Angelina.

Katie didn't relish a dunking tonight. The water truly was too cold. But her long-standing relationship with Shaddoe made it a distinct possibility.

The precedent was set years ago when, as a child, Katie decided to rob a bee tree of its honey. She managed to knock the hive from the limb, but she hadn't counted on the swarm of insects that engulfed her in moments. The young Shaddoe, newly arrived at the Cherokee village, heard her screams. Braving the bees, the boy lifted her in his arms, ran to a nearby stream, and tossed her into the water.

Hurting and in a temper, mad at the world, she had sloshed from the water and launched herself with fists flying at the closest target, Shaddoe. He responded by pitching her back into the water. It took four drenchings before the exhausted girl gave up and lay on the bank, crying. Without a word, Shaddoe tenderly carried her to the Cherokee village, where his uncle performed an incantation and covered the stings with a soothing poultice.

Since that day, Katie had hit her friend in a fit of temper on half a dozen different occasions. Each and every time, he dunked her in the nearest water hole.

The night was winter quiet as they reached the river. "I should have known better than to punch you," Katie grumbled.

"As usual, Kathleen, your arms flew faster than your mind." He lifted her from his shoulder and placed her gently on the ground. "However, you are safe tonight. I did not journey this far only to watch you die of pneumonia." He tilted her chin with his index finger. Softly, he told her, "I have missed you."

"Oh, Shaddoe, I can't tell you how happy I am to see you. I thought you were dead!" She hugged him again, then stepped back and searched his eyes for answers. "Where have you been? What happened?"

Instead of answering, he turned away and busied himself gathering the makings of a fire.

"Shaddoe?" Katie's thoughts returned to the last time she had seen him, July of 1839. Down in the Neches riverbed a horrible event had taken place. "Da and I were there at the Neches River that morning, we watched the battle between the Cherokees and the Texians. So many men, so much blood, everywhere I looked." Katie's stomach churned as the memory of the battlefield came alive in her mind. She could almost smell the gunpowder.

She rubbed her arms as a chill swept her body. "You were beside Duwali, helping your chief, and then, when the Texian shot him in the back, it was so horrible, I couldn't watch anymore. Da looked for you but you'd disappeared. We thought you were one of the bodies, Shaddoe. There were so many of them!"

Shaddoe knelt on one knee next to the dry brush he'd piled together for a small camp fire. He looked up at her, and moonlight slashed across his face like war paint. "No, Kathleen, the Texians didn't kill me, although at times I wished they had."

"Were you hurt? Where have you been? What has happened to your people? You're back for good, now, aren't you?"

"Oh, little one, you haven't changed at all. Still asking

twenty questions at once, allowing me no opportunity to ask my own." He blew gently on the base of a thin ribbon of flame. "I want to know what happened here. I want to know who is the man in your home. But time is short, Kathleen, and other things must come first." He fed a clump of dead grass to the growing fire, stood, and went to her.

Taking her hand, he said, "I have a critical request to make of you, and too, I must speak of my sorrow. I have been to Nacogdoches, where I learned of Steven's death. Know that I share your grief."

"He was lynched. Daniel and I found him hanging from the elm tree at the Starrs' home. They cut him, Shaddoe—oh, the blood! It was—I can't find the words to describe it!" Katie felt the sting of tears as she gazed into his somber black eyes. She said, "He loved you. He never believed you had died. He took care of everything, Shaddoe, about the land, I mean. Da and I, we wanted to forget all about the Cherokees' lands, but Steven wouldn't hear of it. He said that someday you'd return, or at least send someone to settle. We have it, Shaddoe; the land is waiting for you."

Her voice cracked as she added, "Steven and I married. We had a daughter. She . . . died that night, too. They didn't need to set the fire, Shaddoe!"

Shaddoe touched her shoulder. "I am so sorry, Kathleen. Upon my oath, I will discover the one responsible, and he shall forfeit his life."

Sadly, Katie shook her head. *That duty is mine, my friend.* The pitchfork. She'd find the devil, she'd made promises. Besides, Shaddoe could never learn the connection between Steven's death and the Matagorda Bay and Texas Land Company. He would feel responsible when, in truth, it was all her fault.

She moved to the camp fire and sat beside it, tucking her feet demurely beneath her skirt. Like times of old, Shaddoe sat cross-legged on her right. This time, however, Steven wasn't there to complete the circle.

"What is this request you have, my friend?" she asked, anxious to change the subject.

Shaddoe's fierce scowl accentuated the hard angles of his face. In that moment, she saw nothing of the Louisiana Creole that made up half his blood. The man before her was a Cherokee warrior. "Kathleen, I must have Steven's father's supply of smallpox vaccine."

"You want Doc Starr's what?" She could have imagined him asking for many things, but not that. "Why? Is that why you're here? But Doc Starr passed on shortly before Steven died. Why come to me? I don't know what you—"

He interrupted. "Truly, Kathleen, you must learn to control your questions. But, knowing you, I must return to the beginning so that you may know the whole of it. It's an ugly story, little one."

Abruptly, he stood and walked to the riverbank, moonlight illuminating his form. He scooped up a handful of stones and skipped them, one by one, across the water. Katie stared into the fire. Apprehension crept up her spine like a slow-moving spider, and for all of her questions, she doubted whether she really wanted the answers. "Shaddoe, I'm sorry. You don't need to tell me. You're my friend. I'll do anything I can to help you, no matter what. You know I will."

"Yes, Kathleen, I know you will." But after a few moments of silence, he began to tell his story, his voice a low rumble, his words clipped. "After the battle at the Neches, the Texian army took many prisoners, mostly women and children. Corn Tassel, Little Mush, and Running Wolf were killed. Tenata and I helped the remnants of our group travel to Mexico."

"Not Indian Territory?" Katie asked.

"Some went north, yes. I have just come from there. But many of us realized that making a home in the Territory only delays the inevitable, so we went south."

"What do you mean?"

Shaddoe arched a stone over the water. "How long do you think the Cherokee will be allowed to live in peace in the Territory, Kathleen?" The rock plopped into the river. "As long as we lived in Texas? Long enough to build villages, clear the land and plant our crops? Long enough to tame the land for the whites? So they can live in *our* homes, harvest *our* corn, benefit from the fruits of *our* labor? *Just as it happened here?*" He sneered. "I do not think so. Mexico offers something the northern settlement land cannot. Retribution. You see, it is much easier to raid white settlements from Mexico than it is from the north."

Katie wasn't fooled. She flipped her braid over her shoulder. "That may be why others chose Mexico, but not you, Shaddoe Dancer. I know you too well. You might seek revenge, but never against those who have done you no wrong. You may raid Nacogdoches, but never a South Texas ranch."

From the opposite bank of the Angelina came the rusty croak of a bullfrog.

A crooked smile tugged at Shaddoe's mouth, and he nodded. "You have the innocent faith of a babe, Kathleen, but you are right. Steven's arrangements for the East Texas lands will fulfill my need for vengeance, and I wish with all my heart that he could be here to witness it when it happens. But now is not the time for revenge—other needs are greater."

"Smallpox?"

He nodded. "Smallpox is the insidious weapon of the white man. It travels from village to village, an invisible cloud that descends with its fever, chills, and nausea. When it lifts, it leaves behind scarred faces, mutilated lives, and death—black, bloated, stinking death."

After violently pitching one last stone, Shaddoe whirled and returned to the camp fire. In silence he tended the fire. Katie looked into his face and saw the ravaged reflection of a real and personal pain. "Shaddoe?"

His dark eyes glittered in the firelight. "Do you see, Kathleen? It is the perfect weapon. There will be no more Indian Wars. No men will live to fight the battles, no women to bear children, no children to grow into angry warriors."

"What happened, Shaddoe? To you, I mean. What happened to you?"

He was quiet for a long minute before asking, "Do I hide it so poorly?"

"I know you well," Katie answered.

He closed his eyes. She watched his chest expand with a deep breath, then sink as he exhaled in a heavy sigh. "I carried messages from Mexico to my people in Indian Territory. I met a woman, we married. She was Elizabeth, and she walked in my soul. She carried my child, my son. Smallpox took them both."

"Oh, Shaddoe, no!" Katie clasped his hand between both of hers. "I'm so sorry. I know how hard . . . I understand."

"I think perhaps you are the only one who can, Kathleen. We have not been lucky, you and I."

"It doesn't seem fair, any of it. Shaddoe, can the Indians not obtain vaccine from the government?"

He laughed harshly. "The American Congress passed a law that requires smallpox vaccine be given to Indians. But guess what? I visited the Indian Agent before I left the Territory—no vaccine is available, none will be forthcoming. There's an epidemic in the north, Kathleen. It is slowly spreading south and soon will reach the village where the Texas Cherokees have made their homes."

"So you came here to Doc Starr?"

He nodded. "I'd no other choice. I attempted to see Coloneh, The Raven, but he was of no help to his Cherokee brothers."

"Sam Houston wouldn't help you?" Katie asked incredulously. "Why, I can't believe that!"

"I never found him. In Washington-on-the-Brazos I was told he had retreated to a large holding of land near Huntsville, where he intended to build a plantation. On my arrival there—Raven Hill, he calls it—I discovered he had journeyed south to meet with other proponents of annexation." Shaddoe scratched in the dirt with a twig. "My time was growing short. Even had I found Sam Houston, as immersed as he is in the political fortunes of the Republic of Texas, I feared he'd not have time to give to the Cherokees. He is not a god; his efforts to save our East Texas lands failed miserably. It was not guaranteed he could obtain the vaccine for us." The twig snapped as he added, "I knew Doctor Starr would help."

Katie nodded slowly. "Steven's father would have given you the vaccine without hesitation."

"He treated the Cherokee like any other man. But he, too, is dead. As his son's wife, you must have inherited his medicines."

"Yes, I did. But Shaddoe—oh, I hate to tell you this. Shaddoe, I no longer have his supply of vaccine! I gave it all to Doc Mayfair."

Branch glared down at the pocket watch in his hand. Twenty minutes had passed with no sign of Katie or her Cherokee. John and Daniel had given up on him and were deeply involved in a two-handed version of euchre. All the while, the boy's excited prattle regaled him with stories of the illustrious Shaddoe.

Half-Creole, half-Cherokee, he went by the name Shaddoe Marchand while living with his grandfather in New Orleans as a child. But growing to manhood among Chief Bowles's tribe, the medicine man's nephew answered to what translated as Dances In The Night. Katie always called him Shaddoe Dancer.

He fought beside his chief in the summer of '39. "I'll never forget the sight," John said, a faraway look in his eyes. "Chief Bowles was a brave old man. In his eighties, I'm a'thinkin'. Throughout the battle his voice rang out, urging his warriors onward." John shook his head. "You couldn't miss the man. He wore a bright red silk vest and sash, a black military hat, and he carried this fancy sword Sam Houston had given him."

Gallagher folded his arms across his chest and continued. "Toward the end, only a few men were left to stand beside him; the Neches River bottom was red with blood and dead Cherokees. The Bowl rode a handsome horse, a blaze-faced sorrel with four white feet, and the Texians shot it out from under him. The old Indian climbed to his feet and began to walk away." His expression twisted to a snarl of disgust. "A Texian shot him in the back."

Despite himself, Branch's interest was piqued. "You fought with the Texians?" he asked.

"Hell, no!" John exclaimed. "I was after finding me Katie. She'd taken an idea that she could somehow help her friends. The hardheaded girl—she'd run off looking for them."

Branch snorted. "That's not hard to believe," he said. "Did she? Did she save her"—he sneered the name— "Shaddoe Dancer?"

Daniel interrupted his father. "She didn't. Da saw Shaddoe riding right next to Chief Bowles. We figured he died then too."

"Well, it appears everyone figured wrong," Branch grumbled.

After five minutes that passed as hours, Branch could stand no more. "Dammit, John. You're her father. How can you let her traipse off into the darkness with some half-naked half-breed and sit there losin' at cards like nothin's happened? Hell, by now she's probably wearin' fewer clothes than *he* did when he got here."

John sniffed. "A fine thing that you're after worrying about such. And you, sportin' but the skin you were born with that afternoon not long ago. 'Tis the pot callin' the kettle black, in my book."

"It was nothin' but laundry, I explained that," Branch spat. He stared out the window, brooding. "Well," he said a few minutes later, "I haven't had the pleasure of meeting this, ah, friend of the Gallagher's yet." Standing, he strode to the door. "I believe it's time I made his acquaintance." He walked into the yard, his fists clenched at his side. His knuckles shone white in the moonlight.

With their biggest questions having been answered and the problems thoroughly discussed, Shaddoe and Katie sat quietly for a time, enjoying the peace of being together again. Then Shaddoe had to spoil it all. "Tell me of the man."

Katie wrinkled her nose. "Branch Kincaid. He was hunter for Gallagher's for a time. Let's not speak of him. When you went to Mexico, did you see the ocean? I've always wanted to see the ocean."

He was not to be dissuaded. "Kincaid has a claim on you?"

"No," she said, a bit too quickly. "He doesn't even live here anymore. He has a job in Nacogdoches. Don't you want to know what happened to the inn?"

"Yes, but I also have questions concerning your hunter."

Katie chose to tell him about the fire. "Have you heard of the problems between the Moderators and the Regulators?"

He shook his head and she continued. "It's a confusing situation, really. Da has likened it to a clan war in the old country, but it basically is just a bloody feud. It's the old settlers, the Moderators, pitted against the new settlers, the Regulators."

"Which is Branch Kincaid?" Shaddoe asked.

"Forget about Branch. I swear, Shaddoe, you are like a dog with a bone." Katie shook her head. "The Regulators burned us out, because Da is a Moderator and he allowed them to meet at Gallagher's. He didn't choose a side at first, but now just about everyone has declared himself one way or the other. They've had to, for survival."

"So Branch Kincaid is a Moderator, also?"

"You just won't leave this alone, will you? No, Branch is a Regulator. Well, at least I think he is, but I'm not sure. That's part of the problem."

Shaddoe's brows arched in inquiry.

"He made some sort of deal with the Regulator who led the raid on the inn." She fell silent as she thought about the day the tavern burned. Eventually she said, "I get the feeling that there's more to Branch Kincaid than he has let on. He's asked me to trust him. I *want* to trust him. He saved my life; he helped Da and Daniel."

"You love him?"

"No!" she snapped. "I don't. Besides, he's leaving again in the morning. He's Jack Strickland's deputy in Nacogdoches, and everyone knows the sheriff is a Regulator. The only people he arrests anymore are Moderators."

"He is familiar with you, Kathleen. He touches you."

Anger and embarrassment put a sharpness to her question. "You were spying on me?"

"I saw nothing more than what you allowed him in public," he bit back. "I did not peek through your window, Kathleen, though you spent hours alone with him. I have no desire to witness your foolishness, Mrs. Starr."

"Steven is dead, Shaddoe. Twenty long months. And it's none of your business what I do, although I haven't done anything with Branch or anyone else, for that matter." Tears spilled from her eyes and streaked down her face. She scrambled to her feet, intending to leave.

He caught her by the arm. "I'm sorry, Kathleen. So much has changed. I am taken by surprise. I return to find my friend, Steven, murdered and another man dwelling in your heart." Moonlight illuminated his face, and Katie felt the pain reflected in his black eyes. He kissed the tip of her nose.

"One more question, and we will speak no more of your hunter. Would he betray me, Kathleen? Would he speak to others of our plan?"

"You mean about the land or the vaccine?"

"Actually, I was speaking about the vaccine, but the land is important. I do plan to return and proceed with Steven's idea."

Katie pursed her lips. "I don't believe he'd say anything about the vaccine, and I doubt he'd care about the land, to be honest. But I'm not sure."

"Then it would be best if I took no chances?"

"Yes. He'll be gone tomorrow. You should probably stay out of sight until then." She grabbed his hand and squeezed it. "Oh, Shaddoe. I'm so sorry. If only I hadn't allowed Doc Mayfair to take the vaccine, we wouldn't be facing this mess."

"Kathleen, you sound like me now. *Ai!* If only! They are the saddest words in any language. So many times I have said, 'If only I had stopped Elizabeth from traveling to her mother's village, she'd not have contracted smallpox.' Or 'If only I'd chosen not to go to Mexico, we would have had another year together.' It serves no purpose to say 'if only,' Kathleen. Our life path can be walked in but one direction."

Katie nodded. "You're right, I know. It's just that sometimes it's hard to accept." She paused a moment, considering his words, then asked, "Why *did* you go to Mexico, Shaddoe?"

A sparkle entered his eyes and he grinned. "You will enjoy this, Kathleen. I went south because Egg decided he had to have a medicine man in his group."

"What!" Katie said incredulously. "You're no medicine man. Why, you're as Christian as I am. You've told me a hundred times you don't believe in all that."

He shrugged. "It seems I inherited the title when my uncle inherited a Texian bullet. He named me his successor before he died. Chief Egg wanted someone who could say the incantations to hold off evil spirits, and I could do that much." He shook his head. "When the Texians found and defeated us a few weeks later in a battle just north of the Nueces River, I determined that I must have said the wrong one."

"Humph!" The sound was most unladylike. "It's no wonder. As I remember, the only spells *you* cared to learn were the love incantations."

"Well, those *do* work. I earned good money saying erotic spells for members of my tribe, not to mention the young rakes of New Orleans when I visited Grandfather." He paused, then added with studied nonchalance, "I could teach you one for your hunter if you would like."

Katie tossed her head and said, "Don't be silly, Shaddoe."

He drew back, arching his eyebrows. "Could it be you doubt my abilities when it comes to Cherokee magic?" He clicked his tongue.

"I have no doubt you can cast Cherokee love magic around, my handsome friend. But you don't do it with any spell your uncle taught you."

Frowning, he said, "I am insulted. At least, I believe I am."

Katie smiled at him. "Oh, Shaddoe, I've missed you so."

"And I, you." They smiled into each other's eyes for a moment, then Shaddoe said, "Come. I shall prove my magic to you."

Katie allowed him to drag her closer to the water. "Be done with your laughter," he told her. "This is a serious matter."

He straightened his shoulders. "Now, my specialty, love spells, usually require taking the client to the river or stream and reciting a prayer, conjuration, or incantation for said client. However, in the case of a nonbeliever such as yourself, I think it best that you repeat the spell after me. Now, all we have to do is decide which one to use."

He crossed his arms and thought for a moment, then nodded. "I have two that you may wish to choose from. The first would oblige the lover to remain by your side forever. The second compels a lover to leave his partner and not return."

An intense expression replaced Shaddoe's playful look of the previous moment. "Which is it, Kathleen? What do you desire for Branch Kincaid?"

This is ridiculous, Katie thought. I don't believe in this, do I? "Don't you have something that deals with trust or honesty?"

"Love spells were all that ever interested me."

She took a deep breath. "Uh, the first, I guess."

Shaddoe nodded solemnly. "I pray that he is worthy of you. Very well. This one does not require tobacco, so just put your arms around me. That is it," he said as she rested her hands on his waist. "Look into my face, and think of the object of your affections. Your words must rise on the wind, so raise your voice as you repeat what I say. After each line, blow a breath at the middle of the loved one's breast."

"How can I do that? He's not here. Besides, he's not really a loved one."

"Distance does not matter, just do it. We will say each line four times. Ready?"

Katie nodded.

With a bittersweet smile, Shaddoe whispered, "Look at me very beautifully."

Katie said the words, then pursed her lips and blew a puff of breath toward the cabin. She paused for the next line. "Let us talk very beautifully." Then, "There is not loneliness—so let us talk!" She looked up into Shaddoe's gentle eyes and recited a love spell to another man.

As the final repetition rose with the breeze, an angry voice cut across the night. "Kate Starr, where in the hell are you? Your father wants you home this instant."

For the space of a heartbeat, Shaddoe clasped his friend tightly to his chest. And then, fading silently into the night, he let her go.

✺ CHAPTER 7 ✺

$\mathcal{N}$ESTLED IN A VALLEY between two running creeks, Nacogdoches boasted a vibrant mixture of Spanish, Mexican, and Anglo cultures. Arches and adobe blended well with the quaint colonial gables and galleries visible on storefronts and private homes. Residents hastened to assure visitors that their town was quite cosmopolitan for a frontier settlement. Buckskin and homespun had given way to false collars and double-breasted tailed coats, silks and fashionable pumps.

Of course, some members of society resisted the dictates of fashion, and few expected to see the new deputy sheriff strolling about town with a large black fan suspended at his side by a red ribbon, no matter the style.

Deputy Sheriff Branch Kincaid would sooner tie onto a buck-shot coyote than put a ribbon around his waist. However, after nearly a month of acting as Jack Strickland's errand boy, Branch was just about willing to ride anything if it'd get him out of town for a spell. He was sick of running the drunks into jail every night after the saloons closed. He was tired of skulking about with men who were lower than a snake's belly, trying to discover which one of them killed his brother.

He was weary of worrying about Katie Starr and her half-naked Cherokee.

"Hell." Branch flung back the front door and marched into the jailhouse. Dropping into a chair, he propped his scuffed black-leather boots on top of the sheriff's desk and folded his arms across his chest. Might as well sleep, he told himself. Spending so much time in this dismal place was plumb wearing him out.

Sunlight filtered in through the single glass-paned window and shone directly in his face. He grimaced and shifted his chair. although it was impossible to get too comfortable. The jailhouse measured about fourteen paces square, with the front section of the building containing only Strickland's desk and two cane chairs. The back portion was divided into four very small cells, each having a single barred window about the size of a bread pan cut just beneath the wooden roof. On days when bad weather forced the door closed and the windows shuttered, the place smelled almost as good as a pole-cat-infested outhouse.

He sighed heavily, pulling his hat over his eyes to shield the afternoon light, and muttered, "I might as well have stayed at Gallagher's for all the good I'm doin' here."

Oh, he'd learned a few things since coming to Nacogdoches and settling in as deputy sheriff and two-timing spy. He knew that Dennis Beck's wife brained him with a fireplace bellows every time the poor fellow came home after stopping at Cortenoz's Gambling House. He'd learned that Paula Oates had a penchant for slipping ten-penny nails into her apron pocket as she wandered the aisles of Thorne's mercantile. He'd discovered that a preacher's son was meeting a whore's daughter behind the livery stable on Tuesday nights for a little unholy communion.

But as far as the business that had brought him to town, Branch's discoveries had been far from illuminating. Colonel Moorman ran most of the Regulator business from San Augustine, placing Jack Strickland in charge of local action around Nacogdoches. Other than making a few speeches in the town square, the sheriff had left most of the group's business in the hands of the hooded blackguard who'd led the attack on Gallagher's. Strickland hadn't even bothered to ride along on the four retaliatory raids the Regulators had staged since Branch's arrival in Nacogdoches.

The deputy cocked open one eye when a hornet landed

on his arm. It was black and mean looking and reminded him of the anonymous Regulator dressed in black—the one who'd hurt the Gallaghers. Before the wasp could plant its stinger, Branch blew it away with a heave of his breath. Wish it were as easy to deal with the Regulator bastard, he thought, eyeing the insect as it circled the room before escaping through a window. But you can't squash an insect unless you can see him.

On each of the forays against the Moderators, Branch had spent his time trying to discover the identity of the scoundrel. When he had delivered the stack of "counterfeit" shinplasters to the Regulator leader on that first raid, he'd been disappointed that the man never removed his disguise. The villain's eyes had gleamed avariciously through the slits in his hood, and after declaring the notes the best example of counterfeiting he'd ever seen, he'd immediately reiterated his promise to protect Branch when the New York detectives came calling. Branch had figured that'd be his reaction; the promissory notes chartered by a Georgia state bank were legitimate, supplied upon request by William Bell.

The leader's identity was one little detail Branch had promised himself he'd attend to before heading to Riverrun. He owed the man for burning the inn, not to mention the slap the bastard had given Katie, and he didn't intend to leave East Texas without settling the score. "I guess I'll have to go along on more of those devil rides," he muttered. If all else failed, he could confront the Regulator bastard while on a raid and learn who he was *after* he beat him bloody.

Still, that was a minor concern when compared to discovering the identity of Rob's killer. "Unless it turns out they were one and the same," he mused. "Wouldn't that be convenient." But it was probably too much of a coincidence to hope for.

With such troublesome thoughts rumbling around his head, Branch abandoned the idea of a nap. After checking on the jail's lone prisoner, a drunk-and-disorderly from the previous night, he decided to make a circuit around town. Maybe he'd run across an Indian to arrest.

He left the jail and strode up the street toward the square, waving a greeting to the padre who stood pruning rosebushes in front of Sacred Heart Catholic Church. Reaching the corner of Main Street, he slowed his step and casually surveyed the plaza. A jumble of wagons, horses, and people milled about. Children filled jugs from the water well at the center, while nattily dressed gentlemen conversed with others wearing denim and road dust. Branch's gaze skimmed over women clothed in bright gingham and poplin and snagged on a familiar blue homespun disappearing through the door of Doc Mayfair's office. Katie Starr was visiting the doctor.

A hollow feeling gripped Branch's stomach. Was someone sick out at Gallagher's? Had there been an accident? Did that damned Indian hurt somebody? Heart pounding, Branch hurried across the square.

Inside the doctor's office, Katie stood in a rage, her fists clenched at her hips. "One hundred fifty dollars a scab! Why, that's robbery. I don't have that kind of money. Besides, Doctor, I *gave* you those bottles. You can't charge me for my own property!"

Doctor Mayfair curled an end of his long, graying mustache, refusing to meet Katie's gaze. "Mrs. Starr, I'm afraid that I simply don't agree that you need vaccine out at your inn. True, there has been an outbreak of smallpox in South Texas, but any persons traveling in that direction can come on into town, and I'll be happy to administer the vaccination."

"But if they're already at Gallagher's, it'd be a three-hour trip in the wrong direction, Doctor. It'd be much simpler . . ."

"No. You have my answer, Mrs. Starr. Now, if you'll excuse me, Mrs. Cody's confinement is nearing its end, and her husband has requested I attend the baby's birth. I must leave immediately." He snapped his doctor's satchel closed, picked it up, and gestured toward the door. "After you, Mrs. Starr."

Katie folded her arms, her foot tapping the floor like a lucky puppy's tail. "Doctor, I don't need all of the vaccine. I gave you two bottles. You can return one of them to me."

Mayfair's portly belly swelled as he straightened in indignation. "Madam," he demanded, "leave my office at once!"

"Not until you return my property!"

Mayfair's nostrils flared and his lips curled. Then he whirled and walked to a glass-front cabinet. Taking a key from his pocket, he unlocked the door and withdrew two familiar ampoules.

Relief rolled through Katie in waves. "Thank you, Doctor," she said as he locked the cabinet and turned toward her. "I knew that you would—Doctor!"

He placed the two bottles in his medical satchel and closed it. Without a word he started for the front door.

"Doctor Mayfair," Katie screeched, "you can't do this to me."

"Leave here, Mrs. Starr. Now. I've a baby to deliver, and I want you gone from my office."

Katie blinked back angry tears. The odious, mercenary little man. If he didn't outweigh her by a hundred pounds, she'd knock him senseless. She settled for grabbing the bag as he walked by. "Give it to me, Doctor. You want money, fine. I'll get you money, soon. Just give me the medicine now."

They grappled for the satchel, the doctor's face bright red in his anger, Katie's mouth set as she tugged and squirmed, doing her best to steal the bag from a man stronger than she. Intent upon her task, Katie didn't hear the door bang open. But there was no missing Deputy Kincaid's angry roar, "What the hell is goin' on here?"

Doctor Mayfair capitalized on Katie's distraction by wrenching the bag from her hands. He straightened his coat, saying, "Deputy, arrest this woman for attempted theft. I'll explain it all later, I haven't the time now." At the door, he paused and turned to Katie. "You get me the money first, young lady, and you may have your medicine. Good day."

The door slammed behind him.

Branch took one good look at Katie and knew his fears for her safety were groundless. She wasn't hurt or ill. No one could be that furious and sick at the same time. "Is it Daniel or John?" he asked.

"No." Katie turned her savage gaze on him and cursed, "Men!"

That's a relief, Branch thought. She was being her normal self. He took a step back, holding his arms before him as though to ward her off. "Ooh, Sprite. If our army had been equipped with a look like that, we wouldn't have lost the Alamo. Is it your Indian? Did he suffer a haircut or somethin'?"

She glared at him.

"All right, I'll keep quite about the Indian." Damn, but he liked sparring with her. Now that he knew nothing serious was going on, he could take a little time and enjoy it. Sitting on the corner of Doc Mayfair's desk, he folded his arms and tried a sympathetic smile. "Kate, you want to tell me what's goin' on here?"

"No."

"Now, Kate, you'd be well served to cooperate with me. I am the law around here, after all, and one of Nacogdoches' finest citizens has just accused you of stealin'. If you and I weren't friendly, I might've done as he asked and hauled you off to jail. Don't you think you'd best tell me what you took?"

"I didn't take anything," Katie stated, yanking at the ties of her sunbonnet. "And I wouldn't be stealing because it was mine to begin with."

"What was yours to begin with?"

Her mouth snapped shut. Then opened. Then shut again. She took her bonnet off, smoothed her hair, then put the hat back on.

"Mrs. Starr? You hidin' somethin' from me?"

"It's none of your business, Branch Kincaid," she said, turning to a wall mirror and fussing with the bow she tied beneath her chin.

"You can call me Deputy, ma'am, and I do think it is my concern. What did you steal, or try to steal, from the doctor?"

Their gazes met in the mirror. "I could take you to jail, Sprite. It's dark there, and one of the cots has a right nice mattress and it's bug free. I could lock you in." He walked up behind her and rested his hands on her shoulders. "I could lock *us* in."

Slowly, her tongue circled her lips. His fingers traced her neckline, her skin smooth and soft to the touch. She drew a deep breath and smiled at him. Branch waited expectantly.

She whispered in a seductive tone, "Horse liniment."

"What?"

Katie brushed away his hands and turned, stepping toward the desk where her reticule sat. "Pretty Girl has a sore tendon, and I wanted the horse liniment I'd loaned the doctor a few months back. Apparently, he's forgotten that he got it from me."

"Horse liniment?"

"Excuse me, Deputy. My brother's waiting for me at Thorn's and we must be on our way. Good day."

Her lavender scent lingered in the room after she departed. Through the window, Branch watched her cross the street, dodging a dog with a hunk of meat in his mouth being chased by a woman flapping her apron. He didn't believe Katie Starr's story. She was lying sure as Texas has chiggers. It had something to do with the doctor, and Branch would bet his last shinplaster that it had something to do with that damned Indian of hers, too.

Hell. He was getting sick and tired of worrying about Katie Starr and her Indian. He went outside and stood on the boardwalk, leaning against a post as a heavy freight wagon lumbered down the street stirring up a cloud of red dust. As it settled, Branch caught sight of the clerk at Thorn's mercantile loading a bag of flour into the wagon bed of Gallagher's buckboard. Harnessed to the wagon, chewing contentedly on a clump of hay, was Katie's ugly horse, Pretty Girl.

Branch hooked his thumbs in his vest and said, "Horse liniment."

That man. That overbearing, overconfident, overwhelming man. For goodness sakes, why did she have to run into

Branch Kincaid today of all days? Didn't she have enough
problems on her mind as it was?

Katie's heels clicked in rapid staccato against the
boardwalk as she fumed all the way to Thorn's mercantile.
Pretty Girl neighed a greeting, and Katie paused to stroke
the mare's nose, the action as soothing to her as to the
horse. Poor thing, Katie thought, you may very well be
sore. Since the fire Pretty Girl had been forced into
wagon-pulling duty, making Katie thankful she was such a
tame, well-trained horse.

She smiled into the big brown eyes and said, "And you
are beautiful, no matter what that scapegrace says."

Daniel waited for her inside the store. Katie found him
gazing wistfully at a jar containing licorice ropes, and she
requested that the price of two pieces of the candy and a
jar of liniment be added to the Gallagher account. Then,
after loading the rest of their purchases into the wagon,
she and Daniel headed out of town.

Away from Nacogdoches, the towering pines that lined
the road blocked the sky but for the ribbon of blue that
paralleled the red dirt road. Katie's gaze locked on that
promise of color, her emotions as dark as the surrounding
forest. Trouble lay ahead. The knowledge bit into her
mind, sharp and sure, and as she listened to the sparrows
squabbling in the treetops, she wondered from which direction it would come. One thing was certain, however. A
man would bring it, because after all, wasn't trouble always brought by a man?

The March wind was hissing through the forest as
Shaddoe joined them a few miles from town. Daniel
pulled the wagon to a stop, and the Cherokee climbed into
the seat, taking the reins. "Well?" he asked, whipping the
leather straps and signaling the horse forward.

Katie put her hand on his knee and quietly said, "I'm
sorry, Shaddoe, it didn't work." Indignation swept through
her as she recalled her conversation with Doc Mayfair.
"That charlatan allowed that I had no claim on the vaccine, even though I gave it to him to begin with! He cited
the public welfare and then offered to sell me a single scab
for one hundred fifty dollars."

His expression grim, Shaddoe nodded. "You have my thanks for trying, Kathleen. Did he ask you why you wanted the vaccine?"

"Yes. I told him that travelers who stop at Gallagher's often ask about the smallpox outbreak in South Texas and request the vaccination."

"He believed you?"

"He wrote his office location on a stack of cards and told me to hand them out to anyone interested in being vaccinated."

Shaddoe heaved a weary sigh. "As much as I dislike the idea, I guess we must proceed with your father's plan tomorrow night."

John Gallagher had argued against the theft of the vaccine since it was Nacogdoches' single source of the preparation. News had reached the inn of an outbreak of smallpox in Galveston, and it wouldn't have been right to leave the citizens of East Texas without protection. He then proposed an alternate solution to Shaddoe's problem, and as a result, all the Gallaghers were part of the effort to obtain smallpox vaccine for the Cherokees.

Daniel said to Shaddoe, "It'll be all right, you'll see. I can hardly wait, I'm glad it's working out this way. It'll be an adventure."

"Do not fool yourself, Daniel," Shaddoe replied. "This is risky business we are about, and there is nothing romantic in leaving your home and family. If the need were not so great . . ."

At thirteen, Daniel stood poised on the edge of manhood, and his manner as he spoke to his friend proved it. "Shaddoe, this thing that we're doing is important. I'm small enough to squeeze through Doc Mayfair's back window, and I can help convince Keeper to go along with us. If that'll help save a lot of people's lives, what does a couple of years away from home matter? Besides, if we do this right, no one will know for sure that I took the vaccine, and I won't even have to stay away. Katie's real good at telling stories. She'll make it work."

"He's right, Shaddoe," Katie said. "I'm sure I can work up a bucketful of tears when I tell everyone at the ball tomorrow night that my baby brother has run away from home."

"I still do not like it. What if young McShane will not cooperate? Were you able to speak with him today, Daniel, and confirm your father's belief that the boy has not been vaccinated?"

"Yep, Da was right. Keeper told me the only pox his mother fretted about was the French kind."

"Do you believe he will resist our plans?"

Daniel tipped his straw hat farther back on his head. "I don't know. He's awful loyal to the sheriff, and today he yammered on and on about Branch Kincaid." The boy gave his sister a sidelong look.

Katie straightened her spine but said nothing. Her fingers fussed with a ruffle on her skirt.

Shaddoe shrugged. "I know of no other way than to use the boy. By inoculating him and then harvesting the cowpox pustules he produces, we will be able to protect my people without leaving the Texians at risk."

"I *think* Keeper will agree," Daniel said. "After all, you'll be offering him a good bit of money, and hell, how much can he like living in a jail, anyway?"

"Daniel, don't curse," Katie insisted.

The boy rolled his eyes at Shaddoe, who said, "It all depends on Keeper McShane. I hope that he will listen to you and your father, Daniel. Too, we must assure him that the Cherokee will treat him well when his service ends." He sighed, then added, "The time I wasted searching for The Raven haunts my soul."

"Remember what you said to me, Shaddoe," Katie said, adjusting the ties of her poke bonnet. " '*Ai!* If only.' We can't go back, any of us. No matter how much we would like to. We can go forward, though, and we will do so tomorrow. Right?"

An insolent grin brightened the Cherokee's face. "March second, Independence Day. Quite appropriate, actually. Your father will enjoy escorting you to the ball at Brown's Tavern, Kathleen."

~~∋∢ CHAPTER 8 ∢∾~~

$\mathcal{T}$HE FOLLOWING MORNING dawned bright, but by noon, black clouds had attacked the sky, and rain fell in torrents. The Gallaghers and Shaddoe traveled the last few miles into Nacogdoches on a quagmire that passed for a road.

They parted company at the banks of La Nanna Creek. Shaddoe and Daniel would make their way by stealth to Miguel Cortenoz's gambling house, where they would wait for nightfall before breaking into Doc Mayfair's office. John would escort his daughter to the home of an old friend, Adolphus Sterne, and prepare to attend the Independence Day Ball.

With the rain hampering their good-byes, Katie hugged her brother tight. "You take care, love. Mind Shaddoe and hurry back to Da and me."

Daniel endured her embrace with the stoicism of a thirteen-year-old boy. "It'll be grand, Kate. Don't worry, I'll be back before you can miss me."

John gave his boy a manly handshake, then wrapped him in his arms. "God go with you, son," he said. "McShane and I will be a'meetin' you in church at two o'clock tomorrow morning."

Shaddoe thanked John for his help, promised to take good care of Daniel, and turned to Katie. "I may not see you for some time to come, Kathleen. I am in your debt, for this and for your help with Steven's plan regarding the land. Perhaps someday I shall be able to repay you."

Katie smiled through her tears. "Shaddoe, you owe me

nothing but your friendship, and I will hold you to that. Good luck, *oginalii*, my friend. Return to us soon."

"I shall." He bent to kiss her cheek, which was wet with more than raindrops. "Do not give up on my magic," he said. "Be happy, Kathleen."

Shaddoe melted into the trees followed by Daniel, who paused and waved to his sister and father, his sunshine smile a brilliant contrast to the weather.

By late afternoon, the clouds disappeared and a rainbow painted the eastern sky. John stood behind his daughter, watching the heavens from a parlor window in the Sternes' home. "Care to go a'huntin' for a wee leprechaun's treasure, colleen?"

Katie smiled, her gaze fastened on the hazy band of colors in the distance. Often she and her father had done just that. During her childhood, after a storm, they would ride an outrageous race, searching for the end of the rainbow. They would laugh and sing, galloping across fields and meadows until the colored mist faded. Even at a young age, Katie somehow knew that the real treasure lay in the moments spent with her father, occupied in nothing more than play.

"Oh, Da," she said. "What I wouldn't give to find that rainbow's end today with the little black pot filled to overflowing with smallpox vaccine."

Gallagher kissed the back of her head. "Sure but if it isn't a worry, having your brother after a task like this. But the boy is almost a man now, and he needs to be needed. This trip will be good for him, Katie. Shaddoe's quest is noble."

He pulled her away from the window and pushed her toward the stairs. "Time to dress, colleen. Mrs. Sterne has graciously offered the loan of a ball gown for this evening, and I accepted in your behalf. We need everyone in town to notice your presence at the dance tonight. 'Tis on the bed upstairs."

"A dress? Really? I was going to wear my lavender, but if she offered . . ."

"She offered. In fact, I do believe she'd be insulted if you chose not to wear it. Now, get along, girl. As your da,

I hate to admit it, but in that green creation of Eva Sterne's you'll be a grand distraction."

Katie smiled tenderly at her father's compliment. She kissed his cheek, then began to make her way upstairs. "I'm more than willing to contribute to the cause by wearing beautiful clothing. I just hope tonight's activities do not leave us all inquiring after the latest jailhouse fashion."

John turned back to the window and gazed at the symbol of dreams that colored the sky. "Jesus, Mary, and Joseph, hear her prayer," he murmured.

Branch's collar itched. He considered plucking it off and tossing it in the nearest watering trough. *Damn*, but he hated wearing store-bought clothes. Give him a length of homespun cotton and a woman's gentle stitch any day over these mercantile murder devices. The shirt was too tight across the shoulders, the vest too big, the jacket too short, and the trousers were just plain ugly.

Still, they were the best he could do in a pinch. He hadn't planned on attending the Independence Day Ball until Adolphus Sterne told him just who he had for houseguests.

Branch trudged through the mud, all but oblivious to the spatters that appeared on his pants. Something about this evening smelled like an acre of onions, he decided. John Gallagher wouldn't attend a party at a Regulator's place of business unless he had a very good reason. What was the old codger up to?

"Mr. Branch, wait!" Keeper McShane picked his way between puddles, stopping to brush off any speckles of mud that landed on his brand-new britches.

"Come on, squirt. If you're so determined to follow me to this shindig, then keep up. Hell and Texas, these things usually break up by two, and it's already past midnight."

Early that morning, Strickland had waylaid him with a message for Colonel Moorman, who was off doing business with some horse thieves in the canebrakes a good half day's ride east of town. Branch had ridden hell-bent for leather to get there and back in time to attend the dance. Had he known he'd get such a late start, he'd never have promised Keeper he could come along to the "real-honest-to-goodness, society-type dance."

"He's like havin' a lap puppy—wants to follow a man even to the backhouse," he muttered. Of course, the kid wasn't so bad, just lonely. Personally, Branch thought Sheriff Strickland could do a better job of dishing out attention to the boy, considering how he'd taken it upon himself to look after the youngster.

Keeper had told Branch the story of how Strickland had saved him from the whorehouse. The sheriff had settled into the Mansion for a weekend of entertainment when he discovered that the house had run out of his favorite cigar. Keeper had been sent to the mercantile in the nearby town of Red Mineral Bluff to purchase a supply of the smokes. For the remainder of the weekend, he noticed how Strickland eyed him while he went about his chores around The Mansion of Joy.

Keeper had been as surprised as a pup with its first porcupine when his mama traded him and his extra pair of trousers to Jack Strickland for three gold coins. He'd been happy to leave; some of the customers had been lookin' at him a might strangely. From the moment Sheriff Jack allowed him a cot in one of the cells for his very own bed, Keeper had become a fixture at the jail.

Branch thought the whole business a crying shame, but he took to the boy. In many ways, Keeper reminded him of himself.

The lilting strains of a waltz drifted into the street as Branch and Keeper approached the tavern. As they climbed the steps, Branch's pulse quickened in anticipation.

He halted just outside the building's open doors and gazed into the room, searching. He stepped inside the moment he saw her.

Dressed in green satin, Katie outshone every woman in the room. She wore her hair in a coronet with dogwood blossoms woven between the braids, and a patterned silk

fan dangled from her wrist as a gentleman led her onto the
dance floor when the fiddler began a waltz.

"Where'd she get the dress?" Branch muttered. "And
where in the *hell* did she leave the rest of it?" Off-the-
shoulder puff sleeves provided negligible support to a
neckline that plunged entirely too low.

"Wow. Look at Miz Katie. Ain't she just beautiful,"
Keeper said, his face alight with awe.

Her dance partner (some sissified-lookin' fool, Branch
thought) twirled her around, and she faltered a step when
she noticed Branch. But it was the moment she saw
Keeper that she stopped dead still.

The tinkle of shattering glass screamed in Daniel
Gallagher's ears. His heart was thumping like a rabbit's in
a coyote's hind pocket. Carefully, he squeezed through the
small back window of Doctor Mayfair's office. "Sweet
Sainted Mother," he said. "Breaking a windowpane in itself is enough to land us in jail."

"Quiet," Shaddoe demanded in a whisper.

Broken glass crunched beneath Daniel's feet, and only
a sliver of light penetrated the darkness through a gap in
the window curtains. Although he waited a few moments
for his eyes to adjust, he still knocked over a chair while
crossing the room.

A glass-front cabinet stood against the side wall. He
pulled at the door. Locked. Bending over, he peered inside,
searching for the ampoules his sister had described. "Can't
see a blasted thing," he mumbled.

He dug into his pocket for a match, then lit it. The
flare of light allowed him to spot the two small amber bottles marked Smallpox Vaccine, Jefferson Strain. That's it,
he thought.

He blew out the match and lifted a book from Doctor
Mayfair's desktop. Tapping the book spine against the
glass, Daniel cracked chunks from the cabinet front until
he had a large enough opening to slip his hand through.

He was reaching for the second bottle when he heard
the voices. "You should've known better than to go after

your wife like that, Billy. You're not going to win in a
knife fight against a woman as strong as your Sal."

Oh, no, Daniel thought, Doc Mayfair! The lock on the
front door rattled. Daniel grabbed the vaccine and gasped
as his arm snagged on a ragged edge of glass. It sliced
deep, and pain lanced his arm as he yanked it from the
cabinet.

He raced for the back, shoving the bottles through the
open window into Shaddoe's waiting hands. With legs
straddling the sill, Daniel froze when the front door
opened and lamplight illuminated the room.

Doc Mayfair shouted, "What in the—Billy, get the
sheriff!"

Branch winced as Katie trod on his foot. Again. "Sprite,
you take to dancin' like oil to water."

"Oh, hush your mouth and waltz." Katie's flippant
tone hid the tumult of emotion churning inside her as they
glided across the floor. It *had* to happen again. So much to
think of tonight, so much to do, and *he* had to show up.
The untrustworthy wolf in gentleman's clothing who made
her blood race and her knees melt like ice beneath the August sun.

He looked down at her, a question reflected in the
golden glow of his eyes. "Why, Kate Starr?" he eventually
asked. "There must be four men for every woman here tonight. Why did you fight through a herd of admirers to ask
me to dance?"

"I need to talk with you, Branch."

"Why?"

Because I've got to get Keeper out of here. The boy's
presence at the dance muddled the entire plan. Da expected
him to be at the jail. Of course, Katie couldn't tell Branch
that, so she searched her mind for a plausible lie.

Branch continued, "Yesterday, you left me with the distinct impression"—he lifted his fingers and rubbed his
cheek—"that my attentions weren't welcome."

She felt her face flush at his reference to her slap.

His eyes narrowed and he asked, "What are you up to,

Sprite? And why isn't your father here scolding you about your lack of clothing?"

"Branch, I need to tell you something." But before she could finish, the music ended and a dark-haired gentleman slapped Branch on the shoulder. "Deputy, I thought you were on duty this evening."

"Hello, Sheriff. Don't worry, I'm keepin' watch. This seemed the best place to be, since the whole town is crammed in this room." He added silently, *with their eyes on Katie Starr's bosom.*

Though Strickland spoke to Branch, his gaze never left Katie. "Allow me to say hello to this beautiful woman, Kincaid."

Branch's jaw tightened. Working for this man was getting old fast. If the deputy's job didn't suit his needs so well, he'd tell Strickland to take his pearly-white smile and shove it—

He broke off the thought as Katie deftly brought her heel down on his toes. Scowling, he said, "Certainly, Sheriff."

Strickland bowed low over Katie's hand. "Mrs. Starr, it is such a pleasure to see you again. Allow me to say that your beauty brightens this room like a thousand candles."

Branch rolled his eyes as Katie preened. Strickland continued, "Nacogdoches has gone too long without having seen your lovely face grace its streets. You must accompany your father and brother on their trips into town more often. Why, I don't recall your visiting here since that terrible business concerning your late husband."

"She was here earlier this week," Branch pointed out, annoyed at the way the sheriff's words had dimmed Katie's smile.

"It has been difficult for me to leave the inn, Sheriff Strickland," she said. "Business has been good—up until very recently, that is—and in truth, I've not felt much like socializing since Mr. Starr and our daughter died."

"I understand," Strickland said with a consoling nod. "Perhaps had I been able to apprehend the villain responsible for your loss, you'd have found it easier to put the past behind you. I apologize, Mrs. Starr, for my failing."

She shrugged, and Branch figured she'd had enough of this subject. A bleakness had entered her eyes, and she looked a little lost as she gazed around the room.

There was nothing cold or innocent about the way the sheriff was looking at Katie, however. Branch scowled as he watched the man's gaze linger on her neckline. A woman ought to be locked up for disturbing the peace in a dress like that.

"Enough of this," Strickland said. "We've a holiday to celebrate here. Mrs. Starr, may I request the next dance? I watched you earlier, and I must say that your grace on the dance floor overwhelms me."

"Yeah, right," Branch said. "She's as light on her feet as a buffalo. But I'm afraid—"

"I'd love to dance with you, Sheriff Strickland." Katie stepped forward, extending her hand. Strickland led her onto the floor for a waltz.

Branch retreated to the refreshment table, where he tossed back two cups of sweet ginger punch and consumed three tea cakes, trying not to stare at the tall, debonair easterner and his sassy, seductive dance partner. Little witch, she didn't trample the sheriff's toes once. And wasn't Strickland holding her a tad more close than was necessary? Probably had something to do with his height and the angle he needed to look down the front of her dress.

Branch shoved his empty cup onto the table and maneuvered himself over to Katie's side for the final bar of the song. Strickland frowned at him. "I think you need to make a circuit around town, Kincaid."

"I think you're right, boss." He turned to Katie and took her elbow. "Ready for that walk now, Kate?" His smile was grim.

After taking one look at his face, Katie agreed, and then thanked Strickland for the dance. With his hand against the small of her back, Branch guided Katie firmly toward the front door.

The crisp night air brought shivers to Katie's skin. Branch slipped off his jacket and placed it around her bare shoulders. "Ought to teach you not to run about half-naked," he grumbled, detaching the collar from his shirt and burying it in the middle of a pot of yellow daffodils that sat beside the doorway. "You'd best watch out for men like Strickland. In those fancy eastern colleges they teach men how to eat girls like you for lunch. Now, what is it you were thinkin' to tell me before Romeo interrupted?"

Katie couldn't stop her gaze from straying to the cords of his neck that had been hidden beneath the collar. For some reason, now he seemed almost naked. "Oh." She dragged her attention back to the problems at hand. "I just wanted to tell you something."

"Well?"

She pursed her lips and lifted her hands to secure a flower in her hair. Da was right, she told herself, as Branch's stare went right to her bodice. This dress was truly a weapon. "Look, I need to speak with Keeper, and since he follows you everywhere, I decided to tell you first so that you'd not wonder about him when we leave the party for a little while."

Light filtering through the windows illuminated the perplexed expression on Branch's face. "What do you have to say to Keeper, and why do you think you have to leave to do it?"

Mentally, Katie said a quick prayer that Branch would believe her next tale. She'd added a bit to the original plan after seeing Keeper with Branch tonight, and her story might very well have holes the size of watermelons in it, but it was the best she could do at the moment. "Daniel's run away."

"What?" Branch said. "No, I don't believe it."

She nodded. "He left a note. Only, I don't believe it either, and since he and Keeper are friends, I thought perhaps he might know the truth."

Branch held up a hand. "Whoa there, girl. Back up. Start from the beginning and tell me the complete story."

Katie took a deep breath. "When I woke up this morning, I found a note from Daniel saying that he'd left home to join the navy. We think he left late last night."

Inside the tavern, the fiddler began a lively reel. "The navy?" Branch asked. "The Texas Navy?"

Katie nodded. "Commodore Moore once stayed at the inn. He's been a hero of Daniel's ever since he told my brother that the injury to his hand wouldn't prevent him from being a sailor."

Branch shook his head. "What's the kid thinkin' of? He's way too young to do anything like that. Besides, do you know where Moore is right now?"

"I read the newspapers, Branch. I know about the Texas-Yucatan alliance."

Branch sighed heavily and raked his fingers through his hair. "I'll go after him for you. You say he left last night? He can't be too far. I'll see you back to the Sternes' and then . . ."

"No, that's not what I wanted," Katie interrupted. "I don't believe my brother went south, but I do think Keeper might know something."

Branch was silent for a moment, staring out at the empty square. "Your breed, what about him?"

"Shaddoe? What's Shaddoe got to do with this?" Katie's heart began to pound.

"That's what I'm askin'."

"Oh, Shaddoe left last week," she lied. "He's gone back to Mexico."

Branch arched an eyebrow. "Why didn't you tell me that yesterday?"

"You didn't ask me."

"You're a witchy woman, Kate." Frowning, he traced a finger along the bare curve of her shoulder. "Where's your father? What's he have to say about all this?"

His touch brought shivers to her skin, making it hard to concentrate on his questions and her story. She stepped beyond his reach, saying, "Da believes Daniel's hiding in town. He decided to come to this party because he thinks Daniel will see us and it'll hurt his feelings. This is about the sixth time he's left home in the last couple of years, and Da is getting pretty tired of it."

"That doesn't make sense. Why would he come to a

Regulator party just to give Daniel a hard time? Doesn't sound a bit like your father to me."

Katie rolled her eyes, exasperated. "Haven't you noticed both Moderators and Regulators inside that room? This ball celebrates Texas Independence Day, it's not a Regulator gala. Most people can put aside their differences on such an occasion, my father included."

"Don't worry yourself into a snit; all you do then is attract attention. And it's not like you need anymore, walkin' around half-naked. Lord knows, what your Pa is thinkin' of, lettin' you—" He stopped abruptly and scowled. "You never said where John got off to."

Katie snapped. "He felt tired and left a little while ago. Billy Simpkins said he'd accompany me back to the Sternes'."

"Your father left you in the hands of that Lothario?" Branch asked incredulously. "And to think I gave John Gallagher credit for a little sense."

Katie lifted her chin. "What is it about you and Shakespeare, Kincaid? I happen to think Mr. Simpkins is a very nice man. Now I'd like to speak with Keeper, if you please."

Branch reluctantly gave in. "Wait right here. I'll bring the boy outside." He walked toward the door, then stopped, adding, "But you can be damn sure we've not finished this particular discussion."

As he returned to the tavern, Katie absently fingered the petals of a yellow daffodil blooming in a pot set atop the porch railing. The ladies of town did their best to spruce up the tavern for the ball.

Where *was* Da? He was supposed to bring Keeper to the church. Who'd have thought the boy would show up at the dance? Da must be searching all over town for him.

What should she do now? How was she going to get rid of Branch? She shouldn't have stopped him from going after Daniel. *Dumb, Katie, dumb*, she scolded herself. Why had she hesitated in sending him off on a wild-goose chase?

That little voice in her head that enjoyed arguing so much answered. *Because you didn't want to worry him.*

Because you know he really wants to help your family. Because you trust him. "Dumb, Katie, dumb."

The greenery surrounding the flower was smooth beneath her fingers. She looked down at her hand. She was angry with herself, angry at her errant emotions, which had intruded in such an untimely manner. Then she glanced around. Two clay pots filled with flowers framed the doorway. Branch's collar hung over the rim of the one on the left.

She never would have considered it had the little voice not been shouting in her head. Sometimes only actions could quiet unruly thoughts.

Katie smiled.

John Gallagher worriedly rubbed his palm against his whiskered jaw. It was nearing two o'clock in the morning, and Keeper McShane was missing from his cot in his jail-cell home. Where could the boy be?

"I must find the lad, and soon," he muttered. So much of this plan rode on the boy, and he feared they'd need time to convince Keeper to do as they asked. He turned to leave the cell and heard the front door of the jailhouse bang open. Pressing himself into the room's darkest corner, he listened to heavy footsteps shuffle across the outer room. A chair creaked and a desk drawer rasped open.

"That boy! He's done it again," came the disgusted voice. Then Jack Strickland bellowed, "Boy! Boy, get your butt out of bed and come here."

Saints a'mighty, the sheriff wasn't supposed to be here!

The drawer banged shut. "Boy, I am talking to you. You've been in my whiskey again, haven't you? Son, I'm through warning you. Get out here now." He mumbled then, saying, "That Kincaid, this is probably his fault. He evidently encourages the boy. And the nerve of him, taking a woman on his rounds. I should have gone after them instead of ducking out the back. The woman's a jewel. How could I have missed seeing it before?"

Again he shouted, "Boy!" The chair scraped across the floor as he stood.

Hearing the footsteps approach Keeper's cell, John felt around in the darkness for some sort of weapon. His hands closed around the familiar neck of a whiskey jug. A boy Keeper's age shouldn't be a'drinkin', he thought as he lifted the bottle above his head. He prepared himself to strike.

But he made a terrible mistake.

He hadn't figured Strickland would be carrying a lantern. He swung the glass container, clipping Strickland on the forehead, but not before the light illuminated his face. Strickland mumbled the word "Gallagher," and slumped to the floor.

"May the Good Lord strike me for a fool," John said, scooping up the lamp before it could start anything afire. This entire plan had gone to hell in a handbasket. A man wouldn't be a'gettin' by, conkin' a sheriff over the head.

Especially when that sheriff was a Regulator and himself a Moderator.

This would change everything. "Your seein' me face has mucked it up but good," he told the unconscious man. "I'm too near to dyin' to start killing people now." The pains in his gut had been occurring with increasing frequency, and John wasn't one to fool himself about such things. He frowned, glaring at the heap at his feet. "Couldn't you have waited a bit a'fore allowin' the thirst to overcome you?"

Grabbing the sheriff's boots, John tugged the man farther into the cell and slammed the door. Every bit of time he could gain would serve them well, he thought. Whether he liked it or not, it appeared now that a whole passel of folks would be leaving with Shaddoe for the Territory.

"I still have to find the boy, though," he murmured. Stealthily, he left the jailhouse and hurried up the street, checking the windows at the church as he passed. Should I stop and see if Daniel and Shaddoe are there waiting for me?

"No," he whispered. He had to find the boy first.

He reached the square and turned toward Brown's Tavern, thinking the dance might have been what lured the youngster from his bed. The sight of Katie, standing in the street, struggling with Keeper McShane, nudged him into a run.

But the sight of Branch Kincaid, lying flat on his back in the dirt, the broken stem of a daffodil drooping across his nose, and soil and pieces of clay clinging to his dirty white shirt stopped John Gallagher cold.

"Katie me love, what have you done this time?"

ᐓ CHAPTER 9 ᐛ

A SCENT TICKLED HIS NOSE. No, some-thing soft. A woman. Not a woman, something connected with a woman. He opened his mouth a bit. His tongue touched the heaviness at the corner of his lips. Ugh. Dirt. Why was there dirt in his bed?

He wasn't in bed. Damn that Katie Starr. As Branch strained to lift his eyelids, he heard the whispers.

The feminine voice said, "Don't hurt him, Da."

"I'm not hurting him. I'll take the gag from his mouth the moment we reach the church. Boy, you be still now. We'll not be a'painin' you."

Keeper, Branch thought. They're doing something with Keeper.

Katie's skirt rustled as she walked by him. He knew it was her. By God, was that a giggle he heard?

His head pounded mercilessly. Was she using his face for a dance floor now that his feet weren't available? Fi-nally, minutes later, he opened his eyes. He couldn't see Katie Starr, but as he gingerly prodded the lump atop his head, he knew damn well she'd been there.

The music coming from within the tavern ended, and couples began exiting the building. "Why, Deputy!" a woman's concerned voice exclaimed. "What has hap-pened? Are you all right?"

"I'm just fine, ma'am," Branch answered. Beneath his breath he added, "Angry enough to chew nails, but just fine."

An amused voice asked, "What's the matter, Kincaid? Courtin' get a little dirty tonight?"

Branch groaned. Why didn't the blasted dance last just fifteen minutes longer? His smile didn't reach his eyes as he answered, "The lady seemed to believe my language was too flowery."

Couples ringed him as he climbed to his feet and accepted the good-natured ribbing offered by the party-goers. How nice to provide the final entertainment of the evening, he thought sardonically. He flicked the mud from his clothing as best he could, more to give himself time for his temper to cool than from any concern over his appearance.

He waited for the square to empty. All was black and silent. As quiet as the night, he made his way toward the Catholic church, his smile gleaming wicked in the starlight. *Little does she know it,* he thought, *but Katie's party is just beginning.*

Jack Strickland woke up cursing. The stink of the jail floor had soaked into his clothing, and he rubbed something sticky from his face with the sleeve of his shirt. "That graybeard Irishman will pay for this," he declared.

His head pounded like a blacksmith's hammer, and he lifted his hand to touch the tender lump above his ear. Bottle whipped by an old man. It was embarrassing.

Sheriff Strickland did not enjoy being embarrassed.

What mischief took place here tonight? Why had Gallagher been at the jailhouse? Did this business concern his daughter and Kincaid, or did it involve something more sinister?

Jack climbed to his feet and pushed against the cell door. He gave a grim laugh. That fool had locked the door but foolishly failed to search his victim's pockets. Strickland reached into his vest and withdrew his ring of keys.

Once out of the cell, Strickland grabbed his Hawken rifle and left the jailhouse intent on locating Kincaid. He intended to set the deputy on Gallagher's trail, then call out the Regulators. The Moderators might very well have planned an operation for tonight.

Well past two in the morning, only night creatures

roamed the town. Strickland noticed a raccoon digging in the trash alongside the mercantile, and as he passed the doctor's office, he heard a strange thumping noise. Could it be Gallagher?

His left hand held his gun, a finger fondling the trigger, and with his right he tried the door. Unlocked. Cautiously, he nudged it open.

Doc Mayfair was the source of the noise. He and Sidney Wilson lay on the floor, tied and gagged, with the doctor banging his legs against the wall.

Wilson started squawking the minute Strickland loosened the rag around his mouth. "An Injun, Sheriff. An honest-to-goodness Injun. The red bastard got me and the Doc, scared the bejeezus out of me. He said something in one of those crazy tongues and smiled like the devil himself. Naked and painted he was. His entire face was red and black, colored like some creature let loose from hell. Damn, I'm lucky to have my hair!"

Jack frowned. "Are you certain, Wilson? Are you positive he was Indian? There haven't been Indians in this part of Texas since '39."

Wilson shook his head excitedly. "He was an Injun, all right. Tell him, Doc. You saw him too."

Mayfair, still tied and gagged, agreed with a nod. When the sheriff took the kerchief from his mouth, he said, "It was an Indian, all right. Painted and feathered. Comanche, I imagine. And he had the Gallagher boy with him. They came in through the back window and broke into my medicines."

"Gallagher!" Strickland exclaimed. "What is it with that family tonight?" He bent over Wilson and worked the knots. He said, "Something's going on; we may have a Moderator incident on our hands. Doc, I'm calling out the men. You ride over to Davis's place and have him start the word. Sid, you go tell George Taylor to do the same. We'll meet in front of my office immediately."

"But, Sheriff," Wilson piped up, "what if there's Indians out there?"

Strickland gave him a look that would scare a dead man.

"I'm on my way, sir," Wilson said, his voice trembling as he cautiously eased out the front door.

"Wait." Strickland snapped upright and fixed a cold stare on first Wilson and then Doc Mayfair. "I want it clear to every man out there tonight that no one is to hurt old man Gallagher if they discover him. I want information from him—him and his boy."

Twenty minutes later Wilson made the comment to George Taylor, "Sheriff sure looks mad. If that Irishman had any sense at all, he'd be over at that church of his takin' the last rites from the padre."

Votive candles in red and blue glass cast a muted glow beside the altar. Shadow-faced statues flanked the wrought-iron candle stand, and the scent of vanilla hung heavy on the air.

Keeper McShane sat within the circle of light, scratching his head like a flea-bit hound, cogitating on the Cherokee's proposal. "I dunno," he finally said. "You sure something like that will work? It seems kind of farfetched to me."

His eyes searched the darkness for the one person in the group he still trusted in spite of tonight's misdeeds. "Miz Katie, I guess you think I should go along with this or else you wouldn't have brought me here."

Katie moved into the candlelight and sat beside him. She clasped his hands between hers and stared imploringly into his eyes. "Please forgive me, Keeper. I didn't mean to frighten you, and I didn't mean to hurt Mr. Kincaid. It's just that this plan is so important. So many people are depending on us, on you. They are my friends. I love them, and I'm so afraid they'll die without your help." She squeezed his hands tightly and said, "You see, you are the only man I know who can do this. You can save hundreds of lives. You'll be a hero, Keeper."

Keeper swallowed hard. Miz Katie was an angel, one of them statues come to life. At that moment, he'd have jumped off the bell tower if she'd asked. He squared his shoulders and said, "Okay, let's get started." He tried his best not to think about disappointing Sheriff Jack or Deputy Kincaid.

He grew a foot taller beneath Katie's radiant smile. Then she kissed him—on the lips—and he got dizzy in the head. But when he caught sight of the knife in the Cherokee's hand, a knife the size of Mississippi, he thought he'd faint dead away.

"Do you think Miz Katie could do it, please?" he asked the Indian in a timid voice.

Shaddoe's smile reassured him. "Anything you ask, my brave young friend." He passed the knife to Katie.

She lifted Keeper's arm, then hesitated. "I'll be right back."

"What are you about, young lady?" John Gallagher whispered. They were the first words he'd uttered since entering the church with a struggling Keeper in tow. The youngster had wondered what was keeping the usually talkative man quiet.

Katie's dancing slippers made not a sound as she disappeared into the gloom at the front of the church. A moment later she returned, and Keeper could see that the blade was wet. "I was afraid it was dirty," she explained, "and I thought a little holy water couldn't hurt. Daniel, do you have everything ready?"

Daniel Gallagher came out of the darkness like a ghost. A dark red stain seeped through the bandage wrapped around his arm. He passed two bottles to Katie. "I'm going to do this twice," she told Keeper. "Just in case one of the samples is no longer alive, I'll use both. It won't hurt you, and it may prevent this whole effort from being a waste of time."

Uncorking the first ampoule, she withdrew a single thread. "The vaccine has been dried on here. Shaddoe, you remember to remove this from the cut tomorrow afternoon." She mumbled her next words, but Keeper heard them. She said, "I guess that'll be long enough, I hope." She bit her lower lip and raised the knife.

Keeper shut his eyes, scareder than the time he kissed ol' Milly, the droop-tittied whore at The Mansion of Joy. The blade sliced into the fleshy part of his arm, and a blaze of pain called water to his eyes. Blood dribbled from the wound.

Daniel winced. "Hell, Katie. Go easy on him."

"Watch your mouth, Daniel Gallagher," Katie snapped. She stared at Keeper, worry dimming her eyes. "I'm sorry. I think I've done it right. I only watched Doc do this one time, when he did us. I just don't remember."

Actually, the slash didn't hurt too much, Keeper decided. He'd felt worse from the toes of his mama's shoes.

Katie dabbed a fold of cloth to the cut until the bleeding slowed. Carefully, she inserted the thread and wrapped a strip of her petticoat around his arm as a bandage. "Are you in pain?" she asked, frowning.

Keeper grinned. This hero stuff was all right. "Nothing to it, Miz Katie."

When she smiled, she looked like the Madonna statue that stood out front of the church.

He sat up straight and puffed out his chest as Daniel handed Katie a needle and the second bottle. Tipping the amber container, she dipped the needle into its neck. Keeper wrinkled his nose when he saw the thick yellow slime that clung to the darner as she withdrew it.

The next time didn't hurt as much, and Keeper turned his head away when she wiped the matter into his cut. She had just finished bandaging his arm when the unmistakable sound of a pistol being cocked exploded through the quiet church.

The needle slipped from Katie's fingers. Keeper heard it hit the floor.

The slow drawl floated from the darkness. "Anybody care to tell me just what the hell is going on here?"

Shaddoe recognized the voice. So the deputy sheriff had his quarry beneath his gunsight. But would he go so far as to hurt the Gallaghers, hurt Kathleen?

When he spoke, the Cherokee's tone was an open challenge. "Kathleen, is your hunter a *just* man?"

Katie groaned. "I think the paint on your face must have bled over and clogged up your ears. He's not *my* hunter. You know what? You two are really very much alike."

"Quit the yammerin' and answer my question. What's goin' on?" Kincaid had moved since the first time he spoke. Now his voice came from off to the side.

He walks as quietly as I, thought Shaddoe. I wish I could see his face, read his expression. But though she denies it, Kathleen cares for her hunter; therefore, he must be a good man.

John and Daniel were attempting to convince Kincaid to leave the church. Shaddoe interrupted. "I will tell you the whole of it, Branch Kincaid. Your honor will decide."

He turned to face the darkness where he believed Branch was standing. He said, "Not long ago, during the depths of winter, a man from an Indian settlement north of my people's village stole a blanket from a white man on a riverboat. The boat carried smallpox. We heard rumors. A trader reported that within weeks, every member of that man's village had died. I had previously received the vaccination, so I went to investigate."

Shaddoe heard the horror in his own voice, horror that would not leave. "I found bodies, black and swelled to thrice normal size, one atop the other. A stench that is indescribable. The entire village was dead. Those not afflicted with the disease were apparent suicides. Mothers and babies, a buzzard's feast, rotted beneath the sun."

He allowed his pain to show itself on his face and in the tremors of his body. "This was the second time that I witnessed a scene such as this. Once before I traveled to another village where I discovered smallpox's deadly presence. That time it took my wife and my son."

He shrugged away the vision, but his hand remained clenched at his side. "The disease is sweeping south and will without a doubt reach my village and what is left of my family soon." He stared into the gloom, searching for sight of the man who controlled, for this moment at least, the success of his endeavor.

"I came to Texas to obtain the vaccine. The Republic owes my people that much at least. No doctor was willing to share his supply, so I stole it. My new friend Keeper, here, will help carry life to the Territory."

Keeper chimed in, "That's right, Mr. Branch. I'm gonna be a hero."

Katie's voice echoed in the vastness of the church. "The vaccine should have been mine to give, anyway, Branch. Doc Starr owned these bottles when he died. Mayfair wanted it only because it was worth so much money to him, and he wouldn't give it back when I asked. Let them go, Branch, please!" she begged. "They're not even taking the vaccine with them. Just Keeper. In eight or ten days he'll be at the right stage to provide vaccine for the Indians. This could save hundreds of lives, Branch. You have to let them go!"

Kincaid stepped into the light, pistol in hand. He opened his mouth to speak, then stopped. He cocked his head as though listening.

Then Shaddoe heard it too. Metal hinges creaked as the church door swung open.

Branch sprang forward, pushing Katie and Keeper down upon the oak pew. Shaddoe pulled John and Daniel to the ground. "Keep still!" Branch demanded in a whisper. Sticking his head above the back of the pew, he called, "Halt where you are. This is the law speakin'. Who's there and what do you want?"

"That you, Deputy?"

"Who's askin'?"

"Sid Wilson, Deputy Kincaid. Sheriff Strickland has the Regulators checking the town for John Gallagher and his boy. They're wanted for theft and assaulting a lawman. Even worse, they probably got an Injun with them. I seen him, a real Injun. One of them scalp-huntin' Comanches. The sheriff told me and Billy Parker to look around the church."

Branch shouted furiously, "Sonofabitch, can't a man go anywhere to have a little privacy!" He nudged Katie and whispered, "Giggle."

Katie lay on her back staring up at him. He pulled at the buttons on his shirt and glared back. She did as he asked.

"You got a lady there, Deputy?" Parker called.

Branch made a show of rising and supposedly buttoning his pants. "I got a female with me, don't believe she's a lady."

"In church, Deputy Kincaid?"

"On my knees, Parker. What's it to you?" he asked.

"Nothin', sir. Sorry to interrupt you, sir."

"Then get on about your business and leave me to mine. Ain't nobody here but me and the saints." He nudged Katie again and she laughed.

"Uh, I'm afraid we can't do that, sir. The sheriff told us to wait here for him. Seems he's got an idea he'll find the Irishman in church."

"He does, does he." Branch's voice dripped sarcasm. "And I suppose the Gallaghers and a Comanche war party are hidin' in the shadows even now, watchin' the show." He sighed heavily as he stomped up the aisle. "All right, you boys check the confessionals there, and then we'll all traipse up to the bell tower to see if they're gettin' a bird's-eye view."

He followed the men up the narrow, twisting staircase hoping Katie's Shaddoe would have brains enough to hide everyone in the confessionals. They'd get caught sure as Santa Anna's peg leg if they tried to make a break for it now.

A huge brass bell hung from a wooden beam at the top of the stairs. Branch motioned to Parker. "Best check the clapper, someone could be hangin' from it, you know."

"Ain't you the funny one, Deputy."

Wilson grumbled, "Come on, Kincaid." He walked to the arched opening facing east and remarked, "Here comes the boss."

Branch looked down into the street. In the starlight, he could see the sheriff making his way toward the church. "It's Strickland, all right, and he certainly has his dauber down." He called out, "Sheriff, the church is empty. Where do you want us next?"

"Where the blazes you been, Kincaid?" Strickland shouted.

"Uh, just layin' around," Branch answered. The men snickered.

"Well, you certainly were not doing your job. Come down here, I want to talk to you."

"Yessir, boss."

When he came downstairs, Strickland was leaning against a confessional door, a lighted lamp in his hand. Quiet, folks, Branch prayed.

The sheriff said, "It's as dark as a tomb in here. Are you positive you searched the church thoroughly?"

"I'm tellin' you, boss. Ain't a damn thing up around here tonight." Out the side of his mouth he mumbled to Wilson and Parker, "Anymore."

Strickland said, "Kincaid, while you were making cow eyes at John Gallagher's daughter at the Independence Day Ball, he and his son were stealing medicines from the town's only doctor."

"No!" Branch exclaimed, just the right touch of offense in his voice.

"Yes. I hate to believe that the charming young woman was part of the plot, but it is possible her role was to distract the law. From my viewpoint, she succeeded at that quite well."

"Now, Sheriff, Kate wouldn't do anything illegal. Now, I'm not talkin' immoral, mind you. Everyone knows the Widow Starr and I keep company, but I'd bet my last shinplaster that she'd never try anything illegal. She's just not that smart, Sheriff."

Strickland shrugged. "You lived with the Gallaghers for a time, Kincaid, you must know something about them. They have to be aware that their Irish luck has run out. Where do you think they would run to?"

Branch folded his arms and frowned. After a moment of thought, he said, "I'd imagine they'd head for the border. John mentioned a relative, sister I believe, in Natchitoches. Of course, that'd be a first, someone running from the law leavin' Texas rather than comin' in."

"You may be right," Strickland agreed, nodding thoughtfully. "If they fail to turn up during the search of the town, I'll send some men toward Louisiana at first light. In the meantime, I want you to ride out to Gallagher's place and see if they were foolish enough to return there. If so, bring them in. I personally want the pleasure of questioning them."

Parker chimed in, "What about the Gallagher girl, boss? We after her too?"

Strickland opened his mouth to speak, but Branch didn't give him the chance. "She's mine, Sheriff. I made a deal with the Regulator boss before I took this job. You can talk to him, we have an agreement. A man might say I paid for her."

Strickland scowled, but nodded. "As long as she's not part of this crime, she's yours, Kincaid." He looked down and casually brushed a smudge of dust from his shirtsleeve. When he lifted his head, his eyes glowed with a promise. "Of course, now that I've seen the lady dance—as they say, all's fair in love and war."

Branch grinned. "You're just a romantic at heart, boss, what can I say?"

"You can say you are on your way out of town."

"Yessir."

Branch led him to the door and breathed a silent sigh when the other men also stepped outside. Strickland headed back toward the jail after telling Parker and Wilson to search Thorn's mercantile. Branch turned to the men and said, "Looks like I'm haulin' tail. Which reminds me—before I go anywhere, I believe I'll finish what I started in church. After all, the boss can't complain about a man gettin' religion, can he?"

With a couple of lecherous grins, Parker and Wilson left Branch to his business. Relief replaced the tension in his body as he reentered the church.

John Gallagher held Branch's own gun pointed straight at Branch's heart.

In exasperation, Branch flung up his hands and exclaimed, "Now what!"

Katie never noticed the gun as she flew across the room and wrapped her arms around Branch's neck. "I knew it. I knew you wouldn't betray us. Thank you." She pulled his face down to hers and kissed him. "Thank you." She kissed him again. "Thank you." She kissed him three more times.

Cracking a rueful grin, he grabbed her wrists and peeled her off. "Sprite, as much as I enjoy your appreciation, we seem to be facin' another problem at the moment."

Katie stared up at him and blushed. He pushed her behind him, placing himself between Katie and the gun.

John watched his daughter's embarrassment become confusion as she followed Branch's gaze and caught sight of the gun. Of course he'd altered his aim the instant Katie ran to her hunter, but he didn't lower the Colt. Just shifted it a bit. Kincaid had nowhere to run.

"Da?" Katie said, crossing her arms and tilting her head.

He spotted a green dancing shoe peeking from beneath the hem of her dress, tapping furiously.

"Katie-love, I'm a'thinkin' the time has come for your man to answer for his actions."

"What are you talking about, Da? He saved us! He could have turned us over to Sheriff Strickland, but he didn't. That should prove to you that he hasn't forsaken the Gallaghers—it has to me!"

"Then you trust him?"

"Do you know what? I think I do."

"Good." John nodded once. "I do too. Branch Kincaid has looked out for the Gallaghers since he blew into the inn on that norther. He's a good man. I've always thought so. But 'tis a fine thing you should think so too."

He paused significantly before adding, "A wife should believe in her husband."

﹌ CHAPTER 10 ﹌

SHADDOE'S AMUSED CHUCKLE echoed through the absolute quiet of the church. Then the others, except for Branch, burst into speech.

Daniel Gallagher said, "But, Da, Katie's not his wife."

Keeper frowned and clucked his tongue. "Mr. Kincaid ain't gonna like this at all."

"Go get the padre, Daniel," John commanded his son.

Katie shook her head back and forth so fast, John thought she'd shake her teeth loose. "No, Father. You're *not* going to do this to me."

John looked at her and nodded sadly. "Yes, I am, love. I'm sorry as I can be, but this is the way of it. I realized the moment I allowed the sheriff to see my face that our plans must be changed. You cannot stay here with no man to protect you, and I do not want you coming with us."

She braced her hands on her hips. "Well, thank you so much for making me feel wanted, John Gallagher. Fine, I won't go with you. But I don't need a man, I can take care of myself!"

"No, child, you cannot, not alone. It'll be a difficult trip that may last for years—we won't be able to return as long as Strickland is sheriff and the Regulators are in power."

He kept the gun trained on Branch as he insisted, "Life in the Territory is harsh, Katie, and you deserve more than you would find there. I promised your sainted mother before she died that I'd see you found your way to civilized society. Well, perhaps Nacogdoches is not what she had in mind, but it certainly is not Indian Territory. You know

133

that you are not getting any younger, girl. You need a husband and babies to bounce on your knee."

For a second, something showed in her eyes, something alive and filled with pain, glittering as she fumed, "Da, I cannot believe you are saying that to me!"

"John, you need not go to such extremes," Shaddoe interjected, his dark eyes scrutinizing Branch. "I shall be glad to give Kathleen babies if she prefers to travel with us."

Branch's mouth thinned as his jaw tightened, but he remained silent, his gaze fastened on the Paterson Colt.

Katie's voice rose to a hysterical squeal, and she attempted to step around him. "This is ridiculous, Da. I want you to give Branch back his gun this minute!"

"Hush, Sprite." Branch blocked her with his arm and pushed her back behind him. "Don't forget there may be Regulators within listenin' distance."

A shiver ran down John's neck when Branch looked up, his topaz eyes cool and intense. He had the look of a mountain cat ready to spring. "Put away the gun, old man," he said with a touch of asperity in his tone. "There's no need for it. I'll be glad to take care of Kate, only it's goin' to be on my terms."

Well, now, this was something John had not anticipated. Could it be that Kincaid was finally willing to admit his feelings for the girl? He motioned with the Colt for Branch to continue.

Kincaid hesitated just a moment as though weighing a decision. Then he casually dropped onto a wooden pew and pulled Katie down beside him, saying, "Care if I sit down?" He yawned exaggeratedly. "Jeez it's gettin' late. I don't know about y'all, but I could use some shut-eye."

"Kincaid," Gallagher warned.

Branch linked his fingers with Katie's and said, "Sprite, one thing your father didn't consider was just how it'd make me look if you up and left with him and Daniel. You heard what Strickland said here tonight; you heard what I told him. If you disappear now, it'll be obvious you had a hand in this business, and hell, if that's the case, I might as well pull freight with you. I'm not ready to leave Nacogdoches yet."

Gallagher scratched his head just above his ear. The boy had a point. Wasn't he a fine one, though, talking to Katie as if she were the one who was making decisions here tonight. He almost grinned. Branch Kincaid wasn't the least bit threatened by him, and he was taking the time to prove to Katie why she should remain behind. The boy was smart. He'd make her a good husband. "I see what you mean," John said, lowering the Colt. "That didn't occur to me."

"Obviously," Branch drawled. He brought Katie's hand to his mouth and kissed her knuckles, speaking directly to her. "Kate, there's a simple way to solve this problem, and it doesn't involve a gun and a priest. Y'all know, of course, that I'm roomin' at Nacogdoches House? Well, I happen to know that the widow who runs the boardin' house is lookin' for a new place to live. It seems that she didn't inherit the house from her husband; it was actually the Craig family home and went to the old man's sister when he died. Anyway, just last week the Widow Craig's sister-in-law and her family moved back to town after bein' chased off their land out west by the Comanches. Martha and her in-laws don't really cotton to one another, and she's anxious for a new home. I feel certain she'd be tickled half to death to move out to Gallagher's and help you run the inn."

John rubbed his whiskers with his palm. This wasn't turning out like he'd planned. He wanted to see the girl married. "It wouldn't be safe without a man around to help."

"You are right about that." Branch nodded. "What about Rowdy Payne and his boy? Rowdy can get around good enough to run the tavern, and Andrew is a strappin' lad—he can manage the outdoor work."

"Well, I don't know," John said. Rowdy Payne was a widower who had lost a foot to Mexican grapeshot during the War for Independence. He and his son supported themselves by plaiting and selling the finest of braided rawhide quirts out in front of the post office in the Old Stone Fort in Nacogdoches.

Branch added, "I'd be sure to drop by and check on the place ever so often. It'll be fine, John, trust me."

Katie leaned forward, gripping the back of the church bench in front of her, her face beaming. "Da, it's perfect! Mrs. Craig's a dear, and I'd love having her at the inn. In fact, I think she's a little sweet on Mr. Payne. She's done a lot for us, Da, and if she's needin' a place to run to, well, remember what you said about being neighborly? Besides, we need to keep the inn going—don't forget our debt to Mr. Trahern."

"I'm not sure, Katie-love."

"There is one more thing." Branch glanced at Shaddoe and said offhandedly, "You won't have to worry about Kate gettin' man-hungry and takin' up with an Indian."

Shaddoe laughed. "Your hunter is a jealous man, Kathleen."

Katie rolled her eyes and John snapped, "Maybe what I'm worried about is her taking up with you without benefit of marriage, Kincaid."

"Now, John, why would you worry about something like that?"

"Oh, I don't know. Perhaps it was the laundry day you brought me daughter your clothes—all of them. Or maybe the fact she came home from a walk wearing naught but your shirt. Just maybe you should take my Katie to wife because you've already taken her to your bed."

"Da, that's not true!" Katie whispered fiercely.

John waved a hand, dismissing her argument. He looked at Katie, allowing his love and his sorrow to live in his eyes. "The reality of this night is that I must leave you, colleen. The future is uncertain, and it all but breaks my heart in two to think of going without knowing for certain that you will be all right. You've seen so much pain in your young life, and all I want is to help you avoid any more."

As he looked at his beautiful daughter sitting there beside the man he believed she loved, a knowledge engulfed him, a thought so strong and sure that he glanced around the church half expecting to see a vision of an angel or saint who had whispered in his mind. He'd not see his Katie again. His voice was gruff when he said, "I cannot leave this place without Branch Kincaid's word that he will keep you safe."

"But, Da, I'll be fine on my own. I don't want Branch forced to do something he doesn't want to do."

"Sprite, the last time I was forced to do anything, I was knee-high to a mosquito hawk." Branch stood and gently took the gun from John, replacing it with his hand. His golden eyes glowed with honesty and determination. "You have my word as a gentleman that I'll see after her, John."

John paused, then said hesitantly, "I'd prefer just as a man, I'm a thinkin'."

A wry smile twisted Branch's lips. "My word as a Texian, John Gallagher."

He nodded. "Accepted."

"This is all absurd, but if it makes you feel better, then splendid," Katie said, rising from the pew and going to her father. She wrapped her arms around his waist and buried her face against his chest. "I love you, Da. I'll be fine, I promise."

"Are you sure, Mary Kathleen?"

"Yes, Da. I'm sure."

His chest expanded and he slid his arms around her, holding her fiercely, protectively. A deep, abiding love flowed between them. So full of emotion was he, that when he framed her shoulders with his arms and opened his mouth to speak, he choked on his words.

With his eyes like windows to his soul, he swallowed hard and stroked her cheek with his thumb. "Very well, then." Tears ran in rivulets from his eyes as he added, "I love you, my daughter. I shall love you throughout eternity. Have a happy life, colleen."

"Come now, we must hurry," Shaddoe said, his voice gruff with emotion. "I have our horses hidden in the forest near the old Cherokee trail that leads west. Few around here know of it, and we should be safe enough if we waste no more time." He nodded to Branch. "For the vaccine I am in your debt, Kincaid. Watch over Kathleen for those of us who love her."

"I will."

Katie kissed both Daniel's and Keeper's cheeks and Shaddoe's lips. "Until next time?" she asked him shakily.

"Next time."

She hugged her father, her eyes streaming with tears. "God go with you all."

A barn owl hooted in the distance as Branch led a silent Katie toward the Widow Craig's rooming house. They kept to the shadows, hoping to avoid contact with anyone who might challenge her presence on Nacogdoches streets that particular night. The last thing Katie Starr needed right now were questions.

They reached the boardinghouse and he climbed the first porch step when Katie abruptly halted. "No. I want to go home."

Hell, he thought, she looks downright pitiful. "Darlin', we both need some sleep. I'll take you home in the mornin', I promise. But right now there's a nice soft feather mattress waitin' for us upstairs."

She shook her head. "I want to go home now."

"Aw, Kate, be sensible. Neither one of us has enough energy to stay atop a horse for ten minutes, let alone make a three-hour ride. Let's just get a few hours' shut-eye and then we can head out. We need to talk to Martha anyway." He tucked an errant strand of hair behind her ear. "You liked that idea, didn't you, her movin' in with you?"

"Yes."

"Come on, honey. Let's go up."

She heaved a soul-weary sigh. "All right. I need to visit the necessary first. I'll meet you upstairs. Which room?"

"Third on the right." He watched her make a slow trek around the corner of the house before entering the building. She had him worried. He'd never seen her like this. What had happened to the spirit she'd shown in the church, the spunk so much a part of her nature? Maybe she did need a few questions tonight. Maybe he could rile her out of her blue mood. Quietly, he walked to his room, where he hung his hat on a brass wall hook and kicked off his boots.

He sat on the bed and waited for her. Twenty minutes later he yanked his boots back on. Obviously, the stubborn little witch had given him the slip.

Hurriedly he saddled Striker and headed out of town. He caught up with her at the bridge across La Nanna Creek. In the dark of the moonless night, she was a ghostly specter when he spotted her perched on the bridge's railing staring down into the water. "Don't do it, Kate!"

Calmly, she looked at him. "Do what?" Then as he approached her with obvious caution she gave a hollow laugh. "Really, Deputy, do you fear for my sanity?"

He knew then that she didn't plan on jumping. Tension melted from his body, and he put his hands to her waist and lifted her down. "No, I was worryin' you'd jump before I had the chance to push you in. What do you think you're doin', Sprite, sneakin' off like that?"

She gazed up at the sky. "Thinking. Remembering. This is harder than I imagined. I prepared myself for Daniel leaving, but Da ... I didn't expect to lose him too. I can't go inside tonight, Branch. They're out there somewhere, beneath the stars. It makes me feel closer to them."

His voice was a low, soft rumble. "Come on, honey. We're out in the open here. Let's find a spot to rest."

Docilely, she allowed him to lead her along the creek bank until they rounded a bend out of sight of the town. Branch hobbled Striker, then made a makeshift bed with his saddle and a blanket from his pack and pulled Katie down beside him. He tucked her close, his mind on her comfort in the chilly night air rather than the fact that he finally had Katie Starr where he'd wanted her for so long. "Sleep now, Sprite. We'll sort this all out in the mornin'."

He was already half-asleep when she said in a wistful voice, "After my mama died, I remember looking at the night sky. Da told me the stars were distant suns, but I knew better. The sky was really a length of black velvet

God had wrapped around heaven. The stars were pinpricks He'd made in the cloth to give us a glimpse into the brilliance of His Glory."

Branch opened his eyes and gazed at the sky. He gently touched her cheek and she smiled against his hand. "I used to stare so hard, thinking I might catch sight of Mama. I haven't yet. Now I look for Steven and Mary Margaret too." Her voice dropped to a near whisper. "Do you think I should look for Da and Daniel now? Shaddoe, too?"

He had to clear his throat to get the words past the lump hanging there. "No, darlin', they've headed north, not up. They'll be fine, trust me."

She snuggled closer. "I do. You will take me home, Branch, tomorrow?"

"Trust me." He felt her body relax into sleep, and he smiled. She trusted him.

As he drifted off, he knew a twinge of guilt at the blanket of contentment that cloaked him. She'd been through a helluva lot tonight, and she was hurting deeply. He shouldn't be feeling good. But she slept in his arms and it felt so damned right.

When he awoke, she'd gone missing again.

"Sonofabitch." He didn't know how long he had slept; the sky was still dark, but the air had that feel of being near dawn. He sat up and rubbed his hand over his face, then twisted his torso, wincing at the cramped and aching muscles. "Damn, but the woman's nothin' but trouble." He hurried to the creek, where he knelt and splashed water on his face to brush the cobwebs from his mind. How far could she have gotten?

Something rustled in the bushes. Noiselessly Branch rose to his feet and stepped to the brush. He pushed aside a willow and peered into the darkness. Spatters of white lay in a circle around a twisting, squirming shadow.

Katie couldn't get her corset off. Mrs. Sterne had laced her tight as the bark on a bois d'arc tree, and she couldn't get loose. She had slept for maybe an hour before the lack of circulation woke her up. As the night's events rushed back to her, a restlessness had filled her soul and she left

Branch's side, needing to walk or run—or scream. She had settled on the idea of swimming in the cold running water of La Nanna Creek.

She had stripped off Mrs. Sterne's now ruined ball gown and then the ten petticoats she wore beneath it. But when it came to removing the corset, Katie was stuck.

The restlessness inside her transformed into fury. She bent and twisted and turned to no avail. She couldn't manage the laces. When she heard Branch's muttered, "My Lord," she whirled on him and snapped. "Don't just stand there, Kincaid, get me out of my clothes!"

He had her free of her stays in two minutes. Inhaling her first deep breath in hours, she said, "Gracious, you're good at that."

"Mental practice." She felt his gaze upon her, moving slowly up and down as though he inspected every single stitch on her chemise and pantalets. She knew he wasn't thinking of her sewing skills, and suddenly she was glad. The restlessness within her altered, what had been a hum in her blood became a reckless, pounding pulse. Katie wanted to forget, to feel alive.

Katie wanted Branch Kincaid.

She reached for him, grabbed a fistful of linen shirt at his chest, and pulled him to her. The black of the night hid his expression, but she could sense his wariness. An exultation filled her; the roles were altered, the hunted became the hunter.

The hunter became her prey.

"Kate," he rasped as she skimmed her hands over the rippling muscles of his back, then lower to the curve of his taut buttocks. She arched against him, sensuously rubbing her breasts against his midriff, her softness against his steel. He cursed a breathless, "Dammit, Sprite," and she dragged his lips down to hers.

The wildness streaked through her, burying all thought, all emotion, all reality—everything but hot, swamping sensation. She took from him, devoured his mouth, his tongue, his resistance. She pulled him over to where their blanket lay, and they sank to the ground together.

Impatient, she stripped off her chemise and wiggled

from her pantalets. She wanted—no she needed—naked skin against skin. Proof she was not alone. Oh, God, she was so alone. Her fingers worked feverishly at his trousers until he sprang free and she lay atop him, pressing, seeking. "Slow down, honey. Wait." He put his hands at her waist and tried to lift her away. "Kate, this isn't . . . we ought to . . . not like this."

She was having none of it. Why was he talking? She wanted sensation, not words. Words required thought. She would not think. Only feel.

Desperate to resist his tender caress, his murmured endearment, she closed her fist around him. His low groan, his heart drumming fast against her cheek, the surge of his pelvis, told her she had won.

She took him. Mindlessly, passionately. A body pursuing pleasure alone. A mind on a quest for escape. She feasted on his flesh, needing his heat to fill the cold, aching emptiness within her. She wrung from him his desire and in doing so lost herself to the savage, frenzied place where bursts of pleasure exploded into wave after wave of numbing satisfaction.

Branch lay as still as a dead man. Maybe he was a dead man, maybe that explained what had just happened. He'd died and gone to heaven. Or was this hell? He felt like hell.

She had collapsed atop him, and he could feel the slowing hammer of her heart. She was as light as a well-baked biscuit and as warm against him as a tin cup filled with steaming coffee. Except that Katie Starr wasn't coffee-hot inside. She was cold—bitter, icy, vacant.

Not a single word had crossed her lips. They'd been joined in the most elemental way, yet he'd never felt so alone. Where had she gone? Who was she with? A man had his pride, after all.

Still, why should it bother him? he wondered. Could he honestly say he'd never done the same thing himself when he was with a woman? So what did it matter who she'd loved when she'd climbed on him? Raw, instinctive sex, that's what had happened here. Good sex. Empty sex.

It wasn't what he wanted with Katie Starr.

She rolled off him and onto her back. The silence dragged. He licked his lips and tasted blood, hers or his, he didn't know. It didn't matter. The night breeze swept across them, drying the sheen of sweat from his naked body and chilling him.

She sounded a million miles away when she spoke. "My mama taught me to find the constellations. Many's the night we'd spread a blanket over grass and lie back and stare at the sky. I'd find Orion and Leo, Aries. But I had more fun making up ones of my own. Like seeing pictures in clouds only at night. My sky stories, Da would call them."

Branch glared at the sky. Stars? She finally speaks and she talks about stars?

"Shaddoe told me one about the Milky Way," she continued, pointing a finger toward the dusty band of white above them. "The Cherokees call it Gil' LiUtsun' Stanun'yi, 'where the dog ran.' It's a very old story about a giant dog with a silvery coat who stole grain from The People. They set a trap for him and scared him so badly that he jumped into the sky, and the meal he'd been eating poured from his mouth and made a white trail across the sky. The Milky Way."

Branch yanked at a clump of grass beneath his hand. The Indian. She was thinking about the goddamned Indian!

He figured he had near to an hour before sunrise. Plenty of time to take her to those stars she was yammering about. Only this time, she'd damn well know who rode along with her. "Sprite," he said, his voice a raspy drawl, "I know a little bit about the heavens myself. For instance, a star is a luminous body. Luminous means emitting a steady, glowing light. Light means heat. Therefore, a star is a heated body. You're a Starr, Katie." He moved over her, not touching, but blocking her view of the sky. He blew a gentle breath across her breasts. "Tell me, are you hot?"

Her body tensed beneath him. "Branch, leave me alone."

"That's good. The lady knows the man. Say it again, Kate." There was only the sound of the creek burbling against its rocks, a cricket chirping in the brush, his own heavy breaths. He lowered his hips, nudging her. "Who am I?"

"Branch," her voice trembled, "I'm sorry, I went a little crazy, I know."

"I'm a man, Kate. I'm your friend. I'm not a stud horse." He bent his lips to her breast and he laved her nipple with his tongue. She gasped a moan as he locked his mouth around her and suckled.

"I've never done anything like that before," she breathed. "It's not me. I just felt so alone."

He lifted his head and stared into her eyes, his gaze as angry as his touch along her inner thigh was gentle. "Were you alone, Kate?"

She shook her head.

"Who else was there?"

Her tongue darted out to wet her lips. "You, Branch."

Lord, this was a celestial lesson he taught her. His fingers found the hidden, satiny folds of her womanhood. "Who's with you now?"

"Damn you, Branch Kincaid."

That sounded more like his Sprite. A rush of raw, aching need consumed him. He wanted nothing more than to bury himself in this woman, to fill her with himself until he drove all thought of any other from her mind. But more than that, he wanted it to be right for both of them. "You didn't allow me inside before. Why Sprite?"

She nipped at his neck. "I *took* you inside. How can you say that?"

He kissed first one temple and then the other. "In here, baby. You shut me out here. I didn't like it, Kate, it's wrong that way."

Her hands roamed across his chest, bringing fire in their wake. "I'm scared. I've lost them all. I needed. I simply needed."

He slipped a finger into her velvet sheath, and she

tightened around him, welcoming him. "And now? What do you need right now, Kate Starr?"

She traced a finger across his mouth and said in a throaty whisper, "You, Branch Kincaid, I need you."

That was what he wanted. He crushed her lips with his, exultant in the wash of wet heat against his hand, triumphant in the sweet taste of desire in her mouth. He gently released her and rose poised above her. "Ah, my sugary Sprite, I need you too."

This time they rode to the stars together.

With the first touch of sun the willows began to whisper in the breath of the morning wind. Titmice called, and a chittering kinglet jumped from spring-green bough to winter-dead twigs, alternately hiding and flashing his scarlet crown.

Branch watched while the world awoke, cradling Katie in his arms as she slept. So much had happened between sunset and sunrise, he wondered what new surprises the next twelve hours might bring. Probably nothing good, he told himself. By noon the whole town would know that John Gallagher and his boy had fled the county after teaming up with an Indian to steal medicines from Doc Mayfair. How would that affect Katie?

And what about his own situation? As prickly as Strickland was about duty, Branch would have to talk pretty fast to avoid losing his job if the sheriff happened to learn that his deputy disobeyed orders and stayed in town overnight.

I'd best have my story ready in case I need it, Branch thought, tucking Katie tight against him. He wasn't ready to quit Nacogdoches yet. The secrets surrounding his brother's death had been buried for going on two years, and it'd take longer than a couple of months to dig them up.

But dig them up he would. He'd get back to work as soon as he took care of his promise to John Gallagher about looking after Katie. Branch grimaced at the thought; he'd made a head start on that one, and somehow he didn't think it was exactly what John Gallagher had in mind. The corners of his mouth lifted in a grin as memories of the previous night flooded back.

More than likely, Katie would be embarrassed when she woke up naked in his arms, and that meant she'd be meaner than eight acres of snakes. Maybe I ought to distract her, he thought. Kind of ease her into the day.

This time he'd start at her neck. He'd noticed sometime during the night that her breath caught every time he nibbled that spot beneath her ear. He eased away from her so as to get the right angle. The sun's warmth touched the skin exposed as the blanket slid to their waists.

She'd moaned but a single time when the shout rang out. "Halt! Sinners defile this place of God's redemption!"

Reverend T. Barton Howell, founder and sole spiritual leader of the Church of God's Graceful Humanity stood at creek's edge, outrage turning his bulbous nose a bright red. Behind him, in various states of offense, gathered his flock, the majority of whom were women, assembled at the creek to witness the baptism of its newest members, Abigail and Luella Racine, president and secretary of the Nacogdoches Ladies' Society.

Branch looked at Katie. She sat with the blanket clutched to her chest, her eyes as round as a wagon wheel, her skin bled white. From her throat came a mewling like a newborn kitten's.

"Looks like we might have a little problem here," he said, taking a bead on his britches lying a good ten feet away. Miz Starr had quite an arm. With casual nonchalance he rose to his feet and strode across the grass to his pants amid squeals of horror and the flurry of feminine feet. Easing the trousers up over his hips, he noticed Miss Abigail and Miss Luella exchange an approving look. He winked at them and turned to gather Katie's underwear.

She buried her head beneath the blanket. He heard her softly wail, "I'm ruined. Oh my heavens, my reputation is completely and totally destroyed. No good woman will even speak to me after word of this gets around."

Branch lifted Katie, petticoats and all, and carried her beyond the sight of self-righteous eyes. "Now, Sprite, it was just a few women. Delicate women aren't supposed to discuss such business. Maybe they'll keep it to themselves."

She peeked from beneath the yards of cotton long enough to glare at him. "Luella Racine's mouth runs more than the town pump."

"For a woman on the shelf, her eyeballs work pretty fast too," Branch added. Funny thing how spinsters oftentimes knew more about men than wives.

"I'm doomed," Katie moaned. "The scandal of Da and Daniel helping an Indian steal from Doc Mayfair will be bad enough, but once this gets out, folks will be thinking Gallagher's is a brothel instead of an inn. Our business will fail!"

"Oh now, Sprite, it's not that bad."

She couldn't get the gown fastened without wearing her corset. She screeched and pushed the cloud of green to her feet and grabbed her stays from the ground. Presenting her back for Branch to tie her laces, she muttered, "It's all your fault, Kincaid."

He yanked on the strings. "My fault! Honey, I know we've not gotten around to talkin' about last night yet, but even *you* aren't fool enough to place the blame on me."

She gasped for air and pulled up her gown. "I am too a fool. I'm a fool for not leaving with Shaddoe. I'm a fool for listening to your ideas last night in church." She whirled and looked at him. He saw fear and vulnerability hiding in the blue depths of her eyes. "I'm a fool for trusting you."

Hell, he thought, I thought we'd gotten past all that. He tugged on his boots. "You know, Sprite, I gave your daddy my word that I'd take care of you. As well as we know each other—and I figure after last night we know damn near every inch—you ought to have faith in the fact that I keep my word. I promised to watch out for you, and by God I will."

She threw him a scornful look, saying, "And how do you figure to fix this unholy mess?"

Branch raked his fingers through his hair, then very deliberately set his hat upon his head. "Sprite," he said, his voice rich and strong. "Have you ever heard of a marriage bond?"

The Widow Craig's Nacogdoches House was located on a side street, two blocks west of the town square. With her husband's death three years earlier and with her children grown and on their own, Martha had converted her two-story home into a boarding house. She furnished each of the six available rooms with wash stands and mirrors, double tester beds, and a watercolor portrait of Texian heros like Sam Houston and Stephen F. Austin. The recent arrival of her late husband's sister, Ella, and her family of five made for cramped conditions around Nacogdoches House, not to mention ruffled feathers on occasion because Martha couldn't abide Ella's priggish ways. In addition to her in-laws, Martha furnished rooms for five gentlemen and Branch Kincaid.

Martha realized she shouldn't tolerate his behavior, but that Branch just had a way about him. When he bent his mind to it, he could charm the bark off a tree. Or, she thought, sliding a look at the girl staring forlornly at her reflection in Deputy Kincaid's bedroom mirror, the ball gown off a widow.

Katie Starr wasn't wearing a ball gown this sunny spring morning; she was wearing her wedding dress.

Martha puffed the off-the-shoulder sleeves of the white silk gown and said, "Why, don't you look pretty. This dress looked nice on my daughter, Pamela, but it is stunning on you. You're a beautiful bride, Katie dear."

"Thank you Mrs. Craig. I hope Pamela won't mind your loaning it to me."

"Call me Martha, sweetheart, and don't you worry about the dress. She had it put away for special occasions, but after carrying her fourth child in as many years, my daughter would have to add another width to the waist to fit into this frock again. It's yours, darlin'. Every woman should have her own wedding dress."

"I don't know what to say, you've been so kind to me."

Martha waved away Katie's gratitude. "Hush about it now. Anyway, I'm just tickled half to death to have the opportunity to move out to Gallagher's. Why, between you and me, Mr. Craig's sister is near to driving me silly. Bossy"—she drew the word out—"I tell you what, she makes Abigail Racine look like a pussycat. And when Mr. Branch explained to me that Mr. Payne would be making the move also, well"—she lowered her voice and confided—"I'll admit to the hope that someone else might be following you and Mr. Branch to the altar."

Tears pooled in the younger woman's eyes, and Martha frowned, clucking her tongue at the sight. The poor girl wore the weight of Texas on her shoulders. "What is it, child?" she asked gently, tucking a stray auburn curl back into Katie's braid.

"It's not an altar. He doesn't really want to."

"Want to what?"

"Marry me."

"Now, sweetheart, why do you say something silly like that? I've seen how that man looks at you. Last night at the dance he had eyes only for you. It's as obvious as pepper in the sugar bowl that the man's in love."

Katie shook her head. "In lust. Not love. He never mentioned marriage until after the incident this morning. He's only doing it because he promised my father that he'd take care of me." A lone tear slipped from her eyes and trickled down her cheek. "That's why he wants us to sign a bond."

Katie swiped at the wetness on her cheek, took a deep breath, and confessed, "Mrs. Craig, he thinks he's just pretending to marry me so that I won't be shunned by you and the other good women of Nacogdoches! He thinks a marriage bond is no longer binding in Texas!"

Martha met Katie's anguished gaze reflected in the mirror and sighed a *humph*. "Then he doesn't know beans from buttons. Why, what about that fuss over in San Augustine back last summer? Judge Phillmont held in Jane Casey's favor when Ed Black refused to marry her in church, five days after signing a bond and moving in with her and the children. He's still complaining about the five hundred dollars it cost him!"

"I know," Katie said. "I tried to tell Branch that. But he thinks that marriage bonds haven't been in use in Texas since before the Revolution, and that they're only legal when no clergymen are around to say the ceremony. In his mind, this wedding is all for show. He doesn't intend for this to be a real marriage."

Martha folded her arms across her matronly bosom and pinned Katie with a skeptical stare. "He'll be sharin' your bed, won't he?"

Katie dropped her gaze and tugged at the cuff of her sleeve. "I guess so."

"Then it'll be a real marriage, deary." Martha walked to the bed, sat down, and patted a spot beside her. "Come here, Katie, let's have us a little visit. Your bridegroom can cool his heels in my parlor just a tad longer. I think you're needful of a bit of mothering."

Katie did as she was told.

"Now," Martha said, "all this talk-talk-talk about what *he* wants. Let me ask you, what is it *you* want, pumpkin? Admittedly, the only way to save your reputation is to marry Mr. Branch. But is that the only reason you agreed to marry that scapegrace?"

Katie's finger slowly traced the circles on the quilt folded at the foot of the bed. Martha wondered if the girl was conscious of the pattern she stroked—the double wedding ring. Martha placed her hand on Katie's and asked softly, "Why are you marrying him, honey?"

Katie's head snapped up. She gazed at Martha with pleading eyes and groaned, "I'm so confused!"

"Do you love him?"

"I loved Steven, I know that. With Steven I felt warm and happy and safe. I knew where our lives were headed. He loved me."

"How does Mr. Branch make you feel?"

Katie hung her head. "He makes me angry. He makes me crazy. Oh, Mrs. Craig, he makes me feel hot and intense and dangerously alive. It's shameful."

Martha clucked her tongue. "No, honeylove, it's passion. And it's a wonderful thing to be found between a husband and a wife, and it's fertile ground in which love can grow."

"But I don't want to love Branch Kincaid. I loved Steven, he was my friend. We made a child together and they died together." Tears dripped down Katie's cheeks. "I can't love Kincaid because . . . because . . ."

"Oh, sweetling, it's no betrayal to Steven Starr for you to love again. I know you loved that young man, and I know that had he lived, you'd love him even more today. But he *didn't* live, kitten, and you *are* still alive. There's no shame in loving again; it doesn't lessen your love for your first husband."

Katie looked at Martha, a world of hurt in her eyes. "But I'm afraid. Steven loved me; it was a safe love and I barely endured the loss of it. Branch would never love me like that; I could never be sure of him. If I fell in love with Branch Kincaid and then lost him, I could not survive it!"

"My poor little lamb," Martha murmured, gathering Katie to her bosom for a motherly hug. Then she pushed the younger woman away and stood, pulling Katie to her feet. "Enough of this foolishness, I'll not hear another word. You are a stronger woman than that, Mary Kathleen Gallagher Starr, and don't you forget it. You've managed through some of the worst things life has to offer, the death of a spouse, the death of a child. You've done it once, and you can do it again if you have to. But what you can't *not* do is live your life. It's a precious thing, life is. God has granted you the gift, and it is your obligation to make the most of it. Now, you've a man downstairs waiting to marry you. He's a fine, handsome, strapping young man, and he makes your blood sizzle. You go on down and marry him, Katie. You live your life to the fullest. Don't be afraid of love, embrace it."

"But, Mrs. Craig, I'm not sure that I do love him. And he certainly doesn't love me!"

"Pshaw." She waved a hand. "I don't believe that. He loves you; it's written all over him. He's just using this bond business as an excuse."

"I don't think so, Martha."

"I know so. Some men need an excuse to pledge themselves, and your Branch is one of them. You just go on downstairs and look into his eyes. They'll tell you what his mouth is a'feared to say."

In the parlor some ten minutes later, Katie faltered a moment at the first sight of her husband-to-be. No new clothes for Mr. Kincaid, he wore his buckskins, the ones he'd worn the day he blew into her life.

Automatically, her gaze dropped to his pants. They still stretched indecently tight.

"G'mornin', Katie," he said.

Katie? What's this? He never called her Katie. It was always Sprite, or Kate, sometimes Mrs. Starr, but never Katie. What did it mean?

Her heart thumping like a butter churn, she stared hopefully into Branch's eyes. Nothing. Martha was wrong; neither his eyes nor his mouth were talking. He watched her solemnly, intently, with about as much enthusiasm as a chicken eyeing a Sunday skillet.

She nodded a greeting and blinked her eyes against a wave of self-pity. She'd been weepy all morning and it had to stop. She hated feeling this way; it just wasn't like her.

But then, solemnity wasn't like Branch, either. She frowned, puzzled, as he held her gaze, his golden eyes somber. Her eyes widened as she realized what was different. Lust! The lust was gone! He *always* looked at her with lust in his eyes! Every single time. Something was horribly wrong here!

"I can't do this," she said, shaking her head and backing slowly from the room.

Branch reached her in two strides. "It's all right, Katie. Everything's ready, all we have to do is sign our names." He lowered his voice and added, "You needn't worry anymore about John and Daniel. I spoke with Strickland, and looks like they got away clean. I bet they're halfway to the Red River by now."

Katie breathed a relieved sigh. "Thank goodness. What

about you, Branch? I guess the sheriff knows you didn't go out to the inn last night after all."

He nodded. "Yeah, well, this wedding business is going to work out well, because the sheriff's not too happy with me right about now. It's a good time for me to get out of town for a bit."

"Wedding business," Katie repeated, burying her face in her hands.

Branch put a soothing hand on her shoulder. "Now, Katie, I know you're probably feelin' a little anxious, but remember it's all make-believe."

Make-believe, hah. "Branch, I'll attempt this one more time. Marriage bonds are a legal means by which to wed in the Republic of Texas. If we sign that paper this morning, we'll have tied the knot!"

He nodded. "But it's a slipknot, Katie. You needn't worry."

But worry she did. She worried when she read the first sentence of the document: "Be it known that we, Branch Kincaid and Kathleen Gallagher Starr, of lawful age of Nacogdoches County, wish to unite ourselves in the bonds of Matrimony, and there being no Buddhist Monk in the county to celebrate the same . . ."

"Buddhist Monk!" she exclaimed.

Branch grimaced. "Well, the bond I copied had 'priest,' and I couldn't very well use that. There's at least four priests in town today that I know of, and well, I don't like to be messin' around with the Church. Sort of tempts fate, to my mind."

Shaking her head, Katie continued to worry when she read further and saw the words: "We mutually bind ourselves to each other in the sum of five thousand dollars to have our marriage celebrated by a monk when the opportunity offers."

"Five thousand dollars?"

He shrugged. "Round number."

She worried as she lifted the pen from the inkwell and signed her name to the document. She worried when he scratched Branch Kincaid below hers and when Martha made her mark as a witness.

All that worry paled in comparison to the anxiety she felt when one of the boarders spoke from the parlor door-way, "Well done, Kincaid. Now you can kiss your bride," and Branch kissed her cheek.

Just her cheek.

So much for worrying about love. Now she had gone and lost his lust.

⊰⊱ CHAPTER 11 ⊱⊰

*B*RANCH AND HIS BRIDE rode double on Striker along the dusty red road leading southeast out of Nacogdoches. Pretty Girl, having thrown a shoe an hour from town, trailed riderless behind them. Lack of space in the saddle had dictated that Katie remove all but one of the petticoats she wore beneath her long, full riding skirt before mounting her husband's horse. After that, the usually loquacious Branch had held conversation to a minimum, throwing terse, one-word replies over his shoulder in answer to Katie's infrequent questions. Their bodies, however, maintained a constant dialogue.

And Branch didn't like it.

He set an arduous pace, determined to ignore any tingles or tautness or tensions below his neck. His brain had resumed control of his reasoning, and he was busy trying to figure out why in the hell he'd spent those critical hours early this morning letting his pecker do his thinking for him. Hellfire, it wasn't like he was eighteen and constantly on point. No, he scolded himself, you're thirty-four, and one woman keeps your blood too busy in your lower half to ever make it to your top half.

He felt like wash-water scum. He'd given John Gallagher his word, but he'd not given John Gallagher's daughter his name. Not his real name, that is.

Not Britton Kincaid Garrett.

There was no way he could have used that name on the bond, what with half the gossips in town dropping by to confirm the end of the year's most delicious scandal. Besides, if he had used his legal name, he might have re-

155

ally ended up married! It would be just his luck for Katie to be right about marrying by bond, and there was no way in hell he intended to allow himself to be shackled by a name on a piece of paper. He had but a single purpose in East Texas, and marrying a beautiful, passionate, squirrel-swinging spitfire wasn't it.

He was here to find out who had murdered his brother.

His back burned where Katie's breasts pushed against him, and he remembered how they'd looked, how they'd felt, how they'd tasted. Damn, how much farther to Gallagher's? She was beautiful, provocative. And the most wanton bit of woman he'd had in years.

She truly believed she was his wife—he knew it just as sure as a Comanche rides a horse. Undoubtedly, she'd be expecting him to pick up where they'd left off that morning. The thought created a surge of heat in his loins, and he shifted in the saddle, trying to find a comfortable position.

He snapped his attention back to the road. He couldn't allow himself to love her again. There was no going back to before that phony reverend's shout. The differences between that time and this might be subtle, but they did exist. Sure, he'd given John Gallagher his word that he'd see after Katie, and true, the first thing he'd done was sleep with her. But during the whole of that luscious night, the word "marriage" had never once hovered between them. Comfort had been a part of it, pride, certainly on his part, and from what he could figure, for Katie, reaffirmation of life. Neither of them had thought that there was any more to it. Signatures on a single sheet of paper had changed all that.

Now she believed they were married and he couldn't convince her otherwise. But he would never take advantage of her by bedding her under false pretenses. He may not have his name anymore, but he damn well still had his honor.

Since Branch had failed in his efforts to convince the Widow Craig that he and Katie didn't need a honeymoon, Rowdy Payne and his son wouldn't be bringing Martha to Gallagher's for two weeks. Katie's fingers tightened at his

waist as she shifted her weight, and he realized that getting
through the next fourteen days would be trickier than eating red beans with a pitchfork.

He felt her gentle breath at the back of his neck and
muttered to himself, "Fourteen days. Three hundred thirty-
six hours. Twenty thousand one hundred sixty minutes."
Oh Lord, it would be a long two weeks.

Katie hugged Branch securely as he increased their
speed. His scent—musky, heavy, uniquely his own—
penetrated her senses. She suffered the seductive harmony
of his muscles flexing and relaxing in tune with Striker
and thought that she just might not survive the ride.
Branch Kincaid confused her. She confused herself. How
dare she even think such thoughts at a time like this?

The afternoon was warm and wind-wisped with cot-
tony clouds on high blue air. It was a day for banter and
lightness of heart, not for awkwardness and suffocating
grief. She wanted to be home, she needed to be home, and
as the time of their travel neared the three-hour mark, she
listened almost desperately for the familiar bells that
would tell her they'd reached the inn.

The wind chimes in the design of a four-leaf clover indicated the turnoff from the main road to Gallagher's Inn.
A few years earlier, Da had traded two nights' accommodations for the work of a smithy establishing a new business in a nearby town. From the beginning Katie had
loved the hollow music played so furiously on occasion by
strong winds or, at other times, the lone note exposed by
an errant breeze.

But today all was silent.

They didn't speak as Striker carried them the last few
miles to the inn. The closer they came to her home, the
less attention she paid to the way her breasts tingled as
they brushed his back. Striker made the final turn beside
the wind chimes. Home, she thought joyfully. Thank you,
Lord. Her home, her security, her strength.

Unconsciously she leaned forward, waiting for that
first glimpse of Gallagher's. She hardly noticed the caustic
odor of smoldering timber and burned hair.

Branch did. The stench was filed right next to horror

in his mind. He pulled Striker to a halt just beyond sight of the inn. "Wait here," he said, swinging to the ground and grabbing his guns from his saddle. "I mean it, Katie. Stay right where you are."

"What is it, Branch?" Her eyes widened with worry and she nibbled her lower lip.

"Probably nothin'. Just let me check, all right?"

She folded her arms, hugging herself, and nodded. Branch paused at the edge of the stand of pines that blocked their vision of Gallagher's. "Promise me, Kate, you'll stay here this time?"

"Yes."

He walked through the woods. "Damn the bastards," he breathed as he saw the destruction. "Damn them to the lowest pit of hell."

It was only a warning, but oh, what an ungodly threat. The outhouses had been burned to the ground. Two charred carcasses, a milk cow and her calf, hung suspended from the upper porch above the steps leading to the front door. Blood had pooled on the whitewashed step and painted a garish streak down each stair to the ground. An *R* drawn with blood defiled the front door. "Oh, Sprite, I wish I could have spared you this."

A pitiful whimper, like a puppy caught in the steel jaws of a trap, reached his ears. He knew as he turned that Katie once again had disregarded instructions. She stared at the dead calf, her skin drained of color, her blue eyes glazed.

He clenched his jaw and lifted her from Striker's back. "Woman, you haven't the sense God gave green apples," Branch said gently as he turned her head away from the inn and folded her into his arms.

Katie held him like a lifeline, her tears falling relentlessly down her face as she sobbed out her pain. She cried for Da and Daniel, she cried for Shaddoe, she cried for herself. She even cried for Finian Trahern. Branch discovered he was hoping to hear his own name in there somewhere, but she never mentioned him.

He held her for the longest time, the tension in his body making his arms tremble. What he wouldn't give to wrap his hands around a Regulator's neck right then. It'd be a pleasure kill, and he wouldn't feel an ounce of guilt about it. The agony Katie was living wrenched at him, and he ached to give her ease.

But this time he wouldn't ease her body. He would, however, do his level best to ease her soul. Her tears spent, she eased away from him, and dabbed at her eyes with the handkerchief he'd removed from around his neck.

"Come on, Sprite. Your kitchen looks like it's just as you left it. Let's settle in over there, and while you're cooking me some supper, I can tidy things up here. Cornbread and beans'll be fine." As he led her away, he looked back over her shoulder and added, "I'm not rightly in the mood for meat tonight."

Katie washed up, changed from her riding skirt into a serviceable blue homespun, put on a pot of beans, and mixed a batch of cornbread. Then she crawled into bed for a nap. A limit existed to the amount of turmoil with which a mind could deal in a single day, and she had reached it. She slept deeply and without dreams, awaking at dusk to the sound of Branch moving about in the outer room.

Dinner was an awkward affair, with conversation stilted and limited to a discussion concerning proper seasonings for pinto beans cooked meatless. The argument centered on garlic. While Katie had slept, Branch had taken it upon himself to add a full clove to the pot bubbling over the fire. While she appreciated his help—he did, after all, save the cornbread from burning—she couldn't abide the taste of garlic in her beans.

Especially considering the fact that this was her wedding night.

A thunderstorm hit just after dark. Lightning split the sky while rain pounded the earth, and Katie watched the downpour, praying that her family was safely sheltered from the storm's fury. As long as Da, Daniel, and Shaddoe were protected, the torrent was a welcome one. It would wash away the stains on Gallagher's front porch and clear the air of that vile scent of destruction. Too, the intensity—the tension, the electricity—of the storm fit her mood.

Tonight Branch would join her in their marriage bed.

He put on a slicker and left the cabin to see to the horses. Katie lit the lamp in her bedroom, poured water from a ceramic pitcher into a bowl, and washed. Anticipation filled her as she loosened the buttons of her dress. Last night had left her feeling ashamed—she'd given herself outside of marriage. No, she thought ruefully, actually she'd taken a man outside of marriage. Tonight would be different; it was a beginning for her and this hunter who had preyed upon her emotions for so long now. Perhaps tonight could be the beginning of love.

Wearing only her chemise and drawers, Katie reached into her bureau for a night rail. Holding the soft batiste shift trimmed in lace and embroidered with flowers, she hesitated. It was a beautiful gown, her prettiest. But she had worn the same gown on another wedding night. She had worn this gown for Steven.

Quietly and decisively, she shut her dresser drawer. Stripping off her underclothes, Katie slipped naked into bed. She waited.

And waited, and waited even more. Finally she heard his footsteps on the stoop. He entered the outer room, and she listened as first one, then the other, boot hit the floor. She caught a glimpse of white through the half-open door when he tossed his shirt onto a chair. The rustle of his trousers made her swallow.

Then she heard an unexpected sound, an unbelievable, disconcerting, completely frustrating noise. They had not moved the bunk John Gallagher had used in the kitchen up to the new inn, and Katie's chin dropped when the bed ropes creaked as Branch settled himself onto the mattress. "Good night, Sprite," he called.

Two minutes later, his snores bounced off the walls and pounded Katie's heart.

Branch never realized cast-iron pots could make so much noise. But then, he'd never before heard someone sling them around the kitchen with quite so much fervor. Recalling the events of the previous night, he reluctantly opened his eyes to the sight of a violent Texas thunderstorm dressed in blue homespun right there in the kitchen.

Slamming cook pots supplied the thunder, bacon sizzled and popped like lightning, wind whipped through the room in the tempest's wake, and a veil of rain pooled in the black thunderclouds of her eyes. Yep, Kate was a might unhappy.

May as well face the fury now and get it over with, he thought. Storms such as this tend to make a man's afternoon miserable. In his most pleasant tone he said, "What'cha cookin' Katie? Sure smells good."

She turned on him like a twister. "Certainly a peccary like yourself can recognize the smell of griddled ham."

He frowned. "If I'm understandin' what you're sayin', it's *my* butt you like to think you're fryin' up, huh, Katie?"

"Precisely." The sun peaked through the storm clouds. *Damn, but she's beautiful.* No matter how good the intentions, some habits were hard to change. Knowing he shouldn't, but unable to stop, he drawled, "I can hardly wait for you to eat your breakfast."

The Dutch-oven lid she'd held in her hand clanged against the floor, and by the looks of her, he knew he was lucky she hadn't aimed it at his head. Hastily, Branch added, "Look, I know we've got some talkin' to do. We'll feel better if we have a bit of that meal you've gone to the trouble to fix before we get serious."

He pulled on his pants, rose from John Gallagher's bed, and walked over to the woman, who stood facing the fireplace, her back stiff. He tilted her chin with his index finger and stared at her, saying softly, "Please, Katie?"

Moisture flooded her eyes and she nodded.

"I'll go wash up then," he said, and walked outside.

Katie sank into a chair at the table and buried her face in her hands, drained of emotion. Her red russet shoe thumped the dough box beneath the table. After a fitful few hours of sleep, she'd awakened to an early-morning sun, a gnawing hunger, and a biting anger. "Hell hath no fury," she quoted to herself. But her rage had dissolved at the somber expression in her husband's eyes. He has something to tell me, she thought, propping both feet on the box and slumping down in her chair. It was something she wasn't going to like. She could read it in his face.

When Branch returned, she went through the motions of eating, tasting nothing she put in her mouth. His praise of the meal barely penetrated her stupor.

When he was through, Branch leaned back in his chair and stared at her. "Come on," he said a moment later. "The weather's beautiful this mornin'. Let's walk down to the river." Grabbing her hand, he pulled her to her feet and led her from the cabin.

The Angelina's lazy flow carried an occasional green leaf downstream. Wildflowers hugged its bank, and a bee buzzed from an Indian paintbrush to a dandelion. The sweet fragrance of the season filled the air, soothing Katie's soul. It's spring and I'll manage, she told herself. I'll manage no matter what.

Branch opened his mouth to speak, then snapped it shut. Twice more he fumbled before getting a word past his teeth. When he did manage to form a sentence, he said the last thing she expected to hear. "I wanted you in my bed this mornin' more than a bleedin' man wants a tourniquet." He sat on the bank and pulled her down beside him.

He reached behind him for a honeysuckle vine, plucked a blossom and, slowly pulling its pistil, touched the tip of his tongue to the sweet drop of nectar clinging to the thin fiber. "I laid awake half the night rememberin' how tight and hot you were around me and how you made that little throaty groan when you took your pleasure."

Katie shifted uneasily.

A woebegone smile gentled his face as he continued. "It wouldn't have been right, though, Katie. I gave my word I'd take care of you. Takin' advantage isn't takin' care. As bad as I want you, I've figured you out enough to know that you need to be married first. We're not wed, Katie. That marriage bond was no more legal than Houston's Cherokee wife. I know we don't see eye to eye on this, but you don't have all the facts."

Katie's pride prompted her to interrupt. "You've a nerve, Branch Kincaid, thinking that I'm pining for you. But never mind that, just what are these facts I'm missing?"

He hesitated, as though he weighed his answer. Slowly, he said, "Among other things, we live under a different legal system than did your parents. The Republic doesn't require the same conditions for citizenship or marriage as Mexico. Katie, that contract wasn't worth the price of the ink."

Why doesn't he call me Sprite? she wondered. "We've talked about this before, Branch. I told you about the San Augustine case. Your argument's invalid."

Branch pulled off his boots and dangled his feet in the water. "Well, I guess there actually is something else." He paused, grimaced, and added, "I didn't sign my real name."

"What!" She sat still as a snake curled up to strike.

He glanced at her and said, "It's a nickname, you see—Branch. I got it stuck on me as a kid. There's this big old pecan tree at home, and I had a habit of misjudging the clearance beneath one of its limbs. Damn thing knocked me off my horse every other time I tried to ride beneath it. Then there was the time—oh, never mind. Anyway, everyone at home but my pa called me Branch. My name's really Britt. Britton, that is."

"So you're Britton Kincaid, then?"

He looked away and nodded. "Britt." He said it short and quietly.

"How do you think of yourself?"

"What do you mean?"

Katie sighed. "I mean, do you think of yourself as Branch or Britt?"

"I've never really thought about it. I guess I'm Branch except when I'm with my folks. Listen now, Katie, you needn't take this whole thing personal. Actually, it has very little to do with you."

Now that set right well. "In what way?" she asked, staring at her hand and picturing one of his Texas Patersons lying there.

"Now, don't get me wrong. I intend to keep up the act that we're married; I'm partially to blame for the damage to your reputation."

"Partially to blame," Katie repeated tonelessly. Her fingers cocked the imaginary trigger.

"Yeah. I'll make sure everyone in Nacogdoches thinks we have a marriage made in heaven and the fact that we're living apart is just bad circumstances."

"Living apart?"

"Katie, I can't stay here. I have a job to do, a very important duty. This marriage of convenience isn't very convenient for me right now, but I'll hang around until the others move out to the inn. I wouldn't feel right about leavin' you here alone, what with the Regulators actin' up."

Katie kicked off her shoes. The carpet of new grass tickled her toes. She wrapped her arms around her legs and said, "Let me see if I understand you, Branch. You signed a false name to a legal document of marriage with the sole intention of protecting my reputation. You intend for this marriage to be in name only, and you will leave my home as soon as someone else arrives to take responsibility for me."

He nodded. "Yep, that about takes care of it."

"I have a point I'd like clarified, if you will?"

"Shoot."

I've love to, she thought. "How would your plans be affected were there to be a result from our union?"

He looked puzzled and she rolled her eyes. "What'll you do if I'm expecting?"

He shrugged, frowning. "Well, if you turn up carryin', we'll marry for real. I'll just have to deal with it. Anything else?"

She nearly shoved him into the river at that point. Instead she gave him a sunshine smile. "That's all." She stood, saying, "I guess I'd better get to work. If I'm going to reopen Gallagher's anytime soon, I've much to do."

His mouth twisted as though he thought to say something but changed his mind. It was a good decision. One more word, and she certainly would have hurt him.

As they made their way back to the inn, Katie considered his confession. She'd bet her very best Dutch oven that a false name wouldn't nullify the marriage contract. If she remembered right, Ed Black in San Augustine had tried to use something similar in his argument also. Half the people in Texas changed their names when they crossed the border. Britt or Branch, it made little difference.

The man had married her yesterday.

She bit at her lower lip. The way she saw it, she was no longer a widow but a bride. A rejected bride. The question was, just what did she want to do about it?

Looking over at her husband, she took note of his contented manner. So, she thought, he's been to confession and now he's feeling sinless. Well, she was no priest offering absolution. Poor Branch. He would soon learn that his bride had her pride and he shouldn't have trampled all over it. She'd stage the greatest seduction ever attempted, and when he fell at her feet, she'd kick him.

She remembered something her father once told her. "The thing to do with mule-headed men, colleen," John Gallagher had said, "is to treat them like you'd treat a mule you're a'fixin' to corral. Don't try to drive them in, just leave the gate open a crack and let them bust in."

That was her answer. She'd show Branch Kincaid what rejection really was. She knew just how to crack open the gate.

And so began the campaign to win Branch Kincaid's body. Like every good general, Katie had learned from the experience of prior battles. Each tactic he had used during the winter maneuvers, she redefined from a feminine point of view and put into action during the spring.

Her first attack was launched with the arrival of the peddler's wagon three days later. Branch had left Gallagher's early that morning bound for San Augustine after receiving a message from Sheriff Strickland. She'd been working inside the tavern when harmonica music and a freight wagon's rattle had announced the advent of Morsey Johnston, Peddler by Profession.

Katie smoothed her hair as she walked onto the porch and waited for the wagon to come to a stop. She was always happy to see Johnston; he had included Gallagher's on his rounds for years, and he often saved her special items. Usually kitchen utensils, occasionally an extra-fine length of lace or linen, he made a great production of presenting the articles for sale.

Morsey was young, perhaps three years older than Katie, and quite handsome, with emerald-green eyes and cheeks that dimpled with his wicked smile. Women just loved a visit with the peddler, and Katie was no exception. Especially when he came at such an opportune time.

"My divine Mrs. Starr," he said, jumping from the wagon seat. He bounded up the steps, bowed over Katie's hand, and said, "An eternity has passed since I last gazed upon your exquisite beauty. Please tell me you've reconsidered my offer and are willing to travel the trail to life's fulfillment with my humble self."

Katie laughed. "Mr. Johnston, I'm afraid my answer has not changed. I am still unsure as to what you offer with those silky words of yours."

He clasped a fist to his breast. "I'm crushed, madam. But perhaps I could interest you in a potato masher?"

Katie folded her arms. "Steel?"

"Wire."

"No, I have a fine one, thank you." She leaned her head to one side and studied Morsey Johnston's wagon. She had a glimmer of an idea, one that might cause her embarrassment, but one that might just suit her needs quite well. "Mr. Johnston, you've been traveling Texas for some time, haven't you?"

"Yes, my elegant Mrs. Starr. Almost four years now."

"Mr. Johnston, as you undoubtedly know, people in East Texas sometimes lower themselves to gossip. I admit to having heard a few tales concerning yourself."

He dropped all pretense at gallantry and scowled. "Now Katie, if it's about Marvella Davis, I swear to you that I had no idea she was married."

"No, that's not . . ."

"Jessamine Poteet's little boy isn't mine, either. I swear it!"

Katie bit back an exclamation of surprise. She hadn't heard that particular piece of idle talk. "No, Mr. Johnston. What I'm trying to say is that I'm aware that you make professional calls on the women at The Mansion of Joy."

Johnston stiffened. "They are customers, Mrs. Starr, with as much right to merchandise as anyone."

"I agree. But what I'm asking is"—she lowered her voice—"is it true that you keep a particular trunk in your wagon for supplies of special interest to those, uh, ladies?"

His eyes widened and he fell back, leaning against his wagon for support. "Why, Mrs. Starr!"

"Kincaid. I've remarried. Recently. I'd like to look in that box, Mr. Johnston."

Morsey Johnston held her gaze, and a wistful look entered his emerald eyes. "Oh, Mrs. Starr. I'll tell you true, a man spends his life dreaming to find a woman like you."

She grinned. "I'm counting on it, Morsey. Now, if I can just see those items?"

Later that afternoon, although it wasn't wash day, Katie decided to do a little laundry. First she strung a rope from a lower branch of the dogwood tree to the kitchen porch rail a short distance away. Next she built a fire and heated a kettle of water. From her bedroom she took a precious bar of lily-of-the-valley scented soap.

She washed Branch's bedsheets, lathering them well, and hung them out to dry. Then she washed her new purchases.

Those she hung on a second rope so that they dangled against the background of her husband's bright white sheet.

⚘ CHAPTER 12 ⚘

*U*NDER A BLUE SKY pierced high by a yellow thunderhead, Striker thundered down the road at full gallop, kicking up a cloud of red dust along the well-traveled road between San Augustine and Nacogdoches. Branch eyed the anvil-shaped storm, wishing it had built a day earlier and fifty miles east. Perhaps then his head wouldn't still be ringing with the sounds of gunshots. Maybe then he wouldn't be so worried about Katie.

Sheriff Strickland had sent the message just after noon yesterday, and Branch had little choice but to leave her alone at the inn. Honeymoon or no, Deputy Kincaid was needed in San Augustine because rumors of a showdown between the Regulators and the Moderators had reached the sheriff's ears, and Strickland wanted one of his own men there to send a warning if the fight looked to be spreading to Nacogdoches.

Despite her arguments, Branch had known that Katie would be safer at home than in town when destructive passions were running high. It had surprised him how difficult leaving her behind turned out to be, and he hadn't liked that one bit.

After all, he'd be leaving for good in a week or so.

Now as his time away from Gallagher's neared the twenty-four-hour mark, he told himself that as long as Katie had managed all right, the trip had been worth the effort. Holed up in Odd Fellows' Hall on the second story of William Phillips's store, observing the fracas down in the street, Branch had about fallen off his chair when Phillips made an offhand remark concerning counterfeit scrip.

During the ensuing discussion, Phillips had remembered Rob Garrett's visit in East Texas and had confirmed for Branch his brother's location one week before his disappearance.

Rob Garrett had mentioned to Phillips that he had left Gallagher's Inn and was staying with a friend at a farm outside of Nacogdoches. Now Branch had to find the friend. He figured that this fellow—whoever he was—might have information that could lead Branch to the killer.

This friend might even *be* Rob's killer.

It was the most valuable piece of information he'd learned in months. As long as Katie was fine at Gallagher's, he'd be well pleased with the day's work.

The wind chimes sang wildly in the breeze as he took the turn to the inn. Branch gave the dun his head as they traveled the last quarter mile to Katie's home.

Striker rounded the final curve, and the inn came into view. Branch grabbed the saddle cantle for support at the sight that met his eyes—a vision as shocking in its way as the one of a week ago when dead cattle hung from the roof. He abruptly reined in Striker, and the horse pranced in a circle in the yard. "Damn!" Branch exclaimed.

Scarlet underwear. She had scarlet underwear hanging in the front yard where God and everyone could see it.

In a daze he slid from the gelding's back and walked to the clothesline. He lifted his hand and fingered the sleeve of a cambric camisole, a red cambric camisole trimmed in—Branch murmured, "Holy hell"—black lace. Next to the camisole hung a petticoat, chemise, drawers, and—he choked out, "Holy hell on Sunday"—a scarlet corset with black laces and black and purple roses embroidered across the bust and in a line down the front to the—his strangled voice groaned, "Holy hell on Sunday in church!" At the end of the line hung her most demure, navy-blue cotton dress.

He backed away, slowly shaking his head. No, these weren't Katie's. No way they were hers. He'd come closer to believing she'd up and turned Gallagher's into a whorehouse and had been doing the madam's wash.

Something must have happened to her. "Katie," he shouted, turning and sprinting for the kitchen door. "Katie, where are you?" He banged the door open and rushed inside. Nothing. He checked her bedroom. Empty.

Outside, he ran for the inn, his legs pumping, his heart pounding. "Katie, Katie are you all right? Katie!"

"What's the fuss, Kincaid?" She leaned out of an upstairs window, a scowl on her face. "You're interrupting my work. What's going on?"

He stopped and stared up at her, catching his breath as his heartbeat slowed. She looked as healthy and as beautiful as ever. Thank God nothing was wrong. Then his gaze sneaked back to the line of laundry. "Katie, what are you doin' up there?"

"The same thing I've been doing for two days now, sewing mattress covers."

"Is someone with you?"

"It's just me and my needle and thread. I have almost a dozen ready to stuff. As soon as you finish the bed frames, we'll be a big step closer to reopening. How was San Augustine? Was Strickland's information correct? Was there a fight?"

"Yeah," Branch called absently as he tried to figure a way to inquire about her underclothes. Ordinarily he'd have just jumped right up and asked, but ever since their chat by the river the other day, talk between them had been a bit strained. In fact, Katie had been acting downright strange. It spooked him. One minute she was as friendly as a pink-eyed bunny, and then an hour later she wouldn't speak to him.

Framed by the window, Katie waited expectantly for him to elaborate. Branch couldn't manage the words he wanted to say, so he fell back on the reliable. "Um, do you have anything in the kitchen I could eat? I left San Augustine before noon, and I'm as hungry as a coyote with a toothache."

She smiled smugly. "Sure. In fact, I've not eaten since breakfast myself. Why don't you wash up, and I'll put something on the table."

After caring for his horse, Branch made his way to the

well. He'd taken off his shirt and dumped a pail of water over his head when he heard a song drifting from the kitchen. He turned his head, ear pointed toward the cabin. Katie was singing a tune that sounded suspiciously like that bawdy-house song he used to hum all the time.

Funny, he didn't do much humming anymore.

Katie had set out clean clothes for him to wear, and it was while he was buttoning the crisp denim pants that the breeze carried to him the aroma of freshly baked cobbler. Gathering his discarded clothing, Branch followed the scent toward its source. Noticing that the rope no longer stretched from the dogwood to the porch, he approached the kitchen door like a condemned man walking to the scaffold.

What in the hell was she up to?

He stepped into the kitchen and caught his breath at the sight that awaited him. Katie had changed clothes. She wore the prim navy-blue dress that had hung outside earlier. Next to the scarlet corset.

"What's for supper?" he rasped as he stared at the dress, desperately trying to block the mental picture of what lay beneath it. He failed.

She smiled brightly. "Bacon and beans, but I've made a cobbler for dessert. It's going to be good, too. I picked the blackberries yesterday afternoon, and I'm afraid I ate almost as many as I put in my pail. They were *so* delicious—that one bush in particular seems to make the sweetest, juiciest berries. That one out by the oak, you remember which bush I mean, don't you, Branch?"

Damned right he knew which one she meant. He saw her there again, lying on the brambles—only this time she wore a scarlet chemise. "Sounds good, Katie. Only, I really need to split some firewood before dark. I'd best not eat too much. I'll get dessert later."

She shrugged and offered him an enigmatic smile. "Your loss."

Branch ate his dinner quickly and rushed outside to the wood pile. A few days earlier he'd dragged a fallen cedar to the pile and cut it into logs. Now as he went to work splitting the logs for firewood, the image of a scarlet-clothed Katie kept him company. He brought the ax down on a cedar log and found himself talking to the ghost. "Stay away from me, woman. I'm tryin' to do the right thing here, and it's not an easy proposition."

Chickens clucked at him from the henhouse as he argued with the scarlet specter and cleaved a second log in two. "You're a good woman, Katie Starr, and you deserve more than a man who'll not commit himself." He stooped to pick up another hunk of wood and stood it on the block. He swung the ax hard as he recalled the heat of her love-making. "You'll be gettin' no promises from me, lady, no matter how nice the idea sounds when I'm walkin' around stiff as a new rawhide rope." He swung the ax again as he said, "I'll be solvin' my mystery and headin' home soon."

Katie's image vanished to be replaced by the long-dreamed vision of Riverrun with its tall white columns and red brick facade. Branch stared at the ax blade, wiping away a stream of sap with his fingers as the familiar ache washed over him—the need to go home. It was a throb in his soul, something he'd carried with him for twenty years, an elemental part of himself. And now that he'd been given the opportunity to return, no one, not a murderer, not even a very special lady, would stand in his way.

The niggling voice whispered in his mind, "You could take her with you."

"No," he said, tossing down the ax. He couldn't do it. Katie Starr wasn't part of the dream. The dream was Riverrun and Eleanor. The beautiful, elegant daughter whose father's plantation, Bentwood Hills, bordered Riverrun. The woman he'd once loved and planned to marry.

Branch carried the wood he'd cut to the stack, where he laid it atop a healthy pile of wood. Katie must have known he was lying about chopping, and he winced over the foolishness of the lie. Damn, he hated feeling the fool.

Like how he'd felt at his brother's seventeenth birthday party.

Restless, Branch wandered over toward the hog pen, remembering the night he'd left Riverrun and fled to Bentwood. The Nichols family had given him a room in the bachelor's hall, and for four years he had lived there, working and learning sugarcane, falling in love with the Nicholses' daughter. It had been a mutual affection; Eleanor had given him her heart and soon afterward her virginity.

None of that had mattered when her father gave her hand in marriage to Branch's own brother, thereby uniting the two most powerful families in South Texas. That Eleanor went to her bridal bed no longer virgin apparently bothered no one, no one but himself. To a young, passionate Branch, Eleanor's desertion had seemed the greatest of betrayals.

Time had taught him differently, however. Her choice had been logical, the reasonable thing to do. Of course, she *should* have chosen to become the lady of Riverrun. What had Branch to offer her, anyway? He was nothing more than a hired hand. No, Eleanor had made a sound decision based on facts. Her heart had no business in the matter.

Just as now, his heart had no place in his dealings with Katie Starr.

Branch kicked at the slop pail sitting at his feet. "Heart"—where in the hell had that word come from? "My heart is not involved with Katie Starr," he growled at the wide-snouted red hog snorting in the slop. He propped a boot on the railing, determined to repeat the declaration often—until he convinced himself he believed it.

Branch would find Rob's killer, return to Riverrun, and marry his brother's widow. Eleanor was his first love, his only love. She was beautiful, sophisticated, and after years of marriage to his brother, Riverrun's lady. That was her place, she'd earned it. No one could replace her, no one should even make the attempt. Especially not a squirrel-slinging, auburn-haired innkeeper. "My heart is not involved with Katie Starr."

Damned if his body wasn't, though.

The shoats' squeals drowned out the sound of her approach. When she sashayed up to him and flashed a red petticoat hem right at him, his boot slid off the railing and he caught hold of the fence to steady himself.

Katie hooked her elbows over the fence. "I'm on my way to the inn and those mattress covers. I wondered what you had planned for the afternoon, if you might could help me with the stuffing."

He saw cotton ticking and red cambric. "Hell, Katie, I planned on workin' on bed frames. I have seven left to build, you know, and I'll be leavin' in another week when the Widow Craig and Rowdy Payne arrive."

"Oh, all right. Are you through here? We can walk over there together."

Branch envisioned bed frames and cotton ticking and red cambric. "Katie, it's all of fifty yards to the inn. Besides, I need to milk that cow of yours. I swear she could give milk for all of Nacogdoches. Don't you hear her bawlin'?"

"Do you think Lizzie misses Delilah and the calf?"

"Naw, Katie, her teats are full." Oh Lord, he thought as his gaze went right to her bosom—wrong thing to say.

Katie arched her back and said, "Well you'd better do something about it, hadn't you?"

Delilah, bosoms, beds, mattresses, red underwear. Hell and Texas.

He stared at her breasts as he said, "I can't. I've gotta milk the cow." Then he headed for the barn.

Katie sighed heavily as she worked the thread in and out of the mattress ticking. This seduction business was harder than she'd imagined. She knew the underpinnings had affected him, she'd seen it in the way his stare had continually drifted to her bosom during dinner. His gaze had been as hot as a scorpion's sting.

She'd not exactly been a bucket of ice herself. To her surprise, the lacy underclothes had affected her also. They made her feel, well . . . naughty.

As befitted a woman of strong moral principal, embroidery and lace trimmed only those parts of Katie's unmentionables that occasionally might be seen, such as the hems of her petticoats. She never considered adding lace to her corset, and what lace she did wear certainly wasn't red or black!

But when she'd sat across the table from Branch's hot amber gaze, she'd wondered if perhaps the soiled doves didn't have the right idea. There was something to be said for being on the receiving end of a look like the one he'd given.

With thoughts of victory in her mind, she'd thought to escalate the battle by displaying a flash of red and then enticing him up to the inn, where earlier she'd placed a finished mattress on a bed frame Branch had built.

The skirmish never happened. The other party failed to meet the challenge. Branch had milked the cow and gone fishing.

It was one more blow to her pride to know that a lure was more alluring than she. It hurt. Damn Branch Kincaid for having the ability to hurt her.

Her finger slipped and she stuck herself with her needle. As she squeezed her thumb and stared at the drop of bright red blood pooling on its tip, she said softly, "Damn me for allowing him the power."

Nightfall eased over the eastern Texas landscape like a gentle death. The wind lay and the forest fell silent but for occasional sounds made by nocturnal animals as they slipped from their burrows and caves to wander the forest in the pursuit of sustenance. As the moon rose and floated across the sky, beams of milky light bathed Gallagher's in an eerie glow, and from an oak tree at the edge of the clearing, the low, purring *chuck chuck* of a bullbat added to the spectral atmosphere of the night.

Ghosts played inside the kitchen's walls, delving into the mind of the sleeping man, stirring up the nightmare which occupied that corner of the mind reserved for hell.

Branch was Britt again, seven years old and playing with his brother in the attic of Eagle's Nest, the Garrett family plantation home in Virginia. Outside the dormer window, slaves labored in field after field of tobacco, singing a haunting spiritual song in rhythm with their work. Neither Britt nor Rob were interested in what happened in the fields; their concentration centered on the leaves Rob had stolen from the drying sheds.

Britt wrinkled his nose at the production of rolling crushed leaves inside a larger one. "I don't see why you want to light it. It makes a great haystack for my soldiers to hide behind."

"Hush, Britt. You're such a baby. Now, hand me those matches."

The dream altered, and the man in the bed tossed and flung up his arm to guard his face from the phantoms whose features burned black and crusted. They leaned over the young boy Britt, shrieking in his ear. His grandfather, his grandmother. His mother. Fire crackled around them, dancing, its smoke oozing over him and carrying the stench of death. "Your fault . . . your fault," they chanted, reaching for him with bony hands.

"No!" he screamed.

"Branch, Branch, wake up." The soft, soothing angel's voice summoned him back from hell.

As he opened his eyes and gazed at Katie, he knew a relief so encompassing that his naked, sweat-soaked body shook with it.

A lighted lamp cast a golden glow around the room, haloing the woman who sat on the bunk beside him, her gentle hand stroking his cheek, his temple, his hair. Her voice was husky as she said, "Welcome home, Branch."

Panic had wrapped a noose around his neck, but her every touch served to loosen the knot. She said, "Such a terrible place you must have been."

"Oh, God, Sprite." His pulse slowed, and the coppery taste of fear left his mouth. Branch shut his eyes and grimaced. He hated this. He was a man, dammit. Not some snot-nosed boy who cowered at the demons in the night. He hated that she'd seen him this way; he hated that he wanted her comfort. "The fire, I dreamed about a fire."

At his temple, her hand trembled. The catch in her voice betrayed her own nightmares as she whispered a strained, "How terrifying."

Kincaid, you're a bastard. Branch grasped her hand and pulled it to his lips, pressing a kiss to her knuckles. Grimly, he said, "I'm sorry, Kate. I shouldn't . . . you don't—"

She placed her finger against his lips. "Ssh. It's all right. I understand."

Their gazes met and he searched her eyes, knowing a sense of kinship with the tragedy reflected there. "You do know, don't you?"

"Yes, and somehow the dreams are almost more frightening than the reality."

Suddenly, he wanted to tell her. He'd never shared it, not once. But here in the teeth of the night, with this woman whose own trials would render empathy, he needed to share his loss. "My mother died in a fire. When I was a boy. My grandparents, too."

"Oh, Branch, how awful for you." She leaned down to kiss his forehead. From beneath the drape of her high-necked, long-sleeved gown, her breast skimmed his cheek.

In that moment, a totally different kind of fire kindled inside him. No scarlet corset or chemise to tempt, just the downy brush of well-worn flannel and her scent, feminine and warm. Wholesome. A light to the darkness lingering within him.

All thought of honor or resistance vanished as the flame burst to life. He ached for her, hard and hot. Lifting his hand to cup her chin, he said, "Come to me, Kate. Lie with me."

Her mouth curved in a soft smile, and she turned into his palm and kissed him. Her hair spilled across her shoulders in a silky, auburn wave and Branch grabbed it, threading his fingers through its length to tug her gently down beside him. "Sprite," he murmured, his breath ragged with need. Pressing his hand against her lower back and fitting her intimately to him, he rocked against her in a movement as old as time.

Her hips rolled in response, and a great rush of heat threatened his slimly held control. "Slow, sweetheart," he breathed, his fingers working the buttons at her neck. His kiss found first her eyelids, then trailed across her temple to the sensitive skin behind her ear. He pushed the gown from her shoulders, exposing the full round globes of her breasts, and his mouth followed the trail of his fingers.

He knew her arousal; felt the shudder in her bones, scented the musky addition to her fragrance, tasted the salty sheen glistening on her skin. Wild and deep, an answering, primitive force coursed in his veins and battled with the civilized part of himself. Branch rose above Katie, tearing her gown completely away, baring her to his gaze.

She was the most beautiful woman he'd ever seen.

A low moan, almost a growl, rumbled from his throat, and he said, more to convince himself than her, "We'll go slow."

He meant to. He intended to draw it out, to pleasure her inch by inch, to share with her the exquisite torment of lazy loving. But then her hands were touching him, stroking, cupping, and caressing. This was not a night for good intentions.

His control shattered. Rational thought disintegrated. He surged against her, thrusting into her warm, welcoming heat. Taking her.

And Katie reveled in the taking. She watched him, the set of his jaw, the almost painful wrinkle of his brow. The elemental power of the hunger glowing in his eyes.

Such fires, burning in this cabin tonight.

Katie sank her nails into his back as she arched, drawing him deeper. Tension sparked and coiled, tightening as he rode her, her hips hammering back at him. She was as fierce as he, straining, seeking that wild relief that only this man could give her.

That's when she recognized the truth. Somewhere in the midst of that storm of sensation, as ribbons of lightning sizzled down her nerves and the great quaking spilled from her womb, knowledge burst upon her mind.

Her plans had gone awry. This act had nothing to do with seduction. *Oh, Lord, help me.*

She loved him.

.   .   .

The sun was a fiery fingernail on the horizon when Branch awoke, his body weary from too little sleep and too much exertion. For long moments he lay without moving, suspended between heaven and hell; between Katie Starr and reality.

He slipped from the bed, quietly dressing as the first rays of sunlight beamed through the window and illuminated her face, revealing the soft, satisfied smile on lips still swollen from his kisses. For several minutes with his hat in his hand, he stood beside the bed watching the even rise and fall of her breasts, memorizing the classic lines of her stunning face. Gently, he covered her with the sheet.

Silently, he left her.

CHAPTER 13

$\mathcal{M}$AKING HIS WAY along the Nacogdoches streets on his way from the rooming house to the jail, Branch scowled, his dark mood a poignant contrast to the cheerful spring morning. Staring at his feet, he almost plowed right into the oaken wagon parked in front of the mercantile, its bed loaded with wet-wrapped jugs of buttermilk and chickens in cages made of cane.

He glared at a rooster. "It's been long enough, you'd have thought they'd have sent some sort of message to tell me how they're makin' out." Fourteen long days had passed since he rode away from Gallagher's Inn while Katie still slept. Thirteen days since he made sure Martha and Rowdy Payne hightailed it out to stay with her.

He'd heard nary a word of her since then. "I've sent two messages. The least they could do is reply!"

The cock jerked his head, his bright red wattle bobbing as if in agreement. Branch yanked his hat farther down his forehead and continued, "It's just plain rude."

Almost as rude as loving a woman and leaving without a good-bye.

Branch did his best to put Katie Starr from his mind as he sauntered toward the jailhouse. His "marriage" had made his life around town—around both the Regulators and the Moderators—more than a mite uncomfortable at times.

Lately, tensions had surged between the two vigilante groups. Branch was walking a delicate path in his guise as a two-timing spy, and as confrontations between the factions grew bloodier and more deadly, his distaste for the entire venture grew.

Especially since he had yet to discover to whose farm
Rob had moved before he died. Branch had visited almost
a dozen homesteads in the past two weeks and garnered
nary a clue.

He found Strickland seated at his desk, going through
the mail. The sheriff always paid careful attention to the
letters that arrived, and Branch approved of his conscien-
tious attention to "wanted" flyers and requests for information.

"Mornin', boss," he said, attempting to ignore the
stench coming from the back of the building. Nothin' like
the aroma of a drunk's vomit to get a fella's day started,
he thought.

Strickland nodded a hello. "Thank you for the invitation, Kincaid. It sounds as though you and your wife have
chosen an excellent way to mark the reopening of her family's hotel. After all, San Jacinto Day is our biggest holiday, and folks will enjoy an all-day picnic at the inn as a
change from the normal ball here in town. Good thinking."

What the hell? Branch thought. He hung his hat on a
wall peg, missing twice to give himself time to think of a
suitable reply. He turned and said, "Uh, yeah."

Strickland leaned back in his chair. "Sounds like a lot
of fun. I know the children will enjoy the taffy pull." He
frowned then and hesitated a moment before saying,
"There is one thing, though, Kincaid. In truth, it just
doesn't seem right for you to put all that work into that
particular travelers' inn. The Regulators did choose to
burn the inn once. Aren't you afraid the bosses might decided to do it again?"

"I don't think that'll happen," Branch said, shrugging
as though unconcerned. In reality, his muscles were wound
tighter than an eight-day clock. "From what I've been told,
they burned it to begin with because it was a Moderator
hangout. Well, the Moderators sure the hell ain't gonna be
usin' it anymore, what with *my* wife runnin' the place. She
knows where our loyalties lie this time around."

"But what about that trouble her father and brother
caused?"

"Katie didn't have anything to do with that business;

she was with me the whole time. Hell, Jack, that's how I ended up married to the woman, after all!"

The sheriff scowled. "You deserved to be leg-shackled, Kincaid. Really, taking her on a church pew."

Branch forced a grin. "Yeah, well, she's religious about some things."

Strickland leaned back in his chair and folded his arms, his legs outstretched and crossed at the ankles. He gave Branch a measured look. "Tell me somethin', Kincaid. That woman of yours is beautiful, and when I met her at the Independence Day Ball, she demonstrated impeccable manners. She appeared to be a gentlewoman."

Branch sauntered over to the window and looked out into the street. His casual stance was at odds with the emotion churning inside him. He didn't like the way this conversation was going. He didn't like Jack Strickland talking about Katie. "She is a gentlewoman and she's very much a lady," he stated flatly.

"Then why did you tell Trident her father sold her to you? Is she a lady or a whore?"

Branch squared his shoulders, furious that anyone would call his wife whore. He whipped his head around to snap at Strickland when the entirety of the man's question sunk in.

"Trident? Who the hell is Trident?"

"Trident is one of Colonel Moorman's lieutenants. One of his right-hand men. You know him—he leads the raids that originate from Nacogdoches."

"The tall man, always dressed completely in black?" Strickland nodded.

"I know him," Branch agreed, "but who is he? I've been wonderin' about that for some time now."

"Why do you want to know?"

Branch pulled a cane-seated chair from the corner and straddled it. "We do a little business together, and I don't know how to reach him when I need him."

"Kincaid, Trident's identity is a closely held secret, one to which you are not privy." Strickland shuffled through papers on his desk, adding, "You'd best keep your curiosity to yourself; it can be a dangerous habit to indulge."

"Maybe so, but we've an agreement between us, and I might need his help real quick someday. I need to know who to go to."

The sheriff pinned him with his gaze. "Me, Kincaid. Come to me. I know Trident, and I can pass him your information. Now, enough of this. You never answered *my* question."

"What question?"

"About your wife. Is she a whore, a crazy one at that, like you claimed the night Gallagher's burned?"

Katie. What was this business about Katie? Why was Strickland interested in her? What was this business about an invitation? Branch didn't like it one little bit. He didn't like that . . . glow in the sheriff's eyes when he mentioned the woman. He pushed up from the chair, saying, "Goddammit, Katie is no whore. I lied to your Trident that night. She was actin' crazy, and I was afraid he'd hurt her."

"You have a funny way of protecting a woman, Kincaid, destroying her reputation."

"I said the first thing that popped into my mind. It seemed right at the time. But listen, Sheriff, her father didn't sell her. I want you and everyone else in town to know that she *is* a lady."

Strickland nodded. "I thought as much." He picked up a paper and began to read.

Apparently, their discussion was over. Good, Branch thought. The sheriff had best keep his attentions on his work and away from my wife. Then he frowned as he realized he'd referred to the title he'd given the woman in his own mind. Walking over to the desk, he cursed beneath his breath, then asked, "Anything for me?" He lifted an envelope from the stack.

"Keep your hands to yourself, Kincaid." Strickland snatched the letter from Branch but not before the deputy managed to read the return address. *The Matagorda Bay and Texas Land Company.*

Branch's heartbeat accelerated. As commissioner of the

General Land Office for the Republic of Texas, his brother had become personally involved in the investigation into counterfeit land scrip. Phony scrip issued by the MB&T Land Company was what had brought Rob Garrett to East Texas and subsequently led to his death. Why would the Matagorda Bay and Texas Land Company be corresponding with Sheriff Strickland?

Then an agonized moan drifted from one of the cells. Strickland scowled. "Go see to the prisoner, Kincaid. He's in number three. I don't care what you do to him, but make him shut up. That bawl of his is irksome."

"Who is it?" Branch asked, reaching for the keys.

"Oh, a Moderator Trident interrogated last night. Picked him up for stealin' one of Ayer's slaves. Fellow claims he hired a freeman to work at his place, but Ayer says otherwise."

Ayer was a Regulator, an eerie-looking character with one green eye, one brown, who wouldn't think twice about lying or murdering for that matter. This prisoner sure had picked the wrong man to tangle with, Branch thought, shaking his head.

The sight that met him in the cell forced all consideration of the Matagorda Bay and Texas Land Company from his mind. A young man, early twenties from what he could tell, lay tied to the bunk. He was pale as Jim Bowie's ghost—all except for his right hand, that is. Dried, dark red blood smeared the squirrel trap that imprisoned mangled fingers.

"Damnation, boy, what happened to you?" Branch knelt beside the man and removed the trap. Bright red blood gushed with the release of pressure, and Branch hurriedly wrapped his kerchief tight around the wounds to halt the flow. The young man opened pain-glazed eyes, lifted his head, and croaked. "I don't know anything about slave stealing. I swear."

Branch winced as the prisoner fell back into unconsciousness. Damn, who the hell does this fool Trident think he is, interrogating prisoners in such a manner?

Strickland spoke from the doorway. "That boy didn't

hold out more'n five minutes. I'm afraid he'll never make it in Texas."

Branch looked over his shoulder. "Trident did this? Why? You're the sheriff, why aren't you in charge of such things?"

The sheriff simply shrugged. "It's Regulator business, Kincaid. I may not like it, but I've nothing to do with it. I take orders just like you."

Branch picked up the trap and examined it, then tossed it aside. The clank of it hitting the wood reverberated through him. He stood and faced Strickland. "Does he do this often? This Trident sounds like a Texian Torquemada."

The sheriff's blue eyes hardened. "I suggest you not state opinions concerning things of which you know nothing, Kincaid. A man could end up hurt that way."

Branch knelt beside the prisoner and laid the damaged hand gently across the boy's chest. "Did Trident get what he needed from him, or does this child have more of this fun ahead?"

"Oh, he got his information. You'll see, Kincaid, that Trident always gets what he wants."

Not far from the Platte River in Indian Territory, beneath the glare of a brilliant sun, Dances In The Night approached the boy who sat sobbing at the base of a gnarled oak tree. The day was warm, the air sweet and clean, but bitterness filled the man. He laid a hand on the youngster's shoulder and hunkered down beside him.

"It's not fair!" the boy whimpered.

"I know, Daniel. It is not fair. But then, such is the manner of life." Anguish twisted the Cherokee's face. "I loved him also. Your father filled a place in my heart that now aches in emptiness."

"I don't love him—I hate him! He was stupid. A stupid idiot. Coming here, going to that village and never taking the vaccination. He asked for it to happen. Well, I don't care. I'm glad he's dead!"

Shaddoe's fierce shove sent Daniel sprawling. He

loomed over the boy, his blood thundering like stampeding buffaloes. He grabbed Daniel's chin, forcing him to meet his eyes. "Never speak of John Gallagher in such a manner again. I will beat you."

Shaddoe pulled back. He leaned against the tree, teeth clenched and breathing heavily. Reaching above, he yanked at a pencil-thin limb, tearing it from the tree. He stripped the leaves one by one and tossed them to the ground. Heaving a long sigh, he apologized. "Forgive me, Daniel. My grief controlled my actions." He kicked at a leaf with his moccasin and continued, "He was dying. He knew it. He told me of the great pain eating him from within. Could you not read his face and see the agony he lived? Did you not notice the skin shrink around his bones?"

Daniel sat up, frowning. "What do you mean, Shaddoe?"

"He coughed blood, Daniel, had for some time. He was dying slowly and with pain. When he saw a way he could help others, he welcomed the risk involved. Your father died bravely and with honor." Shaddoe stared straight ahead. "Grieve, but be proud."

Daniel's jaw dropped, and tears flowed from his haunted eyes. "I didn't know. Why didn't he tell me? He should have seen a doctor!"

"His choice," Shaddoe replied. "He wanted his days with you unspoiled. Remember the joy of the times, Daniel. That is what John wanted."

The boy wrapped his hands around his knees and lowered his head. Shaddoe tore a second limb from the tree and ripped at the leaves until he realized what he was doing. Disgusted with himself, he flung the limb away, frowning at the green stain on his fingers.

In a tremulous voice, Daniel asked, "Shaddoe, what's going to happen now? To me and Keeper, I mean."

Shaddoe sat beside Daniel. He sat cross-legged and absently smoothed the soft fringe on his leggins. Waiting until the grieving boy looked up at him, he captured his gaze and stated, "Your choice. Your father requested it be so. You know of my plans; I shall return to Texas and finish what was begun there. If you wish to come with me, I will take steps to insure your safety from those who would hold the vaccine theft against you." His lips tightened at the thought. "But if you wish to remain here, with the Cherokees, know that you are more than welcome. I have spoken to the others, and they have assured me that the one who stole the jar of life-medicine will always have a home among The People."

"Keeper too?"

Shaddoe smiled. "Do you have a doubt?" Keeper McShane reigned as hero: the one whose body made health magic. He could live with honor among the Cherokee till the end of his days, and he gloried in the attention he received.

"They don't mind my hand," Daniel said after a time.

Shaddoe nodded, his hearing tuned to the *coo, coo, coo,* of a mourning dove. Daniel was stronger now, having proved himself among The People. This would be a good place for him.

Daniel's brow knotted in thought. "What about Katie, though?" he asked. "We can't just desert her—she's waiting for us to come home. I have to go tell her about Da."

"I can bear that burden, Daniel. You need not worry. And remember, she is not your responsibility; Branch Kincaid now has that honor. He gave his word."

Shaddoe shrugged and the beads on his fringed tunic rattled. "Know that I will watch over your sister, Daniel. Kathleen will have so many people protecting her that she will despise it. And my first act upon my return will be to make sure Branch Kincaid is treating our Kathleen properly."

Daniel heaved a sigh. "I don't know. When will you leave?"

"Soon. I cannot leave this situation unattended for much longer. I cannot allow the sacrifice to be an empty one."

Daniel stood and dusted the dirt from his pants. He wiped the wetness from his face. When he straightened his spine, a young man stood in place of the boy. "I'll stay. I can learn so much from the Cherokees."

Shaddoe rose to his feet and nodded solemnly. "Very well. I shall miss you, Daniel Gallagher, my brother. I shall speak to Keeper, but I have no doubt he, too, will remain." He offered his left hand, and Daniel grasped it firmly.

As Shaddoe walked away, he heard Daniel Gallagher say, "Da, I'm sorry. I didn't mean it, you know." His voice was soft, but strong. "Good-bye, Da."

Alone in her room at Gallagher's, Katie Kincaid stared at her reflection in a mirror and stifled a sob. Freckles. Fine. So she had a few freckles. And true, her eyes were more often red than blue these days. But her hair wasn't too bad, she felt confident of that much. And the bosom that had affected him so from the very beginning still sat right there on her chest.

"Then why?" she asked herself. Tears rolled down her face. If wounded pride was a terminal condition, she lay at death's door. Her husband didn't want her.

He not only didn't want her, he'd rejected her. Twice. Two separate times he'd made love to her, taken her as his own, and then slapped her pride and her feminine senses by shutting her out of his life. Only this time he'd not simply sent her away, he'd up and abandoned her!

Just when she'd figured out that she loved him.

"Honey child," Martha called as she knocked on the door, "are you all right?"

"No, I don't think I am."

Martha was beside her in a minute. "What is it, sweetkins?"

Katie sniffed. "Oh, Martha. I have such a problem."

"Tell ol' Martha all about it, dearling," the widow said as she gave Katie a comforting hug.

"I don't think I can. It's so personal."

"I see." Martha frowned and heaved a heavy sigh. "Katie, my dear, how old were you when you mother passed on?"

Curious, Katie looked at her. "Nine."

Martha nodded. "I'll bet she never got around to explainin' to you about men, did she?"

Katie shook her head.

"Honey child, there is something you need to know. Us women have to stick together, especially when it comes to dealin' with men. They'll just ride roughshod all over us if we allow it, and it's up to each of us to share the tricks of preventing that from happening. Now, I can help you, dear. Tell me what that scapegrace Branch has done, other than disappearing into town for two weeks, that is."

Tears rolled down Katie's face. "Oh, Martha, why is it I always let you see me cry?"

"Oh, baby, tears are just another one of the secrets women have that men haven't discovered yet. You go ahead and cry, there's nothing to be ashamed of. You know you'll feel better afterward."

"But tears don't change anything, Martha, I'll still be awful at it after I cry!"

"Awful at what, darlin'?"

Katie sniffled twice and said, "Sex."

Martha's eyebrows climbed to the top of her forehead. "You! Why I don't believe it. You get passionate about the weather, Katie Kincaid. Now, how did you ever get such a stupid idea? Never mind, I just answered my own question. What did he say to you?"

"It isn't what he said, it's what he did and didn't do!"

Martha gasped. "Don't tell me he didn't bed with you."

"Well, sort of."

"What do you mean?"

Katie stood and paced the bedroom. "He did once, and then he didn't anymore, and then he did a lot, and then he left."

"A lot?"

"Seven times."

Martha pursed her lips and fussed with her sleeve. "Well now, Katie, you were with him only two weeks. From my experience, that was actually quite a bit."

Katie halted and cried, "It was one night!"

"One night?" Martha's jaw dropped. "Seven times!"

Katie nodded.

"Oh, my stars!" Martha exclaimed. "And he had the strength to move the next day?"

"He *left* the next day. He left without saying good-bye and went back to Nacogdoches. Oh, Martha. I must be the worst lover ever born!"

"Um, um, um," Martha said. "Seven times. Katie, you don't need to worry about not pleasin' the man. Why, it's obvious to me that you pleased him *too much*. For a man to get that het up, well, he's got to have some mighty powerful feelin's. He didn't leave you, girl, he ran from you." She rubbed her hands together and giggled. "He's guarding his little baby feelin's."

"I don't think so Martha."

"Well, I do. Seven times—why that Mr. Branch is purely something else." Martha shook her head. "No, Katie, if he doesn't love you yet, he's awful close. He's running from you, and listen to me dear, this is another of our woman's secrets. When he's running from you hard and fast, well ... that's the best time to catch him."

"But I've tried to catch him. I couldn't."

"Tsk, tsk, tsk," Martha said. "You've not been listening, child. Here's how to go about it." She lowered her voice and explained to Katie how to play Branch Kincaid like a fiddle.

When she finished, Katie was laughing.

Branch Kincaid's bride had done come to town.

For three days now he'd been living under carnal siege, and as a result, he stomped around Nacogdoches with his hat covering his crotch more often than his head.

And the little witch had decided to bathe. Again. Katie Kincaid, as she called herself, must be the cleanest damned woman in Texas. One more glimpse of bare legs or naked breasts would have him either running for the border or the bed. Either way, he was doomed.

She'd traveled into Nacogdoches to conclude preparations for the reopening celebrations for Gallagher's Tavern and Travelers Inn, which were to be held a little over two weeks from now on San Jacinto Day. She was hosting a barbecue complete with a Best Dessert of the Day contest. Everyone in town had received an invitation. Everyone but Branch.

Of course, he wouldn't go even if he had been asked. He had more important things to do.

Still, he would have appreciated an invitation.

Katie had arrived unannounced at Nacogdoches House and had moved into Branch's own room and into his own bed, commenting that appearances must be kept up. She kept to her own side, though, never touching him during the night. Not even when he lay awake and willed it. Never once had she referred to the night they'd spent together, nor asked why he'd left before she awoke.

That annoyed him. Damned if it didn't up and get him riled. For the life of him, he couldn't figure the woman out.

For one thing, she'd gone and lost her modesty. She'd settled into the boardinghouse like a wood floor. No matter how careful a fella stepped, she creaked at him. Little things—brushing her hair in the candlelight, kicking off her shoes the minute she entered their room, and wiggling her toes right at him. Katie Kincaid shed her widowhood, and her clothes followed shortly. "Gonna make herself soap-sick," he grumbled.

She should at least yell at him for loving, then leaving, her. That's what a normal woman would do. But as he climbed the stairs to his room, he reminded himself that Kate was no normal woman. What would she be doing tonight? Would he find her naked again? Perhaps he'd finally see her in that scarlet corset and she'd scream and yell at him for running out on her. Then, when she was in a high passion, he'd pull those black ribbons and loosen her stays. Maybe he'd use his teeth.

He took the last few steps two at a time. He dusted off his shirt and straightened the kerchief at his neck before he turned the door handle and entered the room.

She was gone.

Damned if she hadn't packed up and left. Her dresses, her shoes, her blessed sweet-smelling soap, all of it.

A note lay propped on the bed pillow. Branch crossed the room and slowly picked up it. Gallagher's Tavern and Travelers Inn was inviting him to attend their Grand Reopening on San Jacinto Day, April 21, 1845.

Katie had penned a note at the bottom, asking him to judge in the contest.

"Hmm," Branch said, hovering between a grin and a scowl. "I hope she bakes her cobbler."

"I'd like to see the records of land claims filed in this county over the past five years."

The starched-collar clerk in the land office frowned over the tops of his spectacles at Branch's question. "That's quite a bit of paper, sir. What specifically are you looking for?"

Branch slipped his hand inside his vest and pulled his deputy's badge from his shirt pocket. He glared at the man behind the counter. "Just bring me the files."

With a sniff, the clerk turned away to do his bidding. Branch lifted a pencil from the counter and began tapping it impatiently. This was the fourth county land office he'd visited in the last week, and he was getting pretty damn tired of government flunkies.

I have to gather all the information I can about MB&T Land Company, he told himself. He'd wasted too much time cozying up to the Regulators and the Moderators without learning a thing. He'd been so sure that if he wormed his way into their confidences, he'd find his man. He'd imagined that with a little footwork, he could locate the farm where Rob spent his last days and learn just what had happened the day he died. But he'd been wrong.

Branch hated to be wrong.

But this MB&T business felt right. He was close this time, he could feel it. And the sooner he ran his prey to ground, the sooner he could go home to Riverrun. The pencil slipped from his hand as the vision of an auburn-haired spitfire floated in his mind. Tomorrow was San Jacinto Day, and he'd be riding out to Gallagher's, perhaps for the last time.

The clerk dumped an armful of files before him, shaking Branch from his reverie. He stared at the piles of paper. It has to be here, he thought. He damn well knew it.

There were two ways a man could use counterfeit land scrip. He could sell it to gullible immigrants, or he could use it to claim land himself. The volume of folks moving into Texas made the first method of disposing of phony scrip easier to accomplish, but it also was the most risky, because the forger would be forced either to meet his victim directly or allow others into his scheme. While Rob's letters to his father mentioned a ring of counterfeiters, Branch had yet to uncover any evidence that more than a single man, or a single land company—the MB&T—was involved.

That led him to believe the second method of scrip disposal, purchase of the land itself, might just be the one utilized. But for all the offices he'd visited, Branch had yet to figure out just what it was he looked for. He had a gut feeling that he was on the right trail, though, and that instinct had seldom let him down before.

He ran his finger along the stiff edge of the top file and murmured, "Maybe today." If he had any luck at all, maybe this time he'd discover the clue that would put it all together. He was beginning to think he was needing to put some distance between him and a certain innkeeper.

"I'll need the county map also," he said to the clerk as he opened the first folder in the stack, the one entitled donation grants. Donation grants and bounty grants were issued to individuals for service during the Texas Revolution. He skimmed the certificates until one particular name caught his eye, and an old hurt bubbled up inside him. The paper read in part: "Known to all men that James Bowie Having Fallen in the Alamo 6th March 1836 is entitled to Six Hundred and Forty Acres of Donation Land."

Damn, but Jim had been a good man, a good friend, Branch thought, shaking his head. It's good to know that a relative got some good out of his sacrifice—a fine section of the East Texas Redlands—but this business made for a heavy heart. Sifting through the names of those who

fought in the battles of the Revolution revived the faded
nightmare in his memories.

He slammed the file shut, blowing dust up from the
counter. The government man sneezed. Branch doubted
he'd find his answers among the donation grants or the
bounty grants. The muster rolls from the Army of the Republic of Texas were too easy to check—any criminal with
any sense wouldn't risk counterfeiting grants. "I'd bet my
own donation grant on that," he muttered.

Besides, the MB&T dealt mostly in sales scrip—paper
sold to anyone with the purchase price. Headrights, also,
weren't so easy to check. Every man who moved to Texas
had qualified for a headright up until recently. The forger
would have pretty pickings with those. The answer had to
be in either the headright certificates or sales scrip filed in
the counties around Nacogdoches, and in the last week
Branch had checked most of them.

He tossed aside the donation grant file and opened the
headright, second-class, folder. He asked the clerk, "Now,
what are the dates again on what type of classification a
man receives for his headright?"

The clerk answered with a whine in his voice. "First
class arrived in Texas prior to March second, 1836. Married men received one league and one labor of land, while
single men received one-third league."

Branch interrupted. "Just the dates. I know how much
land a man's entitled to."

The clerk tightened his lips into a thin line. "Second-
class rights are issued to those who arrived between March
second, 1836, and October first, 1837. Third is after October first, 1837, to January first, 1840. Fourth is from January first, 1840, to January first of this year."

An idea niggled in Branch's mind. Something about
the dates . . . what was it? He looked more closely at the
map. Most of the claims were in leagues and labors. First-
class headrights. Early settlers.

Branch tapped the pencil rhythmically. Dammit, think.
He'd studied a passel of county maps in the last couple of
weeks. What was it about them that bothered him? He
tried to recall the details of each map.

Very little unappropriated land remained in any of the counties he'd checked; therefore, most of the land was illustrated in blocks. Claimed labors and leagues took up major portions of the counties. Branch stared at the map before him and concentrated.

Rob was investigating scrip when he died. Scrip was usually sold in sections, 640 acres, or even half sections. Branch noted the names of men who filed on less than a league of land, trying to draw a connection between them.

He frowned. This was San Augustine County. He knew this county—he'd hunted the land for the Gallaghers. The prime land in this county had been claimed in 640-acre sections, not leagues of 4,428 acres. That made no sense. Why wouldn't the earliest settlers have claimed the best land?

The answer hit him like a wild mustang's kick. Indians. Chief Bowles's Cherokees. Katie's Shaddoe Dancer. Happy horse dung, *the dates*! Branch sank into a chair and buried his face in his hands, straining to put the information together.

July 1839—the Cherokee War. The phony land scrip that had brought his brother to East Texas began to surface in '42 or '43. Who had settled the Indian land? Was that what this was all about, ownership of the prime, eastern Texas land from which the Indians had been driven? Branch looked up at the clerk. "How was the Cherokee land appropriated?"

The little man looked offended. "Why, the same method as any land, of course. Sam Houston made sure of it. He pushed a law through Congress that insured the land was divided into sections and sold. He wanted all the proceeds to go to the Republic, not landgrabbers."

"Who bought it and how?" He asked the question, but he already knew the answer. He'd bet half of Riverrun that the killer owned that land, and that he'd claimed it using counterfeit scrip.

"Listen, Deputy, I don't mind cooperating with the law, but your attitude . . ."

"Answer me!" Branch snapped, leaning forward with

his hands planted firmly on the counter, glaring at the little man.

"I'll have to check." The clerk glanced nervously at the map, then fingered through the files.

"Why have I been so blind?" Branch muttered. It made perfect sense. The man he searched for must have some connection to the MB&T, and Rob must have found it. The Cherokee land was prime property, extremely valuable, and for someone, worth killing for.

"Here's the file, Deputy," the clerk said, handing him a folder.

Branch opened it and began to read. Most of the land had been claimed with sales scrip—scrip issued by the Matagorda Bay and Texas Land Company. Now he needed to check the certificates. They would confirm the name.

He thumbed through the papers, matching land sections with scrip certificates, and his blood chilled like the Brazos River in January. Most of the certificates were filed by the same man.

John Patrick Gallagher.

⇶ CHAPTER 14 ⇷

SAN JACINTO DAY dawned bright and clear with a warm April breeze stirring through the trees. In Gallagher's yard, gingham cloths covered tables ready to be laden with food. Iron stakes rose from sand-filled horseshoe pits, and along the road, red flags flapped from tree branches, marking the start and finish lines for the horse races planned for that afternoon. Up at the inn, the last of the window curtains had been hung, the furniture dusted, and everything made clean and gleaming in anticipation of the formal reopening of Gallagher's Tavern and Travelers Inn.

Katie, Martha, and the Paynes had been up before the sun seeing to the final preparations for the party. Already the aroma of slow-cooking beef rose from the barbecue pit, leading Andrew to complain of a rumbling stomach as Katie and Martha prepared breakfast.

"Hush your mouth, boy," Martha said, pulling a tray of biscuits from the oven. "You're *not* about to starve. I watched you snatch four molasses cookies not twenty minutes ago, so I'm certain you can wait another five minutes for Miz Katie to get the eggs scrambled."

Katie laughed, saying, "Go tell your father breakfast is ready, please, Andrew. And make sure you wash up before you come back."

"Yes'm, Miz Katie," the boy said, swiping a hot biscuit from Martha's tray and dodging a wrap on his knuckles before dashing from the kitchen.

"Rowdy ought to take a belt to that boy of his," Martha fussed. "He's getting more ornery every day."

"He reminds me of Daniel," Katie said. "I'm happy to have him around for nothing more than that." Dishing the on-the-runny-side scrambled eggs from her skillet into a wooden bowl, she asked, "Martha, were there any strawberries left over from the pies? I've a mind for fruit with my breakfast."

Martha didn't answer. Katie glanced over her shoulder. The landlady stared toward the door, grimacing with concern. Slowly, Katie turned around.

Branch stood in the doorway with thunderclouds on his brow. He hurled his words like hailstones. "Damn you, woman! Tell me *every single detail* of this scam you Gallaghers are running!"

"I beg your pardon?" Katie clipped her words.

"I should damned well hope so. I may be the world's greatest fool, but I don't believe you and your father are killers." He stepped into the kitchen, the fire in his eyes scorching a path to Katie. "I do know that you are thieves. Thousands of acres, patented to John Patrick Gallagher. No wonder the old leprechaun didn't want to take you with him. He needed someone to stay around and keep an eye on his land!"

Katie inhaled a deep breath and set the empty skillet on the table. Branch's gaze never left her as he said to Martha through gritted teeth, "Please excuse us, Mrs. Craig."

Her stare fastened on the pulse throbbing at his temple. "No, Martha. Stay where you are." Katie had learned survival skills at a very young age. "Branch, I can see that you are somewhat upset. However"—she raised her voice to be heard over his guffaw—"however, you labor under a misconception."

Sarcasm dripped from his words. "I labor from the labors of land you've stolen."

Oh, that man! She slammed the spoon against the tabletop. She had never stolen anything in her life—and neither had Da. Outrage at his false accusation starched her spine, but feeding the fury was her sense of guilt.

She hadn't stolen that land, but what she had done was much worse.

Shame and anger forced bravado into her voice. "How dare you! I'll have you know that the last person who accused me of theft found herself taking an unplanned swim in the Angelina. Of all the nerve!"

She put her hands on her hips and glared at him, fuming. "You slander my name, allowing me no chance to explain, and do it in front of a witness yet! Well, I'm of half a mind to show you the door for good."

"You're half a mind, all right," he raged, advancing on her. "And if you don't use that sassy mouth of yours to answer my question this minute, it's gonna see the back of my hand."

"You wouldn't slap me."

Branch's jaw clenched. His words slithered across the room and curled around her neck. "Don't count on it. You've got more nerve than a whore at a tent revival."

His voice was deceptively mild when he spoke again. "You're right, Katie, I'd never hit your face. But you can bet every acre of land in your precious Da's name that I'd give you the spanking you deserve. Now start talkin'."

"Oh, you ... you ...," she stuttered. She glanced around the room, searching for a weapon. The skillet. She stretched for the handle when her gaze snagged on the wooden bowl full of cooling eggs.

"Uh-oh," Martha said. "Honey chile, you'd best not."

Branch's glare promised certain retribution.

Katie didn't care. Guilt was a living, breathing monster inside her. Anything would be better than telling him the truth.

Martha groaned as the gooey, yellow mess tumbled down upon Branch's head.

The bowl clattered to the floor. He raised a hand and calmly brushed the egg from his hair and shoulders.

"I think I'll go find Rowdy and Andrew and tell them breakfast will be a bit late," Martha said, removing her apron and heading for the door. "I'll make sure you two are not disturbed."

Katie watched a slimy, yellow streak dribble slowly down Branch's shirt. *Oh my, you've done it now, Katie-girl.* She clasped her hands in front of her in a futile attempt to control the trembling. "You can't leave me, Martha. He'll hurt me, he'll kill me."

Martha twisted her lips in a frown, then asked, "You gonna kill her, Mr. Branch?"

His gaze locked on Katie, he gave a slow, negative shake of his head.

The older woman nodded once. "Very well. Sweetheart, I'm afraid that short of murder, you've got it coming to you. I'll give you your privacy now."

As her only defense exited the room, Katie faced the enormity of her mistake. He looked down at his shirt, grooming himself like a tawny panther with enormous paws, and she stood frozen in place like a frightened rabbit. With an almost casual air, he lifted his head and impaled her with glowing eyes. A feral grin spread across his face.

Oh, sweet Mother of God, she prayed.

Lord, she makes me horny, Branch thought. She's glorious when she gets this way. The woman could make a starving man forget the meat on his fork. He'd spent half the night calling her every filthy name in the book, but put him in the same room with the lying witch for five minutes, and his blood flowed straight from his brain to his crotch.

He took a step toward her.

She backed away.

With his next step, she looked frantically around her. She grabbed the skillet and, using both hands, raised it above her head like a club. "Stay away from me, Branch," she warned.

"Never."

Her eyes widened. Her tongue darted out and wet her lower lip. In a flash of movement, he whipped one arm out and grabbed the skillet while the other pulled her close. She shook like a willow branch in a whirlwind as he crushed his lips to hers.

His kiss was angry and fury filled. His tongue invaded her mouth, plundering, taking without allowing her the chance to give. Then, as was his habit when he loved her, he cursed her. "Damn you, Katie Starr." He savagely pushed her away. "Tell me. Tell me all of it."

Katie crashed back to earth. What could she say? How could she explain? Looking at him, seeing the torment etched upon his face, she felt tired, weary of both body and soul. She nervously licked her lips and proceeded to choose her words like the choicest of strawberries. "The land is not Da's. He filed in his name because the person who purchased the scrip wished to remain anonymous."

"Who?"

"Please, Branch."

He walked to her worktable and scowled down at the pan of cobbler. "The Matagorda Bay and Texas Land Company issued every one of those certificates. That company is as crooked as a broken nose, and you folks are caught up in its stink."

Katie looked into his eyes, begging for understanding. "That all came later. I swear to you. You're right, we were involved with the MB & T. Steven brokered scrip for the company. He arranged for Da to buy the land for, um, the person who wanted it."

Branch's gaze hardened. He opened his mouth to speak, then snapped it shut and waited, his eyes again angry and accusing.

"It wasn't Steven's fault. Someone else, I don't know who, came to Steven and blackmailed him. That's when the trouble started."

He stared at her for a long moment, the emotion in his eyes fading to blank. Then he turned away. When he finally looked at her again, he wore an impassive expression. She suddenly felt nauseated.

"Names, Katie," he demanded. "Tell me the names, every goddamn one. Tell me who really owns all that Indian land, tell me who counterfeited the scrip, who passed it, and how it was accomplished." His voice soft, smooth, and deadly, he added, "Tell me, Kathleen, who killed the government man who was sent here to investigate your crimes."

Her face drained. *Oh my God! I've been so stupid, I never made the connection.* Branch wasn't in Nacogdoches investigating the Regulator-Moderator War, he was looking for scrip counterfeiters. *I should have guessed!*

Her short laugh was filled with scorn. Just last week the San Augustine newspaper *The Redlander* quoted Sam Houston as saying that the counterfeiting of scrip and bank notes in Texas was no light evil. Of course he'd send someone to stop it!

Katie moved to the window and pushed the blue gingham curtain aside, catching the scent of honeysuckle. The air was hot, heavy, and oppressive. In a flat voice, she said, "Steven established the MB & T Land Company years ago for the purpose of laying claim to blocks of land our friend wanted. When the tracks became available for sale, Steven made sure Da was able to make his claim first using scrip he purchased with our friend's money. Everything was legitimate. We simply desired to make it impossible to trace the true owner of the land."

"Who is . . . ?"

Ignoring him, Katie continued. "After our deal was done, Steven sold the MB & T to a group of easterners—land speculators. A couple of years ago, a man came to Steven having somehow learned the details of our scheme. He threatened to make the story public, which would not only hurt our friend but ruin Steven's reputation in East Texas if Steven didn't cooperate with him by passing counterfeit scrip."

Branch's gaze was skeptical. "How would it hurt his name?"

"Well, it's just that his efforts on our friend's behalf wouldn't have been well received by the citizens of East Texas." She looked over her shoulder at Branch, saying, "My Steven was a proud man. He thought he could outsmart the villain. He wouldn't tell me his plan, though; he thought to protect me. All I know is that he made some sort of arrangements to trap the blackmailer."

Clenching her fists, she turned to face him. "You've no right, Branch. I lost my husband because of this. I lost my daughter. The blackmailer killed them. I don't know who he is. I've tried to find him. Don't you realize how much

I hate that man? Don't you know that I'd have sent him to hell if I knew who he was?"

Branch wouldn't look at her. He stood before the fireplace, his hands clasped behind his back. His spine was as stiff as an ax handle. "Who is it, Katie? Who owns the land?"

"Damn you, Branch." She closed her eyes, smiling sadly, so cold inside she thought perhaps her blood had frozen. "I love you, dearly, but I will not betray this secret. I won't have Steven's and Mary Margaret's deaths go for naught. Let it alone."

His voice was raw. "I can't!" He whirled on her. "A man is dead, Katie, a good man. You have to tell me." He pinned her with his stare. "By God, you're my wife!"

She caught her breath. The words plunged into her heart like the hottest, sharpest of blades, melting the ice inside. "So you finally admit it."

He glared at her.

Katie shook her head. "I don't have to tell you a blessed thing, Branch Kincaid. A government man might be dead, but so is the father of my baby. So is my *baby*!" Her voice cracked, and the words became a wail. "Damn you, don't you understand? She was in her cradle. She was in the cabin, and he set it on fire. She died, Branch."

In a heartbeat, he crossed the room and folded her in his arms. "Shh, Sprite. It's all right." He gently stroked her hair as she sobbed into his chest. "I'm sorry. I'll not ask you anymore, not now. Shh . . ."

Branch grimaced as her tears stung his heart. It hurt to see Katie like this, hear her like this.

She'd given him some information and, by God, it wasn't enough. He knew that Steven Starr, the sainted husband, was a counterfeiter and dead because of it. Rob Garrett, his brother the spy, was looking for a counterfeiter and was dead because of it.

So what did he have? According to Katie's story, he had two mystery men. The land buyer and the blackmailer. She couldn't or wouldn't name either one.

Branch brushed soft kisses on the top of Katie's head.

It was just too much; he'd let it alone like she'd asked, at least for today.

He'd figure it out. After what he'd just learned, it mattered more than ever. He'd find the bastard—for Katie, for Rob. For the hurt so many had suffered. He'd make the connection; it was only a matter of time.

And when he did, someone would die.

As if she had read his thoughts, Katie shuddered in his arms. Branch stroked her hair, thinking, Today, though, I'll let it go. This was a special day for Katie, she ought to enjoy herself, to have fun. He'd do his best to see that she did.

Tenderly, he kissed her lips. His hands dropped to leisurely fondle the curve of her hip, and a profound sadness settled over him. Good Lord, this caring business could hurt.

Imagine how it'd be if he loved her.

In keeping with Katie's concern about maintaining appearances, Branch played host to her hostess as the guests arrived at the inn. He stayed beside her most of the morning, even grabbing the opposite end of the jump rope when Katie interrupted her visiting to turn it for the children.

He'd left to join in a game of horseshoes, but appeared almost magically at her side when Sheriff Strickland had stopped her to compliment her on the success of the party. While she organized the serving of the noon meal, he'd commanded the carving knife and served up barbecued beef and bad jokes as the guests made their way through the line. When everyone had been served, he'd carried a plate for her and two of his own over to a quilt he'd spread in a shady spot beneath a towering elm tree.

He was being so nice that Katie knew he was up to no good. Branch was obviously out after the name she'd withheld, and he wasn't above using any means to get it.

That's why she was so glad to hear Martha call out her name. The Widow Craig's head was bobbing like a chicken's as her gaze searched the crowd for Katie. "Excuse me, Branch," Katie said, standing to go to Martha.

She wasn't surprised to see him rise and follow.

Martha stood beside the dessert table with Luella Racine and a tall, dark gentleman who stood with his back to Katie and Branch. Spotting Katie's wave, Martha met her halfway across the yard.

"I wanted to tell you I made a change in the contest judging. There's a new man in town, a Mr. St. Pierre, and Luella brought him with her today. Oh, honey, he's the most handsome man I ever saw—" She broke off and smiled at Branch as he joined them. "His name is S.D. St. Pierre," she said. "He's from New Orleans—a Creole gentleman. He's purchased land scrip and plans to file his headright this week."

The clang of a ringer and victorious cheer arose from the horseshoe pit, and both Katie and Martha looked in that direction. Branch's narrowed gaze settled on the stranger; something about the way he carried himself seemed familiar. Branch frowned and thought to himself, Trident? Could I have finally found the bastard?

"Anyway," Martha continued after clapping for the horseshoe winner, "oh, sweetie, wait till you meet him." She closed her eyes and exhaled a besotted sigh. "Gorgeous black hair, wavy and thick, but cut quite short, dark eyes, that olive skin. Why, if only I were twenty years younger . . ." The widow preened as she added, "He's promised to judge the dessert contest for us."

"Wait a minute," Branch said sharply. "That's my job."

Martha took his arm and patted his hand. "Well, now, Mr. Branch. Seein' as how you're part of the Gallagher family, and since my Katie here has entered her peach cobbler, I decided it would be more seemly to have someone who's not connected with the inn and who's never had her dessert to judge for us."

Branch scowled, absurdly disappointed, as Martha tugged on Katie's hand. "Come, my dear, Mr. St. Pierre has said he's dying to meet you. Besides, we really should save him from Luella. You know what a magpie she can be. She entered her loaf cake, and she's trying to prime him on picking her as winner." Pulling Katie toward the stranger, Martha huffed with disgust and added, "Foolish woman; why, one time I saw Frost Thorn using one of her loaf cakes for a doorstop down at the mercantile."

"Martha!" Katie scolded. Branch shoved his hands in his pockets and followed the two women.

"Mr. St. Pierre," the widow called. "Allow me to introduce you to our hostess."

The Creole turned. Katie made a choking sound, and Branch looked at her. Her eyes were dancing like fireflies in the forest, and her teeth were nibbling at her lower lip as if to prevent a delighted smile. He followed the path of her gaze to the newcomer.

The devil's black eyes twinkled at Kate, bold as a billy goat after a nanny in season. He wore a double-breasted navy-colored coat expertly tailored to fit his broad shoulders. From his white linen shirt to his highly polished boots, the stranger bespoke money, power, and arrogance. In all of it, Branch detected a haunting familiarity. He pictured the dark-eyed devil with a hood over his head. Could be, he decided. Then the Creole opened his mouth and spoke.

"*C'est magnifique!* Such beautiful women in Texas. Had I but known, I would have made this journey years ago. Please, Mrs. Craig. I beg an introduction to the *mademoiselle*."

St. Pierre's voice was smooth as fresh churned butter and had nothing in common with that of the one called Trident.

Katie smiled radiantly and lifted her hand to the Creole.

Martha said, "Mr. St. Pierre, may I present Mrs. Starr."

"Kincaid," Branch corrected her.

St. Pierre clicked his heels and bent low, kissing Katie's hand. "*Madame.* Please call me Dee, *Madame.*"

"Dee?"

"My initials, S.D. The French tends to trip one's tongue. I find it—friendlier, *s'il vous plaît.*"

"Charming," Katie replied. "And you may call me Katie." Her cheeks flushed a dusty rose, she added, "We Texians rarely stand on formality."

Branch was clenching his teeth. He shoved his hand

between the two, effectively blocking the Frenchman's
view of Katie's bosom. Then he draped his other arm pos-
sessively about her shoulders. "Branch Kincaid."

The black eyes gleamed with humor as the two men
clasped hands. *"M'sieu."*

Damn but the dandy has a grip, Branch thought. And
what's so blasted funny? Katie sounds like she's got a bug
in her throat. "So," he said, "what brings you to our neck
of the woods, St. Pierre? Making a grand tour?"

"Actually, I plan to establish a ranch in Texas."

"Really?" Branch drawled. The Creole's diamond
stickpin glittered in the sunlight. "Well, you seem more
the cotton type to me, Frenchie. You gonna turn your
slaves into wranglers?"

"I do not keep slaves," St. Pierre replied squaring his
shoulders.

Branch lifted an eyebrow. "A New Orleans Creole who
doesn't keep slaves? Well, who'd a thunk it?" Branch
knew he was being difficult, but something about this fella
just stuck in his craw. "Martha says you're gonna file a
headright tomorrow. You just now come to Texas?"

"Oui."

"Then it seems you've plumb run out of luck,
Frenchie. The Republic quit issuing headright certificates
a good while back." He clicked his tongue and shook his
head. "Damn shame."

The Creole's smile didn't reach his eyes. He shrugged.
"Eh, bien! What's a few hundred acres more? I've purchased sufficient scrip to meet my needs."

Tension dripped over the group like cold molasses.
Martha hurriedly assembled the contestants in the dessert
contest and made a production out of presenting the Creole
with a spoon and a fork.

As he sampled the sweets, St. Pierre regaled those
around him with stories of the rigors of his journey, and
listened to suggestions about where he should locate his
land.

Personally, Branch thought Comanche territory an attractive spot.

Katie bubbled like a mineral spring from the Creole's

attention, and it seemed to Branch that she was receiving more than her fair share of it. The stranger actually winked at her when he tasted a molasses cookie. Branch managed to tolerate the Creole's behavior until he sampled his way toward a dish of peach cobbler Branch recognized as having come from Katie's kitchen. As St. Pierre lifted his spoon to dip into the dessert, Branch acted.

He reached over and grabbed it.

"Kincaid!" Katie fussed.

"Mr. Branch," Martha fretted.

St. Pierre flashed an amused smile. "A possessive husband it appears. I take it, sir, that this is your wife's dessert?"

Branch gathered a fork from the table and plunged it into the middle of the cobbler. "Sure is, Frenchie, and I don't like to share. You'd be well advised to remember it, too."

Taking Katie's elbow, he tugged her through the crowd, ignoring her sputtered protests. "Hush now," he said, as he led her toward a spreading oak tree at the side of the inn away from the crowd.

"You make me so mad, Branch Kincaid," Katie pouted. "I wanted to win that contest."

"Sprite, if we're goin' to continue with this little marriage of ours, you've gotta get one thing straight." Sitting, he cradled the pan of cobbler in his lap and waved his fork in Katie's face. "You bake only for me. I won't be havin' another man's mouth on your sticky-sweet baked sin."

She stared at the dessert, and her voice was syrupy as she said, "Branch, it's a deal as long as only my cobbler sits on your lap."

St. Pierre watched Katie Kincaid stare into a pot of boiling sorghum molasses. When she announced the mixture thick enough, the children around her cheered and clapped their hands. She began to pour it onto greased platters. The taffy pull was about to begin.

The youngsters divided up into pairs and proceeded to pull and fold the sticky substance with greased fingers until it lightened in color. Finally, after much work, the taffy could be twisted into a long, slender rope.

Half the fun of a taffy pull was in stealing a well-pulled rope from an unwary contestant. Due to uneven numbers, Katie had paired with a boy of about nine, and they laughed as they yanked and tugged the candy. St. Pierre sneaked up behind his hostess and caught the boy's attention with a coin. The result was that the boy turned his end of the rope over to St. Pierre.

"You slipped him money, sir," Katie said, her lips pursed in disapproval.

"Bribes have never been beneath me."

"How well I know." She tugged hard on the taffy, and they shared a smile. "Tell me the news, I've been dying to hear everything."

St. Pierre looked past her and shook his head. "I'm afraid we haven't time. There is an angry bear headed in our direction."

"Branch?"

He nodded. "We must meet alone. When and where?"

"Why alone?" Katie asked, her expression troubled. "What's wrong?"

"Quickly, love."

"Later, just before dark. He's playing cards with guests up at the inn. Come to my kitchen—I haven't moved up to the inn."

St. Pierre shook his head. "No, more private. Our regular place."

"But it's the first night we have guests. I can't get away."

"Your husband is upon us. Meet me there." He flashed Branch Kincaid a wide smile. "*Monsieur*, you have come to help?"

"Yes. Why don't I just take that off your hands, Frenchie."

St. Pierre tossed Branch the sticky rope, winked at Katie, and left.

"Really, Branch," Katie said, shaking her head. "You've not been very polite to our guests. I do believe you're jealous, Kincaid."

"Jealous? Me? Why, that's a dumb fool idea if I ever heard one." His lips curved in a smirk, but Katie thought his narrowed, golden eyes gleamed suspiciously green as he glared at the Creole's back. Seeing her amusement, Branch yanked on the taffy and snapped the candy rope in two. He stared at the sticky mess dangling from his unbuttered hands and muttered. "The stuff sticks like a goathead to a horse's tail."

Katie's gaze raked him, pausing on the candy and then on his face. "I don't know, Branch. This picture calls to my mind another part of a horse's anatomy."

To allow the visitors who chose not to stay the night at Gallagher's Tavern and Travelers Inn the time to return to their homes before dark, the festivities had been scheduled to end during the late afternoon. In making her plans for the party, Katie had chosen to end the affair with a bang, literally, and Andrew Payne had been sent around to farms and plantations in the area in search of the needed supplies.

Now with everything at the ready, Branch stood beside the anvil, torch in hand, while Katie, Martha, and Rowdy supervised the line of anxious, giggling children. "Ready?" Rowdy Payne asked. At Katie's nod, he handed a long stick to his son, whose eyes shone with excitement as he held it out over the fire. At the end hung a hog bladder, filled with air and tightly tied. When held to the heat, it exploded with a satisfying BANG! At the first pop, the waiting children squealed and called for their turn. Soon the air was filled with noise, bangs and squeals and laughter, a fine way to end a wonderful day.

When all the bladders had been popped, Branch made a short speech about the heroes of the Battle of San Jacinto, then put the final touch on the celebrations. Black powder had been packed into the hollow of an anvil, which had been set upright on a stump. Branch lit the fuse and the anvil exploded into the air with the sound of a cannon. As it thudded back to earth, Branch grinned like a schoolboy.

He and Katie waved to their departing guests from Gallagher's front porch, and for the first time, Branch felt like a married man.

Taking her hand in his and watching the wagons pull out, he told himself, You'd best guard against it, Kincaid. Feelings like that could be fatal to a man's bachelorhood.

After mounting his horse, Jack Strickland paused for a moment, his stare locked on Katie Kincaid as she waved good-bye to a wagon load of her guests.

She's beautiful, he thought. And gracious. He'd found the opportunity to speak with her at length earlier in the afternoon, while that bird dog husband of hers was riding his horse in the race. It had been amusing to watch the Creole beat Kincaid and his dun. The Frenchman rode like an Indian.

Katie Kincaid had proved to be a true gentlewoman. How could he have not seen it before? Although she lacked formal education in the traditional subjects like French and Italian, drawing and painting, she could both read and write. The pillows in her parlor showed a talent for needlework, and she demonstrated a vast exposure to classical literature.

Mrs. Kincaid could hold her own with any of the ladies he'd courted at home in Boston.

It truly was a shame he'd not noticed her before she became entangled with Kincaid. She'd have made a fine wife for the son of a United States congressman, and the benefits that a Texas-bred bride would bring to his political aspirations in the Republic of Texas were extensive.

Of course, if his father managed to straighten things out in Massachusetts, he wouldn't necessarily need a Texian woman for a wife. But then again, a beautiful, witty, charming wife was always an asset. Especially one unafraid to demonstrate her passions, as evidenced by her rendezvous with her husband-to-be in church.

In church!

The woman was wasted on a man like Kincaid.

CHAPTER 15

AUGHTER AND MUSIC filled the tavern as those guests who had taken rooms at Gallagher's continued the day's merriment. Branch paused in the doorway, conscious of the pleasure he derived from having provided this for Katie—even though she'd no idea *he* was Finian Trahern.

She was as excited as a puppy with two tails about getting the inn up and running. She'd been fun to watch, and all in all the day had been quite a success.

If not for the Creole, he thought, a scowl touching his lips. He appeared entirely too familiar with Katie, to Branch's way of thinking. He'd be one worth watching. A loose horse is always looking for new pastures, and Branch figured to make sure that smooth-speaking stud didn't try to feed where he didn't belong. Thank goodness St. Pierre had gone back to town; perhaps now Branch could enjoy the poker game.

Sam Cavanaugh and two other of Gallagher's guests waited for him at a table. Cigar smoke and banjo music swirled around the room, and Branch waved a greeting at Rowdy Payne, who was working the bar.

Branch got a tankard of ale, then straddled a chair and said, "Deal me in, boys."

"You know, Kincaid," Sam Cavanaugh said, "I never have seen you sit a chair properly."

"Well, I don't know, Sam, it's just that some things seem to be a bit more fun when you try 'em a little differently."

The three men looked at him and said, "Hmm."

"Sure was a nice day today, Kincaid." Sam studied his cards with a frown. "You and the Missus put on a right fine festivity."

Branch sipped his ale and said, "I didn't have anything to do with it. The Widow Craig and Rowdy and his boy did all the work helpin' Katie with the barbecue. But you're right, it was a nice day." He grinned and added, "I'm afeared I might have overindulged on the dessert, though."

"Ate too much, huh? Easy to do with a woman as talented as your wife doin' the cookin'."

"If you only knew, gentlemen. Now, I think I'll raise you five." He tossed a coin into the pot.

They'd played for almost an hour when Sam happened to mention his job. "It's been a busy time lately, especially with all the business that friend of yours is doin'."

Branch looked up from his card hand. Sam was the county land agent for Nacogdoches, and Branch couldn't imagine what friend of his had been doing business with Sam. "Friend?"

Sam looked over the wire rims of his glasses. "That Frenchie. The one who bought your land."

The weather that afternoon was warm, the air stifling and difficult to breathe. It was the type of evening that gave birth to twisters, one of those little tricks nature pulled when she got really riled. Branch tugged at the front of his shirt where sweat had plastered it to his skin and repeated, "The one who bought my land?"

The agent's brow wrinkled in puzzlement. "You know, Deputy, those acres that have been held in your wife's name for the past couple of years. She sent a letter through Rowdy Payne verifyin' the purchase four days ago."

Suddenly the slice of Luella Racine's loaf cake he'd been forced to eat sat uneasily in his stomach. "And the purchaser?"

Sam laid his card hand facedown on the table. "There's not a problem is there, deputy? I mean, I recognized her hand, and I knew Payne was workin' for her out here. In fact, he even had a letter from her discussing the sale of those particular acres."

"Payne? She sold land to Payne?"

"No. The fellow from New Orleans. St. Pierre. He bought the land. I even asked Miz Katie about it today, bein' as how she sold it for next to nothing. I didn't want him cheatin' her, but she was insistent. She told me you knew all about it, Deputy."

"Oh, I know, all right." The pieces clanged together in Branch's mind, and a rush of cold rage swept through him.

S.D. St. Pierre was one of the mystery men—the land-owner whose name Katie had refused to reveal. Branch's heart pounded furiously. But who the hell was S.D. St. Pierre?

"Excuse me, gentlemen. I'm afraid I must see to a lit-tle problem." His chair scraped the floor as he got to his feet with great deliberation. Katie had said she needed a nap, and she'd been sleeping, tucked snugly in her bed, when he'd last checked on her.

Following the path between the inn and the kitchen, Branch cursed the fact that she'd lied time and time again. Was the Creole her lover? How was he connected with the MB&T? Did the Creole have anything to do with Rob's murder?

Is my wife protecting my brother's killer? his thoughts raged.

He slapped open the kitchen door and banged open the bedroom door. She wasn't there.

Leaving the kitchen, he started back up the path to the inn when a movement at the edge of the forest caught his attention. What he witnessed cut him like a bowie knife twisting in his gut. His Katie—his Sprite—was locked in the Creole's embrace.

He stood, trembling, as a fury unlike any he'd ever known, a rage even more intense than what he'd experi-enced the night Hoss Garrett banished him from Riverrun, ate through his soul. He stood frozen, unable to speak, as St. Pierre mounted his horse, then pulled Katie up behind him. Damn her, damn her, damn her, he silently cursed. Then, just before the riders disappeared into the trees, a cloud slipped across the sun. Shadows slashed across the

Creole's face, casting a stripe along his cheekbones. Branch realized that he'd seen the man before.

That night in the church. Painted and feathered. Katie's Shaddoe Dancer.

His deceitful, betraying bride was running off for an early-evening rendezvous with her Cherokee lover.

He turned on his heels and headed for the barn and Striker. The dun stamped a foot nervously as Branch flung his saddle on the horse's back, intent upon following the amorous pair. As he fastened the leather girth, though, a thought occurred to him, and he froze, staring at the strap in his hand.

No, it couldn't be, could it?

A chill swept through him. He needed to think—to reason this out. Katie and her Cherokee could wait.

Branch removed the saddle from Striker and left the barn, walking the short distance to Katie's kitchen. Once inside, he built up the fire in the hearth and put a pot of water on to boil. He'd clean his guns while he worked through this idea. He just might be needing them soon.

Branch had a suspicion that he'd found his brother's killer.

"Oh, Shaddoe," Katie sighed against his jacket, her storm of tears subsided. "I knew he was ill, but I never thought . . ."

"He hid much from us, Kathleen. I lived with him for weeks before I noticed anything. But he lived a just life, and he chose his manner of death. It is good."

They stood beside his horse at the edge of a meadow just off the road. She wiped the wetness from her cheeks with her fingertips. Staring up at the sky painted gold and pink and purple from the setting sun, she murmured huskily, "I'll miss him."

Shaddoe nodded. He led his mount as they crossed the field. They walked through muted splashes of yellow, blue, and lavender wildflowers and scared a cottontailed rabbit into flight. The field was peaceful, and full of life. "Does he rest in a place as pretty as this?" she asked, her gaze on a sad-whistled bird perched in a nearby cedar.

"It's a beautiful spot, Kathleen. He chose it himself before he died." They walked in silence toward the Cherokee village that had welcomed them both during their youth. Now, abandoned and destroyed, it offered a place to grieve and remember better days.

Then Shaddoe grinned and spoke in a teasing tone. "*Mon Dieu*, I thought I'd never find a moment alone with you." He picked up her hand and kissed it.

Katie accepted his attempt to lighten the mood, and she gave an inelegant snort as she snatched her hand away and replied, "You shouldn't have baited Branch like you did. Men. Nothing but tall, ornery boys, that's what you are."

"Ah, you wound me, *mon ami*."

"You deserve it. My poor husband is convinced I'm being stalked by a peacock with illicit intentions." She wrinkled her brow in confusion. "Why have you made St. Pierre so gushy, Shaddoe? You were nothing like that when you first came to Texas. Actually, I think the Cherokee civilized you after your savage New Orleans childhood."

Shaddoe frowned and delayed answering her question. He wrapped his horse's reins around a tree, and catching Katie's hand once more, he led her down a familiar forest path. The fragrance of pine and cedar intermingled, triggering memories of her father, and as Katie followed her friend, she thought of better days.

Eventually, he addressed her question. "You wish to know why St. Pierre has become such a gallant? I thought it best to return as a man unlike Dances In The Night. A number of citizens in Nacogdoches remember a half-breed runaway who searched the forests for his father. Don't forget the rewards Emile Marchand posted for information concerning his grandson. I did not wish to spark best-forgotten memories."

"But why 'St. Pierre'?"

"St. Pierre is my maternal grandmother's family name. If it were discovered that Marchand Shipping financed the founding of the MB & T, the connection between Shaddoe Marchand, owner of the former Indian lands, and the 'breed' who fought against the Texians in '39 would be obvious. They hated me then, Kathleen; they would hate me today. You know that."

"They'd never allow you to stay," Katie agreed, her nose wrinkling in disgust.

He shrugged. "There is your hunter, too, Kathleen. He is an intelligent man. I must admit I am surprised he has not recognized me yet."

"You look like a different person now, Shaddoe, with your hair cut short and dressed in gentleman's clothing. The only time Branch really saw you, you wore that awful paint on your face. Besides, he can't see past his jealousy."

"How would he view our deception, Kathleen?"

She pursed her lips and dipped to pick up a pine cone that lay on the forest floor. "Not very well, I'm afraid," she sighed. "He's already done a bit of checking into the MB & T. He discovered the land in Da's name, but he hasn't learned of the sections I sold to you." She flicked her nail along the cone's scales and added, "It seems he had the idea we, the MB & T that is, had something to do with the death of a friend of his."

"Who?"

Katie opened her mouth to answer, then hesitated. "You know, he never has told me the man's name, just that he was a government man investigating counterfeit land scrip. I haven't pressed for details; in fact, I've always tried hard to change the subject."

"*Are* we connected with this man's death?"

She glared at Shaddoe. "What do you mean by that?"

"Kathleen, your father told me the real story behind Steven's death. You should have told me, little one."

She tossed away the pine cone. "No."

"I am responsible."

The wind swooshed through the trees creating an eerie, ghostly sound. Katie shivered and answered, "That's exactly why I didn't say anything. I know all the arguments you can use, and not a one of them will make a difference. Steven and I were with you the day you went to your grandfather's office in New Orleans. We were as much a part of the founding of the MB & T as you, Shaddoe. It was *my* idea to begin with, *I* named the company, for goodness sakes!"

Shaddoe halted abruptly. He gazed around him at the myriad of colors, spring greens of every conceivable shade. He saw birds' nests of straw, heard the chirping of hatchlings. He touched the rough bark of a pine tree and inhaled the musty fragrance of the forest. "I love this land; I'd give my life for it."

Reaching for Katie, he clasped her hands in his. He stared imploringly into her eyes and poured his heart into his words. "Never, Kathleen, I never wanted Steven to give his. And your daughter—oh, little one, sorrow and shame are viper's fangs sinking into my soul."

She yanked her hands from his, then threw herself into his arms, hugging him tight. "No, no, no. You will not do this, Shaddoe Dancer. It is not your fault. I won't have you accept responsibility for something of which you had no part."

Shaddoe swallowed hard, stroking her hair, comforting himself as much as Katie. "But it is my land, Kathleen; he died because he helped me obtain it."

She stiffened in his arms. "He died; they died." She pulled back and looked up at him. "They died because some creature too low to be called a man chose to black-mail, chose to kill. Enough. Enough, now. I choose to speak of this no longer. Today, now, I'll grieve only for my father."

Thunder boomed in the distance as she turned away. She paused, her hand on a leafy green bush that overgrew the path leading deeper into the forest. "Let me be by myself for a little while, Shaddoe. I need some time." She looked around, noticing for the first time where he had led her. "We're not far from the village. Go home, Shaddoe. You've been away too long."

"But rain is coming, Kathleen."

"Please," she said quietly. "I need to go home, too. I want Branch, I need him to hold me. If I take the horse, I'll make it before the rain begins."

THE TEXAN'S BRIDE   219

He stared deeply into her eyes, then nodded, accepting the truth glowing within their depths. After pressing a gentle kiss against her forehead, he walked away.

Shaddoe walked among the charred remains of the Cherokee village and smiled. The cabins were shells burned beyond repair, just as he and Little Mush had intended when they set the fires over three years ago.

The whites may have won the war, but they lost this particular battle. No homes, no crops, not so much as a carrot in the ground had the Cherokees left behind for the whites to appropriate. This was good.

He breathed deeply of the scent of forest, rain, and home. Fertile land—nearby water. A rush of emotion overcame him. Here he would build his ranch. He would build a home to rival his grandfather's Louisiana plantation house. Using his mother's legacy, the gifts of his father, the lessons of his heritage, he would make his dream a reality.

He would name it Le Cadeau d'Etoiles, gift of the stars, because he never would forget he owed everything to Steven, Katie, and Mary Margaret Starr, to the monumental sacrifices they had made in the name of friendship.

Shaddoe St. Pierre now legally owned the land on which he stood—in both the white man's and the Cherokee's eyes. No one would take it from him. He would build Le Cadeau d'Etoiles and someday have a family with whom he'd share his memories of his friend, Steven Starr. He would create a base of power—political and financial—so strong that not a single person in Texas could challenge his eventual goal. Dances In The Night, Shaddoe St. Pierre, would bring The People home, just as Steven and Katie and he had planned years ago.

Cold rain pelted the earth, and he lifted his face to the sky, answering the wind's welcome. He peeled away the trappings of the white man—his coat, his scarf, his shirt. He tugged off the expensive boots and tossed them aside. He dug his toes into the muddied ground and stood with hands on hips, reveling in his homecoming.

He wondered if Kathleen had reached Gallagher's before the rain.

While the storm built outside, a tempest gathered force inside Katie's kitchen. Only this storm was emotional and as cold as a cast-iron coffin. Branch sat at Katie's work table, one Texas Paterson already cleaned and reloaded, the second in his hands.

She entered the cabin soaked to the skin, a pale-faced wraith in a clinging party dress. "Oh, Branch, I'm so glad you're here," she said, crossing the room, ready to fling herself into his arms. "I thought you'd still be playing cards, but then I saw the lamplight through the window, so I came on in—"

"Sit down," he ordered icily. "We've some talkin' to do."

Katie hesitated and her outstretched arms fell to her sides. "Yes, there's something I need to tell you. Let me change and then—"

"Sit down now."

Frowning, she sat, wrapping her arms around herself as though she were suddenly cold. "Branch, what is it?"

He focused his attention on unloading the gun. With a steady hand, he used a ball puller to extract a small sphere of lead from a chamber. "You know, Katie," he said, dumping the black powder into his flask and repeating the process with the second chamber, "for weeks now you've been harpin' that our marriage was legal. Tell me, does adultery come to you as easily as lyin'?"

She gasped softly. "You saw me with St. Pierre."

He tapped the gun's metal cylinder and more black powder spilled into the flask. "Really, an embrace before you even reach the cover of the trees? Not intelligent at all."

"Branch," she said, her voice trembling, "I can see what you must be thinking, but you're wrong. I—"

"Ah, playing the innocent? You do it *so* well," and he sneered the word, "Kathleen."

She closed her eyes. "You recognized him."

"Dances in the Night, St. Pierre, what's in a name? I'm curious, Kate—when he loves you, is he an Indian or a Creole? Is there a difference?"

"Branch, stop." Katie reached across the table and laid her hand on his forearm. "He brought me terrible news—"

He shook off her touch. "Really? Was it something about the land you sold him for a song? Or perhaps he told you he found another slut to bed, that he didn't need you anymore? Maybe that's why you returned here lookin' like hell."

"Branch, listen to me."

He looked at her then. For the first time since she entered the room, he allowed her to see the rage burning inside him. "Shut up. *You're* gonna listen to *me*."

He took the pin from the Paterson, and the barrel slipped into his hand. Then he slid the cylinder off the handle and set the gun's three pieces onto the table. "I'm gonna tell you a story," he said, the ice back in his voice. Dipping his rag into a pot of hot water, he picked up the Paterson's handle and began to wipe it clean. "Years ago, your dear friend, Shaddoe St. Pierre, financed the establishment of a land company using Steven Starr as front man. He arranged for people he trusted—you and your father—to file claims on the land he wanted as soon as it became available. That is, as soon as the Cherokees lost the war with the Texians. Then, when the mood suited him to return to Texas, he'd buy said property from his friends. The Indian would once again own his lands."

Using a second rag, Branch meticulously dried the Paterson's handle. "You told me this morning that someone had blackmailed your husband into dealing in counterfeit scrip. But," he said, putting down the handle and picking up a straight, thin stick, "what if that is a lie? What if your husband and your lover went further with this scheme of theirs? With the company set up already, why not expand their operation and milk a few settlers out of their money?"

His gaze was cold and impersonal as he said, "I think Starr and St. Pierre were partners in dealin' in phony scrip."

"No!" Katie shook her head furiously.

He shrugged, wrapping a strip of cloth around the tip of the stick and dipping it into the water. He rammed the wet rag through the gun barrel. "Suppose, then, that the partners had a fallin' out. Maybe over money—more likely their woman."

"Branch, stop this," Katie interrupted. "You have it all wrong!"

He ignored her, continuing to speak as he plunged the makeshift ramrod through the other end of the Paterson's barrel. "A government man was in the area lookin' for the counterfeiters. You told me earlier, my dear, that Steven Starr had a plan of how to deal with this phantom blackmailer." Branch wiped the gun barrel dry and set it on the table. "Could be," he drawled, "that in a scheme to double-cross his partner, Starr went to this agent and set up a trap. I know for a fact that the government agent moved to a farm near Nacogdoches a short while before he died." Lifting an eyebrow, he asked, "Could have been your farm, right, Mrs. Starr?"

Katie pushed to her feet. "I won't listen to any more of this. I can't, not now, not today. Shaddoe brought news, Branch."

Hearing the Cherokee's name on her lips strained the tenuous hold Branch had on his temper. Viciously, he snapped, "He may as well have brought you the clap for all I care. I've got some questions and, by God, you're gonna answer them."

"No!" She swiped at the cluster of lead balls, and as she ran to her bedroom they scattered, rolling off the table and rapping against the puncheon floor. Branch left them where they lay and quickly cleaned and dried the Paterson's cylinder. After coating the metal parts with bear oil, he reassembled and loaded the gun. Standing, he holstered both weapons and walked to the bedroom door.

She'd latched it. He kicked it open.

Katie stood at the window, peeking through the curtains, dressed in a dry chemise and drawers. A corset dangled from one hand.

Branch leaned casually against the splintered doorjamb, his arms crossed, and spoke as though the conversation had never been interrupted. "The way I figure it," he said, "is that Starr got caught in the teeth of his own trap. I've a notion you can tell me whether the agent was snared at the same time."

Tears glittered in her eyes as she looked over her shoulder. In a weary voice, she asked, "What do you want to know, Branch?"

"This morning you told me that this nameless black-mailer killed your husband and daughter. Was anyone else with them?" He stepped into the room, stalking her like a predator after his prey. "Did another man die that night?"

"Yes." She shut her eyes and her hand gripped the curtain. In a dry whisper, she said, "There was someone else. He'd been staying at the farm helping Steven. He was a carpenter."

"No, he was land commissioner for the Republic. His name was Robert Garrett, and he'd come to East Texas to investigate rumors of fraud connected with the Matagorda Bay and Texas Land Company."

"I didn't know. He said he had family in the government—" Katie's hand dropped to her side as she stiffened. A wild look entered her eyes. "A government man. You said you'd come here looking for the person who killed a government man!"

Branch moved closer. In a flat, cold voice, he said, "I came here lookin' for Rob Garrett's murderer. I've found him."

She swallowed visibly. "What are you saying, Branch?"

"I'm sayin' that your lover, Shaddoe St. Pierre, escaped the trap Steven Starr and Rob Garrett had set for him. I'm sayin' that your lover killed your husband and daughter. He killed my brother."

"Y . . . Your brother?" Katie's face blanched. "Mr. Garrett was your brother?"

He nodded curtly and reached for her, tracing the curve of her chin with his finger. "How does it feel, Kate, to know you've been bedding your daughter's murderer?"

"No! I promise you, Shaddoe didn't do it!" She shoved

his hand away and pushed past him, crossing the room. She stood at the foot of the bed, a hand grasping the footboard. Her head bowed, she murmured, "Oh, God, he was your brother."

Branch stepped toward her, the instinct to offer her comfort reflexive. But he stopped himself. *Hell, how can I feel sorry for her? She deserves any grief she gets. Besides, whether or not she actually cheated on Steven Starr, she damn well cheated on me.* "He's a dead man, you know, your Cherokee."

Katie looked up at him. "You plan to kill Shaddoe because you believe he killed your brother?"

"Among other things."

For a long moment she looked at him, and a myriad of emotions flashed across her eyes. Then she gave a rueful laugh and pointed toward one of his guns. "You may as well take care of it, here and now."

Branch fingered the Paterson's handle. "The Cherokee's at the inn?"

Katie squared her shoulders. Her tongue circled her lips as she drew a deep breath and exhaled it slowly. "No. Not Shaddoe. *I'm* the person you want. *I* shot Robert Garrett."

"What?" He stood still, his face a mask, but inside his chest a huge knot swelled. It took all his effort to draw a breath.

"I'm the one who shot your brother, Branch. But I had a good reason."

His heart pounded, pumping ice-cold rage to every inch of his body. With blurring speed, he moved, grabbing her and shoving her onto the bed. Looming over her, he spat a vile curse and said flatly, "Let it go, Katie. You can't save your Indian with your lies."

"You think I'd lie about something like this?" she cried.

"I think you'd do anything to save your lover."

A single tear slid down her cheek. "You're my lover, Branch," she swore vehemently. "I love *you!*"

His breath hissed between his teeth, and his chest heaved with the force of his wrath. Then he gave a short, bitter laugh. "Me and how many others, Katie Starr?" His callused hand slipped beneath her chemise and roughly cupped her breast. "God, woman, I hate what you do to me; I hate what you make me feel. I look at you and I want you and it makes me sick."

Katie flinched at his words. Dear Lord, it hurt. Why, she wondered, had she allowed herself to love him? Hadn't she learned from experience—the wrenching, devastating pain of losing those she loved? And tonight her loss was doubled. She'd lost her father and now her husband. She saw it in his face—in the disgust so plainly visible in his hard, topaz eyes and in the desire he could not hide.

Branch would leave her.

Damn him.

His lips descended on hers hot and wild. She responded with a whimper—of protest or passion she didn't know—and he used the moment to take her mouth with his tongue.

Burying her hands in his thick hair, Katie pulled him against her with a savagery to match his own. She ached. She burned. She wanted him, this one last time.

With a fluid motion, Branch stripped off her clothing. They rolled and groped and groaned, at war as much as at love. He pulled away and she lay watching him, struggling to breathe and embracing the naked intensity in his eyes. His fingers tore at his shirt and then at the buttons of his pants. The magnificence of the body revealed as he peeled away his clothing burned a picture in her mind, and she knew she'd never forget this man—the look of him, the scent of him, the taste of him.

His knee parted her legs, and as he probed at her, the words burst from her lips, "Branch, I love you so."

He froze. His eyes glittered with fury as he said in a guttural voice, "Sex." He entered her with a surging, driving thrust. "That's all it is. The same as I could get over at The Mansion of Joy."

For just a moment, she believed him. Pain lanced her. Then she felt the pounding of his pulse beneath her hands.

"No," Katie said, lifting her legs to hold him. "It's more than that and you know it."

He rode her hard and she lifted her hips, meeting him, in a primitive rhythm. On and on it went, until she was beyond hearing or seeing, only feeling. As he spilled himself inside her and she trembled with the force of her own release, Katie knew that never before had love been so right or so bittersweet.

When his body relaxed against her, while he was still too drained for anger, Katie explained, "The cabin was on fire, Branch, and Mr. Garrett went inside to save my baby. He burned, Branch. He was in so much pain and dying so horribly. He asked me to shoot him; he begged me."

For a long moment, Branch lay still, his head resting against her chest. Then, in silence, he rolled from the bed and dressed. At the door he turned. "You killed my brother. You betrayed me, Katie Starr."

The rain fell in torrents as he left her.

❧ CHAPTER 16 ❧

*B*RANCH STARED at the flickering candle-light and thought of parlor chairs and a horsehair sofa. He saw a marble-topped table with a single sheet of parchment lying on top—a bond.

Three months ago today. The anniversary of a travesty—a wedding that was not a wedding.

He smirked and raised his glass of French brandy in toast to the bayberry-scented candles.

"Britt, Britt, darling," a feminine voice spoke from the doorway, "Father Garrett is asking for you to join us in the salon."

Branch continued to stare at the gleaming brass candelabra, the only source of light in the library, but he answered in his most civilized tone of voice. "Please tell him I'll be right there, Eleanor."

Her heels clicked against the marble floor as she retreated down the hallway. Ah, Eleanor, his first girl. He had loved her with the hot fire of youth, with the idealism of innocence. He'd humbled himself, begged for her love only to lose it to the one who took everything. Lovely Eleanor had married his brother.

Branch swigged the brandy and lifted the decanter, intent on refilling his crystal glass. Yes, Eleanor. She was as beautiful today as when he first met her. Blond and tall and graceful, she played the part of Riverrun's lady superbly. And now she was a widow.

Widows. What cunning creatures. Aptly named. Eight legs to crawl over a man, distract him with tantalizing touches, then kill him with a bite.

227

The last drops of brandy wept from the neck of the decanter into his mouth. He took pleasure in the ill-mannered act of forgoing his glass—a decidedly ungentlemanly thing to do.

He was nothing these days if not a true Southern gentleman. Wealth, power, prestige, a beautiful woman on his arm—he had it all. Branch swayed and steadied himself by catching a corner of the desk.

He wasn't drunk. No self-respecting South Texas planter allowed himself to demonstrate the effects of overindulgence. Now that he had been named his father's heir, he followed all the accepted precepts of behavior.

Including entertaining the idea of offering for the hand of the lovely Eleanor as expected by Hoss Garrett and all South Texas society.

With a harsh puff of breath, Branch blew out a candle. Why the hell not? He'd put them off for weeks now. And why? Because of some lingering desire for an auburn-haired liar? Because he left a job unfinished in Nacogdoches?

Unfinished, perhaps, but not unattended. He'd sent for William Bell. While Branch took his rightful place as heir to Riverrun—because, after all, he had met the letter of Hoss Garrett's law, he had found his brother's killer—he intended to send William to New Orleans to investigate a half-breed named Shaddoe St. Pierre.

William would bring him proof, and then he'd see to the Cherokee's destruction. Branch spent a good portion of his time envisioning how he'd accomplish the feat. Somewhere private, certainly, where he could administer one or two of those tortures the Comanches had perfected. He could see it now, St. Pierre staked out naked beneath the relentless Texas sun, his eyelids sliced off, maybe some ants feeding on honey applied to slashes across the most tender portions of his body.

Ah, what perfect revenge it would be. In the semidarkness, Branch held out a hand and bowed to the candles. "Mistress Kate, allow me to present St. Pierre, the man responsible for the fire that killed your daughter." Because of course, she would attend the celebration. It wouldn't be the same without her.

Branch stumbled, losing his balance. He fell into a chair. Still holding the decanter in one hand, he propped his elbow on his knee and rested his chin in the other hand. Damn the liar—the beautiful, hideous woman.

He'd told his father he'd destroyed his brother's killer, and he had, after a manner. He'd raped her. Hadn't he? He'd tried to do it. He'd wanted to. She was a slut, and she'd killed his brother. Except, when Branch remembered that last time with Katie Starr, he was afraid that he'd loved her instead.

Love. Branch snorted. She threw the word around as much as she threw around her body. Damn her for saying she loved him. Damn himself for believing her.

I came so close to loving her. Branch's chin slipped from his palm, and he slowly lifted his head to stare unseeing across the room. He shuddered. He must truly be drunk to be thinking such thoughts. Katie Starr was a woman he was lucky to be rid of. Eleanor and all the dreams of his youth awaited him in the salon just a few doors down the hall. Finally, after all these years.

The hell of it was, he didn't want Eleanor. He hadn't wanted a woman since he left his Sprite.

Damn the witch.

Branch heaved a sigh. King Hoss was growing impatient. Required grandchildren, he did. Male grandchildren. The two daughters Rob had sired didn't count. Boys were needed to secure the reuniting of Riverrun with Eleanor's daddy's plantation bordering theirs. Stubborn Britt must perform his obligation.

"Hell. Why not." Branch rose unsteadily to his feet. He caught sight of a ceramic egg sitting on the desk and remembered mornings spent gathering chicken eggs and hauling water. With a curse, he flung the empty decanter at the ornament, knocking it from the table. Both pieces shattered as they hit the ground.

He blew out the candles one by one. Then, crunching the pieces of glass beneath his boots, hard and empty and fragmented like the crystal decanter, Branch left the library. He made his way to the parlor to do his duty and offer his hand.

His heart was no part of the deal.

What use was something broken?

Martha Craig lowered herself gratefully into the rocking chair that sat on the porch of Gallagher's Tavern and Travelers Inn. Closing her eyes and resting her head against the back of the chair, she waved a green silk fan in front of her face and sighed. It was hot this afternoon and sticky. Muggy. What she wouldn't give for a nice summer shower to cool things off a bit.

Hearing the creak of approaching wheels, she cocked open one eye and watched a chaise pull up to Katie's kitchen. "There's more than weather needin' to be chilled hereabouts," she observed, wrinkling her nose with disgust. Sheriff Strickland descended from his carriage and knocked on Katie's door.

The man was on the prowl. At least three times a week he drove out here from town and pestered poor, vulnerable Katie. He claimed he felt responsible, considering Kincaid had been his deputy before he up and disappeared. At first, Katie had turned Strickland away, but more and more she accompanied him on excursions into the country, and on two separate Sundays he'd escorted her into Nacogdoches to church.

Martha was worried. Katie had disregarded all her warnings, saying that the sheriff offered simple friendship. Certainly, Martha thought. Like the fox knockin' on the henhouse door wants to be friends.

She fanned herself faster as she observed Katie greet Jack Strickland at her door. The girl should have made the trip to New Orleans with Mr. St. Pierre, as he had asked. Now there was a good man, a real friend for her little dearling. He had no evil intentions on his mind; he'd made that much clear to Martha when she'd challenged him shortly after Mr. Branch's departure.

She had stopped St. Pierre one morning on his way to Katie's kitchen and ordered him to accompany her into

Gallagher's parlor. There she had told the Creole that although she liked him, he was about as much good for her Katie as a sore tooth. The poor thing was vulnerable, grieving as she was over the loss of her father.

Martha had admitted that, truth be told, Katie and Mr. Branch suffered a spat, but such things happen all the time with newlyweds. And while it might serve Mr. Branch right to return and find his place taken by another, Martha, in good conscience, could not allow it to transpire.

By then, St. Pierre was holding himself ramrod straight, his expression fierce. "Mrs. Craig," he'd said, "I assure you I have no designs upon Mrs. Kincaid. Friendship is all I offer or request."

Martha had believed him. She'd yet to meet a man who could lie to her face and not falter in the doing. It was the mother in her, she believed. The way she folded her arms across her bosom and looked over the rims of her spectacles appealed to the boy in every man and made him feel as if he were lying to his mama.

St. Pierre had not lied, but he wasn't around to help, either. It was simply a crying shame that his grandfather had summoned him to Louisiana at this particular time. As Martha watched Katie allow Strickland into her home, she repeated aloud, "A cryin' shame."

Martha wasn't any happier two days later when Jack Strickland arrived at Gallagher's to collect Katie for Sarah Jane Abernathy's wedding. The sheriff arrived driving a two-person chaise, rather than the larger carriage he usually drove, thereby foiling Martha's plan to interrupt his sinful scheme by playing chaperon.

"That man is up to no good," she grumbled to Katie as the women rose from the swing on Gallagher's porch.

"Now, Martha, you just hush," Katie replied as she lifted a hand and waved at the sheriff. "I'm well and truly tired of your dire predictions. Mr. Strickland is as fine a gentleman as I've ever met."

"Fine like a firefly in the butter churn is fine."

"Martha," Katie scolded. But she couldn't say too much because, in truth, Martha was right. Jack Strickland was courting her. Katie knew it, and she was indulging in a little feminine thrill at the notion. This handsome, debonair man had taken a shine to her, regardless of her questionable marital status. His flattery, the simple gifts he gave her, and especially the respect with which he treated her were balms to her battered spirit. She thoroughly enjoyed these stolen moments spent with a man who appreciated her.

It was such a change from being with Branch Kincaid.

She'd been up front with the sheriff, telling him right off that she considered herself a married woman. That he didn't seem to set any more store in her marriage bond than had Branch didn't surprise or trouble her much. Men were just naturally ignorant about some things. As long as Jack Strickland was willing to accept the limits she put on their friendship, she'd enjoy his company. Despite Martha Craig's grousing.

The drive to the Abernathy farm was a pleasant one, the summer afternoon unseasonably cool with a light breeze blowing from the northeast. Once a flash of white in the woods caught their attention, and they looked closely to see the fluffy white tails of a doe and her fawn disappear into the forest.

Conversation centered on Strickland's family back in the States, something Katie had learned over the past weeks was always a favorite topic of the sheriff's. Today he related a particularly amusing story involving his grandfather, the senator, and former President Van Buren. Watching the smooth, expressive hand movements he employed to punctuate his speech, Katie wondered if he'd touch a woman with such flare. She recognized that with little effort on her part, she could easily find out.

That the thought even occurred to her further proved just how badly Branch had damaged her feminine sensibilities.

You'd best beware, Katie Kincaid, she told herself as they arrived at the Abernathys'. Human nature being what it was, she wouldn't be the first woman to seek solace in another's arms while suffering from rejection by the one whom she loved.

A crowd of people waited in front of the bride's family's dog-run style cabin. Having drawn close enough to make out faces, Strickland muttered, "I thought the Abernathys were Methodists."

"Baptist, actually," Katie replied, fighting a sudden attack of nausea. "Oh, Jack," she added, "I don't believe I'm up to facing the likes of him."

Reverend T. Barton Howell and a goodly number of his goodly flock congregated to one side of the yard. A full thirty minutes before the wedding was due to start, he was warming up the crowd with a dose of hellfire and damnation.

Strickland took Katie's hand in his and gave it a comforting squeeze. "Don't concern yourself with the preacher, sweetheart. I'll make certain he stays out of your way."

Katie noted his use of the endearment, but she didn't fuss at him about it. His reassuring touch and soothing voice were too welcome at the moment. She smiled at him. Maybe I should forget Branch Kincaid, she thought, gazing into Strickland's somber dark eyes filled with compassion and strength. After all, there were times when a woman needed a man—and not just those times when she wanted a man. Instances like now, when half of East Texas would turn their heads and look at her, their minds busily making comparisons between today's wedding and her own, minds deliberating the chances of Sarah Jane's bridegroom hanging around longer than had Katie's husband.

Strickland helped her from the chaise, his hand lingering at her waist longer than was necessary, as one of Sarah Jane's five brothers approached. "Missus Kincaid, am I glad you're here," he said, taking off his hat and wiping a sweaty brow. "Sarah's pitchin' a regular fit, and, well, since Ma is gone and we have no other womenfolk, the boys and I are in a fix. We thought that with circumstances bein' what they are, you might just have a special understandin' you could offer our sister."

His jaw hardened as he continued. "This weddin' is gonna happen no matter what. We'd be much obliged if you could get Sarah to attend without bein' hog-tied and gagged."

"I'll be glad to see what I can do," Katie said, turning a questioning look upon her escort.

Strickland nodded. "Go right along, Miz Katie. While you're busy, I'll have a look at that squeak in my buggy's right wheel." He rested his hand against the chaise as he added, "I'll be right here if you need me."

"Thank you, Jack." His support warmed her as she followed the Abernathy brother inside the cabin. It helped her see her way through the next few minutes with the babbling bride.

Sarah Jane was barely seventeen, a beautiful girl with round brown eyes and springy blond curls. Taller than Katie, but with just as many curves, her only protection from silver-tongued men had been the presence of five burly brothers.

Obviously, upon at least one occasion, the brothers had been lax in their duty. Sarah Jane's apron strings were riding high, and her groom awaited the nuptials out in the shed, tied and under the aim of a double-barreled shotgun.

After a few hugs and bucket of tears, Katie discovered that Sarah Jane wasn't opposed to marrying the father of her child, she feared being made to look the fool before all her friends and neighbors when her brothers dragged a protesting groom before the preacher.

"Now, Sarah Jane," Katie said, patting the younger girl's knee. "Not to worry, I know just how to settle your fears. I've a wedding gift for you that I guarantee will have that man stepping lively toward the altar. I'll be back in a few moments, and while I'm gone, why don't you see to getting out of that pretty dress. I've something for you to wear."

A short time later, the bride, once again dressed but now glowing with happiness, listened with pleasure to the lilting sounds of the wedding music the fiddler played outside the cabin,

Inside the storage shed, one Abernathy pointed the shotgun while another glowering brother untied the bridegroom's hands and handed him a couple of coins and a note.

Morsey Johnston, Peddler by Profession, frowned as

he unfolded the sheet of paper. Then as he read, a slow
smile spread across his face. Soon he was whistling,
brushing dirt from his jacket, and straightening his tie.

Suspicious, one of the Abernathys swiped the note
from his hands and read: "Felicitations on your upcoming
marriage. Included with this note is payment for my purchase this day from a certain trunk in your wagon. It is my
gift to you and your bride. I chose the purple. I think the
color suits Sarah Jane quite well. I'd have made this payment in person, but I am helping Miss Abernathy dress for
the wedding. (Signed) Katie Kincaid."

The ceremony went off without a hitch, considering
that Reverend Howell accepted full credit for saving the
two "wicked souls" from the "fires of hell" for "indulging
in fleshly sin." Jack Strickland stood at Katie's side during
the service, taking her hand as Morsey and Sarah Jane repeated their vows.

The newly wedded couple led off the dancing, and
Katie and her escort quickly joined them. She had a mar-
velous time; Jack was protective and courteous and ever-
the-gentleman. Katie pointedly turned her back on a
disapproving trio of matrons, Martha Craig and the Racine
sisters, and basked in the sheriff's devoted attentions.

It wasn't until she returned home and bid Jack
Strickland good-bye with a sweet, tender kiss—their
first—that doubts began to plague her.

She couldn't keep this up. It wasn't fair to either the
sheriff or to herself. Until she was informed otherwise, she
remained a married woman. Branch had yet to divorce her.
She could not, in good faith, continue to encourage Sheriff
Strickland's attentions.

She didn't love the man. She couldn't. There was no
room in her heart. Dusk fell, bringing with it an attack of the
nausea she suffered nightly. Yes, it was time to be honest
with her suitor. Having bent over a basin and lost her supper,
Katie groaned, "Branch Kincaid, this is all your fault."

Riverrun's Big House rose majestically atop a bluff above
the Brazos River. With three stories plus a captain's walk,

the red-bricked house looked as though it belonged along
Louisiana's River Road. Six huge columns supported a
portico, and all the wood trim gleamed a pristine white.

Ornate gardens surrounded the family home. Rose beds
filled open spaces while shade-loving plants hugged the
bases of live oak trees. Red amaryllis lined brick walk-
ways. Pink crepe myrtle formed a hedge along the side
fence, and bois d'arc separated the decorative landscape
from the more functional vegetable and herb garden near
the kitchen.

Branch took a turn in the garden after dinner, his
fiancée on his arm. Damask roses ringed the gazebo, their
fragrance spicing the evening, while from the slave cabins
came the sound of a woman's voice singing a churning
song to charm the butter into coming.

Branch's gaze roamed over the lady at his side.
Eleanor was a stunning woman, with her big green eyes
and those soft golden curls. Moonlight complimented her
creamy complexion, and the blue silk dress she wore displayed her curves to perfection.

The promise of youth had been fulfilled in maturity.
The children Eleanor had borne his brother had ripened
her tall, willowy figure without marring its perfection.
Branch wondered about her daughters, twelve and nine re-
spectively and attending school in the east. Did they take
after their mother or their father?

He regretted their absence from the plantation at his
homecoming. He liked children, and he didn't approve of
sending such little women off to a distant place to live.
Nor did he understand the reasoning behind such a decision. He wanted family around him here at Riverrun.

Unbidden, the image of twinkling blue eyes replaced
green and the petal-soft hand on his arm became one red-
dened and callused from work. Dammit, he thought, leave
me alone, Katie Starr.

Eleanor prattled on concerning her plans to redecorate
the suite designated to be theirs upon their marriage. She
bemoaned the time required to import costly, but necessary, French fabrics, and pouted prettily over Branch's re-

fusal to take her to Paris on a honeymoon. Eleanor Garrett was the ideal of a Southern planter's wife, beautiful, courteous, and virtuous.

She bored him to tears.

Conversation with Eleanor consisted of puppy-dog admiration and plaintive entreaties for material goods, very nearly a repetition of their discourses years ago. Branch remembered that at one time he'd thought her manner quite enchanting. Her empty-headed worship had boosted his pride and appealed to his vanity. But in the weeks he'd been home, especially since bowing to his father's pressure for the engagement, he'd discovered that what had attracted the boy at sixteen held no allure for a man of thirty-four.

Eleanor gave him a shy smile, and sardonically Branch returned it. The woman was nice but dumb as a box of rocks. How could he have missed it before? Of course, back then he'd not been overly concerned with any woman's intellect. Her looks today were more than enough to quicken a man's blood, and back when they'd both been sixteen, well, she'd kept him hot enough to melt leather.

But now, as her babbling caused him to wonder if there was *anything* in her head, he recalled against his will another woman's quick wit and intelligent conversation. Stimulating conversation. Oh, Lord, how in the hell could he face the rest of his life married to Eleanor? How could he face the rest of his life without Katie Starr?

Damn, I keep forgettin' how much I hate the woman. "Let's go inside, Eleanor," he said. "I'd enjoy hearing you play the piano this evening." A lie, he admitted, but memories of a certain deceitful innkeeper occurred more often outdoors, beneath the moon and stars, than in the ornate rooms of Riverrun.

Hoss Garrett awaited them in the salon. He and Branch took their seats as Eleanor shuffled through a stack of sheet music for the serenade the elder Garrett requested. As sound swelled in the room, Branch fought the melancholy quickly becoming a regular companion of his evenings.

Days weren't a problem. He loved the work of being

a planter, and daylight hours kept him busy. Summer was time to plant a second crop of corn and black-eyed peas, to set the women to weeding the potatoes and cleaning the debris from wells. June was the month to cut the grains: barley, oats, and wheat. Branch worked beside the field hands from dawn till dusk, relishing the labor of farming the land he'd coveted for so many years.

Evenings, however, were a different matter. The contentment he knew during the day fled with the coming of dark. As much as he enjoyed the work of being a planter, he hated the social baggage that came along with it. Social obligations bored him, the people bored him. The rules of proper behavior especially bored him. Sitting in a parlor listening to piano music wasn't nearly as fulfilling as he had once imagined it to be.

It certainly wasn't as gratifying as lying naked beneath the stars atop a woman.

Dammit, she's back again. Branch did his best to concentrate on the music. It was during these hours, when his body rested and recovered from the day's toil, while he spent time with his father's friends and the woman soon to be his wife, that Katie Starr haunted his thoughts. Tonight, while Eleanor demonstrated her considerable talent at the keyboard in a room where summer slipcovers sheathed the furnishings, Branch battled the memory of the swishing rhythm of cotton cards accompanied by the creak of a rocker against a puncheon floor on a winter's night.

Ah, hell, Sprite. Why did it all have to be a lie?

A knock on the open salon door interrupted his musings. "How about some hospitality for a couple of visitors?" William Bell and Branch's cousin, Chase Garrett, stood just outside the room.

The shroud of discontent lifted from Branch's shoulders. William, finally. "Well, William Bell, I never figured you for one to travel with the likes of Chase Garrett."

"I'm smarter than that. I found him on the drive and figured it best to bring him in before he started stealing chickens from the henhouse."

Chase grinned. "Chickens! Why, I was after the horses!"

After a period of polite social discourse, Eleanor said her good nights, and the gentlemen adjourned to the library for some serious drinking.

"I have to say, Branch," Chase commented, accepting a branch and cigar from his cousin, "you certainly look different among these surroundings than you did the last time we met."

"His name is Britt," Hoss Garrett interjected, his brows knitted as he poured his own drink.

Ignoring his father, Branch grinned. "That was just about a year ago, wasn't it? Down near the Rio Grande?"

Chase nodded and then shook his head in wonderment. "I couldn't believe it. Here I was shakin' in my boots because I'd run across a Mexican patrol on the wrong side of the river, and up comes this fellow dressed in a serape and spoutin' Spanish like a native. He throws his arm around my shoulder, a pair of golden eyes gleam from beneath a sombrero, and he says, 'Howdy, cuz.'"

Branch laughed. "The patrol leader, Captain Monterro, and I are old amigos—met up during the war. We were spyin' on each other's army when he snuck up behind me. Right as he was fixin' to put a bullet in my skull, a rainstorm upstream flooded the arroyo we were lyin' in. Ended up, I saved his life and we got to be friendly."

The spoon Hoss used to stir his drink clanked against his glass. "You fought in the War for Independence?"

Although the smile remained fixed on Branch's face, the amusement faded from his eyes. "I was twenty-five when war broke out. What do you think I did, Hoss, run for the Louisiana border?"

"No," the elder Garrett said gruffly, "I knew you were in the army. I didn't realize you were so far south."

Branch turned a mirthless smirk toward William. "Probably hoped I'd manned a cannon at the Alamo."

"Goddammit!" Hoss shouted, "Listen, boy . . ."

Chase held up his hand. "Hold on a minute, folks. I may be family, but I'm not in the mood to hear old family squabbles tonight. I'm glad to see you"—he slid a look at Hoss and added—"Britt. Surprised, but pure-dee pleased. Tell me, how'd you happen to come home?"

Well, Branch thought, if he wanted to avoid family squabbles, he chose the wrong subject to pick. He sipped his drink and said, "I'll let William and Hoss clue you in, cuz."

William stretched out in his chair, crossing his boots at his ankles. "I can't say I know the whole of it. I made a trip to New Orleans after delivering the money that Regulator demanded. I can't say I know how your search has progressed."

"What search?" Chase asked.

Hoss lifted his drink as if toasting and declared, "Britt discovered the bastard who killed Robert."

William slapped his knee. "I knew you could do it, Branch, uh, Britt. Who was it? That Regulator man, Colonel Moorman? He's a slimy weasel for certain."

"No," Hoss said, clipping the end of his cigar with a pair of scissors. "Fella by the name of Starr, may he roast in hell."

William Bell's gaze locked on Branch. "Starr?" He dragged on his cigar, then exhaled a cloud of woodsy-scented smoke. "Starr?" he repeated.

Branch nodded. He tipped his glass, finishing its contents in a single gulp.

"I imagine you killed him," Chase said, noting the tension between William and Branch.

Hoss came up behind Branch, clapping a hand on his shoulder. "Won't tell me how he did it. Must've been pretty grisly."

Silently, William Bell demanded an answer.

Branch said, "I destroyed the person who killed my brother. What's it matter how I went about it?"

"Ugly business," Will observed, his expression unreadable.

The bourbon soured in Branch's stomach. "Damned ugly."

Soon after Hoss retired for the night, Branch turned to Chase and William and said, "How about we walk down to the river and pretend to fish while we set about gettin' drunk."

Chase jumped to his feet, grabbed a bottle with each hand, and said, "I'm overdue for one. After you, cuz."

In the years he'd been away, the course of the Brazos River had shifted, and as they made their way down the bluff to the water, Branch felt a twinge of annoyance that Chase, not he, knew the path to a fishing hole. None of the three men bothered with a pole. Chase built a small fire on the sandy shore and observed, "Why do I get the feeling like I've come in the middle of a nasty little story?"

Dragging a dried piece of driftwood from the edge of the bank back to the fire, Branch laughed harshly and said, "Because you have."

"A very nasty story," Bell added.

Chase fed a stick to the fire. "Would you two rather I leave?"

"Branch?" William asked.

"No. It's all right. In fact, if you've got some free time, I might just need an extra pair of hands, depending on what William learns."

William tipped a bottle to his mouth and shuddered as the whiskey burned down his throat. "Ah, I've an idea I'll soon be making another trip. Did I understand you earlier, Branch? About Rob?"

Branch snapped the stick he held in two. "Katie did it," he stated flatly.

"No."

"Yeah."

"I don't believe it!"

"There's more to it than that, though."

"Hold on a minute," Chase said, grabbing the bottle of bourbon from William's hand. "Y'all are losin' me. Are you saying a woman killed Rob?"

Briefly, Branch told them the story of the fire. When he finished, Chase was the first to speak. "Hell, Branch. I'd have done the same thing, under the circumstances. Did you really hurt her like you told Uncle Hoss?"

Branch was silent for a long minute. "Katie Starr may be a woman, but she fights meaner than any man I've known. Anything I do to her, she has comin' her way. I didn't kill her, if that's what you're askin'. I didn't even beat her, even though I wanted to."

Choosing his words carefully so as not to disclose any of the more personal aspects of the situation, Branch told Chase and William why he suspected that the blackmailer responsible for the fire in which Rob Garrett was burned was named Shaddoe St. Pierre.

When he finished, Chase gave a long, slow whistle. "Hell and Texas, it makes sense, cuz. What do you want us to do?"

Branch fed dry leaves into the fire. "William, I want you to return to New Orleans. The Gallaghers said something once about Shaddoe livin' with a grandfather in New Orleans. Marceaux ... Marcil, some French name beginning with *M*. Anyway, find out who this fellow is and where he's been. If you can place him any one place at any one time since 1839, I want to know it."

"Certainly, Branch. I'll do my best. When do you want me to leave?"

"Well, I know you've been traveling, but the sooner ..."

William held up his hand. "I'll leave tomorrow."

"Thank you, William. I owe you."

"What about me?" Chase asked.

"If William finds proof that a Creole named Shaddoe has been doing business in New Orleans during the times he claimed to have been with the Cherokee, I'll have a solid piece of information upon which I can build my case against him. I may need you, Chase, to return with me to Nacogdoches. I'm too well-known there now to be of much use in spyin' on St. Pierre, and also, I left a little unfinished business there concerning another scoundrel named Trident. I could use an unknown face assisting me."

Chase nodded his acceptance, then he frowned and asked, "One thing, though, Branch. Why don't you just go shoot him? Why bother with proof?"

Branch stood and looked out over the water, his back to the other men. Emotions warred within him—pride, anger, pain—and his sense of honor. The night breeze created ripples across the top of the slow-moving water, crickets chirped, and from the opposite bank a bullfrog croaked. Branch struggled to put his thoughts into words. "I want the man who set fire to the Starr farm dead. I want the man who sliced open Steven Starr's gut punished. Those two acts have earned retribution, and I could administer it with clear conscience."

Bell slapped a mosquito on his arm. "And St. Pierre?"

"Dead. I want him stabbed, shot, and hanged. I want the bastard to die hard. Only it's not because I know for certain that he's the man responsible for my brother's death."

William and Chase exchanged a look at the passion in Branch's voice. Silently, they waited.

Low and raspy, he confessed, "I want to kill him because of Kate. He took what was mine. But as much as I want to, I can't kill the man for that."

Chase stood and walked to stand beside his cousin, handing him the bottle. "And after we prove he's the blackmailer who set that fire, then you can kill him?"

Branch guzzled the bottle. "Yep."

When the bottle was empty and the fire smothered, the three men climbed the path up the bluff. As they topped the hill, they walked abreast, Branch in the middle, back toward the Big House. Carrying the empty bottle at his side, William turned to Branch and asked, "While I'm doing the footwork in New Orleans, what will you be doing?"

Kincaid smiled drunkenly and flung an arm across both men's shoulders.

"What'll I be doin'? Well, gettin' married, of course."

⚞ CHAPTER 17 ⚟

*T*HE CHICKEN SQUAWKED and lunged toward the invader. Katie squealed as she snatched the egg from the nest and lifted her bleeding hand to her mouth to suck at the wound. Tears shimmered in her eyes as frustration boiled in her soul, and she backed away from the hen and out of the henhouse. Then, when the rooster looked at her and loosened a boisterous crow, she drew back her hand and sent the egg sailing, straight and true toward the henhouse wall, where it landed with a splat.

A second egg from her basket flew at the chopping log, a third at a fence post at the hog pen. She shot a fourth against the barn wall, where it smashed and hung for a moment before pieces of tan shell flicked to the ground and the broken yellow yoke mixed with the slimy membrane to slide slowly down the wall.

Katie sank with the egg. She dropped to her knees in the red dirt of the farmyard, cradled the scratched hand to her chest, and wept.

It wasn't starting out to be a very good day.

She was alone at the inn. The two guests they'd hosted overnight had departed at first light, and Rowdy had taken Martha and Andrew into Jefferson to pick up supplies. They'd not return until tomorrow. Katie had total freedom to lie in the mud like a wide-snouted hog and wallow in self-pity. So she did.

She was pregnant and alone. Her poor baby wouldn't have a father. For a time she'd been able to put the problem from her mind, but no longer. Time moved swiftly,

and soon she'd pass the halfway point of her pregnancy.
She could ignore the issue no longer.

She lowered her hand till it lay across her womb and
despite her gloomy state, a faint smile touched her lips.
She was expanding, just a little, but enough that she could
tell. Her body was changing to nurture the life growing inside it, the baby she already loved.

It wouldn't be long before she felt the tiny swells and
kicks that announced the little one's presence. Katie
couldn't wait. She remembered the day she felt Mary Margaret quicken. At first, she'd not known what the funny
bump in her stomach was, but then, as it happened a second time, a joy that eclipsed any she'd known before had
filled her.

The first hello with one's child was a moment a
mother would always remember. The memory stayed with
her, even throughout the good-byes.

The smile on Katie's face slowly died. Other memories
remained throughout good-byes. Branch was never far
from her thoughts.

Where was he? What was he doing? For that matter,
who was he? She remembered their last night together and
his revelation that Rob Garrett had been his brother. At the
time, she'd not questioned the difference in their last
names. Now she wondered at the relationship between
them. Were they half brothers? Was his name really
Kincaid or Garrett? It could be Smith or Simpson or Santa
Anna for all she knew.

Wiping the tears from her cheeks with her fingertips,
she sniffed and wondered, Who does that make me? The
man's my husband. What's my name? What will be my
baby's name?

Maybe she should go after him.

The idea was not a new one; Katie had been considering it off and on since realizing she carried Branch's child.
She'd pondered other, more palatable solutions, even going so far as to write to Shaddoe in New Orleans and ask
him to perform the love spell that calls a wayward lover
home. He must have chosen not to honor her request, or
else he had and it just hadn't worked, because she'd yet to

see Branch Kincaid ride up to her door, proclaim his love, and solve her predicament.

She had to find a father for her baby. She'd face hell itself to see that this child lived a cheerful, protected life—she'd sworn as much at her daughter's grave—and the best way to ensure that happiness was to provide the little one with a large and loving family. It was time for Katie to make a choice.

If she hunted down Branch, she gambled more than the chance he'd deny his promise to accept the marriage if a child resulted from their time together. She risked losing the child to the powerful Garrett family. It was her greatest fear—that they'd take her baby and send her away and she'd have no way to fight.

Her other option was to explain her circumstances to Sheriff Strickland and hope that he'd reiterate his recent offer of marriage. She didn't love the man, but he was kind and gentle. If he could accept another man's child as his own—which Katie honestly didn't feel too certain about—he'd make a good father for her baby.

Branch Kincaid or Jack Strickland? This was her choice. "By the end of the week," she promised herself. "I'll make up my mind before the end of the week."

Baking worked the melancholy from her system and by midmorning she had wheat bread rising on her worktable and a plum-and-peach pie was almost ready to pull from the oven. As she bent over to peek into the oven and check the crust, she felt a warm breeze stir her skirt and encircle her ankles.

Just like before, only warm not cold. Her pulse thundered as she straightened, praying, her eyes squeezed shut as she backed up into a solid wall of muscle. Hands clasped her waist and jubilation grasped her heart. A smile burst across her face, and she whirled around to greet—

Jack Strickland.

Her heart sank to her knees. "Oh," she said. "Why, Sheriff, I didn't hear you come in."

He peered past her into the oven. "What are you baking, Miz Katie? It smells simply delicious."

She took a step sideways, and his hands fell away from her waist. "Pie," she said, tucking a stray strand of hair behind her ear. Why was she nervous? she wondered, slanting him a look as she walked to her worktable. Why was she more comfortable with the table between them?

"I must say, Miz Katie," Strickland said, making a show of sniffing the air around the fireplace, "I've never known a woman with such a talent for cooking."

She smiled wanly. "Thank you. Sheriff Strickland, I hesitate to admit this, but I don't remember making plans with you for today."

With a gentle smile, Strickland approached the table and pulled out a chair. He straddled it, just as Branch always had. Oh dear, Katie thought, is this some sort of heavenly message concerning the decision I must make? If so, what does it mean?

Strickland is nothing like Kincaid, she reassured herself, even as the sheriff helped himself to one of the morning's leftover biscuits. For one thing, Jack Strickland treated her with more gentleness than any man she'd ever known. The lawman was a classically handsome man with his coal black hair and soulful eyes. But that dimple in his chin softened rugged features and gave him a boyish look when he smiled.

He was smiling at her now. "Miz Katie, I have a confession to make. When I awoke this morning, I thought of you and, well, you're a beautiful woman and a pleasure to be with, but I found myself dreaming about your yeast rolls."

Katie punched down the bread dough and turned it onto her table to knead. Dryly she said, "You do say the nicest things to a woman, Sheriff Strickland."

His gaze was a gentle caress. "Please, Katie, I've asked you to call me Jack, and whenever I try to say the things I want to, you put me off."

Her brows knitted in a frown. "Jack, I'm sorry. It's simply so confusing for me. I've decided—well, never mind that for today. Tell me, why are you here? I know, it's more yeast rolls."

His gaze lingered on her bosom, something she'd never noticed him do before. Abruptly he said, "I've had news from home."

"Really?"

"Remember I told you my family's from Boston?"

Katie worked her bread dough and answered, "Of course, Jack, we've discussed it a time or two. Besides, a lady doesn't meet a United States congressman's son very often. It's not something she'd forget."

"I received a message from my father yesterday," Strickland said, spinning a plum on the table. "You see, Miz Katie, some time ago I was erroneously accused of committing a crime against a Bostonian gentleman. I was forced to flee to avoid undeserved punishment. After a brief period in New Orleans, I decided to come to Texas."

Katie stared at him with somber eyes. She knew what it was like to be unjustly accused. "Jack, you are one of many who've settled this country after leaving behind legal problems in the States. You needn't feel it is something you should confess. That's the biggest reason it's considered impolite in the Republic of Texas to ask a man where he came from."

"I'm not confessing here today, my dear. I'm explaining. My father sent word that the charges against me have been dropped. I'm free to go home."

"Why, that's wonderful." She beamed at him as she returned the bread dough to its bowl to rise a second time. Walking to the basin, she washed her hands as she said, "Your father must be so pleased." Then a sobering thought struck her. If he planned on returning home, she might not have to the end of the week to make her decision. Slowly, she said, "I guess that explains why you've visited me today. You've come to say good-bye."

Jack Strickland stood. "No, I've not." His expression was somber as he approached her, his hand held out for hers. "I'm here today to ask you to return with me to Boston. I've run out of time to pay you court. Marry me, my darling."

Katie dropped both his hand and the tea towel she car-

ried. Turning away from his entreating gaze, she walked to
the hearth and swung the metal arm away from the fire.
The aroma of cooking onions escaped into the room as she
lifted the lid from a pot of simmering stew. Using a
wooden spoon, she stirred the mixture and said, "Jack, this
is all so sudden."

He came up behind her and put his hands at her waist.
"Not sudden. I've asked you before, and you promised me
you'd think about it."

"But Boston! It's so far away. I'd have to leave
Gallagher's, and Martha." Katie's teeth worried her lower
lip. *She'd be leaving any chance she'd have of seeing
Branch again.*

The lid banged back onto the pot, and she returned the
stew to the fire. Strickland turned her around. With a finger, he tilted her chin and stared down into her eyes.
"You'll love my family, and my mother will be so pleased
that I've finally married. She's been wanting grandchildren
for years."

Oh, dear. Grandchildren. The baby. Katie bit back a
groan as he continued. "The Stricklands are powerful people in the northeast. We have wealth. I've watched you
with people, Katie, and you'll make a fine politician's
wife. My father is a congressman, my grandfather a senator. Now it's time for me to follow in their footsteps. Who
knows, maybe someday I'll even be President and you my
First Lady."

He kissed her then, with more passion than any of their
previous exchanges. Katie responded to him, more to buy
time than due to any desire he might have kindled.

"Jack," she said, ending the kiss and pulling away
from him. "So much stands between us. There's my marriage, for one thing."

He waved a hand, dismissing her objection. "It's nothing. A bond easily put aside."

"But there's more, Jack—"

He shook his head, and a predatory light entered his
dark eyes. "Katie, none of it matters. I want you. I've
wanted you for some time, now. I've been amazingly pa-

tient." His hands worked the buttons on his shirt, and he shrugged it off.

Katie's eyes widened. This man standing before her wasn't the Jack Strickland she'd contemplated loving. "Jack, stop it. You're scaring me."

He unbuckled his belt and stepped toward her. "I don't mean to scare you, sweetheart. I think maybe you need a little convincing as to how good it can be between us."

"No!" She jumped backward. At his sharp, angry look she showed him a tremulous smile. "I mean, uh, that is, Jack, I know the loving between you and me would be wonderful, but I'd rather wait—"

He didn't wait. He yanked her to him, taking her lips in a long, deep kiss, clamping his arms around her to halt her struggles. Katie could barely get her breath, and when his mouth finally left hers to trail wet kisses down her neck, she gasped for air.

Emotion flared to life inside her, but it wasn't desire. Katie got angry. She'd had enough of men acting like primitive beasts, beating their chests and howling at the moon in the need for a mate to sate their sexual desires. Heavens, if she'd wanted violence in her lovemaking, she'd have never let Branch go. He was a master at it, a genius. Intending to use the handiest weapon she had, Katie turned her head and opened her mouth to bite him.

She froze. There, right at eye level, on the inside of his left breast, was a tattoo. A three-pronged pitchfork set against a background of flames.

Katie stared at it. She shut her eyes, then looked at it again. Fear clutched her heart. *Oh, Lord.* She was transported back in time, to the night that continued to haunt her dreams. To the man whose life she had taken.

Rob Garrett lay dying. His tormented voice croaking, *No name. Pitchfork. Flames.*

A short, hysterical laugh escaped her. A kind and tender gentleman, Sheriff Jack Strickland. How could she have been so wrong?

Katie was in the arms of her daughter's killer.

His hand cupped her breast, kneading and pinching.

Oh, God, it hurt—clear through to her soul. A trembling began deep inside her, and she knew she must get away from him, now, before she screamed and betrayed herself.

But how? His hand tugged her blouse free of her skirt, and she shuddered at the touch of his fingers against the bare skin of her back. Her baby! Was she big enough yet that he'd notice? No, she didn't believe so; after all, he'd never touched her before.

He was touching her. *Oh, God, please!* She'd do anything to protect her baby, she'd lie with him if she must. Anything, just as long as her child remained a safe, hidden secret.

She'd have to take care not to retch.

Think, Katie! How? How do I get away from him? His heavy breaths lifted hackles on her neck. Bile rose in her throat, and she swallowed hard before attempting the only ruse that came to mind. She began to kiss him back.

Passionately, she pressed herself against him, rubbing and wiggling. "Oh, Jack," she sighed.

He lifted his head and smiled triumphantly, the male beast whose dominance has been assured. "I knew you'd be a hot bit of fluff," he said, dipping his hand down her drawers to cup and brace a bare buttock as he ground himself against her.

Now, the gamble. In her most provocative voice, she said, "Sheriff Strickland, you've convinced me. I find I fancy myself to be a politician's wife." At her words, he loosened his hold, and she yanked away from him, showing a saucy smile. She began a campaign of distraction. "Will we marry here or in Boston? It'd be nice for your family to attend, don't you think? Probably good politics, too—the handsome young candidate and his Southern belle."

Strickland's gaze lifted from her bosom to her mouth, and she found encouragement in the fact. He was listening to her. "Maybe the President could come! What do you think, Jack? Would President Polk come to our wedding?"

He wiped his mouth with the back of his hand. "Yes, I do believe he might. That's a wonderful idea, Katie. See, you'll make a grand political wife."

He moved to take her in his arms again, but she held up a hand. "What about my divorce? We must make certain that not a breath of scandal reaches Washington. It could be disastrous."

"I'll see to the divorce," Strickland said. "Don't worry. I will not allow anything to interfere with the future I have planned."

Please, Katie prayed, *let this work.* She sank into a chair at the kitchen's table and sighed heavily. "Then we'd best wait, Jack. One thing your political career cannot tolerate is a baby prior to nine months after the wedding." Pleasure or politics, had she read him right?

Jack frowned and picked his shirt up from the floor. "You are right, Katie. As much as it pains me, we'll wait until we're wed." He put his shirt on and flashed her the smile that less than an hour ago she had found so appealing. "I'll want to be on the road tomorrow, though, taking the fastest route to Boston."

She forced an answering smile. "I'll have my bags packed and waiting at dawn."

He kissed her once more before he left. She heard his carriage rattle on its way as she rushed to the basin and vomited.

Her first impulse was to flee. She went so far as to grab up a bag and stuff it with clothing and keepsakes. Better sense prevailed, and she left her bedroom and sat at her worktable, thinking, planning, and shelling peas. She always thought better with busy hands.

Three problems faced her: two immediate, one more distant but certainly as urgent. First, she must leave Gallagher's before Strickland returned. Second, she must see that the sheriff received the punishment she had envisioned for the killer of Steven and Mary Margaret Starr. And third, she must see to finding a father for the child she now carried.

Repeatedly as she considered her options, Katie snapped the end from a pea pod, yanked off the string, and gouged out the peas. She deliberated everything from running away and hiding, perhaps at Shaddoe's Le Cadeau d'Etoiles, to remaining right where she sat with a loaded shotgun pointed at the door. Glancing down at the mess of smashed green peas in the wooden bowl in front of her, Katie shoved away from the table. Frustration made for messy shelling.

She sighed as she made her decision. Of all the choices available to her, only one addressed all three of her concerns. One man could solve all her problems.

She'd leave a note for Martha up at the inn and tack another one to her front door for Strickland. Surely she could come up with some kind of excuse not to be here when he arrived. Then she'd go to Riverrun Plantation and find Branch Kincaid.

An immediate trip to Brazoria in South Texas would put her beyond Strickland's reach and solve her first predicament. If luck was with her, Branch would be at the Garrett family home, but if not, surely someone at Riverrun would know where to find him. She would explain what had happened—well, most of it, anyway—and he would realize that the major part of the blame for his brother's death lay at the sheriff's feet.

Together, she and Branch would see that the wheels of justice rolled right over Jack Strickland, thereby dealing with her second concern.

But the third, well, that was the thorniest of the bunch. If she burned a few red-onion peels for luck, maybe Branch would forgive her participation in Rob Garrett's death and believe her when she said she'd not betrayed him with Shaddoe.

Then she could tell him about the baby. She dare not risk it before she knew Branch would honor their marriage—the powerful Garrett family was too big a threat to an innkeeper's daughter. Katie still loved her husband, and she knew she could forgive his lack of faith if Branch could forgive her and accept her love and the child they had made together.

They could be a family. Her child would have a father. And, just perhaps, she would have Branch's love.

It was the grandest of all dreams.

Daybreak the next morning found Pretty Girl and her mistress headed south on the road toward Liberty. Traveling at a steady pace, Katie hoped to make Brazoria and Riverrun Plantation within the month.

She'd have a nice little belly growing by then.

Katie smoothed her skirt, unhappily aware of the idleness of the gesture. Over three weeks of hard traveling couldn't be so easily erased, and besides, after traveling in this open wagon all morning she'd be covered in road dust when she finally arrived at Riverrun. She might as well have ridden Pretty Girl straight from camp instead of going into town and catching a ride out to the plantation.

She winced and brushed a layer of dirt from the sleeve of her yellow gingham. She should have planned better, worn a traveling cloak, and changed into this dress just prior to arriving at the Garrett home. But she simply hadn't been thinking straight—the nerves rumbling around in her stomach demanded too much attention from her mind.

At least she'd thought to wear the yellow dress. Of the three she had packed in her bag, it alone had the fullness required to hide the signs of her advancing pregnancy. Even so, she'd have to be careful how she stood; it wouldn't do for a Garrett to get a good look at her from the side.

The driver interrupted her thoughts. "Missy, we'll be there directly."

"Wonderful," she replied, not thinking it wonderful at all. I can't believe I'm doing this, she thought. I'm going to meet the Garrett family and ask for their help. Really, I ought to be shot for even thinking of crossing Riverrun's boundary.

She swallowed hard as the wagon turned onto a road marked by two brick pillars. Mounted on each was a metal sign with raised letters that read *Riverrun*.

A hedge of Cherokee roses lined the road. "Where is it?" she asked the driver in a squeaky voice.

"The Big House? Why, it's two miles yet. The cane fields are off to the left, behind that stand of oaks. See, there be the slave quarters, look through that open space."

Katie caught a glimpse of a cluster of frame cabins, probably twenty by twenty feet, with brick chimneys.

The driver asked, "You seen a cane plantation before, Missy?" Katie shook her head, and he continued. "You'll have to look close to get a look-see at this'un. Hoss Garrett, he keeps it all hidden back amongst the trees, blacksmith's shop, the overseer's house, the carriage house, barn, stock pens—all of it. He don't want nothing distractin' from a visitor's first glimpse of the Big House."

Shortly, Katie understood Hoss Garrett's reasoning. "It's beautiful," she breathed. No wonder Mr. Garrett had spoken of his home with such love. On the west bank of the Brazos, the afternoon sun bathed the red-brick dwelling in shimmering light. A lump grew in Katie's chest as she realized what Rob had given up in his attempt to save her daughter.

For the first time, she looked forward to meeting Hoss Garrett. Perhaps she could find some way to convey her gratitude to the man whose son had died in violence that awful night. But first, she'd inquire after Rob's brother.

The road circled in front of the mansion, and as the driver pulled the wagon up to the front steps, he whistled. "Glory be, they've done a fine job of gettin' the gardens ready for this party tonight, that's for sure."

Katie whipped her head toward him. "Party?" she asked.

"Ain't that whatcha comin' out here for?"

"Oh, no. I didn't realize the Garretts were entertaining today."

The driver climbed out of the wagon, nodding as he did so. "Sho'nuff. Big dance here this evening. You know what? The whole top floor of that house is a ballroom. Fancy that, these rich folks are somethin' else." He walked to the wagon's side to assist Katie down from her perch.

She looked to the house with dismay. "I shouldn't have come."

"Well, you're here now," he said, "and I gotta get these things around to the kitchen. If you're ready to head back before me, hitch on around that way."

He climbed back into his seat, and with a click of the reins, the wagon squeaked round the drive. Katie took a deep breath, dusted off her skirts, and climbed the steps to the front porch.

A gentleman, not yet thirty, Katie guessed, answered her knock. With his dark hair and blue eyes, he looked so much like Rob Garrett that he took her breath away. "Come in, come in," he said. "We are so pleased you could join us. Actually, you're our first guest to arrive, so . . ."

"Excuse me, I'm afraid I'm not a guest. Well, that is, oh—" Flustered, Katie gave a quick toss of her head and said determinedly, "I've come to speak with Mr. Garrett. Mr. H. R. Garrett, if you please."

The young man's brow lifted in an amused slant. He ushered her into the house, where she marveled at the beauty of the long hallway. Baskets of flowers lined the walls leading to a circular staircase draped in garlands of magnolia blossoms.

"Oh, my goodness," Katie said, gazing around in awe. "How very beautiful everything looks."

"Really?" The young man scowled at the flowers. "I think it a bit overdone. Smells something like an undertaker's in here. Of course"—he grinned then, watching her with an absolutely wicked expression in his eyes—"now that *you're* here, the old place definitely holds more allure. Have we met before, Miss . . . ?"

Katie smiled at him. "Mrs., Mrs. Kincaid."

"Wouldn't you know." He exaggerated his sigh and shook his head. "I'm Chase Garrett, Mrs. Kincaid. Welcome to Riverrun. May I offer you a refreshment?"

"No, thank you. I—"

"Here, come into the parlor. I need something to drink even if you don't, Mrs. Kincaid. Your beauty leaves me positively parched." He gestured toward the first doorway on the right. Katie smiled and walked into the room.

Elegant rosewood tables accented the handsome marble hearth. Wool damask draperies hung over two floor-length windows, and Katie caught a glimpse of herself in a large, gold-framed mirror that reached almost to the stenciled ceiling. She saw that Chase Garrett watched her behind with undisguised enthusiasm.

She whirled around. He wore a look that reminded her so much of Branch—the innocent angel's look—that she gave an inadvertent "Oh!"

Immediately he frowned and asked, "Mrs. Kincaid?"

She shook her head. "Nothing, I'm sorry. I'm here to speak with Mr. Garrett about a matter of some urgency. I only learned upon my arrival of the event you are hosting this evening, and I apologize for my untimely intrusion. But do you think it would be possible for me to have just a moment of his time?"

"Why, Mrs. Kincaid, a woman of your beauty could never be an intrusion. Let me hasten to assure you, the only way you could possibly be more welcome would be if there were no Mr. Kincaid."

Katie stiffened momentarily. Chase Garrett leaned against the doorway, his arms crossed and a besotted smile on his face. She relaxed. "I do believe, Mr. Garrett, you have, as my father would have said, a true gift for the blarney."

"Thank you, madame." He bowed his head, and when he looked at her, he wore his wicked grin once again. "I must admit I learned it all at my cousin's knees."

"Cousin?" Katie asked, hoping to hear something that could help her bring up the subject of Rob.

"Yep, quite a lady-killer, he is. That's why I can't believe he's actually going through with it. I never thought I'd see the day when good ol' cuz . . . oh, there's my uncle. I'll go tell him you're waiting."

Katie heard his voice echo down the hallway. "Hoss, there's a beautiful woman here to see you. Says it's a matter of some urgency." Katie could almost hear Chase's grin as he added, "Where do you find them, Uncle?"

Just what I need, she thought. He'll think badly of me before he meets me.

From a distance away, upstairs, she imagined, a deep voice boomed. "I'll be right down."

Chase returned and, seeing Katie's expression, looked somewhat sheepish. "I guess you heard all that, huh? We Garretts tend to forget our manners sometimes and shout our way around this drafty old place."

Katie smiled but didn't reply.

"Please have a seat, Mrs. Kincaid," he said. Walking to a table, he gestured to a pitcher that sat beside cut-crystal decanters. "Lemonade?"

Katie had never tasted lemonade, though she'd heard of it. Although she felt guilty for accepting anything from the Garretts, the temptation proved to be too great. "Please."

He handed her a tall glass of the pale yellow, pulpy beverage, then fixed himself something from a decanter. Blended whiskey, she supposed.

"While we're waiting, and since I've already demonstrated my capacity for rude behavior, may I inquire as to this urgent matter that brings you here today?" He sat on the arm of a brocade sofa and waited for her answer.

Katie sipped her drink. She puckered, whether from the sour taste of the drink or the question, she knew not. "I'd rather not say," she finally answered. "It's a personal matter."

Garrett shrugged, but the curious look remained on his face. Katie was relieved to hear the approach of heavy footsteps. A large man with graying hair entered the room. Dressed in a casual, though elegant, white ruffled shirt with black string cravat and navy pants tucked into tall leather riding boots, the man looked hauntingly familiar.

Chase stood and performed the introductions. "Mrs. Kincaid, may I present my uncle, Hoss Garrett. Sir, Mrs. Kincaid." He sat right back down as though he intended not to miss a word.

"Welcome to Riverrun, Mrs. Kincaid. Do you know my wife was a Kincaid? Could it be we've a relative come to call?"

Katie ignored the wings fluttering in her stomach. "Yes, Mr. Garrett. I believe so."

When he raised his eyebrows, she noticed the color of his eyes. Gold.

Garrett clapped his hands and said, "Wonderful. You know, my wife had cousins by the dozens, and we're always glad to have Kincaid's visit us here at Riverrun. Especially today. I hope you will stay for the entertainment, Mrs. Kincaid. We're giving a dinner to be followed by dancing this evening, and we'd love to have another guest."

Katie shook her head. This was turning out to be much more difficult than she had anticipated. "I'm sorry, sir," she said. "I'm looking for someone; that's why I'm here."

"Looking for someone, huh?" Garrett repeated. "Well you've certainly come to the right place. Half of Texas will be here soon. Chase"—he looked at his nephew—"go upstairs and get the man of the hour. He's the one to help Mrs. Kincaid. He has the guest list."

Chase left the room before Katie could stop him. Oh dear, she thought, why not take out an advertisement in the local paper, "Wanted: Lost Husband."

"Mr. Garrett, I'd rather keep this between us if possible." She clicked her tongue and shut her eyes for a moment, gathering the strength to admit the truth. "You see, this is somewhat embarrassing. I believe the man I'm searching for is your son."

"What?"

Katie hung her head. Miserably, she continued. "He's probably told you about me. I'm the woman who—"

"Just a moment, young woman. Here's the boy now. Let's see what he has to say about all of this."

"But, Mr. Garrett," she pleaded.

She turned her head away, mortified, as another person entered the room. She'd never been so embarrassed in her life. She took a sip of her lemonade. Perhaps it would cool the heat in her face.

Garrett was saying, "Here he is, Mrs. Kincaid. Britt, do you know this relative of your mama's?"

Katie's head snapped up at the strangled sound the

newcomer made. The lemonade spewed from her mouth. "Branch Kincaid!"

"What in the hell are you doin' here?" Branch's words cut across the room like a bowie knife.

When she heard his voice, the delicious timbre she'd dreamed about, Katie felt her baby kick.

≫ CHAPTER 18 ≪

SILENCE LAY LIKE a corpse in the parlor.

Hoss Garrett's face wrinkled in scorn, visibly appalled at his son's outburst. Chase pursed his lips in an inaudible "Ooh," and took a step backward. Katie clutched her glass of lemonade, her lips parted in disbelief.

Branch stood as though turned to stone. Riotous emotions coursed through him at the sight of Katie Starr, and he called on every skill he'd learned at the gaming table to keep those feelings hidden.

His mask slipped for a moment when a petulant, feminine voice inquired, "Darling, are you acquainted with this woman?" For chrissakes, he thought, *Eleanor*!

A flush stole up Katie's body, and her blue eyes flashed at Branch. Deliberately, she folded her hands in front of her and turned a vapid smile toward the woman who'd followed him into the room. Mockingly, she said, "I certainly would say so, wouldn't you, Branch?"

Branch looked from Katie to Eleanor, then back to Katie again. Eleanor, prim and elegant in a green poplin morning dress, looked like one of Hoss's prized thoroughbreds while standing next to Katie, disheveled and dirty—a perfect match for her unsightly mare, Pretty Girl.

Of course, Pretty Girl ran a mighty fine race.

Hoss found his voice, and in clipped tones he said, "Britt Garrett, your language is inappropriate."

Branch grabbed Katie's hand and pulled her to her feet. "Come on." He dragged her past his outraged father, his amused cousin, and his pouting fiancée into the entry hall, beyond the baskets of flowers, and down toward the library.

Katie punched his ribs. "You river rat, you low-down snake, you . . ."

He put his hand over her mouth.

She bit him.

"Ow!" He had a death grip on her upper arm. She stumbled and he kept her from falling. "You've enough brass in your butt to make a kettle, showin' your face around here," he muttered.

Hoss Garrett had followed them into the hall. "Britt, what is going on here?" he called. "The guests will arrive soon, and we're scheduled to announce your betrothal in one hour. I trust you'll have this problem dealt with by then?"

"Later, Hoss, please," Branch snapped. He slammed the library doors shut behind him. When he turned, he saw her hand brush a lamp on the desk. By the look of her he thought she just might throw it at him.

"You lied to me," she said, "the entire time, you lied. You told me you were Branch Kincaid. It wasn't real, any of it!" Suddenly, her eyes flew wide and her face bled white. "Betrothal?"

He might have taken great satisfaction in her shock, but instead she was killing him with every word. She looked like a disillusioned waif. He took a step toward her.

"You're Britt Garrett," her voice was ragged, her eyes bleak. "And that woman—she's Britt's fiancée." Katie shut her eyes. "You're getting married to somebody else!"

Hell, he'd missed her so damned much. He yanked her into his arms and kissed her, knowing it was madness. His mouth slanted across hers, angry fire that covered and consumed. He tasted lemon and sugar and a little bit of heaven.

Then he felt the bulge in her stomach.

He shoved her away.

She lifted her hand to her mouth, and they stared at one another, chests heaving, gazes locked.

"You're pregnant!"

She lifted her chin defiantly. "I had hoped you wouldn't notice."

"Damn you, Katie Starr," he cursed softly, raking his fingers through his hair. His gazed dropped to her waistline. "It's the Indian's kid, isn't it?"

"Oh, you . . . ," she said, her voice tight with rage. Her eyes bright, her cheeks flushed, she drew back her hand and slapped him viciously across the cheek.

He lifted his hand to slap her back, but the same bulge that made him want to hit her stopped him.

With a wounded cry, Katie stumbled to a chair and sank down. Branch stared at his upraised palm, hating it, hating himself. What had he become? How could he feel such rage, such hate for the woman that he'd . . . He didn't finish the thought. He couldn't.

Branch dropped into a chair beside Katie. He stretched his legs out straight, the heels of his boots resting on the floor. Though they sat but inches apart, the distance between them stretched as wide as the Gulf of Mexico.

Five minutes passed before either spoke. Though the questions in his mind numbered in the dozens, Branch asked for an answer with a single, soft word. "Why?"

Katie rubbed her eyes with her fingertips and took a deep breath. "I came here looking for Branch Kincaid. He was Rob Garrett's brother, this was Rob Garrett's home. I'd hoped Branch would be here, or if he wasn't, the Garretts would know where I could find him." She mocked herself, saying, "But I won't find Branch, will I? Because you're Britt. This is your home. This is where you'll marry your elegant fiancée."

Branch grimaced at the truth so baldly stated. He pushed out of his chair and paced to the window, where he stared out at the beauty of roses in bloom. "Dammit, Kate, why the hell were you lookin' for me? If you think to try and bring up that bond business . . ."

"I found him, Branch."

He slanted her a piercing look.

"I found the man who killed my Steven and Mary Margaret. I know who set the fire."

Branch spoke with icy rage. "Well, you're still tryin'

to save the father of your bastard, aren't you? You must have figured out I wouldn't let it rest until I sent your precious Shaddoe to his grave!"

Cold eyes scorned him as she lifted her chin, unthreatened. "Your jealousy blinds you. I never took you for a fool, Britt Garrett, and I guess that makes me one. Very well, you don't believe me. Allow me to speak with your father so I may share his son's dying words and offer the proof I have discovered."

Branch cursed. Threading his fingers, he cracked his knuckles as he sat on the corner of the mahogany desk and said, "Very well. Let's hear the lies it's taken you two months to concoct."

Katie measured him with her look, trying valiantly to bury the pain this day's revelations had brought. Dealing with the killer came first. "I can handle the man myself if I must. However, vengeance must wait until I've delivered my child—I'll not put this baby at risk."

"You're a nervy witch."

She smiled blandly and said, "Sheriff Jack Strickland."

Something dangerous flickered in Branch's eyes. "Explain yourself."

She began her story at the beginning, with Rob Garrett's tormented words. "I always wondered what he meant," she explained. "In my mind I took to calling the killer Pitchfork."

Branch rose from the desk and paced the room as Katie related the days following his flight from Gallagher's. He sneered at the mention of Strickland's frequent calls and scoffed at her claim of belief that the sheriff had offered only friendship. "If any of this is the truth, which I'm not sayin' it is, mind you, you were bein' downright dumb to believe him. That man's wanted in your skirts for months." He picked up a paperweight from the desk and studied it as he casually asked, "Did he get there?"

Katie's teeth clenched. She refused to answer, continuing her story. "Strickland is from a powerful political family in Boston. He claimed he'd come to Texas because he'd been unjustly accused of a crime. Proof of his innocence has been unearthed, and he's now free to return home. He wanted me to go with him. He asked me to marry him."

She paused to organize her thoughts, the memories vivid and frightening enough to set her to babbling. Branch stood with his back toward her, ramrod straight and attentive. Katie smoothed her skirts and spoke in a flat tone of voice. "He tried to convince me."

"Convince you?" Branch repeated sharply, twisting around to look at her. "How?"

She pinned her gaze on the shelves of books lining the opposite wall. Ignoring his question, she said, "That's when I saw it, on his chest. I realized what it was, who he was. He was trying to make love to me, and it was all I could do not to retch."

She vaguely heard his whispered, "Make love to you?" Hanging her head, she pressed her hands to her temples and grimaced. "I didn't kill him. I could have, he was right there. But I had the baby to protect. I was alone at the inn and I couldn't be certain, so I let him—"

"Oh, God, Kate, did he hurt you?"

She lifted her gaze. Branch knelt before her, his face flushed with fury, anguish glittering in his golden eyes.

Her voice small, she said, "It was a tattoo on his breast. It was a pitchfork in flames, just like Rob said."

Branch grasped her shoulders with trembling hands. "Sprite, did he rape you?"

She flinched at the words and believed that the look in his eyes, the white-hot murderous rage, was reflected toward her. "Damn you," she hissed. "Is that all you care about, how many men have my body? No, he didn't rape me." She slapped his hands away from her, "I didn't let him do it. I outthought him, outsmarted him. I'll allow no man to hurt me, Britt Garrett! Not even you."

Swiftly, he stood and backed away from her, his expression cold and impassive. "You think this tattoo proves he's the killer?"

Angry, she nodded.

He took a sheet of paper from the desk drawer and inked a pen. He laid the pen beside the paper, gestured toward the desk. "Will you draw it?"

Katie stood, distressed to find her knees a bit wobbly. She bent over the desk and mentioned as she drew, "It really is appropriate for the man. He's the devil himself."

Finished, she stepped back, allowing him to see the sketch. She sensed rather than saw him stiffen and when she looked at him, he was staring at the paper, his expression stony.

"Well?" Katie asked.

He lifted his gaze, looked at her with probing eyes. "Kate, if ever anything between us was true . . . No, wait. On your Mary Margaret's soul, Katie Starr, is this true? Is your story true? If St. Pierre sent you to me with this tale, I demand you tell me now. Otherwise, swear to me on your daughter's soul that you tell me the truth in this."

Katie hadn't realized she had anything left within her to hurt, but his words found something. A wave of pain buffeted her as she answered, "How dare you, how dare you say that to me! I hate you, Britt Garrett, and yes, I tell the truth."

Branch nodded once and turned a deadly look at her drawing. In a cold voice, he stated, "It's a trident. He's Trident. Goddammit, Katie, he didn't settle with killing your family and my brother. He's also the bastard Regulator leader that burned Gallagher's!"

He quizzed her then, sitting at the desk and taking notes of every bit of information she remembered Strickland imparting. He shook his head when she mentioned the sheriff's desire for a politically minded wife and threw down his pen when she mentioned his intention to seek the presidency.

They'd been in the library an hour when a knock sounded on the door. Hoss Garrett opened the door and stiffly said, "Britt, your guests have arrived. You must excuse yourself, *now*, to prepare for the celebration of your engagement."

Branch threw him an absent look. "Sure, Hoss. I'll be

finished here in a few moments." Hoss Garrett frowned at Katie, then withdrew.

Katie laughed, and the sound echoed in her ears like shattered crystal. "How inconsiderate of me to arrive on the day of your engagement ball. What a social quandary—a wife and a fiancée at the same event."

Branch scowled. "We were never married, Kate."

Katie whipped around and glared at him, her hands planted firmly on her hips. The legitimacy of the child she carried was at stake here. "Yes, we were."

"No. I signed that bond Branch Kincaid. There *is* no Branch Kincaid."

Her fingers itched to hit him. Instead, she crossed the room and put the desk safely between them. Throwing him a contemptuous look, she said grimly, "You fool. Half the men in Texas call themselves a name other than the one their parents gave them. You signed the marriage bond. It matters not whether you signed it Britt Garrett or Napoleon Bonaparte, you married me that day."

He stood and placed both hands on the desk. Against her will, she noted the slender strength of his fingers supporting his weight as he leaned across the highly polished wood to snap, *"No, I didn't."*

"You signed the bond."

Branch threw up his hands. "Okay, the bond. The goddamn bond. I signed it. What did it say? I'll marry you or pay you, if I remember correctly. Well, by God, woman, I choose to pay!"

He grabbed a key from a desk drawer and went to the bookcase where four volumes of Shakespeare concealed a safe. He shoved in the key and turned the lock. Then he reached in and withdrew a blue velvet coin pouch.

He poured out a handful of gold.

She backed away from him as he approached her. But then she remembered that she was just as mad as he, so she stopped and lifted her chin. He slipped his fingers inside the scooped neckline of her dress, pulled out the bodice, and shoved the money into her corset.

Katie angrily blinked back tears. "Damn you, Branch Kincaid!" she cursed, reaching down her front for the cool metal that scorched her skin. "I don't want your money." She threw the coins at him with all her strength.

Katie wrenched open the door. Faint sounds of music and laughter floated from the third-floor ballroom. The two Garrett men and Eleanor waited outside, their expressions ranging from embarrassment to fury. For the baby's sake Katie turned and spoke to Branch before them all. "We're legally married, sir, whether you like it or not. You can have as many other wives as you care to collect, but make sure you divorce me first."

"I'll not allow you to give my name to your bastard, woman."

Katie opened her mouth to deny his accusation, but then she hesitated. Obviously now, her grand dream would not come true. There would be no Mr. and Mrs. Branch Kincaid and family.

But if she was careless here with her words, her greatest fear might come to pass. Branch's father might see to it that Mr. Britt Garrett's new wife, Eleanor, took a stepchild into Riverrun to mother.

They'll have to bury me first. Katie gave a short, unamused laugh. "Don't fret, Britt," she said. "I would never consider bestowing such a dishonorable name as Garrett upon my child. You have my word that this baby will carry his father's name. Besides"—she paused and smiled sweetly—"the French language does roll so pleasantly from one's tongue, don't you agree?"

Katie marched across the hall and out the front door, ignoring the cacophony of questions being hurled at Branch by the members of his family. Seeing the wagon and driver waiting at the bottom of the steps, Katie sent a quick prayer of thanks heavenward. She climbed into the seat and said, "Please, sir. I'm ready to leave now."

The driver's expression was quizzical, but he whipped the reins and turned the horses down the drive.

Katie couldn't stop herself from looking over her shoulder. Britt Garrett stood framed in the doorway, watching her. A single tear slid from her eye. *Damn you, Branch Kincaid. I loved you.*

And I know that you loved me.

Damn you, Katie Starr. Is it true? Did you betray me? Or could it be that the child you carry is in truth mine?

Inhaling a deep breath, Branch turned around and faced the family. Aw, hell, he thought, exhaling in a rush.

Eleanor stood with her hands clasped to her heart, a stricken expression on her face. Chase looked past him at the retreating wagon, an eyebrow quirked speculatively. Hoss Garrett had swelled in indignation, his mouth moving silently open and shut. Branch thought of a riled-up catfish in a waistcoat.

"Well, folks, shall we adjourn to the parlor?"

Hoss found his voice. "Perhaps it would be best if you and I had a private conversation." He turned to his nephew and said, "You will escort our Eleanor upstairs to our guests, Chase?" In an undertone he added, "We'll join you directly."

Hoss led Branch back to the library, his brows lifting at the sight of the coins strewn on the floor. He settled into his chair and folded his hands on the desktop. "Care to explain what's going on around here?"

Branch scooped a coin from the floor as he sat in a chair. "I was wrong about Rob's killer. I'll be goin' after him first thing in the mornin'."

"This man Starr didn't kill my boy?"

Branch flipped the coin. "Actually, Starr is a woman, and yeah, she was the one who pulled the trigger."

"A woman killed Robert?"

"The woman who just left here. My wife." As the color drained from Hoss's face, Branch said, "Let me tell you the whole story."

It took him the better part of half an hour. He told him about Shaddoe St. Pierre and how he'd believed him to be the blackmailer. He explained why Katie had shot Rob and relayed his brother's dying words. He spoke of Katie's subsequent discovery of the tattoo. By the time he finished, Hoss had paced the room, lit and crushed out three cigars, and rearranged the entire section of Shakespeare on the shelves. Into the silence, Branch's father asked, "Did you ever check on her claim concerning the legality of a marriage bond?"

"Yeah."

"And?"

"It's tricky. I didn't sign it Britt Garrett. My lawyer's checkin' into it now."

"Divorces can be granted by the legislature. Have you made the arrangements should they be necessary?"

"No."

Hoss slammed his hand against the desk. "Then how in the hell did you ever intend to marry Eleanor?"

Branch looked him right in the eye. "I'd have checked it all out before a wedding. But to tell you the truth, I don't believe we'd ever have reached such an occasion."

"My God, Britt. You are married to your brother's killer!"

"Hell of a note, ain't it."

Hoss sputtered and spat. Branch shook his head. "Listen, Hoss, it's not really like that. I explained it to you, she acted humanely. You or I'd have done the same thing."

"You'll divorce her at once," Branch's father demanded, lighting a fourth cigar.

Branch's mouth thinned as he said, "No, I'm goin' after Strickland at once. He's the one responsible for all this death and destruction. I'm goin' to find him and kill him." Softly, he added, "Before he tries to do any more convincing."

Hoss's eyes widened. "By damn, you care for the woman. I don't believe it. She's about to present you with a bastard, and you have feelings for her." He shook his head in wonder. "My God, boy, I've always known you were weak. Even so, I never thought you'd sacrifice everything for a chit." His whisper trembled with loathing: "God, you make me sick."

God, you make me sick. A repeat of the words father had said to son decades earlier, a return of the same bony fingers of pain seizing Branch's gut. He could smell the smoke and hear ten-year-old Rob's voice whisper in his ear. "Don't tell him, Britt. Please! He'll skin me for sure. You're tougher than I am, you can take it, he can't hurt you. Please, Britt, please promise you won't tell him it was me that started the fire!"

"I promise."

"What?" Hoss Garrett's voice penetrated the haze of Branch's memory, pulling him back to the present. But the past still held him in its tormenting grip, so he asked the boy's question in his man's voice.

"Why have you always hated me, Papa?"

Garrett sat back heavily in his chair. "What do you mean?"

Branch repeated his question. Hoss stared open-mouthed for a long minute; then a blaze of pure fury burst upon his face. "Damn you, boy! You cost me everything, every single thing I valued through your carelessness. Garretts wrestled the Virginia plantation from the wilderness, built it in the midst of hostile Indians, defended that house in the American Revolution. You destroyed my heritage! You and your damnable reckless ways."

The boy within Branch screamed silently, *Papa, it wasn't me. I didn't do it.* Branch the man thought, *You're a fool for not having seen the truth.* Aloud, he said, "I was a child, a boy. You've held that against me for twenty-seven years, Hoss Garrett. Don't you think it's time to let it go?"

"Dammit, that's what I'm doing. I've made you my heir. You've got it—Riverrun's yours if you don't throw it all away now. Don't you know how much it galled me to offer that to you?"

"I'm beginning to." Branch drew his lips into a long, thin line and approached the desk. It hurt. After all these years it still hurt. Well, he'd made an attempt at being a dutiful son, and look where it got him. For a while he'd thought . . . oh well, what did it matter now?

He leaned forward, resting his weight on the fingers he splayed on the desktop. Softly, he said, "It's too late for regrets now, Hoss. You've made me your heir. I'm goin' after Strickland, and when I come back, I'm comin' back here to stay. You'll get to see my pretty face every day the rest of your life."

"I'll change it back. I'll disinherit you," the elder Garrett snapped, his eyes flashing.

"Just try it, old man. I made sure that agreement we

signed was irrevocable before I ever went to Nacogdoches."

"No, you haven't met the terms. You didn't kill the murderer."

Branch's laugh sounded hollow to his own ears. "Read the paper. All I had to do was *find* the killer. Period. You just assumed that a killer like me wouldn't hesitate to kill again.

"Besides," he added, "Jack Strickland's the real murderer. You can bet your sweet cigar that he's already a dead man. And if you try usin' the fact that Katie Starr pulled the trigger to weasel out of the agreement, I'll do something you'll really love."

"What?"

Bitterness lay behind Branch's threat. Twenty years' worth. Why in the hell couldn't the man have loved him, even just a little bit? He smiled evilly and said, "Why, I'll bring my wife home to Riverrun."

Hoss turned a mottled red as he shouted, "You'll not bring that murderess into my home!"

Branch straightened, braced his feet wide apart, and crossed his arms. "Even better, I'll claim her child." He cocked his head and nodded. "I'll bet she has a boy. Yep, you fight me on this, and I'll declare her infant—her Indian half-breed's son—as my own. How do you like that Hoss? We'll give Riverrun back to the Indians."

He lifted his hand in a cocky salute and turned to leave. But Hoss had another question. "What about Eleanor?"

"You marry her," Branch said over his shoulder. "I promise you that as long as she remains lady of Riverrun, she won't care who the hell she's married to. In fact, she'd probably rather have you, anyway. All she really wants is to get new furniture for the room upstairs and go to Paris."

Hoss flinched visibly from the slap of Branch's words. "Damn you, boy. Damn you to hell."

"Ah now, Daddy, you did that years ago." The door shut silently behind him.

.   .   .

Branch left Riverrun early the following morning headed for Nacogdoches. Upon his arrival in the city, he learned that Sheriff Strickland had resigned his office some six weeks earlier and had left instructions for his mail to be forwarded to the home of Congressman William Strickland in Boston, Massachusetts.

Gallagher's Tavern and Travelers Inn wasn't actually on the route to Boston, but Branch believed the slight detour to be a necessary one. Time spent in the saddle gave a man the opportunity to ponder, and Branch had spent a good bit of his travels thinking about Katie Starr.

He had a notion that he'd made a mistake. He wanted to talk to Katie.

Martha Craig met him on the inn's front porch. "No, Mr. Kincaid," she said, all signs of friendliness wiped from her face. "Katie hasn't returned home as of yet. She sent word from Galveston that she intended to visit a relation in Alabama for a month or longer."

Branch didn't believe her. Katie wouldn't make a trip like that when she was in a family way. "You wouldn't mind then, Martha, if I took a look around?"

She nodded. "Be my guest. Temporarily, that is."

Branch knew then that he wouldn't find his wife at Gallagher's. Probably she's with her Cherokee, he thought disgustedly. Damn, and he really wanted to talk to her before he headed out after Jack Strickland.

Tilting his head at an angle, Branch gave Martha a considering look. Then he screwed up his courage and said, "Martha, there's somethin' I need to know. Katie and I have had a bit of a misunderstanding, and I'm wonderin' if . . . well . . . I know she's expectin'. Is the baby mine?"

In answer, Martha stepped inside the inn for a moment, reappearing with a shotgun in her hands. The blast landed just short of his feet. "Get out of here, you wormy scoundrel. Unless you find some sense, don't ever bring your ugly face around this place again." The door slammed shut behind her.

Branch made the three-week journey to Galveston in a week and a half. He boarded a steamboat for the two-day trip to New Orleans. Five days later he stood on the deck of a sleek English ship as it left the Mississippi River and entered the Gulf of Mexico. The towboat cast off, and Branch walked toward the ship's bow, looking forward to the end of his journey, Boston, Massachusetts.

But a yearning within himself summoned him to the stern, and he looked westward, toward Texas, toward Katie. After this business with Strickland was done, he'd find her again. They had some unfinished business between them.

Katie Kincaid had left Texas following her disastrous trip to Riverrun, only she hadn't traveled to Alabama. She'd gone to New Orleans seeking the comfort of her friend, Shaddoe St. Pierre.

Shaddoe was furious when she told him about Strickland, and he offered to hunt the man down himself. Katie discouraged him, knowing in her heart that Branch, or Britt, as she must learn to think of him, would see the matter dealt with. In New Orleans she shopped and socialized with some of Shaddoe's friends. Most of her time she spent sewing a layette for her baby—a child who seemed anxious to greet the world, so forceful were his tumbles and kicks.

Shaddoe finished his business on behalf of his ailing grandfather and escorted Katie back to Texas in early October. So happy was she to be home that when Martha related the story of Britt Garrett's visit, Katie didn't once fret about missing him. It was good news, actually. It proved to her that she was right in trusting him to deal with Strickland.

A few weeks before Christmas, Shaddoe St. Pierre stood in the bitter cold outside the door to Katie Kincaid's kitchen. Hours dragged by, and he found himself half-frozen and very nearly drunk when the scream split the air: "Kincaid, this is all your fault!"

Katie gave birth to a boy.

CHAPTER 19

$\mathcal{I}$N HER ROOM at the Eberly House hotel, Katie lay across the middle of her bed, heedless of wrinkling either her gown or the bedspread, cooing and clucking as she coaxed happy smiles from her two-month-old son, Johnny.

Martha stood before the wall mirror tying her bonnet strings, her expression a poignant contrast to the pair playing on the bed. "I feel like I'm attending a funeral," she said, sniffing back a sigh.

Looking up, Katie nodded with understanding. "I know, Martha. As much as I support annexation, I can't help but feel a little sad. But remember, although today we'll witness the death of the Republic of Texas, we'll behold the State of Texas's birth."

Martha turned and lifted her shawl from a hook beside the door. "I know it's for the best, but as independent as we Texians are, I wonder just how well we'll blend."

A memory of a golden-haired Texian standing tall with two Patersons on his hips rose in Katie's mind. Gently, she fingered a tuft of her son's blond hair and said, "Some men simply aren't meant to blend."

"Men like Mr. Branch?"

Katie pushed off the bed and smoothed her skirts. "Please, Martha."

The older woman donned her shawl and picked up her reticule, her lips pursed in a frown. She tapped an impatient foot against the floor, and Katie put a white knitted hat on Johnny and bundled him in two thin blankets and a thick quilt.

"Katie Kincaid," Martha fussed, "you'll give that boy a heatstroke."

Defensively, Katie lifted her chin. "I don't think it's advisable to have my baby out in February. I should never have allowed you and Rowdy to talk me into this trip. If Johnny takes a chill, why, I'll likely expire with guilt."

Tsk, tsk, tsk. Martha clucked her tongue. "Missy, your protectiveness is slopping over. You're gonna have to learn to step back and allow that boy to grow."

"Well, he can't grow if he catches a chill and dies, now can he?" Katie snapped, lifting Johnny to her shoulder, where she patted his back furiously.

"Darlin'," Martha said, her eyes softening at the picture of panic standing before her. "I know you're worried. It's a fact of life that the odds run against little ones here on the frontier." She reached out and stilled Katie's hand, then wrapped mother and son in her arms for a comforting hug. "The trick I learned with my little ones holds true today, honey child. Let them climb the hills by themselves, confident that you are right beside them ready with a steadying hand should they fall. Your children will be stronger for it, Katie, and so will you."

"I know, Martha, it's just that he's so little, and it's February—"

"And it's an absolutely beautiful, warm, windless day outside. Bring the boy to the doin's, pumpkin; he'll be tickled over it when he's grown and can tell his own babies that he witnessed the birth of the Lone Star State."

With a surrendering shrug, Katie cuddled her son and left the room. Walking down Colorado Street toward the statehouse, Katie listened as Rowdy Payne, who had joined them in the hotel lobby, described the plans for the ceremony inaugurating the new state officials. Due to the large crowd expected and because the weather had cooperated, the chairs and benches had been removed from the representative hall and senate chamber and placed on the long gallery east of the capitol building. Flags and greenery decorated the area, and hundreds of citizens congregated on the lawn waiting for the formalities to begin.

Rowdy turned to Katie and said, "I sent Andrew along quite some time ago to reserve us a good spot for the seein'. He took that handkerchief we washed with the red long johns to tie onto a stick and wave so we could find him."

They wandered through the crowd, shaking hands with politicians, nodding greetings to diplomats, and trading looks of amusement at some of the silly fashion on display. One particular lady's hat caught their eye, and Martha and Katie burst into giggles at the sight of the stuffed prairie chicken nesting in a froth of ribbons and straw.

Katie and her friends found Andrew and had just settled onto the quilt spread across the ground when the President and governor-elect made their appearances at the podium.

Conversation ceased; a hush of expectation draped the area like a shroud. As introductions were made, Katie glanced around. Faces displaying a mixture of joy and sadness watched the proceedings with rapt attention. The Honorable R.E.B. Baylor rose and recited a prayer rich with fervor. At its finish the crowd applauded wildly.

Then as President Anson Jones arose to deliver his valedictory, the noise died. He began, "Gentlemen of the Senate and the House of Representatives . . ."

Katie listened to the moving and dignified speech and saw not the men at the podium, but scenes from the past ten years. She recalled the nation's struggles with Mexico, both the victories and defeats, the confrontations with the Indians, and the unceasing battle with the land itself.

She thought of her personal involvement in the effort to build a home and a homeland. Feelings she could not define overcame her. The dreams were not dead but evolved into something new, something different, hopefully something better. But Texas, the State of Texas, had a bittersweet birth here today.

President Jones spoke the words, "The final act in this great drama is now performed. The Republic of Texas is no more."

Katie rose to applaud Anson Jones with tears streaming down her cheeks. Sorrow for the past, joy for the present, and hope for the future melded within her as she watched the beloved flag of Texas drop slowly toward the ground and the banner of the United States of America rise in its stead. She grinned in sympathy as Sam Houston stepped forward, crying vigorously, and clasped the Lone Star flag to his bosom.

As Governor James Pinckney Henderson and the other state officials were sworn in, the atmosphere of the crowd lightened. Merry shouts interrupted the proceedings as celebrating commenced. Katie saw jugs of spirits being passed among members of the legislature. A resounding cheer swept the assemblage as a boom of artillery announced the fact that the State of Texas had been born.

Such was the merriment, the whooping and chortling of men and women, young and old, that no one paid notice to the serious, somber expressions of a trio of men in the section of reserved seats close to the podium.

Branch Kincaid bent his head toward his father and quietly said, "There. He's on the fourth row behind the speaker."

Hoss Garrett scowled and said, "I'd rather he be in hell than Texas, but I guess it is best to take care of our dirty laundry locally. Your idea was a good one, son."

"Couldn't have been done without your pull," Branch replied grudgingly. It had stuck in his craw to have to ask Hoss Garrett for anything, and he'd sworn when he'd done it that it'd be a one-time deal. But Hoss had the power to get the deed done, and truth be told, that was more important than Branch's own pride.

He folded his arms and leaned back in his chair, his hard eyes focused on the man he planned to kill. "I was bettin' he'd be here, but it sure is nice seein' him with my own two eyes."

"I thought you tailed him all the way back."

"Lost him St. Louis. Wished then I had gone ahead and killed him in Boston when I had him in my rifle sights."

Chase Garrett, who'd been listening intently to the hushed conversation, inquired, "Why didn't you?"

"Because a gunshot is too easy a death for a worm like Strickland; not near personal enough. I couldn't get any closer, not with him hidin' out at his father's estate after the scandal involvin' that poor girl."

Hoss studied Strickland from a distance. "I have to say I'm looking forward to our little soiree for the newly appointed judge. I can see the politician in him. He's a nice-looking man, the picture of a gentleman."

Nice-looking man. Branch's jaw hardened as he remembered the young Irish girl whom Strickland had been accused of beating to death in Boston. When Branch investigated the incident, the grieving father had shown him the girl's portrait. She'd borne an amazing resemblance to Katie Starr. "The bastard."

Luckily for Branch, the one thing that had seemed to appeal to Jack Strickland more than women was politics. Branch had capitalized on the weakness and put into motion a plan to bring Strickland out of hiding and back to Texas.

With rumors of his misdeed floating around Boston and ruining his immediate political plans, Strickland had jumped at the chance to return to Texas for a judgeship and the guarantee of a future senatorial seat. His firsthand experience with crooked politics during the Moderator-Regulator War led him to accept Judge Terrell's underhanded offer without question. Branch looked at his father and asked, "Did Terrell balk at involvement in our scheme?"

Hoss took a cheroot from his pocket and waved it beneath his nose, saying, "Billy Terrell owed me a favor. He was glad to help. Told me Strickland paid the bribe without a complaint. Bribes and corruption—that's something that won't die with the Republic." He cocked an ear toward the podium. "Sounds like the speeches might be winding down. You got the men positioned?"

"Three of them dispersed through the crowd," Chase answered. "Britt, you think it's time for us to move around back?"

Branch nodded and Chase explained to Hoss. "The

dignitaries are scheduled to file around to the back of the capitol buildin' where food tables have been set up. We figure to nab Jack Strickland between the barbecue beans and the pickled beets."

One corner of Branch's mouth lifted in a wry grin. "Hurts like hell when you get it in the beets."

Beneath the shade of a sprawling elm tree, Andrew turned his attention from the podium and said, "Boy, am I glad that's over." He peered into the white wicker basket that sat on the winter-yellow grass at the edge of the quilt, sniffed, and asked, "What'cha bring to eat, Missus Kincaid?"

Katie kissed Johnny's waving fist, then settled a speculative look on the curious youngster. "Andrew Payne, what makes you think I had anything to do with our picnic lunch?"

He grinned and patted his stomach. " 'Cause I heard you tellin' Missus Eberly you'd help her make dewberry tarts."

"Scamp." Standing, Katie ruffled his hair. "I'll tell you what, Johnny's getting a bit fussy, and I'd thought to walk him for a bit. Why don't you come with us, and we'll see if we can't find a bottle of milk to buy to go along with those tarts."

Martha, whose right hand was linked with Rowdy's left, looked up at Katie and said, "Katie, I'll take Johnny for a walk if you'd like."

"No, thank you." Katie bent and kissed Martha's cheek, adding for her ears only, "If you think I'm going to interfere now that Rowdy's finally swelled up the nerve to court you, you're a fool."

"I'll carry Johnny if you'd like, Missus Kincaid," Andrew offered. "Even though he is as heavy as a turkey."

Katie smiled wistfully into her son's face. "He is large for his age. I guess he takes after his father in that respect." She adjusted the baby's bonnet, then said, "I'll carry him, Andrew. You lead the way. I might need you to clear a path for us through all these people."

The light breeze swept the scent of cedar through the crowds as Andrew very seriously took a position in front of Katie, his hands at the ready to shove if need be. With her baby cradled in her arms, Katie crooned as she walked, patting her son in the hopes that he'd settle into sleep.

She paid scant attention to their direction, enjoying the unique experience of moving among a sea of people. Colors and textures abounded, sounds and scents assailed her. Being part of a crowd like this wasn't anything she'd want to get used to, but this first time she found it stimulating. "Imagine, Johnny, it must be like this all the time on the streets of New York and London."

A hand took her elbow, and a deep-toned voice spoke, "Or the streets of Boston at Christmastide."

Katie looked up into the face that roamed in her nightmares. "You're not supposed to be here!" Katie said, the words bursting from her lips before her mind had a chance to call them back.

Dressed in gentleman's attire, his gold brocade vest glistening in the sun, Jack Strickland grinned down at Katie. His smile was as stunning and as evil as ever. "I'm wounded, my dear. Is that all you have to say to your fiancé?"

"Fiancé?" She repeated weakly.

"We did have an agreement, didn't we, my darling?"

"But . . . but . . ."

Strickland cupped her chin and lifted it, studying her face in the sunlight. "Such a blessing the smallpox marked you not at all. I worried over it."

Frozen in bone-numbing fear, Katie forced herself to think. *Smallpox. Yes, the note I left tacked to my kitchen door explaining why I couldn't leave with him for Boston.* "No, no scars."

"You are still a beautiful woman, Katie. Tell me, whose child is it you hold?" His gaze dropped to Johnny, and Katie's arms tightened involuntarily.

This was the man who'd killed Mary Margaret. She must keep him away from Johnny. "Um, Andrew. I mean, he's Andrew's brother." Trying desperately to keep the panic from showing on her face, Katie looked around for the boy. There, he was in the milk line. *Oh, Andrew, why didn't I let you carry Johnny?*

"Really," Strickland said, extending a finger for Johnny to grab. "I wasn't aware that Rowdy Payne had remarried."

"Martha," Katie said, staring hard across the crowd to where Martha and Rowdy sat engrossed in one another.

"Martha Craig? Isn't she rather old to be having children? Here, let me hold him. You know, you look good with a child in your arms, Katie. I'm anxious to see you holding one of ours." Jack Strickland plucked Johnny right out of her arms.

Terror gripped Katie's heart and her knees threatened to buckle. Then as she watched her greatest enemy tickle little Johnny's chin, his blood-red ruby ring glowing dully in the sunlight, a calm descended upon her. Her thoughts sharpened, becoming quick and crisp.

She'd kill Jack Strickland before she'd allow him to hurt her son.

She pasted a smile on her face and extended her hands to reclaim her son. "You must tell me how it is you've returned and why I meet you here of all places."

Jack maintained his hold on the baby. "Gladly. It is providence, you know, us meeting this way. It saves me a trip to Nacogdoches. Come, I'll tell you all about it while we eat. I'm to sit with Judge Terrell and his wife."

He took her arm and escorted her through the crowd around the side of the capitol building. "You and Mr. Payne, here, will join me."

Katie smelled the aroma of fried chicken and almost gagged. She could not sit at a table with Jack Strickland. She couldn't do anything with Jack Strickland. *Oh, Lord, help me.*

From behind them, a man's voice called, "Judge Strickland, sir? A moment of your time, please. I'm an aide to Judge Terrell, and I've a message for you."

Strickland turned, and Katie seized the moment to take Johnny from his arms, saying hastily, "Don't allow us to intrude on business." She backed away a step, hoping to disappear into the crowd, but he grasped her elbow and held her at his side.

Katie stared at the ring on Strickland's finger as his hand held her prisoner. When Judge Terrell's aide approached and began to speak about Strickland's appointment, she listened with half an ear, her thoughts busily calculating an escape.

"Wonderful," Strickland said. "Come, my dear. We've a stop to make before our dinner."

She and Terrell's aide spoke simultaneously. "No!" he said.

"Thank you, Jack, but—" Katie and the newcomer looked at one another, and two sets of eyes widened in recognition. Strickland tugged her along toward the back entrance to the capitol, and Katie heard Chase Garrett mutter beneath his breath, "Oh, hell."

Branch gazed around the courtroom and smiled. He fully intended for Strickland to have his day in court. A short day, to be sure, considering prosecutor, judge, jury, and executioner all had claimed Rob Garrett as a relation. To Branch's way of thinking, killing his brother's murderer in a courtroom of the capitol building of the State of Texas had the ring of poetic justice. He could hardly wait for the trial to begin.

Hoss Garrett sat behind the broad, oaken judge's bench. Branch propped a hip atop the prosecutor's table, one of his Texas Patersons drawn and resting on his thigh. They awaited Chase, whose assignment had been to lure Judge Strickland into the building with the promise of a black robe and gavel.

Hinges creaked as the courtroom door swung open. Branch tightened his grip on the Paterson's handle, grinned, and lifted his head. *Damn, he wasn't alone.* Branch noticed only frightened blue eyes as his gaze swept past the woman and settled on the child in her arms. *Shit.*

In an aisle between rows of pine benches, Jack Strickland paused, his brow knitting as his gaze flicked from Hoss to Branch. Then, like a striking snake, he moved, yanking the woman at his side in front of him, shielding himself from the gun Branch had aimed at his chest.

Branch heard a faint, feminine whimper of fear. Something cold slithered around in his belly as suspicion crawled up his spine. Briefly, but long enough for time to grind to a halt, he darted another look at the woman.

Oh, Lord. Katie. And her baby.

"Chase?" Branch's quiet voice was deadly.

"I've got a gun on him."

Black eyes glowed, and Strickland's smile gleamed white with menace as he said, "And I have one on the lady."

The air inside the room was heavy, thick with tension. "Let her go, Strickland," Branch said, his voice hard, his finger tickling the Paterson's trigger.

"I think not." Strickland sneered, an evil chuckle shaking his shoulders. "Isn't the lady here the object of this exercise? I assume I'm facing the jealous husband?"

"No," Hoss Garrett called out from the judge's chair. "You are facing your victim's father, brother, and cousin. Remember killing a man named Garrett? Land Commissioner Garrett?"

Strickland frowned and slowly nodded. "I remember him, but I sure as hell didn't kill him."

"Not directly, perhaps." At Branch's nod Chase spoke from behind Jack Strickland, reminding the judge of his presence. "But you started the fire that burned him."

"A gunshot killed that man." Strickland tightened his hold on Katie as she began to squirm. He said, "Surprised me at the time—I was sheriff, you know, and investigated that fire. Garrett hadn't even been at the farm that night as far as I knew. You, Kincaid, have the wrong man for that particular crime."

Branch's voice was cold and flat. "No, *Trident*, I have you dead to right on this."

"So, you know that too? It took you long enough to figure it out." His lip curling in an amused smirk, Strickland added, "I had you completely fooled, didn't I? Even the lady, here." He shook his head and grinned. "I never did think you were much of a man, and I knew it for certain when your lady came running after me before your dust had even settled." Tracing the barrel of his gun down Katie's cheek, he said, "She's a fine lay, don't you think, Kincaid? Spirited. Why, when I had my mouth on her titties, well—"

Branch's finger tightened on the trigger.

"Branch?" Katie pleaded, fear dulling her blue eyes. "Branch, please. My baby!"

Strickland poked her breast with the gun.

"Hoss," Branch said through gritted teeth. "Come here and get the child."

Strickland gave his head a curt shake. "No. The other one. Have him come over here where I can see him."

"Do as he says, Chase," Branch ordered.

Chase moved with careful steps until he stood an arm's length away from Katie. "Give me the baby now, sweetheart," he said, both hands extended, his gun still trained on Strickland.

"Not yet." Strickland turned sideways, his grip on Katie tight and the gun held beneath her chin. "Kincaid," he asked, "is this your kid?"

What? Branch wondered. Why the hell is he asking that? He hesitated, not knowing what to say. Would Katie's child be in more or less danger if he claimed it? He simply didn't know.

But it felt good when he said, "Yes, that's my baby."

Strickland grinned. "Then catch it."

Everything happened in an instant. Strickland grabbed for the infant, stripping him from Katie's arms at the same time he pushed her into Chase. As Katie knocked Chase to the ground, Strickland flung the child in the air toward Branch.

Each second passed as an hour. Branch shifted his aim as the baby came at him. He saw a flash at the barrel of Strickland's gun, heard Katie scream and the infant shriek. Dropping his gun, he lifted his hands to catch the child. A bullet rammed into his shoulder.

Both his hands clasped the infant's waist. A second

gunshot tore into his side. Blood spattered the baby's white bonnet.

Jack Strickland ran out of the courtroom.

"Son!" Hoss Garrett's hoarse voice shouted. "Britt!"

Branch sank to his knees still gripping the child, suddenly desperate to see beneath the hat's ruffled bill. *What color hair did this fair-skinned baby have?*

Gently, he laid the infant down before tumbling to the floor, unconscious.

The craggy-faced doctor lifted his hands from a white basin filled with bloodied water, wiped them on a towel, and said, "You understand that if he dies, I'll tell the truth about the bullet in his shoulder."

Hoss Garrett shrugged, afraid to speak. Afraid he'd retch. That was his boy's blood staining the water, the towel, the white sheet spread across the table.

"I don't want him moved for at least twenty-four hours—if he makes it that long." The doctor rolled down his shirtsleeves and donned his jacket. "Somebody needs to stay with him. When he gets feverish, he's liable to roll right off that table." He paused at the door and barked a short laugh. "Helluva place to do surgery, you know. Usually my job's done before it ever gets to the courtroom."

Hoss stared down at his son's pasty face, his emotions a jumble of anger, grief, and guilt. It was the second wound—the one in Branch's side—that now threatened his life. The gunshot that Hoss himself had fired. He'd drawn a bead on Strickland, right at the heart. And then Branch had moved. "Hell boy, why didn't you let that damned baby fall?"

A knock sounded and Hoss turned to see Chase enter the courtroom. "Uncle Hoss, how is he? The doc wouldn't say a word, just rushed on out."

Hoss had to clear his throat before he spoke. "He ... uh ... we'll just have to wait and see. The doc wouldn't make any promises."

Chase walked up to the table. "Damn, he's as white as

bleached bones. When I catch up with Strickland, I'm gonna—"

"He hasn't been caught?"

"No. I don't think the sheriff much believes the tale we told him either. Seein' how we couldn't very well tell him we'd planned a murder that doubled back on us, well . . . I imagine we're the only ones that care much if Strickland gets found."

Hoss brushed a lock of hair from Branch's brow before turning away and saying, "It's all that goddamn woman's fault. Is she still out there?"

"Yes, but—"

Guilt ate through Hoss like an acid as he walked the aisle toward the back of the courtroom. He shoved open the doors, his gaze raking the hallway until it came to rest on the petite woman who knelt on the hardwood floor, her head bowed in prayer.

So great was his pain that he lashed out against the one person in the world whose love for his son equaled his own. "Yes, pray, God damn you! Pray for the salvation of your soul. He's dying, woman, and it's all your fault."

Katie lifted red-rimmed eyes to look at him as Hoss pointed a trembling finger at her. "You," he fumed. "Your fault. You couldn't settle with killing only one of my sons, could you? You had to take them both." He spat on the floor beside her and said, "Better for my family that you had never been born."

A tear dripped down her cheek as she softly agreed. "I know."

Nudging her with his boot, he said, "Stand up, witch. Leave here. Now. I don't want you here. I won't have you tending a death watch for my son. I won't have you at his funeral."

Katie climbed to her feet, not meeting the fury of his glare. Head bowed, shoulders slumped, she walked the length of the hall, then paused. For a full minute she stood there unmoving.

Then her spine straightened and her shoulders squared. She turned around, head held high and said, "I'll grieve for Branch Kincaid whenever, wherever, and however I choose. You cannot stop me, Hoss Garrett."

Her cold eyes narrowed as she smiled, and the air about her fairly shimmered with malevolence. "Neither can Jack Strickland. Although he'll undoubtedly wish he could."

Garrett stood at a window watching her as she walked outside and met an older man and a woman who held that cursed babe. A boy helped her into a carriage, and as it pulled away from the capitol grounds, Hoss shuddered. *A man has to be mighty careful when he chooses a woman for an enemy.*

There's never any tellin' what one of them'll do.

By the time the travelers returned to Nacogdoches, Katie's plans were made. With the former sheriff on the loose, Gallagher's Inn wasn't a safe haven for her loved ones, and Martha, Rowdy, and Andrew readily consented to settle in with Johnny at Le Cadeau d'Etoiles. They were not so quick to agree when Katie declared her intention to leave Shaddoe's home in search of Jack Strickland.

Katie ignored their protests and slipped away one night armed with numerous weapons and a burning need for revenge. Locating Strickland was surprisingly easy. Bold and without fear, he'd assumed his judgeship and set about doing his duties as Shelby county judge.

She shadowed his movements for two weeks, planning and revising until she'd perfected her strategy. On a Monday, she penned and posted her note.

Wednesday morning found her alongside an overgrown trail that once was a path between Cherokee villages, a wild green onion stalk held in one fist, the other clasped to her breast. " 'By this leek, I will most horribly revenge. I eat and eat, I swear.' "

A hysteric giggle escaped Katie's throat. One seldom quoted Shakespeare while setting a bear trap, but then, one seldom began the day intending to torture and murder a man before noon.

Dawn illuminated the vivid greens of early spring in

the eastern Texas forest as she strained to turn the screw that would open the rusty steel trap. Crushed bits of animal flesh clung to its dull metal teeth. She wrinkled her nose and swallowed hard as a wave of doubt washed over her.

No, she thought, hardening her heart, this man has destroyed everything I have held dear. He's an evil man, who merits this end. He deserved it years ago.

He deserved it that day in Austin.

The widening jaws of the trap emitted a tormenting creak. It echoed through her mind like the smoke-smothered cries of her daughter.

She wedged a clamp over the leaf spring and moved to set the second lever. Fleeing Austin a lifetime ago, she'd clamped her emotions just as securely. She allowed but one desire to exist, and it was a fever in her blood.

Katie lived for vengeance.

The trap lay open wide. She pulled up the pan and set the trip lever. Swallowing hard, she removed the clamp and stepped away. A grim smile tugged at her lips as she swore, "Jack Strickland dies today."

Carefully, she hid the trap beneath decaying leaves and brush, then checked her cache of weapons and supplies. The shotgun, bullwhip, and knife lay in readiness, tucked beneath an evergreen. She could reach them with ease from her position between the trap and the holly.

Her fingers brushed the cool, smooth neck of a bottle of Irish whiskey, and she pulled it from its hiding place. Staring at the amber liquid sloshing inside, she thought of her father. Da *had* loved his whiskey. "That's something else I owe Strickland for," she vowed. But for Sheriff Strickland, Da wouldn't have traveled to Indian Territory; he'd not have contracted smallpox. A doctor might have saved him from the stomach ailment had he had the chance.

Yes, Jack Strickland more than deserved the torment she planned for him. For Da, for Mary Margaret, for Steven, and Rob Garrett. For Johnny, especially Johnny, who would grow up knowing his mother as a murderer— the woman who killed his uncle Rob.

And Branch. Oh, God, Branch. And herself.

"No!" she cried. She'd not think in this manner any longer. The clamp in her chest wiggled dangerously.

She pulled the cork from the whiskey bottle and took a good-sized swallow. Fire burned her throat, and she choked and coughed while her eyes watered. "Oh my," she wheezed, "how do men do that?"

By now the sun rose well above the trees, bleaching the cloudless sky an oyster white. The temperature climbed steadily and perspiration trickled down the back of Katie's neck. He'll be here soon, she thought, inhaling a deep, calming breath. The trap was set. Now came the time to bait it.

Katie reached beneath her skirt and loosened her petticoat. She wiggled, and it dropped to the ground as her fingers worked the buttons at her bodice. She'd chosen this dress for its color; the lilac would show up well against the dark green foliage of the holly. It would never do to have him ride by without noticing her presence beside the road.

She pulled her arms from the sleeves and pushed the material over her hips. The morning air kissed her bare skin and she shivered—but not from cold. Grabbing the petticoat, Katie tossed the garment toward the center of the trail. The skirt billowed and floated gracefully to the ground. "A blind man would see that," she assured herself.

Line of sight would lead him to the splash of color she hung on the evergreen. But just seeing wasn't enough. She had to make sure he'd want to touch. Of course, she didn't really doubt he would, but a little extra effort never hurt. Katie took the bottle of liquor and stepped carefully around the trap to the sliver of space in front of the holly.

After taking one small sip, she tipped the bottle, and the liquid with its potent fumes cascaded down her front. The thin white cotton of her chemise and drawers absorbed the wetness and clung to her curves, outlining the fullness of her breasts and the gentle flare of her hips beneath a slim waist.

That's what I want him to see, she thought, looking

down at the transparent fabric. She counted on those curves to bring Jack Strickland into her clutches.

A mirthless smile curled Katie's lips. She was ready.

Jack Strickland tied his horse to a dogwood tree at the spot where the Indian path crossed the road. He continued his journey on foot, gun drawn, and senses alert. He tasted danger on the wind, smelled it. He knew he walked toward a trap, only he did so with anticipation.

Yesterday he'd received the note, read it, and promptly tossed it into the trash basket. But a strange feeling made him retrieve the letter. Smoothing the crinkled paper, he'd reread the words: "If you want to know who really killed Land Commissioner Garrett, meet me tomorrow at nine o'clock at the Cherokee village on the banks of Rocky Springs Creek." The handwriting was hauntingly familiar. He remembered a note warning of smallpox tacked on a cabin door.

Katie Kincaid waited for him at Rocky Springs Creek.

Leaves rattled as a cool breeze swept through the trees and scooped up the edge of something fluffy and white. A petticoat danced across the red dirt trail, bringing Strickland to an abrupt halt.

"Hello, Jack," Katie purred from a grassy spot just off the trail. She drew a pointed toe slowly up her leg and rested her foot along her inner thigh. "I thought you'd never get here."

His pistol at the ready in his right hand, Strickland tipped back his hat and flashed her a leering grin. "Why, Mrs. Kincaid, I must say this ambush you have arranged is unique to my experience—delightfully original."

"I'd hoped you'd appreciate my efforts, Judge. After all, you did seem rather taken with my charms on a number of occasions."

Lust burned in his eyes as his gaze locked upon her breasts. "It's safe to say I'd like to take your charms, Miz Katie, but I'm not a foolish man. Where are you hiding your weapons?"

She showed him her empty hands and carefully rose to

her knees. "The only weapons I have, Judge, are these." She arched her back and gestured toward her breasts, the dark, erect nipples clearly visible through the wet muslin.

"Such a feast could kill a weak-hearted man, but there's nothing feeble about me. Not my body *or* my brain. So tell me, what's the purpose of this morning's exercise?"

Katie's fingers played with the ribbon at the neck of her chemise. "Branch Kincaid died in that courtroom, and Hoss Garrett is after my neck because of it. You see, Jack, *I'm* the one who shot Rob Garrett."

"What?" His stare was fixed on her hands as they slowly pulled the muslin from her shoulder.

"He was going to arrest me for larceny. Steven was dead, and Garrett claimed he couldn't go back to the capital without a counterfeiter—Sam Houston had ordered it. So you see, Hoss Garrett feels that I cost him both his sons, since Branch died trying to save my son from being hurt."

Strickland's voice sounded strangled. "What is it you want from me?"

Katie rolled her shoulders, and her chemise slipped to hang at the tips of her breasts. "Protection. I'll be your wife or your whore, it doesn't really matter, as long as you protect me when Garrett's men track me down."

Strickland took a step forward, his hands tearing at the buttons on his shirt. She felt detached from the entire scene, simply a casual onlooker. "Why did you bring me all the way out here? Why not approach me in town?"

"Too dangerous. Hoss Garrett's nephew has already been to Gallagher's looking for me, and as easy a time as I had finding you, Chase will be right behind me."

Strickland scoffed as he unbuckled his holster and allowed it to slide carefully to the ground. "The Garretts can't hurt me here. East Texas is my stronghold. They can come at me all they want, but I have the men and the power to stop anyone they send."

"I know. That's why I came to you." Katie looked at his chest and the tattoo that stained his breast. Inside, she was shaking like a tree in a gale, but outwardly she remained calm. Her hands hovered at the drawstring of her drawers. "Are you ready to seal our bargain now?"

He unbuttoned his pants. "Nothing can stop me, Miz Katie."

Pulling off his brass-toed boots, he tossed them to the ground. How many men, Katie wondered, had he kicked with those particular items of footwear? He stepped toward her. Closer . . . *He'll scream.* . . . closer . . . *There'll be blood, lots of it, more than when Steven died.* . . . closer . . . *crushed leg, slivers of bone, maybe severed* . . . closer . . . *I really will be a killer.*

"*Stop!*" she screamed, grabbing the shotgun. She shoved the gun into the trap, tripping the spring, thereby saving the man she hated with every ounce of her soul from the fate she had dreamed for him.

"What the hell!"

Katie's shoulders slumped as she sank back onto the ground. The very last bit of fight she possessed flew out of her, escaping into the endless Texas sky. "I couldn't do it. Oh, holy saints above, I couldn't do it."

Strickland's gaze burned a furious path toward her. He bent, scooped up his gun, and leveled it at her head. Obviously, he now understood what had been her intentions.

"Why, you goddamn bitch!"

Katie raised her head and looked at him through life-weary eyes. "I want to kill you. Lord, I need to kill you. But I can't." She shook her head and laughed incredulously. "Can you believe that? I can kill a friend, but I can't kill the river scum responsible for the deaths of people I loved."

Keeping his gun pointed at Katie, Strickland reached down and pulled hard, dragging the trap out of his way.

"You are crazy, aren't you? Just like Kincaid claimed the night I burned down your inn. Now," he said, straightening and walking toward her, "as you know, I've been appointed Shelby County judge. I guess it's time to haul the criminal before the law, isn't it?"

He rubbed his hand slowly across his crotch.

It was as if another person lived within her body, watching Strickland shuck out of his pants. That person didn't even flinch as his sex sprang free, reaching grotesquely toward her. He set his gun aside and squatted down before her. With a vicious yank, he rent the thin cotton chemise in two, completely baring her breasts. "Damn, you have a pair of melons on you. This time, bitch, I'm finishing what I started long ago."

Melons . . . fruit . . . peaches. Oh, Branch, I loved you so. The thought summoned her resistance from the wind. As Strickland groped, she reached and found the knife hidden beneath the bush.

She stabbed him in the shoulder.

He screamed, she pushed, and scurried away from him. Quickly, she pulled on her dress, pausing only long enough to say to the writhing man who reached to pull the knife from his back, "Go to hell, Jack Strickland. My greatest regret is that I haven't the strength to start you on your journey."

Katie ran for the horse she had tied in the woods. The bay pricked his ears and nickered as she nervously untied the reins and mounted. Now that she'd decided to live, she'd best be about making sure he didn't catch her.

"Let's go, boy," she said, slapping the horse's rump. She couldn't return to Shaddoe's, she didn't dare lead him to Johnny. People were her best hope. She doubted she could hide from him in the thicket; Strickland was known to be a good tracker. Her best protection would be to surround herself with people until she could find a way to send for Johnny and disappear completely. When she reached the road, she turned the horse toward Nacogdoches.

It proved to be a poor choice. Before dark, the county sheriff and two deputies had taken Katie into custody. By nightfall, she was ensconced in the Nacogdoches jail charged with, of all things, the murder of Robert Garrett, Jr.

Katie wondered why she'd not been accused of the attempted murder of Jack Strickland. But when the authorities deemed the crime against Rob Garrett had occurred in Shelby county and transferred her trial to Shelbyville, understanding dawned. Scheduled to begin in two weeks, the case against Katie Kincaid would be heard by the newest county judge, the one who'd already condemned two men to hang—Judge Jack Strickland.

He was out for her blood.

CHAPTER 20

$\mathscr{F}$RAGRANT WISTERIA crawled along the red-tiled roof line and drooped down into the patio of a hacienda halfway between Austin and San Antonio de Bexar. Chase Garrett sat at the edge of a bubbling, double-tiered fountain in the center of the courtyard, one bare foot splashing lazily in the water. He used the other to balance himself as he stretched out on the blue-tiled font.

For the past ten minutes or so he'd been fighting the hiccups, a result, he felt certain, of too much cayenne pepper in the gumbo served tonight at dinner. "That's what I get for tryin' to teach a Mexican cook how to fix Creole food," he grumbled, followed at once by another *hiccup*.

He groaned and thumped his chest with a fist as he heard his cousin's roar explode from his bedroom in the east wing of the house. Well, from the sounds of that yell, I give him less than a week, Chase told himself. He'd be strong enough to sit a horse for the trip to East Texas by then.

Branch Kincaid did not make a good invalid. It was bad enough that Hoss Garrett imposed on the hospitality of old friends for a private place where Branch could recover from a serious gunshot wound. What Chase's ailing cousin especially didn't appreciate was the fact that Hoss kept sending the daughter of the hacienda, a black-eyed señorita named Concheta upstairs to nurse him.

Heartburn got the better of Chase, and he rolled off the fountain. Padding around the courtyard toward the kitchen with the intent of pilfering a glass of buttermilk, he glanced inside as he passed the library doors. That's strange, he thought, watching as his uncle knelt at the hearth and put a match to kindling. The air tonight had a muggy, headaching edge. It was not the night for a fire.

Chase's brow knotted as he moved back into the shadows. Why would Hoss be building a fire when it had to be eighty degrees outside? And at this time of night, in Don Andres Montoya's library of all places?

Hoss rose and walked over to the desk. He picked up a stack of newspapers and tossed them one by one into the flames. The fire flared as it fed upon the paper. Chase took a look at his uncle's expression and blinked in surprise. Hoss's eyes were as hard as the marble hearth, his smile nothing short of malevolent.

What in the hell was in those newspapers? Smothering his hiccups, Chase waited until the fire died and Hoss had left the room. A thick carpet cushioned his feet as he crossed the room to the fireplace.

Only ashes and the distinctive scent of cedar kindling remained.

He pursed his lips, staring at the grate. He couldn't shake the feeling that something important had taken place here moments ago. But what?

"Damn, what was in those newspapers?" They'd arrived in today's batch of mail. A boy brought it out twice weekly with his deliveries from the mercantile in Austin. The Garretts had been here long enough that they were receiving their own mail in the bag with the Montoyas. "I wonder," Chase said quietly. "Would the lovely Concheta sneak me her father's newspaper?"

It took him only a few minutes, three Spanish phrases of adoration, and one stolen kiss to find out. The señorita met him back at the fountain, paper in hand.

"It's the *Telegraph and Texas Register*," she said. "Will that do?"

"I think it might, *querida*."

She handed the paper to Chase, who immediately glanced at the headlines. Political news and the editorials dominated the front page. He could see nothing of special import in such information.

The paper rustled as he opened it, and Señorita Concheta said, "I imagine you're anxious for news about the trial, aren't you?" She shook her head. "It's such a sad thing. Your poor Uncle Hoss."

Chase looked up sharply. Concheta's smile was full of pity as she continued. "The article's on the back page. The trial's getting press all over the state, so I've heard, what with the scandal of it all."

The headline blared at Chase. *Woman charged with murder in Shelbyville. Trial begins Monday.*

Chase felt the color drain from his face as he read the account. Hell, Katie, why couldn't you have stayed out of trouble, at least until Branch got well? Chase raked his fingers through his hair. He'd bet his bottom dollar Branch didn't know Katie was in the Shelbyville jail right now. Hoss apparently did. Sonofabitch! By the appearance of things, he didn't want any other Garrett to learn what was happening in the East Texas forests. Hoss must really hate Katie Kincaid to pull a stunt like this. Chase knew his uncle held her responsible for Rob's death, although to Chase's way of thinking, Hoss ought to be glad she'd spared his son from lingering on in pain. But Ol' Uncle G. didn't feel that way and, in fact, he blamed her for Branch's being shot, too.

His thoughts spinning, Chase absently thanked Señorita Montoya with a distracted kiss and headed to his room. A thunderstorm building in the west obstructed the dawning stars. Watching the cloud steadily dim the sky's light, he felt as though something similar had a hold on the Garrett family.

What should he do? Branch couldn't travel yet, it'd kill him. Learning about this would kill him. That copy of the *Register* was a week old; could the trial be over already? Dear Lord, they wouldn't hang a woman, would they?

It looked like they'd hang her, for a fact.

Katie sat on the splintery defendant's bench in the courtroom and watched a parade of witnesses—most of them strangers—come forth to malign her character. After the first day and a half, the outcome of the trial was a foregone conclusion, punishment being the only question remaining. With Jack Strickland sitting as judge, she feared the answer was inevitable.

She had held out some hope even after realizing the judge counted her own lawyer among his cronies. Katie never liked to give up a fight, but the day the prosecution read a letter from Hoss Garrett urging for swift and strict justice, she conceded. Apparently, the way out of this mess didn't lead through a courtroom.

Martha Craig laid a comforting hand on Katie's shoulder as she rose to hear the verdict. It would have been nice if Shaddoe had been here, she absently thought. Had news of the trial reached him in New Orleans? A weak smile stretched across her face. She certainly could use one of his spells right about now!

Strickland's smirk revealed the judgment before it was read. Despite herself, Katie's stomach clenched, and perspiration wet her brow as she waited to hear her sentence pronounced.

Seizing upon the presence of reporters from across the state to further his political ambitions, Judge Strickland lectured, "The murder of a government official cannot go unpunished. This woman, despite her gender, committed a vile, contemptible crime. We've heard testimony as to the watonness of her conduct, of the audacity of her actions. Who here can forget this woman married the brother of the man she murdered to secure his wealth? I tell you, people of the great state of Texas, this we cannot abide."

He looked directly at Katie. She read the hate in his eyes and her stomach soured. A blackmailer and a murderer prepared to serve her with a penalty for a crime for which he was responsible. How's that for justice?

She fixed her gaze upon the red, white, and blue Lone Star flag hanging on the wall above the judge and thought, Holy saints above, I don't want to die.

"Kathleen Gallagher Starr Kincaid, you have been tried and convicted for the murder of Commissioner Robert Garrett. By the power afforded me by the State of Texas, I hereby sentence you to death by hanging."

The courtroom erupted, cheers and jeers, and a horrified shriek from Martha Craig. Strickland raised his voice to be heard over the commotion. "In order to provide the opportunity for the citizens of Texas to witness the execution, and to allow sufficient time for the erection of a scaffold, I declare the punishment will be delayed until one week from today. At that time, Katie Kincaid, you will be hanged by the neck until dead."

Gleefully, he declared, "This court is now adjourned."

Shelbyville merchants knew from experience that executions swelled profits. But even the most knowledgeable of businessmen never expected the extent of interest hanging a woman had generated. The night before Katie's scheduled execution, every bed in every hotel, residence, tavern, and whorehouse in town had been claimed. Hundreds of visitors waited impatiently to see the State of Texas stretch Mrs. Kincaid's lovely neck.

Hoss Garrett could be counted among the multitudes, and his presence did not escape notice. One man in particular made note that the head of the Garrett family traveled to watch his daughter-in-law die. Muttering an obscenity, he decided that with this, Garrett had gone too far to be forgiven.

Puffy clouds concealed the crescent moon, plunging the streets into near blackness. A tall, solid shadow separated from the building opposite the jail, then faded into the inky alleyway. Information had been gathered. Two guards, four guns. Simplicity itself.

Feeling his way with his good hand, a specter dressed completely in black crawled atop the mercantile's roof. From that vantage point, he scanned the top of the building next door, searching. There, just as he had hoped, a thin wisp of smoke rose from the stove pipe.

On the courthouse lawn, the scaffold flashed beneath the intermittent moonlight. A near-silent scrape of metal on metal betrayed the attendance of mischief beneath the trap door. The creak of a twisting screw gave evidence of tampering on the crossbar. However, only the one who did the work heard the sound.

Footsteps paced the wooden planks of a fancy-house room outside town. A muffled curse escaped the walls as an ankle twisted in unfamiliar feminine shoes. The notched tip of a forged steel bowie pricked the deep pockets of the dress. In lieu of an ammunition pouch, extra bullets went into the flowery plumage of a stylish hat. The occupant checked his rouge, then left the room.

He poured an equal amount of black powder into each hole of the Paterson Colt's cylinder. Then he took a bullet from a soft leather pouch and placed it on the mouth of one chamber. Rotating the cylinder until the ball was under the loading lever, he rammed it home. He whistled a tune beneath his breath as he repeated the process for each chamber.

A small box sat beside him on the bed, and from it he took small brass percussion caps and placed them one at a time on the five nipples at the back of the cylinder.

The smile that crossed his face was ugly. He cocked the Paterson, and as was its design, the trigger dropped. He fingered the cool steel carefully, an imaginary scene playing out in his mind. Lamplight cast a dull blue gleam on the well-oiled surface of the gun as he uncocked it and tucked it into his belt.

He stood, gathered his other weapons, and set a wide-brimmed, low-crowned hat upon his head. The door closed silently behind him.

· · ·

Beneath the light of a single candle, Katie affixed her signature to the letter with a sense of finality. It was done. Thank goodness for that. Never before had committing her thoughts and feelings to paper proved so difficult. Probably the fact that she'd not defined those emotions to herself beforehand made the difference.

For the past week, she'd spent her time composing this letter to her son, hoping all the while that he'd never see it. Hour after hour, she'd worked to find just the right word, the perfect sentence to convey her thoughts.

The letter explained and denied, requesting and defended. It was a mother's deathbed letter to a son she'd never know, a man who would grow to adulthood under the stigma of family scandal. She'd cried over the missive, and laughed. She'd confessed her deepest secrets and warmest memories. Most of all, she'd told her son of the great, undying love she'd felt for his father.

More than anything else in the world, she longed for the chance to tell him all this in person.

But just in case she couldn't, if this plan she'd also composed during the last week failed, the letter would be delivered into Shaddoe St. Pierre's hands as she had requested. Shaddoe would keep it for her, for Johnny. He'd make sure her son received it when the moment was right.

Shuffling footsteps interrupted her reverie. A key jangled in the lock and the cell door squeaked open. Sheriff Llewellyn massaged the back of his neck as he said, "Mrs. Kincaid, the streets are fairly clear now. If you've still a mind for that bath you asked for, I've informed the hotel to clear a room for you and heat up some water."

His fingers pulled at his beard as he continued, "This is pretty irregular, and you have to know I'm obliged to stand guard over you. But seein' how it's your last request, I'll take you on over there if that's what you want."

Katie stood. "Thank you, Sheriff. I appreciate your kindness."

He ducked his head, shifting uneasily. "Sorry I couldn't get ya a better table to write at than that old barrel. Nothin' else would've fit in here, though. Hope ya got all the writin' done ya needed. I'll take good care of your letters."

Katie smiled at him. As he took her arm, escorting her from the jail, Katie fretted over her intentions. Of all the men who had a part in this farce orchestrated by Jack Strickland, Sheriff Llewellyn had proved to be the single honorable man. He upheld the law and performed his duty, although he obviously felt uncomfortable dealing with a woman prisoner.

She liked the man. It's a shame, she thought, that he'd be the one to get hurt.

A harmonica played a melancholy song in the distance as they made their way to the hotel. The proprietor gawked at Katie as he led her and the sheriff up the stairs to a room at the end of the hall. Inside, all small objects had been cleared away; only heavy furniture and the brass bathtub filled with steaming water remained. Katie smiled with satisfaction.

She turned to the sheriff, a God-fearing, family man she'd been told. "Will you be inside or out, Sheriff Llewellyn?"

Color crept up his face. "Uh, I'm sorry, ma'am. I gotta stay in the room. I'll give you privacy as best I can, though."

"Very well," Katie said, shrugging. She inhaled a steadying breath. So far, everything was going according to plan.

But now, with the moment upon her, could she follow through? Could she physically assault a man she respected, a man who acted only as his position required?

It's either that, or die, she told herself. She had to take matters into her own hands, so to speak. No one was coming to save her. She could depend only upon herself.

And that's the way it ought to be. She'd forgotten it for a while, that's all. Da had always told her, "The Good Lord helps those who help themselves."

She'd not forget again.

Lifting her chin, Katie presented her back to Sheriff Llewellyn. "If you'd be so kind, sir, to undo my buttons?"

Whump. Thud. One jailhouse guard went down.

Whack. "Ugh." Both men lay unconscious on the floor.

Shaddoe St. Pierre, disguised in buckskins and the traditional Cherokee turban, turned to the cell ready to speak and stopped. The door stood open wide.

Kathleen was not there.

He stared, gawking, and was therefore taken by surprise when the tall, ugly, loudmouthed woman burst through the door wailing, "You can't kill her. Not now. I tell you, I work at Gertie's place, and Katie Kincaid came there not two months ago asking for a way to rid herself of a babe. Well, of course we didn't tell her, us knowing her husband so well and all. You cannot put her to death, Sheriff. She's pregnant!"

Then her sharp brown eyes gleamed at Shaddoe. The handkerchief came away from her face, and a gun came out of her pocket.

"Don't I know you?" a gruff, male voice asked.

Shaddoe said, "You are Garrett, Chase Garrett."

In that moment, a billowing cloud of black smoke gushed from the pot-bellied stove.

Daniel Gallagher grinned as the sound of choking coughs came from the jailhouse. He picked his way over the side of the roof. Then, to his dismay, his damaged hand lost its grip and he slipped.

He fell square atop a man who was standing on a box and peering inside Katie's cell window. "What the hell," Keeper McShane gasped, attempting to catch his breath.

"Keeper? Is that you, Keeper?" Daniel asked in a whisper as he rolled off the other man.

"Gallagher? Well, I'll be damned. How ya' doin', Daniel? It's been a while, ain't it? Whatcha been up to? Been in the Territory all this time?"

"McShane, you are as dense as ever," Daniel growled in a whisper. "My sister's going to hang tomorrow unless I save her, and you're interrupting my plan."

"*Your plan!* You're the one interruptin' *my* plan."

Daniel shook his head. "Well, never mind. Listen, I've blocked the stove pipe, and the place is filling with smoke. I've got to get in there *now* and get her out."

He got to his feet and sneaked around to the door with Keeper following on his heels, whispering, "Say, I rigged the scaffold. There's no way she's gonna hang off that bit of lumber tomorrow. My plan's perfect, I've got a wagon all set to go and black powder charges hidden all over town."

Daniel crashed through the doorway, pistol drawn. Through the smoke, he saw the craziest sight he'd ever witnessed. A big, ugly, short-haired woman was bent over double, coughing like a lung-shot sailor, holding a gun on Shaddoe Dancer, who beat at the stove with a lady's scalp.

Keeper held a kerchief to his face and drawled through the cloth, "Well, I'll be dipped in shellac."

With the fire out and the door wide open, the smoke began to clear. The four men stared at one another, then straightened as one at the clicks of a pair of guns.

Silence hung like the smoke on the air. Then a voice familiar to them all growled, "Goddamn! She's gone and done it again."

Sheriff Llewellyn's fingers trembled as he worked the buttons at the back of Katie's dress. Poor man, he was as nervous as a hen on a hot griddle.

She'd caught him by surprise with her request for assistance in undressing. He'd had to choose between helping her himself or leaving her to hunt down a woman who could act as lady's maid, and he'd approached her as though *he* were the condemned.

Katie had rather hoped, for his sake, that he'd leave her alone. As it was, she'd have to hurt him, and she dreaded that as much as he flinched at undoing her dress.

She almost made her move while his fingers fiddled with the buttons and hooks at the back of her neck. His gun was in easy reach, and he appeared unaware of his vulnerability. But she hesitated, unsure, as her teeth nibbled at her lower lip.

She'd only get one chance.

Besides, she thought, seizing on the first excuse that flitted through her mind, if I act now, I won't get my bath. After almost a month in jail, she wanted a bath almost as much as she wanted to avoid the hangman.

The sheriff managed to finish the job, then he marched to the door where he stood with his back to her. The skin above his collar scorched red. Rocking on his heels, he shoved both hands in his pockets and waited.

Katie didn't wait. She stripped off her clothing and climbed into the warm, lilac-scented water with a heartfelt sigh. Never again would she take such a simple pleasure for granted. A bar of soap and a washcloth sat on a chair within reach. After scrubbing the stale scent of the jail from her body, she stretched her neck and dipped her head back into the water. The soap didn't lather nearly as well as what she once made, but she washed her hair as best she could.

A wooden bucket of fresh water sat at the foot of the tub. Should she do it? The more flustered he was, the better. Aloud, she said, "Sheriff, I hate to bother you any more, but I need to rinse my hair and I can't lift the bucket. Would you please help me?"

"Oh, umm, ah, Mrs. Kincaid, I don't think so," he stammered.

"Please? I know this whole situation is a bit difficult, but Sheriff Llewellyn, it's very important to me that I meet my end with as much composure as I can muster. A clean person will help me *so* much in that regard. Please, sir?"

"Oh, all right." He shuffled to the tub. Lifting the bucket, he started to pour the water over Katie's long hair. She saw his Adam's apple bob as his eyes darted a look. He dumped the rinse water in a rush, dropped the bucket, and scurried back to his position by the door.

A quick little smile flashed across Katie's face as she climbed from the tub, wiping water from her eyes. He really was a nice man.

Drying herself, she considered her plan of action one last time. Was this the right thing to do? Would it work? She had no earthly idea how she'd get out of town, but then, a few days ago she'd had no idea how she'd get out of jail. Surely, even if she got caught, it would be better than sitting around waiting to feel the noose tighten around her neck.

And she really didn't want to die.

Chatting all the while, she quickly slipped into her underthings. She consciously milked every rustle out of every feminine frill that she could as she donned her dress. She talked about the weather; how she hoped the visitors in town wouldn't be hurt by the heat expected the following day. The first time she sat on the bed, the ropes didn't creak. She sat again and they did.

Sheriff Llewellyn jumped.

Katie kept talking. Changing her topic, she began to speak of Branch. "He was such a fine husband. Why, for such a strong man—he's big like you, sheriff—oh, let me tell you, he was just the most gentle thing. Those hands of his, his touch, umm, so soft." She sighed. "I miss him. But I guess I won't have that problem much longer. Still, I wish I could have felt a man's touch just one more time."

She stood and lifted her hair, presenting her back to the sheriff. "I need you to do me up, Sheriff," she said.

Katie could hear his strangled gurgle. His footsteps approached as though *he* were climbing the scaffold steps. His fingers never touched her skin, but she could feel him tug at the button, and his nervousness stood like a third person in the room.

Now, she thought. She whirled and grabbed his gun. Before he had the presence of mind to as much as speak, she scooped up the empty water bucket and whacked him on the side of the head.

Sheriff Llewellyn slumped to the floor. Following a quick apology, she hit him again and he lost consciousness.

Katie ran to the window and peered out, reaching around to fasten what buttons she could. Pursing her lips, she made a decision. She'd go out the window.

Stripping the sheets from the bed, she tied them together, then looped one end around the iron bedstead. She frowned. The white would be a beacon hanging down the side of the hotel, but there wasn't much else she could do.

A prolonged creak announced the opening of the window, and Katie winced. Tossing the sheet-rope out, she cautiously began her descent to the street.

Branch Kincaid walked down the deserted street, cursing beneath his breath. He'd been at it most of the past ten minutes, ever since he realized the jail cell was empty. The fact that four other would-be rescuers muddled the picture hadn't helped his temper much either. No one, not a cursed one of them, knew where the hell she'd gotten off to. What an ineffective bunch of clods they all were, himself included. It had never occurred to him that the sheriff might move Katie from the jail.

Branch had demanded explanations from each man. They'd all had pretty good plans, although he'd had to shake his head at Chase's ill-begotten plot. "I thank you for your help, cousin," he'd said, "but I've got to tell you, as a woman, you're a two-bottle nightmare."

Chase agreed, declaring he'd arrived in Shelbyville just that afternoon and had taken the only course he could think of on such short notice.

After a brief discussion, the five men concluded that Keeper's plan would be the one upon which they relied. His was the only scheme set for daytime. Katie's life depended on them, and they were prepared to do anything to save her. Branch had set a meeting place and time for the following morning, and each man declared to do his best to discover what had happened to the missing prisoner.

"I wonder where they've put her," Branch muttered as he headed for his hotel room and a bit of thinking. "But I'll find her, and when I do, hangin's gonna look to be a peaceful bit of livin'." *Humph!* The damn fool woman had done her level best to get herself killed and he'd known nothing about it. He never would have seen the newspaper if Senorita Montoya hadn't stormed into his sickroom complaining about Chase's abrupt departure. Branch had been shocked to read the newspaper account of her trial wondering all the while just what she'd done to get tangled in Strickland's net. It must have been bad, for him to have staged this medicine show.

Yes, his bride definitely had some explaining to do—and not just about this Strickland business either. For one thing, she up and ran off before he even got the chance to look her baby over good. In those few seconds in the courtroom before everything went black, he'd seen something in that child that left a funny feeling in his gut.

Then, too, was the fact that she'd left at all. That's what really chewed his jerky—that she'd hightailed it when he lay there squirting blood like a patio fountain spurts water. His wife left Austin not knowing whether he was dead or alive.

The thought brought Branch to a halt at a bench on the boardwalk in front of the mercantile. He sat, propped his elbows on his knees, and thumped his chin with his fisted hands. Above him, a wooden sign squeaked as it swung slowly in the light breeze.

Maybe she didn't care whether he was dead or alive.

Well, hell. He pushed to his feet and turned toward his hotel, kicking along a rock as he walked Shelbyville's Main Street. He was gonna find his bride and do some serious talking. There were certain things he just had to know.

Maybe she didn't love him anymore.

⚛ CHAPTER 21 ⚛

*T*HE ROPE WAS too short. Dangling fifteen feet above the street, Katie twisted her head, looking for signs of life below. Empty. Good. So far, her guardian angel was hard at work.

She inhaled a deep breath, closed her eyes, and let go. She landed in the dirt with a thud. On her behind. "Ouch." Cringing, Katie climbed to her feet. She glanced over her shoulder and checked to see if anyone noticed her not-quite-silent descent. All quiet. "Thank you, Lord."

Now where? Off the street first. She took a step toward the alley beside the hotel when a board squeaked somewhere behind her. She dashed for the darkness. Hide, Katie, hide, she told herself. You can't outrun anyone barefoot. Fool, what were you thinking of when you left your shoes upstairs?

There, a shadow, at the end of the alley, big and dark. Moving toward her. "Oh." She ducked behind a staircase, flattening herself against the wall, thankful her dress was forest green. A whisper of wind touched her as he passed. Boots crunched debris, then silence.

Slowly, Katie counted to one hundred. She'd have liked to make it five hundred, but Sheriff Llewellyn could be waking up at any moment. She'd had no rope with which to tie him, and she didn't think wrapping his wrists with her petticoat would hold him for long. He'd spit the pillowcase from his mouth and call for help, if nothing else.

Time to go. A horse, she needed a horse. Stepping out from behind the staircase, she moved on silent feet toward the back of the alley. An arm snaked out of the darkness and grabbed her about the waist, pulling her back against a wall of hard muscle. A hand covered her mouth.

Fear. Despair. She didn't want to die!

Then, the scent of him—oh, Merciful Lord.

"Well, well, well. If it ain't the missin' Mrs. Kincaid," a familiar drawl whispered.

Her heart skipped a beat. Terror gushed from her head to her toes, and her knees went weak. "But you're dead! Oh, my God, they must have hanged me after all."

Branch was so relieved that he was furious. Damn the woman for putting him through this. No doubt she'd shortened his life by at least a decade with her shenanigans. He felt her sag against him, and he grumbled in her ear, "That's it. Get comfortable. I'm not lettin' you loose anytime in the near future. You've a nasty habit of disappearin' on me."

"Oh, Branch." Katie twisted and flung her arms around his neck, burying her face against his chest. "Are you really alive? Am I still alive? What are you doing here? I'm so glad you're here. How did you get here? Is Johnny here?"

"Here, here, hush." He tilted her chin and gave her a quick, hard kiss before saying, "I'm alive and you're alive, and if we want to stay that way, we'd best get to movin'."

"But Branch, he told me you were dying! And there was so much blood—I didn't see how—"

"Come on, Sprite. There'll be time for questions later. And believe me, there'll be plenty of them. Now, though, I've got horses hidden just outside town."

He pulled her back toward the street just as Sheriff Llewellyn stuck his head out of the upstairs window and shouted, "Escape! Sound the alert. Prisoner escape. Mrs. Kincaid's disappeared."

Branch muttered, "Damn," as the immediate uproar in the street indicated a search would soon be underway.

Nervously, Katie babbled, "I should have tied him and gagged him better, I guess. I didn't have much. He's just such a nice man and I didn't want to hurt him and . . ."

"And your benevolence'll get you hanged, woman. Just be glad I'm here to help you. Now hush and let me think. We need a place to hide—fast. We'll have to hole up and wait for the posse to head out of town before we make a move to the horses."

Branch cautiously stuck his head around the building's corner. Already a dozen or more men gathered, carrying lanterns and flickering torches, waiting for instructions. Katie tugged at his shirt. He waved her back. She tugged again. Pulling back into the alley, he snapped, "What?"

"I don't need to be grateful to you—I was doing just fine on my own. I escaped. You didn't help. Of course, I thought you were dead, so I didn't expect you to help. But I *did* do it all on my own, so quit being so all-fired mannish about it." She crossed her arms over her chest and huffed.

Branch gritted his teeth. "Save it, Sprite. You've bigger problems to deal with. Come on." He dragged her to the back of the alley, looked up and down the back street, then led her north.

"Where are we going?" Katie whispered.

"I want to be nearer the horses before we settle in."

"Do you have a hotel room? We could wait there."

Branch shook his head. "They're liable to search the buildings first, especially if they've heard I'm in town. We need a spot where nobody'd think of lookin'."

They sneaked behind a tavern where news of Katie's escape swept through the drunken crowd like a flame. Branch sneered in disgust as he heard a man's loud voice complain, "I rode over a hunnerd miles to git a look-see at a woman bein' hanged. Heard she's a right purty gal too. I'm gonna be pissed as hell iffen they don't get her back in time to stretch her neck."

Katie gasped. Branch gave her hand a comforting squeeze. They worked their way across town, hiding in shadows, darting across streets when the moon disappeared behind a cloud. By now the sound of fists banging on doors and shouted demands filled the night. Lamps burned in places previously dark.

"All right, this is as far as we go for now," Branch

said. They stood behind a two-story building, and he pointed toward a window at the second-floor right corner. "That's my room. I can watch you from there, drive off any trouble if needed."

"What?" Katie asked, a frown in her voice. "Watch me where? Why? Won't I be with you?"

"Can't you hear? They're searchin' the buildings, just like I said. I've a place in mind that'll be safe for you. I've done this a hundred times and it always works. Come here, we don't have much time." About twenty feet from the back of the hotel was an ash pit. He led her to its edge and said, "Lie down."

"What?"

Branch dipped one hand into the black, dusty ash and caught Katie's chin with the other. He brought his fingers to her cheek, but she reared back. "I'm not going in there, Branch. I won't do it. You just think of something else."

"No time. Hurry now." He smeared the ash across her face.

"B . . . ra . . . a . . . anch," Katie wailed, "I just took a bath. My first one in weeks. I'm clean again. Don't make me!"

"Quit your bitchin'. What's more important, your life or sweet-smellin' skin? I swear, if you're not just like a woman."

He scooped her up and deposited her, facedown into the smut. She immediately bounced up on all fours, spitting the ash from her mouth, blowing it from her nose. "Dammit Kate, get down. This is a perfect place to hide. No one's going to notice you unless they step on you, and even then all you have to do is keep your mouth shut."

Branch tugged at her skirt, pulling her knees out from under her. He rolled her onto her back. Standing with hands on hips, he looked down. "That's pretty good. Now, hold still." He gathered a few leaves and a couple of sticks and covered her haphazardly. Stepping back, he looked again. He shook his head and sighed. "Nope, you stick up too far. Roll back to your stomach."

Katie propped herself up on her hands and glared at

him. "One of these days, Branch Kincaid, I'm going to make you pay for all this."

Branch pushed her to the ground and tossed some leaves atop her. "Every day for as long as I live will be just fine with me. You just lie here quiet like. I'm goin' up to my room, and I'll signal you when it's safe to come up. You *can* climb a rope, can't you? Hush now, Sprite. I think I hear someone comin'."

Katie muttered just loud enough for him to hear. "This is what I get for depending on a man. When will I ever learn?"

Branch faded back into the darkness beside the building. Footsteps crunched down the alleyway, and he saw the figure of a man stop and look above to the second-floor windows. Branch's room and one other had a lamp burning. The figure tossed a pebble at the other window.

The window opened, and an elderly woman stuck out her head. "My lands, is there no peace to be found in this place? Quiet out there!" She slammed the window shut.

"Well, I'm as sorry as a whore in church," the figure muttered, thereby identifying himself to Branch.

He stepped out into the moonlight. "Chase," he said.

The figure turned. "Branch? That you?"

"Yep."

"Branch, have you heard the news? Katie was in the hotel, and she knocked the sheriff over the head and escaped. What'll we do now? We've gotta find her. They're gathering a posse and searching the town. She can't have gotten far."

"I wouldn't doubt her too much. After all, there were five of us trying to help her, and she managed to get it done all on her own. If she could hear me now, I'd tell her I've learned a thing or two."

"Or three." The muffled words carried to the cousins' ears.

Chase jumped. "You found her!"

"Damn right. Just took a bit of thought," Branch drawled. "Look, since you're here, maybe we can get out of this a little faster." He whispered over his shoulder, "Sprite, I've got a few things to take care of. You keep still. They'll be sure to search my room right off, then I'll have you upstairs in no time." Throwing his arm around his cousin's shoulder, Branch led him away, whispering his plan in the younger man's ear.

He ignored his wife's angry hiss.

Katie cried silently. Big, sloppy, soggy drops that created streaks in the grime ground into her face. After five hours in the stinking ash pit, with people stomping near, with at least one rat and a multitude of beetles crawling all over her, she figured a couple minutes of self-pity wouldn't hurt a bit.

Chase tugged her toward the hotel. "Come on, darlin'," he whispered. "Branch said you'd handle this rope with no trouble—said ya had lots of experience in trees."

Katie eyed the rope that hung from Branch's window and grimaced. What next!

Chase tugged the line, making sure it held fast. He handed it to her, saying, "Be quick about it now, it's almost dawn."

With a sobby sigh, Katie began to pull herself up. Chase put his hands on her behind and pushed. These Garrett boys were certainly free with their hands, she noted. With her feet propped against the hotel wall, Katie inched upward. The hemp bit into her hands, stinging. She pooched out her lip and cried a little more.

"You got it, Katie," Chase whispered. "Just hurry, it's getting light; and remember, Branch is waiting for you right the other side of that window."

The sound she made was a cross between a whine and a snarl.

Halfway up. Her arms ached, splinters speared the soles of her bare feet. Clenching her teeth, she took a deep breath to bolster her strength. "Oh, my," she gasped. She smelled gamy as a goat.

Then she heard it. That song, that stupid little song he hummed all the time, the one he called his battle hymn. The sound called her, wrapped around her, and lifted her toward his window. She grasped the sill with one hand, then the other. Where was he? Why didn't he help her? Why hadn't *he* pulled her up?

She heaved herself through the window and fell headlong into the room. The whistling stopped as she looked up.

Branch sat in a steaming brass tub, a cigar in one hand and a whiskey in the other.

It was just too much. Her eyes overflowed and her shoulders began to shake. A long, thin wail escaped her throat.

Branch's cocky expression faded. "Aw, hell, Sprite, don't cry. It was only a joke. The bath's for you," he assured her. "Don't cry anymore, please! Here." He rose naked from the water and walked toward her. Droplets of water reflected the room's muted light, and his frame glistened, reminiscent of the fine sheen of sweat he wore at the end of their lovemaking.

A great sob escaped her before he wrapped her in his arms and silenced her with a kiss. He tasted of whiskey, smelled of tobacco, and felt hard and soft and ever so safe.

"Come on now, Sprite," he murmured against her forehead. He held her while she cried, rocking her, cooing and kissing until the tension melted away.

"You weren't the least bit funny, Branch Garrett."

"Kincaid," he corrected. "Sorry, love, it just seemed the thing to do at the time. You'd yelled at me for helpin' and said you'd do better alone, so I figured I'd let you. I didn't think climbin' a rope would be a step for a stepper like you. Why, I've seen you shimmy up a tree quick as a hiccup."

Katie sniffed and wiped her nose with the handkerchief he handed to her. "It's not that, it's everything. Oh, Branch, I thought you were dead! It was all my fault. Hoss was right. I'd cost him both his sons. Rob was dead and you were dying. He sent me away." Trembling, she repeated softly, "I thought you had died."

She felt his pulse pound as fury flexed his muscles. For a long minute he was silent. Then softly he asked, "And did you care?"

Katie stared at him. She looked deep into those haunted golden eyes and recognized the vulnerable light. Well, fancy that, she thought. Her answer mattered to him. Maybe a lot. Her heart twisting in her chest, she answered him in the way she thought he'd best accept.

High in the stomach, well away from his wounds, she punched him with her fist. "Of course I cared, you stupid fool! I love you!"

Wincing, he coughed twice and said, "Lord, woman. You ought to bottle that wallop and sell it. It'd make me rich."

She buried her face in his shoulder. "You are rich."

He pushed her away from him and placed his finger beneath her chin, tilting her head to look at him. "Yes, Sprite, I am."

Dropping her gaze, Katie pleated her gown nervously. What does that mean? she wondered. Is he talking about money?

Or was he referring to her love?

And how did he feel about her?

Unwilling to face that particular truth, she said, "Branch, tell me what happened. The wounds—"

His hand stroked her arm. "The bullet in the shoulder caught me high and missed all the important parts. The one in the hip, well, I lost a good bit of blood. Took me a while to come round; apparently I had a fever. Don't worry about it, though, Sprite. I'm fit just fine. It's all over."

She nodded. "I'm glad you're alive, Branch."

"Well, you know, I am too." He clicked his tongue and added, "If I were dead, I couldn't tell you how all fired angry I am at you for pullin' whatever stunt it was that got you into this fix. Care to tell me about it, Kate?"

Katie gave him a weak smile. "I tried to kill Strickland."

"I was afraid it was somethin' like that." Branch muttered a vile curse. "Why, Kate? Why risk yourself like that? And your baby, for God's sake. You put that child at risk of growin' up without a mother."

Katie pushed angrily away. "Don't you dare try to

second-guess me, Mr. Garrett. I considered every angle before I made my plans. Jack Strickland killed my Steven, he killed Mary Margaret. I thought he'd killed you. I thought it best not to allow him the opportunity to kill anyone else I loved, primarily Johnny."

"Johnny?"

"My son."

Slowly, like honey poured from a chilled crock, a smile lit Branch's face. "A boy, huh? Well, we need to talk about him too, but let's get done with Strickland first. If you made such careful plans, how come you're the one scheduled to hang come ten o'clock?"

Katie's face paled. "Oh, I'd almost forgotten."

"What happened, Sprite?" Branch asked, wiping a smudge from her cheek.

She was silent for a long minute. From out on the street came the sounds of life beginning to stir, readying to meet the dawn. She trembled and her voice was a mere whisper. "I couldn't do it. I had him, and I couldn't do it."

He sighed. "I figured as much. You're about as vicious as a sucklin' lamb." He pulled her into his arms. "But you try, don't you? You're faithful to those you love."

She looked up at him, the question in her eyes.

Branch wasn't quite ready to answer it. "Guess we're lucky the good sheriff didn't allow your bad temper to send you to the scaffold early."

"I was nice. Poor Sheriff Llewellyn, I wish I hadn't been called on to hurt him." Her teeth worried her lower lip. "It's not over though, is it? We're not safe yet."

"Nah, it's all right. Men searched my room twice, Sprite. I feel certain they don't know I'm your husband, or I'd have had a personal visit from the sheriff by now. You can quit your frettin'. Didn't I promise I'd take care of you?"

"No."

"Oh. Well. You have my promise, Katie Kincaid. Now that I've found you again, there's not a power on earth that could take you away from me. Fair enough?"

"I still think I'm better off depending only on myself,"

she grumbled. So much lay between them, so much left unsaid. Johnny.

"Fine. Then I'll depend on you," Branch said, grinning. "And right now I'm depending on you to climb into that bathtub. Frankly, love, you smell like drowned possum."

"I hate you."

"I know, love. And listen, be quieter would you? The walls in this place are pretty thin."

Katie stood unmoving while he tenderly removed her clothing. He carried her to the tub and lowered her slowly into the warm, soothing water. Then with gentle fingers, he lathered her skin with a floral-scented soap, massaging the stiff muscles of her arms, neck, and back. "Mmm," she sighed, and sank lower into the tub, her head resting on the rim, her eyes closed.

A rough cotton washcloth dragged across her face, trailed by his soft kisses. He washed her hair, sudsing and rinsing, speaking to her in soft, comforting tones of inconsequential matters. His touch lulled Katie into a sensual dream where realities of the moment were but other-life nightmares.

She must have fallen asleep in the bath, because the next thing she knew, she woke curled against him beneath soft, clean sheets. Tired still, she tucked his arms more tightly around her and wiggled her rump to get a tad closer.

His response brought a smile to her lips. She wiggled again and he nuzzled her neck. "I've not had a decent breakfast since I left Gallagher's, Kate," he growled into her ear before nipping at her earlobe.

Not opening her eyes, she smiled. She all but purred when he licked that certain spot on her neck.

"I'm a starvin' man. Cook for me, Sprite."

She wanted to. Oh, how she wanted to. But she couldn't. Not without things between them settled. Lamplight cast a muted glow in the room as she rolled over and put a hand against his chest as he lay on his side. "Branch?"

He sighed. "You want to talk, right? You gotta bring it all out in the open?"

She nodded.

"Aren't you just like a woman." He let the silence spin out.

His gaze roamed over her, and he brushed a strand of hair away from her face. Katie waited; she'd been waiting so very long. Then, his golden eyes glowing soft and warm like the lamplight, he said simply, "I love you, Sprite."

He pushed her back against the pillows and propped himself above her. "I think I must have loved you from the beginning"—and he flashed her his crooked grin—"from the minute you introduced me to those squirrels. If not then, then at least by the time we rambled in the brambles."

"Branch, I . . ."

"Shush. You got me started, let me get it all said. I may never get my courage up again. Hell, if I don't do this right, I may never get anything up again." His finger trailed the curve of her cheekbone. "When you left Riverrun that day, it like to tore my heart out. That's when I began to suspect. And then, between goin' after Strickland and layin' up in the bed shot full of holes, I had plenty of time to think. I believe I've figured some things out.

"I was scared. What I felt for you frightened me near to death, and I was so jealous, I couldn't see straight." He lowered his lids for a moment, and when he lifted them, bleakness filled his eyes. "About your Cherokee, well . . . I don't believe you betrayed me, Kate. Not at first, anyway."

"Branch!"

"No." He put a finger to her lips. "If my leavin' like I did drove you to him, I figure I deserved it. But I love you, Kate. I want you with me. And even if the child isn't mine, I want you both to come and live with me and be my family."

Katie's pulse quickened and she inhaled audibly. Branch Kincaid had the sense of hanging beef. Pure-dee ignorant, to up and ruin a moment like this for a woman. Furious, she bit his finger, heedless of his yelp, then crossed her arms and fumed.

Rolling away, Branch stared at her while he lifted his hand to his mouth and sucked at the bite. His golden eyes twinkled, and a grin hovered on his lips as he said, "I take it back. You are a vicious thing. Johnny, huh? After your father?"

She nodded curtly.

"Did you give him a middle name?"

"Robert."

"John Robert." Branch scratched the whiskers on his cheek. Then he nodded and said, "I like it. It's a good name—a strong name. John Robert Kincaid."

Katie didn't miss the sharp look he sent her way. She remembered her words from so long ago. *You have my word that this baby will have his father's name.* "You know?"

The look he gave her could have melted steel. He leaned over and softly said, "I've been a fool, Katie Kincaid. Forgive me?"

She sniffed. "I want you to say it."

He lifted her hand and kissed the tender center of her palm. "I know you didn't betray me, Kate. I know you didn't bed that Cherokee."

"And?"

He grinned. "Won't give an inch, will you? All right, darlin', I admit that you did the right thing with Rob. No one should have to suffer that way. I'm glad you were there to do it for him. You've my thanks." He leaned back against the pillows, his fingers laced behind his head. He cocked an eyebrow and asked, "Now, anything else you want while I'm grovelin'?"

"You, grovel?" She sat up and punched her pillow, fluffing it before lying back down. "Let me know ahead of time so I can sell tickets."

Branch leaned over and whispered in her ear. "Katie Kincaid. I love you. You will forgive me, won't you?"

She sulked. She pouted.

He kissed her.

She forgave him.

A long shudder captured Branch's body at her touch, relief merging with desire as he fit his aching need between her thighs. As she lifted her hips in welcome, he crushed her to him, driving deep and strong, making them one. He loved her as he'd never loved before, with his whole heart. With his soul. And over and over again, accompanying every movement, every touch, he vowed, "I love you, Kate. I love you."

When next she opened her eyes, sunlight sparked the hints of red in his blond hair, making it glow alive and bright.

Sunshine. Alive, Oh, dear. Today's the day she was to die. Worry clouded her eyes. "Branch, what time is it? We have to get out of here. Where's Chase? Is he going to help us? What do we do next?"

"Breakfast." Sleepily, he leaned over and kissed the corners of her eyes. His hands began to roam beneath the sheet. "Mmm. I have missed my meals, Katie Kincaid." She slapped playfully at his hands, and he grinned and told her, "By the way, Chase isn't the only champion you have in Shelbyville. A regular crowd met at the jailhouse last night to spring you. Only you'd decided not to wait for us."

Katie frowned, trying to keep her mind on the matter under discussion while her body was busy responding to him. "What are you talking about?"

"It was quite a sight." He trailed kisses across her collarbone. "Umm, you taste sweet. Yeah, I walked in with pistols drawn only to find your brother, my cousin, that scamp, Keeper McShane, and your ever-lovin' Cherokee there ahead of me, guns pointin' at each other and everybody starin' at an empty cell."

Katie pushed away from Branch and sat up. "Daniel? Shaddoe? Here for me? Keeper too?"

"Yep. And by the way, in the future I expect you to keep your number of gentleman admirers to a bare minimum. Like one." He pulled her back down and began to circle her breasts with his tongue. His fingers stroked her thighs.

"Where are they?" Katie asked.

"Out layin' a false trail—four different directions.
Ought to keep the law busy and off our backs. We'll stay
here until nightfall and then head out. Now, enough conversation, Sprite, feed me."

Katie buried the niggling fear and opened her heart to
the man she loved. Stretching sensuously, she smiled and
asked, "And what will be your pleasure, sir?"

Branch lifted himself above her, his weight resting on
his hands. He licked his lips and said, "I've a mind to start
with dessert."

Traveling at such a furious pace in the darkness was dangerous, Branch knew, but it couldn't be helped. They had
waited through a long day up in the hotel room, loving and
sleeping, resting for the rigors of the journey ahead.

Periodically, he had left the room, checking on the posse's movements and purchasing supplies. The mood in
town was ugly; people had dressed for a party that wasn't
taking place. St. Pierre, sneaky Indian that he was, had encountered Branch in the mercantile, and quickly and quietly they made arrangements for a rendezvous in two
weeks' time at the spot on the Neches River where the
Cherokees had met their defeat back in '39. There Branch
would meet his son for the first time.

During the early hours of the morning, Branch and his
bride escaped the hotel without detection, heading east toward the canebrakes. Many a Texian criminal had lost his
pursuers in the thick, wide expanse of cane that grew
along the Louisiana border. With luck, they could do the
same. The crescent moon provided a mixed blessing; less
light in which to be seen, but also, less light by which to
see.

They retrieved Striker and the quick palomino filly
Branch had bought for Katie. They'd traveled two hours
before Branch heard the sound he dreaded.

Dogs. Somehow, someone had picked up their tracks.
With each minute, the barking grew closer.

Branch peppered the trail, hoping that would hold

them off. An hour later, he heard the dogs again, closer this time. Dawn cast a rosy glow in the eastern sky, and he could see the terror reflected in Katie's face at the sound of the animals. Damn dogs, he thought. Somehow he'd have to get rid of them.

"What are you doing?" Katie asked incredulously when he began to take short detours from the trail.

"Sprite, the horses are whipped. The dogs'll be on us quick unless we figure a way to lead them away. There's got to be water or somethin' else around here to get them off our trail."

"What can I do?"

Branch pursed his lips, then nodded. "You check the right, I'll take the left. We've got fifteen minutes at best. Good luck."

She veered off the trail and found just what they needed almost immediately. But it didn't make her one bit happy. She continued to search desperately and unsuccessfully for water. Turning back to look for her husband, she begged, "Please, Branch. Please find water."

The rustle of brush announced his return. A worried frown etched deep lines in his face. "Not a lousy thing," he said, pulling up next to her.

Katie sighed heavily. He lifted an eyebrow. "Oh, all right," she said. Turning her mount around, she led Branch to the uprooted tree, saying, "Where's a river when you need one?"

Exposed roots of a huge old oak tree stretched toward the sky like an elderly widow's gnarled fingers. The tree had crashed to the ground some time ago, felled by a storm, most likely. Dirt clung to the roots that remained in the ground, while vines, poison oak, and poison ivy guarded the entrance to the depression in the earth left by the stripped roots. An unmistakable scent clung to the area.

Katie dismounted and gave him a sickened, grim smile. "I counted on you to find water. I should have known I'd have to depend on myself; I should have kept looking for a creek. When am I going to learn?"

He was already unloading necessities from his horse: a

little food, water, blankets, clothing for himself—Katie had no extra—coin, guns, and ammunition. "Now, love, you did a fine job. Nothing could be more perfect."

"I know," she moaned.

Branch grinned. "Settle on in, sweet, I'll get rid of the horses."

Katie shook her head. "Huh-uh. You first."

The dogs' barking grew louder. Branch hurried the horses back to the trail and slapped their rumps, sending them off. Quickly he returned to the downed tree.

"I don't think they're in there now," Katie said, wrinkling her nose. "At least, none have stuck their heads out."

"Oh, well, if they are, they'll just have to make room for us." Branch shrugged and used the barrel of his shotgun to poke the hole. Immediately, the air filled with the odorous announcement that, indeed, the hole was currently occupied.

Katie and Branch jumped back as a flash of black and white scampered away. Luckily, a nice breeze blew away from them at the time, so they were not sprayed directly. Still, their eyes watered and Katie choked and coughed.

Branch prodded the hole again. Nothing. Turning to Katie, he handed her his extra shirt. "Wrap this around your hair. I'd hate to have to cut it off due to the stink." He bowed and said, "After you, madam. Your bower awaits."

"Oh, my heavens," Katie wheezed, but she settled into the hiding place, just big enough for the two of them and the pungent essence of skunk.

"This really is good, you know," Branch said, squeezing down beside her. He pulled the vines over them and continued, "The dogs won't come near this place. They'll have lost our scent, and they'll be useless to whoever's sendin' them out. And after a while, we won't smell anything."

"And to think I thought my guardian angel wasn't paying attention," Katie marveled sarcastically.

Branch wrapped his arm around her and settled her comfortably against him. "Why do you need a guardian angel? I'm here, aren't I?"

Katie didn't bother to reply. They waited silently, she doing her best to retain the contents of her stomach.

Yap, yap, yap, yap. The dogs bounded toward them. They slowed just beyond the skunk hole. She stiffened in fright.

Branch kissed her cheek. "Quiet now, darlin'," he whispered in her ear.

Through the vines, she could see the hounds darting to and fro, tracing the steps she and Branch had made in their efforts to find sanctuary. The sound they made chilled her and she shivered. Branch squeezed her tight.

Then the dogs were off, following the riderless horses, away from them. Katie heaved a heartfelt sigh of relief and began to rise.

"Kate," Branch snapped. "What are you thinkin'? Those dogs aren't out here on their own. Sit still and hush."

"Sorry," she muttered beneath her breath.

He patted her thigh absently, his gaze intent as he watched for the man who tracked them.

Branch's muscles flexed. She heard his soft, hate-fed whisper, "Bastard." She stared through the cover until she, too, made out the figure of the lone man on horseback who approached.

Judge Jack Strickland.

Branch's expression turned hard, evil. He reached ever-so-quietly for his gun. Katie's eyes widened as he pointed the barrel.

The hounds had doubled back. Branch cocked his Paterson and the trigger dropped. Strickland was in spitting distance. Katie's gaze locked on the sight of Branch's finger wrapped around the trigger.

He'd do it. For me, not just for Rob. Rumors of her attack on Strickland had been bandied about. Branch would have put it together. It all could end right here, right this minute. Vengeance taken.

"No, love." She pushed the gun, disrupting his aim. She whispered in his ear. "I can't allow it. I've been there, I've learned. This won't bring them back. It's dishonorable, and it would haunt us both for the rest of our lives."

A muscle twitched above Branch's clenched jaw. He aimed the gun once more. Strickland had passed them now, his back a perfect target.

Katie watched Branch's finger tighten on the trigger. For a long moment, she held her breath.

His hand dropped. He turned a tortured expression toward her. "Why? You know who he is, what he is, what he's done. Why, Sprite? Why shouldn't I end it now?"

Katie touched his face, smoothing the angry furrows in his brow, and quoted, "Vengeance is mine, and requital for the time when they make a false step. For it is close, the day of their ruin; their doom comes at speed."

He looked puzzled. "Shakespeare again?"

She kissed his cheek. "No, my love—the Bible."

Four days later, they could almost live with themselves again. Branch found himself thanking Katie's guardian angel that the wind had been blowing right when the skunk sprayed.

Striker had shown up at their camp sometime during the second night, and Branch had bought another horse for Katie from a farmer later that day. The farmer's wife had sent clothes for his bride with instructions not to set a foot closer to the house.

They'd cleaned the fellow plumb out of the last of his summer tomatoes, squeezing them and bathing in the juice. That had helped some—been pretty fun, for a fact. With Katie he was always doing something new. He'd never taste a tomato again without thinking of his bride.

He sat with his back to a cottonwood tree, watching her step from the spring. Beautiful. But as much as he loved the sight of her naked, this stopping to take a bath at every bit of running water was slowing them down something fierce.

Dressed in only her chemise and pantalets, she knelt beside him and cuddled against him. She combed her long auburn hair with her fingers. He wiped a droplet of water from the tip of her nose.

They sat quietly for a few moments, then Branch

leaned away from her. Reaching into his pocket, he withdrew a stick of peppermint he'd acquired at the mercantile in Easton, where they'd stopped for food. He snapped it in two and waved half before her face.

She snatched the candy with glee, then shut her eyes and licked the stick, savoring its sweetness. At times, she could be such a child. He said softly, "Don't ever disappear on me again, Sprite."

She stopped midbite and slowly took the peppermint from her mouth. "What makes you think I'd do that?"

"You have a funny habit, Sprite, of not stayin' where I put you. I want you to promise me you'll break that little practice."

Katie looked down at the candy, suddenly sick at her stomach. Had he guessed that she'd been thinking of leaving him? "What do you mean?"

"It's not like you, wife, to refrain from askin' about our future plans. Somehow it gives me the idea that you've some of your own."

Tossing the peppermint into the stream, Katie searched her mind for a plausible diversion. "I'm worried about Gallagher's, Branch," she finally said. "What's going to happen to it? When I was in jail, I sent a letter to Mr. Trahern explaining the circumstances. I suggested he allow Martha and Rowdy to continue running the inn, but there wasn't time to hear back from him." She paused and nodded as a new thought occurred. "But maybe now that Daniel's back, he could help."

"I don't think that's a good idea, Sprite," Branch interrupted, frowning at the hunk of red and white lying at the bottom of the clear stream. "Shelbyville's not all that far from the inn, and I hate to think of Daniel anywhere near Jack Strickland. Actually, I think Keeper McShane has decided to try his hand at innkeeping. And Kate," he added, "next time you don't want your candy, give it to me, all right?"

Katie's eyebrows rose. "Keeper?"

"I talked to him a bit in town. The boy's done a lot of growin' while he's been with the Cherokees."

She sighed heavily and tugged at a clump of grass at

her feet. "I guess that with both Keeper and Andrew there to help, Martha and Rowdy will be able to keep Gallagher's running." She pitched the grass away with a short, violent motion. "But I didn't even get to *see* Daniel, Branch. Where is he going? What's he going to do?"

A squirrel played on the high branches above them, leaping from limb to limb before scampering halfway down the trunk to take a flying leap at low-growing brush. Her heart was heavy as she watched the bushy-tailed critter disappear with the sound of kicked leaves.

Branch took her hand. "Listen, Kate, don't worry about Daniel or Trahern or Gallagher's, everything will be just fine. I promise. Now, let's talk about what *you're* gonna do."

"Don't you ever tell me not to worry about my brother, Branch Kincaid," Katie fussed, snatching back her hand. "I can worry about him all I want. And stop trying to change the subject." Really, she thought, the man had a one-track mind. He was determined to ferret out her plans, and she simply wasn't up to discussing them yet. Just a few more days of happiness—that's all she wanted—at least until they met Shaddoe and picked up Johnny.

Flashes of silver in the stream caught her attention as a school of minnows darted back and forth above the melting candy. She asked, "How do you know everything'll be fine at Gallagher's, Branch? We owe Mr. Trahern a substantial amount of money. He may just decide to take the inn itself as payment and Daniel will lose his property!"

"It's not gonna happen," Branch said, testing the point of his peppermint stick with his tongue.

Katie folded her arms. "And how can you be so sure?"

Through hooded eyes, Branch watched her. He took a long, slow lick of his candy, then flashed his wicked wolf grin. "Because Trahern has another method of payment in mind."

Now Katie was distracted. The man could start a prairie fire with that look. Her blood began to hum in response, and unconsciously, she licked her lips. He had definitely lit a fire in her.

"Well," his voice purred, his hand slipping beneath her

chemise and sliding up her bare back, "aren't you gonna ask what that payment is?"

She shrugged. She couldn't care less about Finian Trahern at this particular moment. Branch kneaded the muscles in her back. Her toes curled.

His teeth nibbled the lobe of her ear, and he said, "Lovin'. He wants regular daily, make that twice-daily, lovin'. With you."

"What!" Katie's spine snapped straight. "Why that dirty old man. I never—"

Lowering her gently to the ground, he rose above her, planted a wet, sweet-candy kiss on her mouth, and said, "Actually you have. Not an hour ago, in fact."

Katie found it hard to think when he was doing all those delicious things to her body. She fought for control for a full minute and a half before giving herself up to his magic. And, after all, she had wanted a distraction, hadn't she?

Only after they both found their pleasure, as they lay side by side, their hands linked while the warm breeze dried the sheen of perspiration from their bodies, did she remember. "You," she groaned. She freed her hand and punched him. "Finian Trahern. All the time, it was *you*."

"Aye," he said in a false brogue, wiggling his eyebrows lecherously, "and I'm a'thinkin' it'll take a lifetime for ye to work off the debt." Then suddenly he sobered. "So just make sure you're around to do it, Katie Kincaid."

"Oh, Branch." She realized that the time had come to tell him. As much as she hated the idea, there was no more putting it off. There had been enough lies between them; there was room for no more. "I can't go to Riverrun with you, Branch. I have to disappear. No matter how rigged that trial was, I'm still a convicted murderer sentenced to hang. I know how much Riverrun means to you; I know how long you waited to return. It's your future, and I'll not take that from you."

"You and my son are my future, woman." Branch got to his feet, raked his fingers through his hair, and began pacing the spring's bank as he railed at her. "Do you really think a house and a few lousy acres of sugarcane are worth more than my family to me? Dammit, Kate. If you left me again, you'd take my heart with you."

"It's not like that, Branch. I only thought—"

He braced his hands on his hips. "I know what you thought. St. Kathleen of Nacogdoches, martyred for money. For the sake of an inheritance. Well, by God, woman, that doesn't show much respect for me, now, does it? What makes you think I can't build a home as grand as Riverrun? Am I that much less of a man than my father? Am I so little a man that I must wait for someone to die to amount to anything? Well, thank you, Mrs. Kincaid. It's so nice knowin' you've such confidence in your husband."

"Oh, Branch." Katie reached for him, but he turned away. "That's not it at all," she chided. "What about your father? All these years you've been estranged, and now . . ."

"What do you mean 'now'?" he roared. "Now that he lied to my wife and told her I was dyin'? He was there, Kate, in Shelbyville, to watch you hang. You think I could live with him after that?"

Katie looked down at her hands clasped in her lap. Softly, she said, "I've already taken one son from him, I'll not take another."

"Shit. That's a bunch of goddamn shit." At the venom in his tone, she reared back.

"Look," he said, "you are not responsible for what happened to Rob. Rob's responsible, Rob and Jack Strickland."

Katie looked at Branch in surprise.

"It's true," he demanded. "Rob was an adult; he made his own choice, for reasons you know nothing about. Kate, you helped my brother when he needed help, and for that I'm grateful. I don't ever want to hear any guilt out of you over that again."

A hollow ache tightened Katie's throat as she argued, "But, Branch, he went into that cabin for me, for my baby. He didn't have to . . ."

"Yes, he did," Branch stated flatly. "He was ten years old when he started a fire in the attic of our grandparent's home. It got away from him. He ran and hid instead of tellin' anyone about it. Pa's folks both died in that fire. So did my younger sister and my mother. I was seven. He let them believe I did it."

Branch picked up a rock and tossed it into the stream. He added, "I think eventually it got to him. He regretted it. That's why he went after your daughter. He was trying to make up for the other. I've got an idea he'd have told Pa then what really happened in Virginia. Only he died." Branch plopped back down on the grass a few feet away from Katie.

He looked at her and said earnestly, "Pa didn't have diddly-squat to do with me from the time I was seven. Hell, he sent me away from home for ridin' a goddamn horse. Your bein' with me has nothin' to do with how much or how little of his love comes my way. I gave up on him long ago."

Katie's heart wept for him. He wore the stoicism of an emotionally battered child impervious to pain after repeated abuse. And when he continued to talk, speaking of herself, his expression didn't change. "Katie," he said, "after Ma died, I forgot what love meant. Then I met you, and you filled that emptiness inside me. But Pa had dangled Riverrun before me, and like a fool, I thought that was what I needed."

He leaned back on his elbows, turned his face toward the sky. "God," he confessed, "the time we were apart near to destroyed me. I know now what's important in life, Katie Kincaid. It isn't Riverrun and Hoss Garrett. I've finally grown up, Kate. He can't hurt me anymore."

Then he looked at her, honest in his vulnerability. "But you can, Sprite. You have the power to tear me into such little pieces, there won't be any gluin' back together. I can't lose you again. It'd kill me. Promise me, Katie, promise me you'll never leave me."

"Oh, Branch." Her voice caught in her throat as she stood and went to him, kneeling before him and laying her head in his lap. "I promise. I promise, Branch Garrett, I'll never leave you again."

He stroked her hair, softly saying, "Kincaid, I want to be Branch Kincaid again, if it's all the same to you. And

Branch Kincaid has a notion to raise cattle, build a ranch. You don't need slave labor for that, and there's plenty of land in the west." His lips twisted in a wry smile as he added, "Besides, you've always gotten along well with the Indians."

He pulled her into his lap. Hugging her tight, he asked, "How 'bout it, Mrs. Kincaid? Want to get our boy and head west?"

Katie lifted her head and smiled through watery eyes. "There's nothing I'd rather do more, Mr. Kincaid."

≈⊲ CHAPTER 22 ⊳≈

DOUBLE K RANCH, 1848

*B*RANCH KINCAID APPROACHED the final turn on the road to the ranch house with two thoughts on his mind—peach cobbler and Katie Kincaid. Together, they were the closest thing to paradise his tongue had ever tasted. And it was just about the right season, too. The new baby turned two months old today, and the fruit hanging on the trees ought to be ripe for the picking.

Damn, it'll be good to get home, he thought. The trip into Dallas had taken only two days, but he worried about Katie and the boys. Of course, Daniel Gallagher would defend his sister and her family with his life, of that Branch had no doubt. Even had they not been family, his position as ranch foreman would have assured Daniel's protectiveness.

Branch didn't expect trouble, however. Soon after settling here a little over a year ago, he'd gone out of his way to make peace with the Tonkawa Indians that lived around the new settlement of Dallas. No, he didn't worry, just missed his family something fierce.

Taking the road's curve at a gallop, Branch smiled at the welcome sight of the dog-trot style cabin that was his ranch's "Big House." No six columns here, but a two-room dwelling made of rough-hewn logs chinked with mud, and a couple of limestone fireplaces to warm them in the winter and cook on year round.

No home in the world could be more grand.

From one chimney, a thin wisp of smoke curled into the endless blue sky. Branch wrinkled his nose and sniffed. Did he imagine it, or was he catching a whiff of that heavenly concoction of his dreams? "Sprite, you certainly know the way to a man's heart," he said to himself, grinning. Feeling his heat rise, he added, "Not to mention other parts."

Katie came out onto the porch to meet him. A smudged, once-white apron covered her dress of buttercup yellow, and ringlets of auburn escaped her braid, framing the face that shone with happiness. "You're back!" she cried, leaping off the porch and into his sweaty embrace.

"How did you guess?" he teased.

She pulled away, wrinkling her nose. "I could smell you coming."

"Witch." Placing his hands around her waist, he lifted her up and kissed her, long and thoroughly. He tickled her as he set her down, then swatted her fanny. "Where are my boys?" he asked, turning to step onto the porch.

Katie held him back. "Wait, Branch," she said. "There's something I've got to tell you." At his look of alarm, she hastened to assure him, "They're fine. Everyone is. But we have a visitor, Branch."

He lifted an eyebrow. Katie wiped her hands on the apron. "Just give him a chance, love. Listen to him."

Branch's gut clenched. Well, if that didn't sound like trouble, he wasn't a new papa. He took a deep breath and opened the door.

Hoss Garrett sat in Katie's rocking chair, reading a book to Johnny. His gaze held Branch's for two squeaks of the rocker before Johnny interrupted, clapping his hands and shouting, "Papa, you're home! Look who came to see us. It's my Grampa. He likes to read to me just like you. Can we finish this story, please, Papa?"

"Sure, son," Branch said. He hung his hat on a peg hammered into the wall beside the door. "Where's the baby?"

Katie said, "He's asleep in the other room." Branch headed for the side door to peek in on his infant son, but Katie stopped him. "Give him a few more minutes, please love? I've just put him down, and I want him to get good and asleep before you go in there."

Branch nodded and crossed the room to the fireplace.

He bent down and peered into the kettle that hung above the glowing coals. "Stew for supper?" he asked.

"Brunswick," Katie answered.

"What's the meat?"

"Squirrel."

Branch pursed his lips. She'd not served him such a stew since the day they met. What was she up to? He shrugged and asked, "Your muffins hot?"

"The corn bread is ready. We'll have dinner as soon as you wash up. Dessert will wait until after you talk with your father, or"—she sent him a pointed look—"later. We'll just have to see if it turns out all right."

With brows lowered thunderously, Branch grabbed Katie's arm and pulled her near. He whispered in her ear. "Don't you be tryin' to blackmail me, Sprite. I don't cotton to it, you ought to know by now."

Katie smiled sweetly and said, "On your way to the well, would you check the squirrel traps for me, please? I just might need a couple more before the evening's done."

Branch shook his head at her and walked outside. Tension made his movements sharp and awkward as he washed. He entered his bedroom and changed into a clean pair of denims and a brand new homespun shirt Katie had made before crossing the dogtrot to confront his unwelcome visitor.

Johnny's excited questions and innocent chatter kept the supper conversation light. Branch told of his trip to town and mentioned a barn raising they'd been invited to in two weeks. He never spoke directly to Hoss Garrett, but he did ask after his brother-in-law. Daniel usually ate supper with them.

"I took him something earlier," Katie answered. "He thought maybe just the family should eat together this evening."

Branch glared at his father. "Daniel is family."

Katie rolled her eyes and stood. "Come on, Squirt," she said to Johnny, "you get to sleep with Uncle Daniel tonight in the bunkhouse."

"Yippee!" the boy scrambled from his chair. He headed for the door, then stopped and turned. "Papa, in the morning can I come wake you up and you and me go fishin' like you said we might before you took your trip?"

Branch frowned but allowed the boy to see the teasing sparkle in his eyes. "I don't know, how early you plannin' on wakin' me?"

Johnny shook his head. "Not before two or three."

Branch grinned, "Make it five or six, and you've got a deal." Johnny ran to his father and threw his arms around his waist. "Thank you, Papa. I love you. I'm glad you're home."

Branch ruffled the boy's strawberry-blond hair. "I'm glad, too. And I love you, too. Now, skedaddle off to bed, young'un, and don't you dare show yourself in my room before five o'clock."

"Yessir. G'night. G'night, Grampa." Johnny flew out the front door. Katie gave Branch a measured look before following her son outside and shutting the door behind her.

Hoss Garrett leaned back in his chair and folded his arms across his chest. "You're real good with your boy."

"Yep, well. It's easy to do. I love him." Branch rose from his seat. He carried his dishes to the water basin and began to wash them.

After a few minutes of tense silence, Hoss asked, "You do dishes around here?"

"She mends fences."

Hoss nodded. "She does at that." He stood and finished clearing the table, then picked up a towel and a dish to dry. He cleared his throat a couple of times before gruffly saying, "I remember when I used to take you fishin' when you were about his age. Once you caught a catfish almost as big as you were. You recall that?"

"I make it a practice not to remember my life before the Virginia fire."

Spitting an obscenity, Garrett tossed down the towel. "Fine, here it is. I came to tell you I was wrong. I'm sorry. I never should have sent your wife away from Austin."

"You told her I was dyin'," Branch interrupted flatly.

"Dammit, son, I thought you *were* dying. I should have known that you were too stubborn to do it, especially since it was my shot that would have killed you. I died a thousand deaths when I saw you step in front of that bullet."

Branch said nothing, holding a crockery bowl up before his eyes, checking its cleanliness. Hoss pushed his fingers through his thick gray hair and said with a sigh, "Guilt was a devil ridin' my shoulder that day, and I said some ornery things to your woman. I've already apologized to her, and I'm trying to do the same here with you."

"You went to watch her die."

Hoss scowled. "It was the boy. I thought to check on him, discover the arrangements she'd made. I wondered if he was yours."

He waited, but Branch remained silent. "Won't you at least look at me?"

Slowly, Branch lowered the bowl. He swallowed hard, then turned and stared his father in the eye. "What do you want from me?" he asked quietly.

"I want you to come home. Bring your family and come live at Riverrun. Rob's girls are home with us now, and Eleanor, well, I married her and she's havin' a baby." Hoss paused to let that sink in, then continued. "She'd like, we'd like the rest of our family with us."

Branch tried to picture Eleanor and Hoss together. It made a certain kind of sense. "My wife is a convicted murderess livin' under a death sentence," Branch said. "What's the deal, Hoss, you got a sheriff waitin' at the plantation ready to hang her from the nearest oak?"

"Aw, hell, you stubborn cuss." Garrett whirled and went to his saddlebags that lay across the bed in the corner. Pulling out two sheets of paper, he stomped back over to Branch and shoved them beneath his nose.

Branch scanned the lines and his chin dropped in amazement. "Pardons? You got her pardoned?"

"Straight from the governor to you. For both the killing and the escape. You too. I wasn't sure how much you had to do with her getting loose, but I figured it wouldn't hurt to have it."

Branch forgot the dishes and carried the documents with him to the rocking chair. Turning up the flame in the oil lamp, he sat and stared at them for a full minute. Then he raised his head and looked at his father. "Why?"

"It took losing just about everything for me to admit the truth. I know the story. I knew it then. Katie Starr only tried to help my boy She was never responsible, only Jack Strickland. By the way, here's something else you might be interested in." He pulled a folded newspaper from his saddlebags and handed it to Branch. "Bottom right corner," he said.

Branch read the headline. *County Judge ambushed near Shelbyville: Indians in East Texas.* He snapped his head up to look at his father before continuing to read. Judge Jack Strickland had been riding with two other men when he suddenly fell from the saddle. The other men dived for cover, and when no other attack was forthcoming, they returned to Strickland. He was dead when they turned him over. An arrow lay buried in his chest.

"Shaddoe," Branch murmured.

Garrett shrugged. "Wasn't me."

Branch struggled with his thoughts, trying to figure a reason for his father's actions. "If you didn't hold Katie responsible, then why?"

Garrett sank onto the bed. He sat there and spat, "Because it was *my* fault he went into that cabin to begin with."

Branch stared incredulously at his father. He felt he was looking at a stranger. Then something he never could have imagined happened. Tears began to fall from Hoss Garrett's eyes.

"I know you didn't start that fire. It was such a mess— all of them dead, your mama dead, I was crazy with grief. Rob had guilt written all over his face that night, but when I found you with the matches and you didn't deny it, I lost all sense."

He looked at Branch, the tears of sorrow and shame etching the wrinkles in his face. "You know, you were so much like me. From the day you were born, I felt something special for you. So I got angry when you let me down. Later when I came to my senses, I suspected the truth and I waited for one of you to let on about it. Neither of you ever did." He shook his head wonderingly.

He was silent for a few moments before he continued. "Rob was always weak. You were younger than he and already twice the man at seven that he was at ten. I should have done something, and I didn't. I thought the competition between you two would eventually harden him, make him into something."

"Why did you send me away?"

"For him. I thought if you weren't around, he'd work harder to make something of himself. He always competed with you, and he never could win."

Hoss stared at Branch, his whole body shuddering in anguish. "I thought you could make it by yourself. Besides, every time I looked at you, I felt guilty for lettin' the charade continue. But I ended up killin' one son and makin' the other hate me."

"You didn't kill Rob, Pa. That can be laid at Jack Strickland's feet, and I'm sure the judgment he faced for it wasn't pretty."

Hoss slapped his hand against the wall. "It *is* my fault. If I'd made Rob admit what happened, he might have dealt with his guilt over the fire. I think that's why he went after your Katie's baby."

"I do, too," Branch said. "But that was his choice, Pa. His and no one else's, not yours, not Katie's, and not mine. His."

Emotions were whirling inside Branch like a tornado. He didn't know yet just what he felt about all of this, but he did state the one conclusion he'd drawn some time ago. He said, "Pa, I don't think you should feel guilty. Katie's told me what he said, how he looked before he died. I think he was glad he'd done what he did."

Garrett swallowed. "Why?"

"He smiled, Pa. He looked to be at peace with himself."

Garrett nodded as silent tears continued to coarse down his cheeks. "He didn't die weak, did he son?"

Branch looked out the window where a lamp glowed in the bunkhouse. He took a deep breath, then exhaled. He walked over to the bed, sat beside his father, and put his arm around his shoulders. "No, Pa, he didn't. Rob died a brave man."

Together, they wept.

The summer sun rode at the eastern treetops as Hoss Garrett swung into his saddle. A bittersweet smile spread across his face as he turned to his family. Branch held a cane fishing pole in one hand and Johnny in the other, while Katie's arms held the cooing bundle whose single tuft of blond hair stuck straight up.

Hoss said, "Would it do me any good to ask one more time?"

Katie and Branch both smiled and shook their heads. Branch drawled, "Now, Pa, there's a road runnin' between here and Brazoria. I wouldn't be surprised if you had some visitors at Riverrun come Christmas."

"Don't expect me to quit askin'. I'll probably send a pitifully lonely letter with Chase when he comes this way." His horse whinnied as though in agreement.

"Why don't you and Eleanor deliver it personally, Hoss?" Katie told him with a smile.

"That's not a half-bad idea," he said, nodding.

Branch stepped off the porch and held out his hand. "You're welcome on the Double K any time, Pa. Remember that. And thank you for all you've done."

Hoss shook his son's hand. "I can't tell you how happy that makes me, Britt—uh, Branch, I mean. By the way, any chance you'll change the name of your spread now that the Garrett name wouldn't be so dangerous for you to use?"

Stepping away from the horse, Branch looked at Katie. She lifted her shoulders and grinned. Branch said, "We'll think about it, Pa. My wife's had so many names, maybe it's gettin' to be time to change it again. We'll let you know when we visit at Christmas."

"Well, good-bye, son."

"Good-bye, Pa."

Hoss pulled the reins and turned his horse. They took

a few strides before he yanked the mount to a halt and twisted around in his saddle toward Branch.

"Son?"

"Yeah, Pa?"

"I, um, y'all take care now."

"Sure Pa, we will." Branch paused significantly. "You too, *sir*."

A beaming smile spread across Hoss Garrett's visage as he kicked his horse into a run. Just how many years had it been since the boy had called him "sir?"

Long after his father had disappeared from sight, Branch stood staring at the horizon. Quietly, Katie slipped her hand into his. He heaved a sigh, gave her fingers a squeeze, then turned to her and asked, "You goin' fishin' with us, Sprite?"

"I don't think so," she said. "I've a bit of wash and some baking to do."

Branch angled his head toward an elm tree, where a mourning dove cooed her melancholy song. "Ah, Kate, I want you with us. You work too hard, you can take the morning off."

A slow smile spread across her face, and she shook her head. "This isn't something I need to do, it's something I *want* to do."

Branch folded his arms and gave her a measuring look. "Laundry? You do laundry on Monday. This is Wednesday."

Her expression was as innocent as an angel's, an imitation of the one he so often used. "A lady can't wash her red things with her white things, now, can she?"

"Red things?" Branch repeated in his slow molasses drawl. He grinned. "And bakin', too?"

Katie stood on her toes and pressed a kiss to his cheek. "What's your pleasure, sir? Blackberry or peach?"

"Hell, Sprite, I'm working' up quite an appetite. Make 'em both."

ABOUT THE AUTHOR

After growing up in a home on Alamo Drive in
Wichita Falls, Texas, GERALYN DAWSON was
destined to write about Texas history. In addition to twice being a Romance Writers of
America Golden Heart semi-finalist, she has
won numerous writing awards. Today she lives
in Fort Worth, Texas, with her husband and
three children.

On sale in early 1994 . . .

CAPTURE
THE
NIGHT
by Geralyn Dawson

A desperate French beauty, the ruggedly handsome
Texan who rescues her, and their precious stolen
"Rose" are swept together by destiny as they each try
to escape the secrets of their past.

Here is a sneak preview of the award-winning Geralyn
Dawson's next fabulously entertaining historical
romance.

Antwerp, Belgium, 1855

"Kidnapping is such an ugly word," Madeline Christophe murmured, gazing into the angelic face of the infant she cradled in her arms. It was an ugly word for a monstrous deed—taking a child from its parents for the purposes of extortion. That's how the police and the newspapers would label her crime, but they would be wrong.

She had absolutely no intentions of ever returning the child she had stolen.

Madeline was a thief, a talented thief, and she'd been stealing all her life. Her earliest memory was of slipping her hand into a green brocade reticule and silently removing the jeweled hand mirror into which her beautiful mother so often gazed. Though only four years old, she had already possessed the delicate touch and dramatic flare that would serve her well in the years to come. That day, however, all she'd wanted was to see for herself just how ugly one must be to merit abandonment by one's mother.

While her beautiful parent had tossed a bag of coins onto a desk at a English boarding school, her scorn-filled voice saying, "See to the loathsome child," Madeline had stared into the mirror and decided it must be the brown eyes and sprinkling of freckles that made her ugly. Mama had sparkling green eyes and unblemished ivory skin.

Now, twenty years later, Madeline's eyes remained a velvet brown and a dusting of freckles had yet to fade from the bridge of her nose. She also still owned the mirror.

Madeline never returned the things she stole.

A biting wind swirled across the wharf, the salty scent of the North Sea mingling with land's dust in a dervish that swept over the queue of colonists waiting to board ship. Madeline shivered and tucked the yellow lamb's wool blanket snugly around the sleeping child. Her life had become a whirlwind—cold ashes of lies, betrayal, and death twirling around an aching emptiness. But the barest hint of refuge rode the squall and she clung to its promise as she advanced a position in line.

On board the *Uriel*, the packet-ship on which Madeline and the baby would sail, final loading of equipment and supplies was under way. Ropes creaked as heavy bundles swung from shore to ship. Dock workers shifted crates and lowered hogsheads into the hold.

A hand touched her on the shoulder. "Madeline? Madeline, did you not hear me call?"

She turned to see a woman with sparkling green eyes and a round, smiling face. "Oh, Lillibet, I'm sorry, I only—" *I only forgot the name I'm using*, she thought. She must be more careful, mistakes like that could be dangerous.

Self-disgust swept through her as she searched her mind for an excuse. One would have thought that the quantity of time she spent during her childhood playing roles from beggar-child to princess would have better prepared her to slip into a new identity. But apparently, after twenty-plus years as "that poor little orphaned Mary Smithwick," she needed more than two weeks to accustom herself to the name Madeline Christophe.

She touched the soft velveteen of Lillibet Brunet's cloak in apology. "It's the excitement of it all—such a distraction. I vow I'd begun to believe the weather would never clear."

"Is that not the truth. Why, these past two weeks have been the longest of my life, well, except for the two right before little Thomas was born." Lillibet bestowed a prideful, maternal look upon the bundle nestled in her plump arms.

"He is a precious child, Lil."

Madame Brunet beamed, "Yes, yes he is. But then, your little Rose is too. Why, in the week and a half that I have been caring for her I've come to love her as my own. Of course, with a mother like you she's bound to be special. You've more courage than most, continuing with your plans when so newly widowed."

Guilt rolled through Madeline like a North Sea swell. She winced, saying, "It was his dream, our dream. What else could I have done?" She reached for Lillibet's hand and gave it a friendly squeeze. "I'm so thankful that you offered to assist with Rose. I searched desperately for a wet-nurse willing to emigrate, and I'd almost abandoned hope when we met."

Lillibet dropped kisses first on Rose's forehead and then on her son's. "Think nothing of it, Madeline. I'm happy to help. After all, isn't that what the Colonization Society of Texas is all about? Man helping his fellow man for the betterment of all, or in our case, perhaps I should say woman helping woman? The fact is that the shock of your husband's death dried up your milk." She fingered the edge of the blanket framing Rose's face. "I, on the other hand, can easily provide both for my son and your daughter. I would be failing in my duty to my beliefs if I refused to help you."

She shrugged sheepishly and added, "Besides, she's as sweet as spun sugar and I enjoy her tremendously. I'm hoping some of Rose's good nature will rub off on my little scamp."

Madeline shifted the sleeping baby to her shoulder and gently patted her back. "Still, I am in your debt, Lillibet. If you'd not agreed to feed Rose for me, we could not have joined the La Réunion colonists. You truly are a kind and generous woman."

Lillibet shook her head, dismissing Madeline's praise. "Now don't start in again, Madeline. I do not wish to hear it. Besides, I haven't the time. My André has already checked us aboard and he's waiting in our cabin. I must get back to him before he wonders whether I've changed my mind about sailing."

She giggled, then lowered her voice. "Darling, I must tell you. André did speak with the captain about changing our assignment from steerage to the cabin next to yours. Madeline, you're such a friend to spare the coin and especially to do so unbeknownst to my husband."

She huffed. "Men and their silly pride—I think we should outlaw such nonsense at La Réunion. While admittedly we are not nearly as wealthy as most of our fellow colonists, in a true Utopian society like La Réunion that won't matter." As she spoke, indignation lifted her chin and sharpened her tone. "My André may not have gold like most of the émigrés, but he was the best farmer in the entire south of France! He'll be of much more use to the colony in Texas than will Monsieur Robards, the musician, or Monsieur Correll, the banker, or the hatters or the artists or countless others who are members of the Society!"

Madeline nodded, laying her hand atop Rose's ear. As much as she liked Lillibet Brunet, she wished she'd muffle her voice. "You are right, Lil, André will be central to the success of the colony. It was my pleasure to upgrade your accommodations, so you mustn't think a thing about it. Why, it would be nonsense to have you anywhere but at my side—what with your caring for Rose—not to mention the fact that you've quickly become my very best friend."

As she made the vow of friendship, Madeline realized that she spoke the truth. Suddenly, an intense and unprecedented need to confide brought the entire ugly story to her lips and she bit back the confession just in time. With her jaw clenched tight, she scolded herself, *You fool, the madcap dash across Europe must have scrambled your brains.*

Why, never before had she entertained such a foolish notion. Madeline prided herself on her superior intelligence—she could plot and scheme and connive better than anyone she'd ever met. But talking about the baby would be nothing more than stupid. Even alluding to Rose's true identity could only lead to disaster.

Madeline had risked too much in stealing this child from Château St. Germaine, and she mustn't allow her own desire for comfort to jeopardize her plan at this critical time. Europe was too small a place in which to hide from one as powerful and wealthy, someone as evil as Julian Desseau.

She swayed beneath the weight of the burden she'd assumed, closing her eyes as the fear voiced itself in her mind. *Is Texas big enough to hide us? Will anyplace be safe?*

"Madeline, are you all right?" Lillibet touched her sleeve. "You're as pale as the mizzen sail. Why don't you sit for a bit, I'll hold your spot in line."

"I'm fine, Lil." Madeline forced a smile. "I was thinking about—"

Nodding wisely, Lillibet finished for her, "The baby's father?"

"Yes, the baby's father." *Well, at least I'm mixing some truth in with the falsehoods.* She swallowed a self-mocking laugh and waved toward the ship. "Now you go on to your André, Lil. I'll bring Rose to you when she awakens."

Watching her friend make her way aboard the *Uriel*, Madeline sighed heavily. Lying, unlike thievery, bothered her.

Suddenly, the seabirds' caws and sailors' curses were muted by the angry roar of a man who stood before the gangway. Dressed in a simple, navy blue sailor's jacket over a chambray shirt and denim trousers, he braced his hands upon his hips and glared down at Victor Considérant, the colonist's leader and the man who had chartered the *Uriel*.

"*Mon Dieu,*" the stranger shouted in the most horribly accented French Madeline had ever heard. "I tell you I'll do anything, pay anything, to get aboard this ship. I must go home to Texas immediately!"

Madeline frowned as Rose stirred in her arms, disturbed by the man's bellow. *Don't wake up, darling, please,* she thought. She'd purposely waited for the child's nap time to arrive at the ship—the last thing she wanted was to attract the attention of the hawkers selling their wares around the docks. Memories of a crying infant might linger where danger could follow.

At the gangway, Considérant turned his back on the dark-haired man whose blue eyes blazed at the insult. Madeline watched the Texan as another couple gave their name to be checked against the manifest.

His jaws hardened as his gaze trailed the boarding passengers. He appeared completely out of place in his surroundings and totally at ease with himself in spite of it. Standing straight as a mainmast and seemingly as tall, he towered over Considérant. He wore no hat; his hair was unfashionably long, a straight curl of black past his collar. He lacked but guns at his hips to fit her image of a Texan, what with his sun-darkened skin, a face set in rugged, though attractive angles, and broad shoulders that stretched the seams of his wool jacket.

He conformed to her picture of a Texan until he turned and caught her staring, that is. Then he looked like any other man whose thoughts more often originated beneath his belt buckle than in his mind.

One corner of his mouth lifted in an appreciative grin as he very deliberately scrutinized every facet of her appearance. Madeline resisted the urge to pat her windblown hair back into place.

Disgusted with both herself and the stranger, she lifted her chin and looked past him, focusing on a crate

marked "farm implements and musical instruments."
From the corner of her eye she saw him stick his hands
in his back pockets and rock on his heels. Tall and broad,
he blocked a good portion of the gangway.

"Mr. Sinclair, if you would please move away?"
Considérant asked. "Boarding procedure cannot take
place with you blocking our path."

"But we've not finished," the Texan said.

"Wait in line, please."

Madeline groaned as the man called Sinclair strode
toward her. *This is all I need,* she thought.

He stopped beside her and dipped into a perfect
imitation of a gentleman's bow. Eyes shining, he looked
up and said in his deplorable French, "Madame, do you
by chance speak any English? Apparently, we'll be shar-
ing a spot in line. I beg to make your acquaintance."

She didn't answer.

He sighed and straightened. Then a wicked grin
creased his face and in English he drawled. "Brazos
Sinclair's my name, Texas born and bred. Most of my
friends call me Sin, especially my lady friends. Nobody
calls me Clair but once. I'll be sailin' with you on the
Uriel."

Madeline ignored him.

Evidently, that bothered him not at all. "Cute
baby," he said, peeking past the blanket, "best keep him
covered good though. This weather'll chill him."

Madeline bristled at the implied criticism. She
glared at the man named Sin.

He grin faded. "Sure you don't speak English?"

She held her silence.

"Guess not, huh. That's all right, I'll enjoy
conversin' with you anyway." He shot a piercing glare toward Victor Considérant and added, "I need a diversion,
you see. Otherwise I'm liable to do something I
shouldn't." Angling his head, he gave her another sweeping gaze. "You're a right fine lookin' woman, ma'am, a

real beauty. Don't know that I think much of your man, though, leavin' you here on the docks by your lonesome."

He paused and looked around, his stare snagging on a pair of scruffy sailors. "It's a dangerous thing for women to be alone in such a place, and for a beautiful one like you, well, I hesitate to think."

Obviously, Madeline said to herself.

The Texan continued, glancing around at the people milling along the wharf. "'Course, I can't say I understand you Europeans. I've been here goin' on two years, and I'm no closer to figurin' y'all out now than I was the day I rolled off the boat." He reached into his jacket pocket and pulled out a pair of peppermint sticks.

Madeline declined the offer by shaking her head, and he returned one to his pocket before taking a slow lick of the second. "One thing, there's all those kings and royals. I think it's nothin' short of silly to climb on a high horse simply because blood family's been plowin' the same dirt for hundred of years. I tell you what, ma'am, Texans aren't built for bowin'. It's been bred right out of us."

Brazos leveled a hard stare on Victor Considérant and shook his peppermint in the Frenchman's direction. "And aristocrats are just as bad as royalty. That fellow's one of the worst. Although I'll admit that his head's on right about kings and all, his whole notion to create a socialistic city in the heart of Texas is just plain stupid."

Gesturing toward the others who waited ahead of them in line, he said, "Look around you, lady. I'd lay odds not more than a dozen of these folks know the first little bit about farmin', much less what it takes for survivin' on the frontier. Take that crate, for instance." He shook his head incredulously. "They've stored work tools with violins for an ocean crossing, for goodness sake. These folks don't have the sense to pour rain water from a boot!" He popped the candy into his mouth, folded his arms across his chest, and studied the ship, chewing in a pensive silence.

The nerve of the man, Madeline thought, gritting her teeth against the words she'd love to speak. Really, to comment on another's intelligence when his own is so obviously lacking. Listen to his French. And his powers of observation, why, she knew how she looked.

Beautiful wasn't the appropriate word.

Brazos swallowed his candy and said, "Hmm. You've given me an idea." Before Madeline gathered her wits to stop him, he leaned over and kissed her cheek. "Thanks, Beauty. And listen, you take care out here without a man to protect you. If I see your husband on this boat I'm goin' to give him a piece of my mind about leavin' you alone." He winked and left her, walking toward the gangway.

Madeline touched the sticky spot on her cheek damp from his peppermint kiss and watched, fascinated despite herself, as the overbold Texan tapped Considérant on the shoulder. In French that grated on her ears, he said, "Listen Frenchman, I'll make a deal with you. If you find a place for me on your ship I'll be happy to share my extensive knowledge of Texas with any of your folks who'd be interested in learnin'. This land you bought on the Trinity River—it's not more than half a day's ride from my cousin's spread. I've spent a good deal of time in that area over the past few years. I can tell you all about it."

"Mr. Sinclair," Considérant said in English, "please do not further abuse my lanaguage. I chose that land myself. Personally. I can answer any questions my peers may have about our new home. Now, as I have told you, this packet has been chartered to sail La Réunion colonists exclusively. Every space is assigned. I sympathize with your need to return to your home, but unfortunately the *Uriel* cannot accommodate you. Please excuse me, Monsieur Sinclair, I have much to see to before we sail. Good day."

"Good day my—" Brazos bit off his words. He turned abruptly and stomped away from the ship. Halting before Madeline he declared. "This boat ain't leavin' until morning. It's not over yet. By General Taylor's tailor, when it sails, I'm gonna be on it."

He flashed a victorious grin and drawled, "Honey, you've captured my heart and about three other parts. I'll look forward to seein' you aboard ship."

As he walked away, she dropped a handsome gold pocket watch into her reticule then called out to him in crisp, King's English. "Better you had offered your brain for ballast, Mr. Sinclair. Perhaps then you'd have been allowed aboard the *Uriel*."

Brazos Sinclair patted his empty pocket and scowled. What else could go wrong this afternoon? Some little urchin had up and stolen his watch, the one his father had given him the last time he'd visited Silverthorne. Damn and blast, he thought, I've gone as soft as a queen's feather pillow not to have noticed.

Many a time during his trek around Europe had a light-fingered thief attempted to divest him of his valuables, but this was the first time anyone had succeeded. Of course, as distracted as he'd been by the circumstances, a cutpurse could have purloined his pants and he'd probably not have noticed.

It was time to go home.

Brazos lifted a half-empty glass of brandy from the table in front of him. Staring into the shimmering amber liquid, he wished the tumbler were half full, but life had managed to knock the optimism right out of him. Right about now he needed every scrap of confidence he could muster to force himself to climb aboard that boat.

After his row with the Frenchman he had come directly to the alehouse across the pier from the *Uriel*. Choosing a table by the window, he'd ordered a drink and bent his mind toward figuring a way aboard that boat. Time, seldom a concern in this vagabond existence of his, had become his greatest enemy.

On this side of the Atlantic, that is.

The letter from Juanita lay like a hot brand against his chest. "Salazar," he cursed. Hatred electrified his nerves and his muscles tensed reflexively at the name. Captain Damasso Salazar, prison guard extraordinaire—thief, sadist, butcher. Brazos felt the black tide rise within him and he quickly slammed back his drink.

He must get on that ship. Juanita's life was at stake, the children's happiness and safety at risk. He'd put it off a long time—almost two years—but now it was time to go home. Salazar had found Juanita.

Absently, Brazos pressed his jacket's sleeve, feeling for the silver arm band he wore above his elbow. Embossed and engraved, the band had originally belonged to his friend, Friar Alaman, before Damasso Salazar had claimed it for his own. Brazos wore it not as jewelry, but as a symbol of his escape from Perote Prison, a reminder of the night when he'd stripped the band from the Mexican captain's arm and made a grievous mistake.

He should have killed the bastard then. Now Juanita and the children were suffering as a result of his cowardice.

Why had he allowed the man to live? Brazos didn't know and Juanita had been unable to tell him. He couldn't remember anything about the months he'd spent in The Hole. Even his memories of the escape and the subsequent return to Texas were sketchy. One particular moment stood out in his mind, however. He could clearly picture himself standing over a terrified Damasso Salazar, his fingers itching to wrap themselves around the captain's beefy neck, instead wrenching the silver band from his arm and leaving a long, deep gash in the skin.

Brazos remembered the blood and how it had frightened him. The sight of blood bothered him to this very day.

Salazar was the only man alive who could tell him why.

Had that been the reason he'd spared the captain's

life? Brazos twirled his glass on the tabletop. *Fool*, he told himself, *you put Juanita at risk for something you've no intention of pursuing*.

Three and a half years following his escape from Mexico, Brazos was certain of one fact. Whatever evil had occurred in the dungeons of Perote Prison, he was better off not knowing about it. Something told him he couldn't survive the truth.

Ordering another drink he considered his present predicament. For months now, he'd wandered around Europe, wanting to go home but being too damned scared to do it. Climbing a ship's gangway was like crossing a bridge into hell. Sailing brought on the terror—a hard lesson learned on the trip over.

He held up his glass, admiring the warm glow of light shining through the liquid, and mumbled, "And now, when the price of staying here is more than the cost of haulin' my tail aboard a boat for an ocean voyage, I have to run up against the Napolean of Utopia, Victor Considérant. Grand, simply grand."

Lifting his glass to his lips, he sipped and the drink scorched a delicious fire down his throat. "Mmm," he said, savoring the taste. That's about the only thing he'd miss when he left this godforsaken continent. French brandy was not easy to come by at home. "Maybe I'll take a case with me."

Because he would make it home—somehow, someway. He looked out the window toward the vessels lining the wharf and grimaced. "I'll be on a ship in the morning if I have to steal one and sail it myself."

For some time now, Brazos had absently watched the people go about their business along the quay. Except for the woman, that is. He had watched her with considerably more interest. Glancing toward the docks, he noticed that the flaxen-haired beauty hadn't moved since the last time he'd look, all of three minutes before.

Seems he wasn't the only one having trouble getting on board that boat.

She'd tweaked his curiosity when she had her own confrontation with Considérant. She'd been the last in line, all alone—her husband never put in an appearance. Brazos had lifted his glass in salute when she'd reached the gangway. He'd almost dropped it when he saw Considérant shake his head forcefully and deny the woman entrance. She'd argued, he'd seen her brown eyes flashing from where he sat. Watching her arms flailing about he'd worried she'd drop the baby.

She'd talked for the best part of fifteen minutes, her agitated movements sending her full pink skirt to swaying. He'd gotten a good peek at a pair of trim ankles and her stiff spine showed off a right fine bosom. Nursing women did have a certain advantage in some areas.

The fussing hadn't done her any good, apparently. After dragging herself and her child away from the ship, she'd sat atop a short stone fence and had been staring out at the water ever since.

Maybe I ought to go check on her, he thought. Nah, she didn't need him. He shrugged and ran a finger along the rim of his glass. Half a dozen times he'd seen scurvy looking sailors or rought-cut men approach her. Half a dozen times he'd risen to go save her, but by the time he'd made the street, the men were gone. "I wonder what she says to them," he muttered into his drink.

"Ah, never mind the woman." He slammed his glass on the table. This was no time to worry about a petticoat, he had to get on that ship. The lives of his loved ones depended on it.

Sighing, Brazos took another sip of his brandy. Perhaps he could stow away and count on the captain's mercy. The hand holding the glass trembled a bit at the thought. But the *Uriel* was the only ship bound for the United States scheduled to sail from Antwerp in the coming week and he dare not waste any time.

Juanita was in trouble. Salazar had found her once; it'd be easier the second time. After all, it was hard enough to hide one beautiful woman, how in the hell could you conceal five extra children? Nope, as much as he hated the idea, somehow he'd get aboard that god-damned boat. Tomorrow he'd sail for Texas.

Then he felt it, that tickle at the back of his neck. He looked around. Behind him, a timid, vulnerable expression on her face, stood the beauty. He arched an eyebrow, the question in his eyes.

Without asking his permission, she took a seat at his table. She settled the baby on her lap and looked up at him. "Mr. Sinclair," she said, her voice husky and earnest. "May I ask you a question?"

Brazos nodded.

"Mr. Sinclair, are you married?"

He frowned and shook his head. What was this about?

"I see." She looked down at her lap. He saw her swallow hard and when she lifted her gaze, he felt as if he were face to face with a wounded doe.

"Then perhaps, Mr. Sinclair," she said, "perhaps you would consent to marry me?"